PRAISE FOR

FROM BAD TO CURSED

"I am happily and completely under the spell of The Witches of Thistle Grove series."

—Emily Henry, #1 *New York Times* bestselling author of *Book Lovers*

"The only flaw in Lana Harper's magical, whimsical, sexy-as-hell The Witches of Thistle Grove series is that I can't set up shop in Thistle Grove myself right this second! These books truly do cast a spell."

—Erin Sterling, *New York Times* bestselling author of *The Ex Hex*

"Clever, fiery, and so much fun. *From Bad to Cursed* is a sharply written romp with wicked imagination. It's pure magic."

—Rachel Harrison, author of *Cackle*

"Packed with mystery, danger, lots of love-to-hate-you foreplay, family drama, and an identity crisis thrown in. Sound like a lot? It is, but still oh so fun. Highly recommended."

—*Library Journal* (starred review)

"Atmospheric and lush, this captivating story ignites the senses. The magic lends itself to big, cinematic scenes, while conflicts about familial expectations and mental health struggles ground the story with realness. The romantic relationship is emotionally rich and deliciously sexy." —*Kirkus Reviews* (starred review)

"These books are intensely queer, honest, and essentially kind. I adore them so."

—Seanan McGuire, *New York Times* bestselling author of *Where the Drowned Girls Go*

"With a fresh, fun voice, Harper brilliantly blends romance, mystery, and magic. Series fans will not be disappointed."

—*Publishers Weekly*

"Rarely is the second book in a series better than the first, but as Harper continues her Witches of Thistle Grove series, following *Payback's a Witch*, the world-building and exploration of family cultures enhances this already fascinating setting . . . Harper's latest is imaginative and captivating."

—*Booklist*

PRAISE FOR

PAYBACK'S A WITCH

"The sexy Sapphic modern Gothic I didn't know I needed . . . fresh, sharp, and often frankly hilarious . . . a perfect winter read, highly recommended for one of the longest nights of the year."

—*The New York Times Book Review*

"*Payback's a Witch* is the book I've been waiting for all my life. A sexy, funny, charming romp of a novel that scratches that witchy, autumnal itch just right. I read this story in one breathless, giggling sitting, and at the first fall nip in the air, I know I'll be reading it again. One of my favorite reads in years."

—Emily Henry, #1 *New York Times* bestselling author of *Book Lovers*

TITLES BY LANA HARPER

Back in a Spell

LANA HARPER

BERKLEY ROMANCE
NEW YORK

BERKLEY ROMANCE
Published by Berkley
An imprint of Penguin Random House LLC
penguinrandomhouse.com

Library of Congress Cataloging-in-Publication Data

Names: Harper, Lana, author.
Title: Back in a spell / Lana Harper.
Description: First Edition. | New York : Berkley Romance, 2023. |
Series: The Witches of Thistle Grove
Identifiers: LCCN 2022021262 (print) | LCCN 2022021263 (ebook) |
ISBN 9780593336106 (trade paperback) | ISBN 9780593336113 (ebook)
Subjects: LCGFT: Novels.
Classification: LCC PS3608.A7737 B33 2022 (print) |
LCC PS3608.A7737 (ebook) | DDC 813/.6—dc23
LC record available at https://lccn.loc.gov/2022021262
LC ebook record available at https://lccn.loc.gov/2022021263

First Edition: January 2023

Printed in the United States of America
1st Printing

Book design by Alison Cnockaert

For Cindy, who loves these books—and Thistle Grove—
as much as I do. Thank you for everything.

Back in a Spell

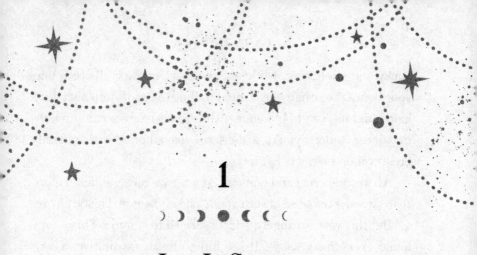

1

Let It Snow

I'VE NEVER BEEN what one might call a *winter person*.

Witches are supposed to feel naturally aligned with the Wheel of the Year, receptive to the charms of every season—and nowhere is that easier than in Thistle Grove, where every type of weather is utterly and gorgeously flamboyant, the most extravagant cosplay version of what it might look like anywhere else. In theory, I could appreciate the extremeness of its contrasts; all that diamond-faceted white, blazing against the blue of windswept skies and the stark black silhouette of Hallows Hill. I could even get behind winter chic, when it came to sleek après-ski wear. And then there was Yule, with its fragrant wreaths and crackling logs and sea of candlelight. Arguably the most luminous and magical of the solstices.

But in practice? Winter is horribly inelegant and messy, almost impossible to calibrate. One too many layers leaves you sticky and sweltering, while one too few lets the chill creep into your bones. Your hair turns into kindling, or poufs into a staticky halo immune even to glamour spells. You can't even run properly in winter, unless you're a die-hard marathoner with no self-preservation instincts left intact.

All around cruel and unusual. At least we rarely suffered more than two months or so of such yearly punishment in Thistle Grove.

But this year, strangely, winter seemed to suit me. This year, I found every fresh snowfall soothing, almost meditative. There was one raging right now beyond the frost-rimed window of the Silver Cherry, where I was grin-and-bearing my way through a jewelry-making class; a feathery whirlwind, like being inside a shaken snow globe filled with drifting down. It felt hypnotic, a chaotic escapade of white that made it hard to hold on to any single thought for long. Which, these days, was more than fine by me.

These days, my thoughts and I didn't tend to be on the best of terms.

"Sweetheart," Jessa said, in that delicate tone she'd taken to using on me, like one harsh note might topple me over, damage me in some irreparable way. She didn't have to be quite *that* careful with me, but I loved that she wanted to be. "You're doing your depressed-mime face again."

The words themselves didn't tend to match up with the spun-sugar tone all that often, because she was still Jessa, and I loved her for that, too.

"What?" I mumbled, finally tearing my eyes from the window. "My . . . *what?*"

"You know." She rearranged her adorable, ringlet-framed features into a truly dismal expression, drooping puppy-dog eyes and a dramatically downturned mouth like a melancholy bass. "Like you're about to perish of chronic woe. Or possibly planning to re-create that scene from *The Giver* where the kid and his little brother escape into the snow to die with their emotions."

"It's been a while since middle school English class, but even so, I'm *fairly* sure that wasn't supposed to be the takeaway," I told her with a snort. "And hard pass on that cold demise. If I absolutely have to die somewhere with my emotions, I'd rather go all nice and toasty."

Dragging my attention back to my little work tray, strewn with a glittery mishmash of wire and beads, I saw that I'd been halfheartedly tooling around with making earrings before the blizzard got the best of me. Once upon a time, I'd have crafted something gorgeous given an opportunity like this, painstakingly applied myself until I had it just right. Too bad "once upon a time" felt like several eons and an infinity of wrong turns ago.

"Burn you at the stake, then, noted," Jessa quipped—though of course, thoroughly normie as she was, my best friend had no idea how close to home that hit. As far as I knew, Jessa had never once seriously considered the notion that our charming postcard of a town really *was* settled by witches, exactly like Thistle Grove legend would have you believe.

To her, I was just Nina. Best friend and partner in crime from our shared law school days, now in-house counsel to my family's extensive business interests. Not Nineve Cliodhna of House Blackmoore, second in line to the most powerful witch dynasty in Thistle Grove.

"Don't worry, buddy," I assured her. "I do still have considerable will to live. Just not, like, enough *zest* to care about these earrings, apparently."

Jessa pooched out her lower lip, abandoning the complicated

(and suspiciously BDSM-looking) beaded choker she'd been working on.

"But that's the *point*," she insisted, smooth brow wrinkling with concern. "That's what these classes are for, Nina. We're supposed to be nurturing our creative selves, meeting new people, rediscovering your zest. Unearthing it."

She looked so crestfallen that for the barest moment, I entertained the idea of assembling the pitiful bead hodgepodge into something pretty with a simple transmutation spell of the pumpkin-into-carriage variety, but even more basic. The raw materials were already right in front of me, half-threaded. I could have done it with just a few words, using a single, purely distilled thought as a vehicle of my will.

But that wouldn't have been honest or fair, which was part of the reason I never did magic in front of my best friend. For the safety and the continuing preservation of our town, as per the Grimoire—the spellbook that also held sway over the conduct and governance of Thistle Grove's witch community—only long-term, witchbound partners were permitted access to that secret. And for all that I adored Jessa to pieces, our friendship wasn't the kind of love the founders had had in mind when deciding who should be privy to our magic.

Letting the oblivion glamour that was cast over the town take hold of her, erasing her memory of whatever spell I'd worked, would have felt . . . traitorous. A little gross, even.

And it would have been a cop-out at best. Jessa was the kind of delightful whirlwind of a person who effortlessly transformed strangers into friends—or short-lived partners, as the case may be—wherever she went, and I knew she'd been hoping a little of that joie de vivre might rub off on me. Tonight's jewelry-making class was the fourth hopeful outing of its kind, following a disastrous wine-and-paint night (during which I'd gotten the not-artistically-conducive kind of wasted), an equally catastrophic pottery class that had reminded me of Sydney's love of ceremonial teacups and sent me spinning into a meltdown, and a flower-arranging class that had only managed to unearth memories of the ivory-and-rose-gold palette I'd chosen for the flowers at my own wedding.

A wedding that was never going to happen, much like the perfect life with Sydney that had been meant to materialize thereafter. A life that now seemed not just fictional, but so fantastically unbelievable that I, a flesh-and-blood descendant of the sorceress Morgan le Fay, couldn't conceive of it as a reality.

"You're talking about me like I'm some archeological dig, Jess, and we're troweling for ancient potsherds of joy. What if there's no zest to unearth? What if I'm just a barren wasteland?" I dropped my chin, the familiar, hateful well of tears pressing against my eyes. I was so damn sick of crying at the slightest provocation, like some weepy damsel stuck in a mire of never-ending distress, but I'd apparently won the sob lottery. Team #Leaky4Life over here. "Permanently broken?"

"Everyone's fixable, sweetheart," Jessa assured me, slipping a soft arm around my shoulders and tilting her temple against mine. She favored those subtle skin-musk perfumes that you couldn't detect on yourself—the kind I'd never go for, because what was the point if you couldn't catch indulgent whiffs of it throughout the day?—but that made her smell gorgeous, a vanilla-cedar scent that hit somewhere between gourmand and woody. Being hugged by her felt like free aromatherapy.

"Even that guy you dated with the towering manbun?" I asked, a little damply.

"You say that like there's only been one . . . which, *would* that were the truth."

"The one who drank so much Bulletproof Coffee it was like he was speaking in fast-forward all the time," I clarified. "And did biceps curls while taking dumps."

"Fuck no, not him." She shuddered delicately against me, sticking out her tongue—which was pierced, something no other estate lawyer I knew could ever have gotten away with. Apparently a deceptively angelic face like Jessa's covered a multitude of sins, even when it came to the most uptight of clients. "Everyone but Chasen, then."

"*Of course* that was his name. And what about dictators? Or sex cult leaders? Or serial killers?"

"Now you're just being difficult. Allow me to rephrase, counselor." She shifted sideways against me, just enough to boop me on the nose. "*You* are fixable, sweetheart. Eminently so."

"Then why can't I get into even this, the most emotionally undemanding of activities?" I asked her, that relentless ache lurching in my chest again. A panging disorientation that felt almost like homesickness, as my gaze skimmed over the dozen or so other people happily crafting beneath the cherry cutouts dangling from the ceiling, the recessed lighting spilling over them in a mellow glow. Mostly clusters of women around Jessa's and my age, along with a few mothers with their tweens in tow.

Even the solitary goth enby with the pentagram neck tattoo— likely a tourist drawn to the Silver Cherry by its affiliation with Lark Thorn, who not only was teaching this class but also sold her line of enchanted jewelry here—looked to be having a more exuberant experience with this mortal coil than I was.

"What kind of mess can't focus on stringing beads together?

Or letting loose on a pottery wheel?" I swiped at my eyes, trying in vain to keep from smearing my eyeliner. "It's been a whole year, Jess. How long is this emotional fugue state even supposed to last?"

My voice rose enough that on the other side of the room, Lark Thorn abruptly straightened from where she'd been instructing one of the tweens. She turned just enough to flick a concerned glance at me over her shoulder, deep brown skin glowing against the vivid turquoise of her scoop-neck sweater, her dark eyes liquid with sympathy. The Thorns were empathically attuned to one another's feelings, and acutely sensitive to others' emotional landscapes, too. Though I doubted Lark even needed their particular brand of ESP to detect the seismic rumble of my distress.

The Nina I used to be had been unshakably sure of herself, vacuum-sealed into her composure. But these days, the old me felt like a fossil, a crumbling memory. These days, I was more of a tempest in a teacup.

A flailing, distractible tempest that just could not seem to get it the hell together.

I twitched my lips into an "everything's just *peachy* over here" smile, wincing inwardly as she gave me a lingering look before turning away. I wouldn't have agreed to come here tonight at all, had I remembered Lark's connection to the studio. Given how the Blackmoores' standing in this town had declined since the debacle of last year's Gauntlet of the Grove—not to mention the fact that my little brother, Gawain, had briefly come under suspicion when one of the Avramovs' dearly departed ancestors cursed the Thorns this past Beltane—the last thing I needed to be doing was signaling weakness in front of a member of one of the other families.

The thought spurred me into taking a breath, stiffening my spine a little, and leaning away from Jessa as if she weren't, in fact, my load-bearing support column. Trying to act as though I at least remembered who I was supposed to be.

"I don't think heartbreak's an exact science, sweetie. Though I will concur that maybe we've been going about this the wrong way," Jess concluded thoughtfully, nibbling on her lip. "You know what, why don't we ditch this and grab some drinks instead? Rethink our strategy?"

"But what about your . . ." I gestured vaguely toward the abandoned snarl on her work tray. "Fetishwear-in-progress? It had such promise."

She chuckled through her nose, not bothering to deny it. "I can always take it home. It was going to be for Steven, anyway . . . Ooh, maybe I can make him finish it for me, before he gets to wear it! You know, like a meta-kink moment. Foreplay for the foreplay."

I stared at her for a second, equally confounded by the rigorous intellectual component her most recent bedroom exploits apparently called for, and the fact that her flavor of the week had already earned himself an actual name. By Jessa's standards, that was unusually rapid progress. Most of her conquests went by evocative nicknames the likes of "Lacrosse Jesus" or "Emo Clark Kent" until they dropped out of the rotation; maybe she actually *liked* this guy.

"I do not claim to understand your ways, Jessamyn Singer, but I respect them," I finally said.

"Just the way I like it." She slid the jewelry into a little ziplock, grinning to herself. "So, where do you want to go? Dive bar? Nice bar? Weird bar?"

"Nice bar," I said automatically, suppressing a sniffle. My spirits rose a little at the idea of delicious craft cocktails and low lighting, the utter relief of not having to funnel any more energy into forcibly enjoying, or pretending to enjoy, yet another form of alleged entertainment.

"See, *there* you are," she said warmly, reaching out to give me another squeeze. "Knew my favorite fancy bitch was in there somewhere."

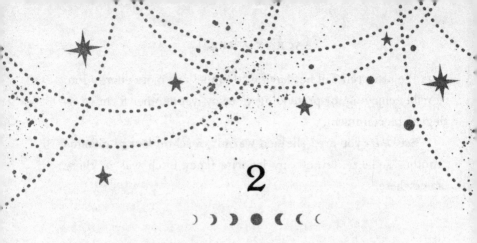

2

Whimsical Bitches and Trickster Gods

TEN MINUTES LATER, Jessa and I wedged ourselves into an empty booth at Whistler's Fireside, a waft of cold still clinging to us as we shed our layers and stamped our snow-crusted boots under the table, wind-lashed cheeks both numb and glowing.

Whistler's majestic black walnut booths, with their intricately carved backs and must-and-varnish smell, looked like they'd begun their lives as pews in some medieval abbey. Bare Edison bulbs cupping twists of glowing filament swung above each table, and to our right, the bar top gleamed copper from the vintage pennies preserved under its glass slab, fat pillar candles flickering along its length. Even the cool blue cast of early-winter dusk drifting through the Victorian windows couldn't chill the aura of warmth.

There was no actual hearth to be seen, despite the name—probably the owner's idea of an ironic joke—but the whole ethos of the bar *did* feel like sitting at a fireside.

I loved it here. It reminded me of my favorite New York speakeasies, the ones that had brazenly ridiculous thousand-dollar concoctions tucked into the drink menus like dirty capitalist secrets, and all but demanded a password and secret handshake to get in, even though everyone and their mother knew where to find them. I couldn't help but enjoy that little thrill, the sense of being part of an exclusive club—especially when it wasn't *real* elitism, but just for fun, the way it was at Whistler's.

"What are you thinking?" Jessa asked, once the server had dropped off menus and a complimentary bowl of honey-and-harissa popcorn. Truly, this place was the bomb. "They have the spiked hot chocolate today, and *oooh*, a new buttered rum hot toddy. Shit, but does that even sound good, in reality? Or are they counting on the butter to gaslight us into believing it must be delicious?"

"Hmm, as yet unclear."

I gave the happy hour specials a cursory skim even though I already knew what I wanted, wondering whether I should at least try to be more adventurous. As sometimes happened at moments like this, the Ghost of Sydney Past materialized by my shoulder to whisper in my ear. (Though not, to be clear, her *literal* spirit, as Sydney had been alive and aggravatingly well in Chicago last I'd checked. And in any case, ghost whispering was more the kind of ghastly trick you'd expect to find in the Avramovs' repertoire than the magic my family preferred to practice.)

Why do you always have to order the exact same thing, the memory of her voice sniped at me in that coldly exasperated tone that always used to make my shoulders hunch. *Why not just* try *something new for once, so we can share?*

But I happened to *like* the mulled wine here. And furthermore, I *liked* the tried-and-true reliability, the comfort of an order that you knew for a fact would make you happy. That was one of Syd's and my most well-worn fights—her desire for spontaneity, set against my craving for structure and routine. The core disparity between us that had seemed like a charming opposites-attract deal at first, her the fluttering kite and me the grounded ballast. Us together, a rare alchemical balance that would elevate our relationship beyond the sum of its parts and into something golden and enviable.

No such elevation had, in fact, transpired. In hindsight, as happy as much of our relationship had made me, Syd and I had been the definition of fool's gold.

"I'm sticking with the mulled wine," I decided, banishing the Ghost of Sydney Past with as much firmness as I could muster.

"Foolproof choice." Jessa pursed her lips and squinted at the menu for another moment, the bulb's ruddy light picking out wavering highlights in the rings stacked above and below her knuckles. She had a metallic rose-gold French manicure this week, too; seriously, what the hell kind of amenable clientele did she even have? "Okay, yup. I'm gonna take a gamble on the hot toddy and see if I live to rue the day."

I huffed a laugh into my handful of popcorn, shaking my head. "As if 'regret' even figures into your vocabulary."

"Just because I choose to look back fondly on most of my mistakes doesn't mean I don't learn from them."

Once our order was in and the menus whisked away, Jessa

draped an arm over the table and rested her chin in the cup of her other palm, giving me a frankly assessing stare.

"How worried do I really need to be about you, sweetheart?" she said, matter-of-fact but still in that sweet tone that dissolved anything sharp or accusatory before it could make me shrink into myself. "This two-step of meltdowns and existential malaise is starting to seem like more than you should have to handle on your own. What does Sassy Sue have to say about this situation? Is it time to consider meds?"

Sassy Sue was my much beloved and, yes, profoundly spicy and no-nonsense therapist. WWSSD—What Would Sassy Sue Do— had long been Jessa's and my tough-love code for "Get your shit together and make the right call."

"We've discussed it," I said, wiping popcorn grease off my hands and then folding the napkin into a neat little square before setting it aside. "But she thinks, and I agree, that my issue is more situational. Meds might give me a little boost, sure. But the thing is, I don't actually *feel* the chronic kind of depressed, Jess. I still like my job, and I enjoy working out. I get pretty reliable jollies from my preferred forms of retail therapy, just like before."

And I still adored the magic in my life every breathtaking bit as much as I ever had, not that I could share that with Jessa.

"No issues getting out of bed in the morning or motivating," I went on. "So it's not that I've become constitutionally incapable of producing happy feelings. I'm more or less fine—as long as I don't venture beyond my comfort zone."

Jessa gave a pensive nod, mulling it over. "Got it, I think. So, what is the problem, then? Is it that you still miss her?"

Our drinks arrived, just in time to help choke down the tangle of emotions clambering up my throat like climbing vines. I closed my eyes, took a therapeutic inhale of the boozy steam followed by a semi-scalding sip of red wine. Cinnamon and nutmeg and the bright, sweet tang of hot alcohol seeped into my mouth, blunting the thorns in my throat into something more manageable.

"No," I said, fighting the tremble in my voice; even though the real answer was unfortunately still *sometimes*. "It's when I start trying to move forward, to do *anything* new. It makes me feel so lost, Jess. So . . . disjointed, permanently off-balance, somehow. Like I woke up one morning and suddenly found myself a castaway, stranded in the wrong life. I should be *married* right now, to the love of my life. Maybe even starting to think about having kids."

Jessa suppressed a little eye roll, presumably bored stiff by the unforgivably vanilla spouse-plus-2.5-kids slant of my life goals. I felt a stab of annoyance back at her, for not understanding the way she usually did, with ample empathy. I certainly expended enough of it on her, trying to wrap my brain around the offbeat way she conducted her relationships.

"Look, I'm well aware those aren't your things," I said, a little sharply, "but they *are* mine. You know that."

Her round face softened immediately, brief chagrin glinting in her brown eyes. "It's not that, Nina. I'm just not sure I'd call Sydney 'Jacqueline-pronounced-Zha-KLEEN' Grant the great love of your life, you know? She did call the wedding off a *week* before you were supposed to get married. Might as well have ditched you the day of, at least let you have your beautifully tragic moment at the altar if you couldn't get your damn deposits back."

I gritted my teeth at the memory of Sydney sobbing in our loft apartment—she'd cried much more than I had at the time, which struck me now as quite a bit of bullshit—as she trailed me from room to room, wringing her hands and pleading for my under-standing while I paced back and forth, my entire life dissolving around me like an ice palace under a blowtorch. *I just can't* breathe *when I'm with you, Nina,* she'd said through shimmering tears; Sydney somehow even cried prettily, like she was creating content for her Instagram reels just by existing. *It's like there's not enough air around you, like you create this vacuum wherever you are. And I . . . I don't want to live the rest of my life that way, so joyless, so* arid.

I can't do that to myself. I won't.

You'd have thought she might've been struck by this tragic revelation at any other, more convenient time in our four years together—before, for instance, proposing to me, and insisting on a December wedding even though she knew how much I hated winter.

Now, instead, *I* had to live the rest of my life knowing I was the kind of "joyless," suffocating person who made other people feel like they'd been vented out of an airlock.

I hadn't told anyone, not even Jessa, the damning details of what Sydney had said to me. The dramatic way things had un-folded, everyone hated her enough as it was, which was fine by me. But what if I went beyond the broad strokes, and it turned out they *agreed* with her? This fragile eggshell version of me couldn't roll with a punch like that.

I'd shatter into a sticky mess of shards, and not even Sassy Sue would be able to glue me back together again.

"I just don't understand how things could've gone so wrong," I said instead, a half-truth that at least skimmed the surface of the awfulness iceberg floating just beneath. "And I'm . . . hon-estly, Jess, I'm a little scared that I'm the problem. That if I try again, with someone new, the same exact thing will happen. But

I don't think I know how to fix myself. Or whether I even really *want* to."

"First off, you are brilliant and generous and considerate, and certainly in no need of some kind of elaborate personality overhaul—let's take things down a notch," Jessa said, admirably restraining herself from launching into a full-bore Sydney takedown, though I could see the mutiny brewing on her face. Even though I'd thrown them together at every opportunity, hoping they'd eventually come around to each other, there had never been much love lost between my ex-partner and my best friend. "Second, your ex-fiancée was an obnoxious, self-centered, *whimsical* bitch with tremendously overblown notions of her own worth. So let us never again refer to that shitty manic pixie gallery girl as the 'love of your life,' 'kay?"

And boom, there came the drag.

I burst out laughing, marveling at how deftly she'd turned a generally positive word into an insult with such bite to it. Sydney *had* been almost methodically quirky, but even still, I'd been charmed by her. Her appeal had never struck me as manufactured. "Whoa, buddy, tell me what you really think. And she *was* a curator, technically."

"Let it be known that I do not give a solitary, last-of-its-kind fuck about Sydney Zha-KLEEN's former job title," Jessa declared, giving the French pronunciation an even prissier twist. "The one thoughtful thing she did for you was clear out in the aftermath, and let you have this town to yourself. At least we don't have to look upon her precious wee *Amélie* face ever again."

"To small mercies," I agreed, clinking my glass against hers—though, obviously, I'd thought Sydney was beautiful, and still occasionally stalked her social media when I felt low enough to want to inflict on myself the stiletto-twist pain of seeing her be happy. "Full disclosure, I had no idea you loathed her whole Francophile thing so much."

"Eh, didn't seem like a helpful take at the time," Jessa replied with a shrug. "But boy, am I stoked to talk about it now! Feels downright *cleansing*, like it's clearing out all those years of pent-up shade. Gotta be good for the skin."

"Makes one of us, then." I bit down on the inside of my cheek to stave off the inevitable tears. "Because talking about her just makes me feel hopeless. Like I already had my shot at my dream life, everything the way I wanted it, the way it was *supposed* to be. And I screwed it up, just by being myself."

"Oh, sweetie," Jessa exhaled, pert face scrunching up with almost painful sympathy. "So that's why there haven't been any second dates."

I'd been cautiously trying to put myself back out there the past few months, at both Jessa's and Sassy Sue's urging. But even the handful of first dates I'd been on made me queasily anxious, and the prospect of a second date flung me into full-blown panic. I ruthlessly overanalyzed myself at every turn, as if each prospective partner might be scrutinizing my every choice and mannerism with Sydney's witheringly critical gaze. The pressure felt buckling, enormous, as though what drink I chose and whether I agreed to taste the other person's tapas could derail my whole future with them before it even began.

So I'd decided, hey, maybe better to just tap out before I proceeded to lose my entire mind.

"That's why," I admitted with a whooshing sigh, taking another slug of my wine. "I can't relax enough to even think about letting someone get to know me. The pressure is just . . . untenable."

Jessa rocked her head from side to side, the endearingly Machiavellian expression she always slipped into when thinking stealing over her face.

"What if," she said, lifting her eyebrows, "we took the pressure off? Picked someone so unlikely, so obviously not a realistic prospect for you, that you could just chill a little, have fun with it? Go on a date or three, possibly even enjoy a solid bang, as God knows you need one in the direst of ways. Have a shallow-end-of-the-pool experience, you know? Just doggy-paddle around a little bit before you go full-on snorkeling."

I knit my brow, trying to parse this tortured metaphor. "So, you want me to pick someone I'm not into? How is that supposed to help?"

"No, duh, *of course* they still have to be a smoke show. I'm thinking someone super hot, but relatively low investment." She snaked her hand across the table, palm up, and wiggled her fingers at me. "Hand over your phone, and I'll show you what I mean."

"I don't know, Jess," I said slowly, balking. "This feels like a very ill-advised experiment. Or worse, a reality dating show with seriously low production value. Which, as you know, is the opposite of my bag."

"Oh, just try it *once*, Neenie," Jessa wheedled. "One little date. Think of it as a change of scenery!"

I tilted my head against the booth's slick back, mulling it over. I knew that I was stagnating; one way or another, it was past time to implement a different strategy. And once upon a time, I used to be a very proficient dater, if I did say so myself. If I was being honest, the idea of a no-pressure date with some hot yet ludicrously unsuitable individual sounded about a million times less excruciating than the glow-paint-and-goats yoga Jessa was probably planning to foist on me next.

Sensing my softening, Jessa doubled down, a cunning gleam kindling in her eye. "Aaaand if it's a total catastrophe, I'll owe you a batch of my gourmet pigs in blankets—*and* I'll even throw in a *Lost Girl* marathon."

"Ugh, you know me far too well, friend," I groaned, dropping my face into my hands. Puff pastries of any kind were my bizarre mortal weakness, the savory version of my kryptonite. I probably had my parents' epic dinner parties to thank for that, and all the stealth scavenging my brothers and I had done at them before we'd been allowed to formally attend. For the right kind of flaky hors d'oeuvre—especially one of Jessa's rare homemade treats, and in conjunction with my favorite TV—there was troublingly little I wouldn't do.

Lifting my head, I unlocked the phone and plopped it into her palm with a grimace. "Deal, I suppose. But to be clear, the terms of our agreement do *not* extend beyond the one date."

With a gleeful crow, Jessa swiped over to the third screen and pulled up my dating apps. Seeing as she'd created the folder and downloaded them for me in the first place, even wordsmithed my profiles so I couldn't hide behind the excuse of not having the energy to write about myself, she knew exactly where to find them all.

Rolling my empty mug between my palms, I watched her with a mixture of trepidation and the slightest brush of intrigue. It *did* feel just a little refreshing to cede control over this, instead of swiping through prospective partners in the late nights after work, with an eagle eye toward how many of my boxes they checked. Sitting alone in the dark bedroom that sometimes still smelled faintly of Sydney's dainty Jardin sur le Toit—for no good reason, given how many thorough scrubbings my loft had gotten since she left—peering into that rectangle of sallow light like it was an exam I badly needed to pass, had felt depressing and lonely and borderline desperate.

This, astonishingly, felt like it might even be fun.

"Too perky . . . too basic . . . oof, *way* too messy," Jessa was muttering under her breath as she swiped through possible candidates with decisive little flicks, nose wrinkled in thought. "Too Aritzia-catalog-model—"

"Excuse me, what? Let me see!" I snatched at the phone, but she batted me away.

"Hands to yourself, missy," she ordered, cradling my phone to her chest. "This chick is not the one we're looking for, trust me on this. She's basically brunette you, which means instant disqualification. And might I remind you, I'm in charge of Operation Doggy Paddle? You just sit back, relax, and let me do this good work."

"Yes, *ma'am*."

"That's what he said."

Snorting, I flagged down the server for another mug of mulled wine, while Jessa speed-swiped through so many profiles it was like watching a live-action carpal tunnel PSA. Then she paused, lips parted, fingertip hovering over the screen. "Well, *hello* there, sir. Finally, someone with actual promise."

"Sir?" I echoed, my heart sinking a little. "It's a dude?"

I'd been trying to keep my options open in the apps, seeing no reason to throw up any additional obstacles for myself. But while I'd slept with a handful of guys, and briefly dated a trans man back in college, my serious relationships had all been with women. When I could bring myself to imagine the hazy outline of a future partner, my mind always conjured up a woman of its own accord.

Which, possibly, meant that *not* a woman might be perfect for this absurd experiment.

"Well, maybe not entirely," she corrected, still engrossed in the profile, a tiny reflection of the phone screen glowing blue in her pupils as she flicked through the photos. "Nonbinary, pronouns are 'he/they,' and pan orientation, just like you. TBH, I'm more concerned with this *face*. Here, take a look."

She passed me the phone, still warm from her grip. I reared back a little at the profile picture, my eyebrows rising as I saw what she meant. Bright blue eyes glittering like gems against the shadows of black liner, a tousled shock of dark brown hair falling into them. Stubble roughening what was otherwise a clean-cut face, with features so fine they were nearly feminine, closer to pretty than handsome. A lazy, crooked half smile, the "stick with me, I'll show you some things" kind that looked like a gauntlet thrown.

Okay, well. *Maybe.*

Intrigued despite myself, I swiped through more of his photos, defaulting in my mind to the masculine pronoun since he'd listed it first. In one of the pictures, he wore a dramatic corset and midnight-blue lipstick, galactic flares of silver paint and glitter swooping over his cheekbones. A fuchsia feather boa wrapped around his neck and strung across the shoulders of the two grinning, similarly festooned people crowding in on either side to press their cheeks against his. In another, he was shirtless and upside down, suspended in aerial silks; caught in a pose that high-lighted the striking definition of his abs and obliques, bright stage lights illuminating waterfalls of Technicolor tattoos coursing down his arms. He had the kind of muscle so sleek it looked car-ven, somehow feline.

Something that I tended to like a whole lot, in women and men and everyone in between.

Not all the pictures were quite as flattering. In one, he wore a plaid shirt under suspenders—which, what—and had his mouth massively open as he prepared to chow down on a monstrous-looking burger that appeared to include both chili and a smooshed doughnut. In another selfie, he was giving duckface and flashing the shaka hand sign, while having clearly gotten a makeover from a little kid. His lips a mess of bubblegum pink, yellow eyeshadow indiscriminately smeared all over his upper face.

But in the final photo, he was swimming; submerged up to the bridge of his nose, dark hair bristling in waterlogged spikes. Only those mischievous blue eyes were visible, narrowed against sun-shine and reflecting the sequined shimmer of the waterline just below them, beads glistening on his forehead and clinging to the defined arches of his eyebrows. I could see the distinctive ring of evergreens and the bright purple splash of thistles on the distant shoreline behind him; so he was bold enough to swim in Lady's Lake, something very few Thistle Grove normies seemed to do, as though the lake beckoned specifically and almost exclusively to witches.

I felt an unexpected little flutter in the depths of my belly, even as I acknowledged that he looked . . . risky. Impulsive, unpredict-able. Sydney had been quirky and flighty, yes, but in the most polished, socially acceptable, Zooey Deschanel of ways. More Anthropologie, a lot less Burning Man. Before we fell apart, she and I had held similar values, the same ultimate goals for what we wanted our lives to look like.

This person looked like the embodiment of a dare, someone I'd never in a million years have picked for myself.

"So you want me to go out with the trickster god of circus and burlesque," I said to Jessa, looking up to fix her with a flat stare, "is what you're telling me."

"Is that the vibe you're getting here?" She canted her head, considering. "I'm thinking more like *Lord of the Rings* elven, but with just the right dash of black sheep."

"Dash?" I demanded, brandishing the phone at her. "His username is literally 'lowkeyloki,' which, okay, possibly I'm a tiny bit here for that. But *look* at him. He looks like someone who'd get cast to play a sexy chaos demon on *Supernatural.*"

She shrugged, like, *And this is a problem, how?* "A little CW bone structure never hurt nobody."

"That's not the point. He likes dangling upside down at a perilously great distance from the ground, on purpose. He eats heart-attack burgers with freaking *doughnuts* in them, like some kind of carpe diem cliché. He posts terrible pictures of himself of his own free will and not under any obvious duress." I crossed my arms over my chest, like, *Rest my case.* "I cannot date this individual."

"You can, and you will—because I picked him for you, and that was the deal, remember? One date. You're not going to go back on your word *now*, are you?"

She grinned hugely, knowing she had me there. No Blackmoore ever reneged on an oath once given. Though she wasn't privy to the witchy background behind this code of honor, Jessa certainly knew it to be true based on her experience with me. Once I committed to something, I always followed through, no matter the cost to myself.

Which wasn't to say that being honorable didn't occasionally suck the big one.

"Fine," I groused, slumping back against the booth. "Swipe right it is, then. Maybe we won't even match."

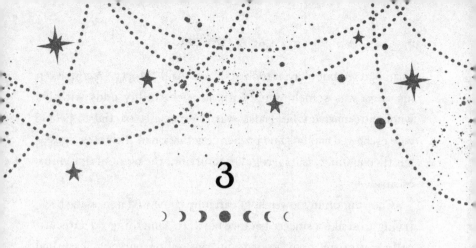

3

A Winter Spell

WE MATCHED.

My phone pinged with the notification before I even got home, soon followed by a message from none other than @lowkeyloki himself. I waited until I'd curled up on my couch with a glass of wine, my heart racing just a little, to even open the app DMs.

"You can do this, Nina. Here's to . . . *whatever,*" I muttered to myself, lifting the glass in a wry toast and taking a hearty swig as I swiped the message open, grimacing preemptively.

> **@lowkeyloki:** heya this is morty! thanks for the like 😊

I wrinkled my nose, swishing the Bordeaux around my mouth, tannins seeping into my tongue. Not a tremendous fan of "heya" as an opener, but okay, it took all kinds. And "Morty," *really*? Even his *name* was somehow uncouth, at such stodgy odds with his whole alternative vibe. I also wasn't especially partial to people who eschewed capitals and proper punctuation in their messages— but then again, was its irregular nature not the point of this entire escapade?

Chewing on my lower lip, I carefully composed a message back, trying to strike a sincere balance between something I'd authentically say of my own accord and the online persona Jessa had painstakingly constructed for me: a bubblier, glossier, more emotionally available, and definitively less neurotic version of myself.

Certainly less *arid*, at any rate.

I typed back, cringing at the fact that I'd completely forgotten having allowed Jessa to saddle me with such a ridiculous handle of my own.

> @AttyQueenNeens: Hi! I'm Nina. Fantastic pictures . . . love the silks!

Leading with a flat-out lie was probably not the greatest, but to be fair, I *did* like the way he looked in them. Just not the potential lethality of the endeavor.

> @lowkeyloki: thnx, nina, right back atcha. love the halloween costume, wicked cute 😈

The "Halloween" costume was actually what I'd worn to the Beltane First Dew festivities two years ago: the Blackmoore onyx-and-gold ceremonial robes over a clinging yellow maxi dress, a peony-and-feather wreath perched on my head. Jessa had demanded that I include it in my pictures—she'd also been under the impression that the photo was from a "themed" event—because she thought I looked both beautiful and genuinely happy, which she insisted was important. I was holding a goblet of spring wine, head thrown back midlaugh, my balayaged blond curls pouring over my shoulders in honeyed waves. Teeth shining against rosy lipstick, cheeks flushed from the wine.

It wasn't one of my favorite pictures of myself—I looked so *unraveled*—but maybe she did know a thing or two about crafting these profiles, after all.

As I typed back, my cheeks heating a little, I was surprised at how good it felt to be admired even in this small, chill way.

> @AttyQueenNeens: Thanks! It was from a party by Lady's Lake. Looks like you enjoy swimming up there!

> @lowkeyloki: for sure. that water's got some sweet zing to it, u know? idk why more folx don't take advantage of it

> @AttyQueenNeens: I agree! I spend a lot of time up there myself; it's one of my favorite places in town.

> @lowkeyloki: right? the view, the vibes, the whole deal. love takin my niece up there for picnics, too

Ellipses bubbles pulsed, appearing, then disappearing, then appearing again as he typed. I discovered, with an uncomfortable little jolt, that I didn't want this conversation to end.

@lowkeyloki: hey, what do u think about grabbing a
drink soon?

Oh. I leaned back into the cushions, feeling a pleasantly giddy
lurch of surprise. So he was one to cut to the chase, then, rather
than wasting everyone's time by texting for days or weeks before
we actually met up.

Efficient, and time-saving. This, I liked.

@AttyQueenNeens: Sure, I'd really like that! When/
where were you thinking?

@lowkeyloki: u know the moon & scythe? how's this
sat at 8?

I sucked in a breath, gritting my teeth at the choice of venue.
The Moon and Scythe was the closest thing Thistle Grove had to
a dive bar—the kind of place one might unironically refer to as a
"joint"—and therefore so far from my scene that it wasn't even in
the same zip code. I swiped out of the app and shot off a desperate
text to Jessa, in dire need of guidance.

Nina: Soooo, I'm chatting with @lowkeyloki

Jessa: YASSSSS ATTYQUEEEENNEEEEENS

Nina: Yeah, we're gonna have some words about that handle, you
and I. But, beside the point rn. First off, his name is MORTY, what.
And he wants to go to the Moon and Scythe on Saturday ☹ Jess,
do I have to?! Like, really have to?

Jessa: Bitch YESSSSS, bonus points for sticky beer floors, THIS
IS PERFECT.

Nina: But but

Jessa: Remember the plan, soldier. Operation Doggy Paddle, full steam ahead

Nina: 😬😬😬

Jessa: Just think of the pigs in blankets!!!

Who could argue with that logic, certainly not me. I texted DAMN YOU, FIEND to Jessa and swiped back into the dating app, steeling myself.

@AttyQueenNeens: Sure, sounds great, let's do it!

@lowkeyloki: dope. c u then nina

@lowkeyloki: really lookin forward to meeting u

@AttyQueenNeens: Same! Have a lovely rest of the week, Morty 😊

The weirdest part was, I kind of meant it. For the first time since I'd resumed my white-knuckled approach to dating, I actually *was* looking forward to this date.

Even if it meant an unfortunate foray to the Moon and Scythe.

I HAD TO admit, the pressure-valve psychology of Jessa's plan seemed to work, at least as far as getting ready went. On Saturday night, I managed not to triple-guess my outfit, my shoes, or my choice of perfume—already a minor miracle in itself—and just a single glass of malbec took the edge off what nerves I had. It felt like a marked enough change of pace from my previous attempts to fill me with a tentative swell of hope as I gave myself a final once-over in the mirror, feeling only the barest, creeping tendril of self-doubt.

Maybe this could work. Maybe I could be the old Nina again, sooner rather than later.

I'd given myself so much extra time to get ready that I wound up with more than half an hour before I needed to make an appearance at the pub. Sitting alone with my thoughts would only leave room for the doubt to claw its way back to the surface, wriggling through my cracks. So I did something I hadn't done in almost a month, not since it had gotten properly cold.

I wound a scarf around my neck and shrugged into my warmest Moncler parka, then portaled up to Lady's Lake.

Portal magic was some of the most demanding spellwork a witch could cast. It required finesse, a vast reservoir of magical strength, and an iron will; the kind of unflagging focus that didn't falter even for a breath. In essence, it allowed you to craft a vessel of magic for your body, a spellbound capsule to whisk you through the fabric of reality itself, without letting all the opposing forces at play shred your flesh—and spirit—into its most minute component parts.

To pull it off, you had to be capable of holding two opposing convictions in your mind, cemented alongside each other—that you were a perfectly cohesive unit, unassailable and self-contained, *and* that you were made of the same fluid, malleable matter as the rest of the universe. Both wave form and particle at once.

An absolute mindfuck, one which also happened to be my specialty. Holding coexisting yet contradictory lines of thought as truths was exactly the type of mental contortion lawyers engaged in all day. Only a handful of other living Blackmoores could pull a portal off, my grandmother Igraine and my mother, Lyonesse, among them. My little brother, Gawain, had always been too chickenshit to even try, and my older brother, Gareth, could travel only relatively short distances.

But to me, it had always felt like second nature.

Closing my eyes, I lifted my hands and chanted the words to Lightborne Folly, concentrating intently on both my inviolable individuality and my oneness with the cosmos as ribbons of light with a pearly rainbow sheen shimmered into being, weaving themselves around me. Magic rushed under my skin, a glittering flood like liquid lightning crackling through my veins. My pulse quickened, thudding in my ears as I wrested the swirl of light into the proper shape around me, and thought myself toward the lake.

For a brief, jarring moment, gravity and direction winked out altogether, and I tumbled through a vast expanse of nothingness.

The bottom of my stomach fell out, the lurching feeling of having missed the final step in a staircase, even as I lost any sense of myself as a physical object anchored in space. The closest analogue to the feeling was falling—but falling *upside down* somehow, like Alice plummeting down the rabbit hole. If you let your focus slip while you went hurtling like a wayward comet through this formless sea of in-between, no part of you would emerge on the other end.

A very powerful motivator to keep your will and mind firmly in check against a rising tide of instinctual terror.

From one heartbeat to the next, the world snapped back into place. A crisp skin of snow crunched under my boots as my feet suddenly found purchase, and a bracing gust of pine-scented wind curled around me like something old and sentient, stealing my breath and combing through my hair.

I stood atop Hallows Hill, with Lady's Lake sparkling in front of me and the lights of Thistle Grove at my back, blinking like fireflies down by the mountain's distant base.

This time of year, the lake somehow looked even more elemental. Like some primordial origin story, the place where winter's cold heart had been born back when everything began. Up here, the sky had a brittle quality to it, a chilly purity so keen it made the slew of stars look nearly sharp, a frozen, milky spill shattered across the glassy sky. The pines ringing the banks looked like darker brushstrokes flicked against the night, their branches etched with white. The black mirror of the water held an emerald waver along the edges, a phantom ripple that echoed the flicker of the northern lights that danced above.

Thistle Grove had spectacular displays of aurora borealis in the winter, despite not being anywhere close to far enough north; another of those beautiful quirks that those of us who lived here simply took for granted.

All Thistle Grove witches loved the lake, but I *loved* it. The way you loved something that was only yours, even though of course Lady's Lake belonged to all of us. Maybe to the Harlows most of all, since they were the ones who sieved its remarkable magic into something we all could use. But I'd felt connected to the lake ever since I could remember, as if part of it lived inside myself. Back when I'd gone to college and then law school in New York, I'd had the privilege of being able to portal back up here anytime I wanted, to sit on the shore and let the lake's sustaining magic roll over me—with the significant fringe benefit of my own talent never waning with distance, as happened to other witches who spent significant amounts of time away from Thistle Grove.

Maybe, more than the fact that I loved it, sometimes it felt like the lake loved *me*.

Or maybe that was just the infamous Blackmoore egotism at play, our sense that this town revolved around us just because we happened to be the strongest of the families. I tried not to think like that when I caught myself doing it—being powerful didn't make you *better*, not in any way that mattered—but when it came to the lake, sometimes I let myself slip.

I took a few crunching steps closer, wind lifting my hair as I approached the water's edge, that muffled, wintry silence pressing into my ears. Each exhale turned into a spinning ghost in front of me, tumbling away into the night. It was so cold that my eyeballs burned with it, and I could feel a shiver start up even under my heavy-duty parka. Still, contentment curled catlike in my belly, that sense of pure belonging I only really felt up here.

Like I was known, and I was perfect, and I didn't need to be anything beyond what I already was.

I sighed a little, wrapping my arms around myself and closing my eyes, wishing I could feel this untroubled all the time. Wishing I were different, stronger, better . . . that *everything* was different, but in a way that would let me make peace with myself. Discover the version of me that had it in her to be happy and confident, truly at home in her own skin.

The wind died down as if a switch had been flipped, so completely and abruptly my eyes sprang open.

Just in time to see the lake flare white.

It was brief but utterly dazzling, like a colossal flare had gone off somewhere in the depths, a controlled explosion that somehow didn't so much as ripple the water's surface. Then the blinding white seemed to *fracture*, dissolving into a glittering mosaic of silver and platinum, like a shower of falling stars—if stars could fall upside down, rising like bubbles from the bottom of the lake up to its smooth surface.

I stood rooted in place, shading my eyes and gaping as the water finally cleared, shifting back to black and green, a simple reflection of the night. I had *never* seen the lake do anything like that in my whole life, not even during the Gauntlet last fall. It had looked, for all the world, like some kind of enormous spell being cast somewhere deep beneath the water, farther down than anyone had ever reached.

But what kind of spell could that possibly have been?

And who could have cast it, when there was only me up here?

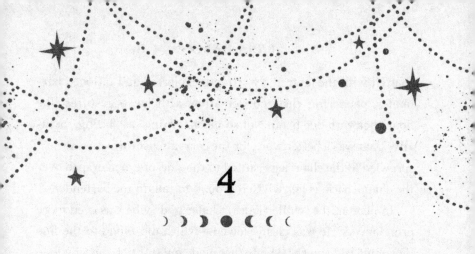

4

You're That Nina

I WAS STILL RUNNING through possible explanations for what I'd seen at the lake when I walked into the Moon and Scythe, scrubbing snow off my boots on the dingy welcome mat. Could it have had something to do with the winter solstice, a little less than a month from now? Or, maybe, some kind of natural magical shift, a new ley line convergence? No one really understood ley lines besides some of the more metaphysically inclined magical historians of the Harlow clan—and those arcane conduits had never seemed to account for Thistle Grove's overflow of magic, anyway. Certainly *I* wasn't likely to get to the bottom of it, when none of us even knew what it was that made the lake tick in the first place.

Even with only half my mind attending to the crowded, noisy tavern, my gaze immediately snagged on Morty.

He sat at one of the tables closer to the bar, grinning as he chatted with the (extremely attractive) pierced and tattooed bartender, peppering their conversation with loose gestures like flourishes with one hand. Not so much "sitting" as "lazing," actually. That was a better word for the easy, almost careless way he'd sprawled in the chair, legs canted to the side, one arm draped over the chair's back as he swiveled around to talk to the bartender.

In person, the "chilled-out trickster god" vibe was even more pronounced. He was clean-shaven—which did *things* to the fine line of his jaw and cheekbone that made my stomach flip a little—but his longish dark brown hair was mussed, flopping into eyeliner-shaded eyes. His outfit landed somewhere between "1920s British gangster" and "Byronic poet," with brogue boots, gray tweed trousers and waistcoat, and a penny-collared white dress shirt with billowing sleeves, unbuttoned to the hollow of his throat.

A highly questionable sartorial situation that on anyone else would've looked like a costume, like someone doing *way* too much—especially considering where we were. On him, the whole thing managed to seem bespoke, like an offbeat *Esquire* spread.

I felt that little frisson of excitement you get when someone turns out to be even hotter in real life than they were on the internet. In general, I wasn't the biggest fan of surprises, but this was the kind even a rigid Virgo like me could get behind.

It made me feel marginally better about the shoe-sucking floor and cloying old-beer smell, the TV droning sportsball above the weathered bar. Not that I had a problem with divey bars, per se; I just didn't see any compelling reason to ever set foot in one. To be fair, I hadn't previously been meeting punked-out Shelby brothers in them, either. And now that I was here, it seemed the Moon and Scythe *did* have some character to it; the walls were lined with battered but still handsome wooden panels, along with an outsize vintage map of Thistle Grove with elaborate depictions of the four family demesnes, the cemetery and the Witch Woods, and other town points of interest.

Maybe a drink or two here would be . . . tolerable.

Morty had noticed me, too, as I wove my way through the tables toward him, shucking my parka and slinging it over an arm. He cut off his conversation and turned slowly in the chair, fixing his entire focus on me. Eyes drifting from my face down to my body, a corner of that pretty mouth lifting a little as he took me in.

I'd gone for my version of casual, which was still way overdressed for this place. A lacy black Zara bodysuit under a navy blue blazer, high-waisted jeans tucked into knee-high Hermès riding boots (that were much warmer than they looked, thankfully), three slim, connected chains layered around my throat like golden cobwebs.

I'd have felt cringingly out of my element, with my tiny diamond earrings and meticulous balayage and nylon laque parka—like I was being the worst kind of entitled asshole just by barging in here—had it not been for the warm, appreciative way Morty was looking at me. Not to mention his own bold outfit choice.

"Nina," he said, rising to meet me, eyes glittering even in the muted light. They were even bluer in real life, that electric azure that looks photoshopped. "Hey."

So, no "heya" in person. Promising.

Both of us leaned in for an introductory hug, something I rarely did on a first date. But the chemistry was instant, an unmistakable jolt, tingles teeming in my belly as his cheek brushed mine. He was the barest span taller than me, one of his hands landing lightly on my lower back to draw me in. We lingered for just long enough to let me draw in a deep breath of his scent. I don't know what I'd been expecting: Axe body spray, damp wool, patchouli? But it certainly wasn't this expensive-smelling unisex perfume, both crisp and sultry, heavy on the ambergris. Distinctive but balanced, in the way I liked best for my own fragrances.

He didn't seem like the type of person to drop serious money on cologne, but hell, who was I to make elitist assumptions about someone I didn't even know? *Don't be such a snotty jackass, Blackmoore*, I chided myself. *For all you know, trickster gods have champagne tastes in perfume, too.*

When he drew back, I could see the way his pupils had dilated, the black flaring into the bright blue.

"Wow," he said, gaze still locked on mine, "you smell fucking phenomenal."

I did, in fact. I'd spritzed myself with Tom Ford Santal Blush—the one Jessa referred to as Taylor Swift's Blessing after she read somewhere that it was T. Swift's favorite perfume—for a little confidence boost in the car. The opening notes of sandalwood and jasmine lingered, heady and creamy and generally showstopping.

But as soon as he said it, I recoiled, unable to suppress a reflexive wince. It wasn't that I didn't swear myself, far from it. It had just been ingrained in me since early childhood that first meetings demanded an ironclad protocol in order to make a good impression. A very unforgiving code of conduct that deemed curse words to be coarse, uncouth, and completely unacceptable most of the time, but *especially* when meeting someone new.

"Sorry," Morty said immediately, brow furrowing as he took a step back from me, palms out. He had a tattoo in the center of each palm: the blurry outline of a shamrock inside a black heart on one, an Eye of Horus in the other. "Was that . . . too forward?"

"No, not at all!" I assured him, feeling my cheeks heating. I was a terrible blusher, splotching with embarrassment at the slightest provocation, and once the ignition sequence fired up, I'd yet to discover an abort button. "Thank you. I, uh, I love this perfume, too. I just have this knee-jerk reaction to swearing, sometimes, it's incredibly stupid. Should probably bring *that* up in therapy, right?"

He nodded a little warily, clearly torn between respectfully acknowledging my mental health journey and respectfully pretending I hadn't brought it up within the first ten seconds of conversation with a near-total stranger like the world's most unwieldy icebreaker. Then he rallied, flashing me a half smile.

"Okay, well, as long as I haven't managed to fuck things up before we even sat down." His eyes slid closed, crinkling at the corners. "Shit, sorry—I mean, *damn*. Honestly, I had no idea I cursed this much."

"It's *really* not a big deal!" I insisted, my cheeks now fully aflame, heat pooling down my neck. I could practically feel the chemistry evaporate between us, evanescing in a sad little *womp womp* cartoon poof. "I swear all the time myself, seriously. It's just a whole thing in my family—they can be kind of sticklers about it—and sometimes it gets stuck in my head in an extremely unhelpful way when I'm meeting someone for the first time. But it's fine if you do it. Completely fucking fine, even!"

He cocked his head, squinting, probably wondering what long line of perplexing killjoys had managed to spawn a neurotic mess such as myself. Well, Jessa had been right that picking someone unlikely would change the vibe. This was, in fact, notably more tragic than what usually transpired in the first few minutes of my dates. I was starting to feel unhinged, like a supremely awkward body-snatcher had hijacked my mouth and mental processes.

"You know what, why don't we just . . . let's just maybe have a drink?" I said a little pleadingly, draping my coat over the back of my chair.

"Absolutely, I'll go grab some for us," Morty said, springing into action with a *tad* too much zeal, like a trip to the bar might provide momentary refuge from me. To be fair, the hot bartender had seemed a lot more capable of normal human conversation than his date was turning out to be. "What'll you have?"

"Gin martini, please," I replied, flashing a mental middle finger to the Ghost of Sydney Past before she could admonish me for ordering my go-to drink, even on a night engineered to be free-wheeling. *Take that, you garbage ghost, I'm a grown woman and I drink what I want.*

Morty paused, rocking his head back and forth and chewing on the inside of his cheek. "I don't know that I'd recommend getting one of those here. My buddy Alisha over there and the rest of the Scythe crew are fantastic folks, but not what you might call *mixologists.*"

To my knowledge, gin martinis weren't the bartending equivalent of quantum mechanics, but okay. "A glass of malbec, then," I said, feeling proud of myself for adapting to this evolving situation.

Morty sucked air through his teeth, scrunching up his nose. "They really only do a house red, I think. Does that work?"

The idea of some hypersweet ambiguous red made my sprawling blush threaten to level up into hives.

"Mm, I'll pass. Seems like you come here a lot, though," I added, striving for a judgment-free tone, even though I was coming to loathe the Moon and Scythe more with every further moment it denied me palatable alcohols. "What would you recommend?"

"Their drafts never miss, if you're into beer," he said, brightening at the opportunity to *not* be a drink-choice downer. "If not, I'd stick to straight liquor, or your more basic mixed drinks—Jack and Coke, vodka tonic, Long Island iced tea if you're feeling that kind of wild. You can always trust you'll get that good and heavy pour here."

A good and heavy pour was beginning to sound like such a medical necessity that my insurance would probably cover it.

"A gin and tonic would be perfect, thank you," I said, combing my fingers through the curling ends of my hair, a nervous gesture that had the benefit of at least appearing flirty.

Before he turned toward the bar, I could see Morty's gaze linger on the fall of "effortlessly" beachy waves that had taken me a solid twenty minutes to achieve; maybe all hope wasn't yet lost. I watched him slide through the knot of people who'd gathered between us and the bar, my gaze snaring on the lithe way he moved even in a crowd. The fluid shift of his weight as he leaned against the bar top, resting his forearms against the edge and flicking his head to clear the hair from his eyes. There was a certain kind of seamless feminine elegance to it, almost like charisma in motion.

The lowkeyloki version of BDE, if you will.

By the time he made it back with the drinks, I'd snuck his glass of water and held it pressed against both cheeks, for long enough that they were probably at least inching back toward normal. He slid my drink in front of me with a wink, and wonder of wonders, I found it *sexy*, even though I'd once given Jessa an entire unsolicited TED Talk on why I believed being winked at repulsed most women on a cellular level.

"The pour was, indeed, heavy as hell," he said solemnly. "I made very sure to supervise."

I laughed, curling my hand around the sweating glass. "This one's to you, then," I said, lifting it up. "For still having my back on drink ordering, even though I managed to swear-shame you pretty much first thing."

"Occupational hazard," he said, grinning as he clinked his beer against my glass. "Can't stand to see someone overpay for their alcohol—*even* if that someone is policing what's apparently my primary mode of expression. That's actually why I like to come here, besides the good vibes and excellent company. Makes for a nice break from more complicated beverages."

"So, you're a bartender, too?" I asked, taking a welcome swallow of the gin and tonic, thankfully every bit as strong as promised. "And here I was, wondering whether worker's comp covered risking life and limb while hanging upside down."

"Believe it or not, I do not get paid fat stacks to fuck around with silks," he said with a soft chuckle. "Or even hired, in any conventional sense. More like, I audition for the privilege of getting to perform a hobby. And yeah, I do bartend. Have you been to the Shamrock Cauldron, over on Myrtle? My family owns it; I actually took over running it from my dad, just a few years back."

The name rang a faint warning bell in the backmost belfries of my brain, even though I could have sworn that I'd never been anywhere with a name like that. Stranger still, there was an amorphous but distinctly negative association attached to it.

I let it go, unable to pinpoint it any further. "I work with my family, too. In-house counsel for all our business concerns."

"Ah, so you're a *lawyer*," he replied, feigning a shudder, a reaction that annoyed me to no end no matter how many times I encountered it. "Can't say you all make up one of my favorite groups of humans. Present company very much excluded, of course."

"Well, everyone's entitled to their opinion," I said, a little huff-ily, the butterfly swarm in my belly stilling in their fluttering. "And hating on lawyers never seems to go out of style—until, you know, you end up needing one! But I happen to love my job."

"To each their own," he said with a neat shoulder flick of a shrug, lifting his beer for a swig. "Didn't mean to rag on you. I've just had enough unsavory dealings with 'em to leave a bad taste in my mouth, is all. Shouldn't have tarred you with the same brush."

"Right," I said, crossing my arms over my chest. "Well, in re-turn, I'll try my very best not to hold every shitty drink I've ever had against you, too."

Another husky chuckle, almost like a whispered laugh, and a brief flash of that gorgeous crooked grin. He spread his hands like, *mea culpa*. "Okay, touché. That was out of line, I'm sorry. Love to see that fighting spirit, though."

"Oh, trust me on this," I said, lifting a challenging eyebrow. "Got enough of *that* for ten."

"'Do not be fool enough to argue with this woman, lest you meet your untimely end,'" he intoned, jotting down imaginary notes. "Got it now."

"Oh, I meant to ask," I said, reminded by the reference to "woman." "I wanted to make sure I had your pronouns right. What do you prefer?"

"'He/him' is fine, but I also get a lot of 'they' when I perform, and honestly, that works great, too. I've always been pretty fluid with it. I default to 'he' at the bar and at home, since it also feels true and it makes my mom more comfortable about . . ." He ges-tured vaguely at his eyeliner, the outfit, the entirety of his person. "Thank you for asking, by the way. Not everyone thinks to."

"Of course. Basic courtesy, right?" I gave him a small smile, glad to be back on less contentious ground. "Must be tricky, navigating that with your family if everyone's not on the same page."

For all their many—*many*—faults, my parents had never had any issues with whom I chose to date—which, of course, wasn't really the same thing at all.

"My pops is actually awesome about identity shit, and always has been," Morty said, knuckling away that stubborn hair from his eyes with a graceful whisk of the hand. He wore even more rings than Jessa, a dense collection of chrome and gray and matte black that highlighted the taper of his fingers and the muscled broadness of his hands. "But for my mother, it's a cultural *and* generational thing. She's almost ten years older than he is, and emigrated from Ireland thirty-ish years ago. Her upbringing was on the, shall we say, more uptight end of the Catholic spectrum."

I made an expressive face, sucking air through my teeth.

"Exactly," he said, with another breathy chuckle. "She loves me, and she tries her damnedest, but sometimes she just . . . doesn't quite *get* it, you know? Still. She does her best, I know that."

"I'd think her maternal instincts might be more triggered by how potentially fatal your hobbies seem to be."

"Dang," he marveled, a slight but unmistakable edge of annoyance to his voice, "you're really still stuck on that risk factor, aren't you?"

"I just have a strong desire to not die any sooner than absolutely necessary." I shrugged, took a sip of my gin and tonic. "And difficulty understanding when someone doesn't seem similarly invested in living to a ripe old age."

"Well, like everything else, when it comes to silk safety, you can be smart or stupid about it," he said, recrossing his legs and shifting in the chair in a way that somehow came across as adversarial. "I tend to choose smart. But not gonna lie, I do it for the thrill, too. That's a built-in part of the appeal."

"To each their own," I said primly, echoing his own earlier dismissal of me. "I'll stick with my marathons."

"So you're a runner," he said, in the same lackluster tone one might say "probate accountant," all but wrinkling his nose. "Cool."

"It gets me moving!" I chirped, trying by sheer force of will to reignite that early spark between us, even as it became increasingly clear that having next to nothing in common was not, in fact, incredibly conducive to conversation. "I've also done a couple Tough Mudders, even ran the Boston Marathon a few years back. It's tough during winter, being stuck inside on a treadmill."

"You could still run outside on the nicer days," he pointed out. "People do."

"I am aware," I said, gritting my teeth. "But it's really not the best idea. It locks up your muscles and joints, and if you fall—of which there's obviously a much higher likelihood—you can do a lot more damage to your body than you might in warmer weather."

"Definitely very risky," he agreed, in that same deadpan tone that made it sound like he was humoring me, as if the objectively enhanced risks of winter running were something I was exaggerating to a paranoid degree.

I dug my fingers into my palms, reminding myself that this was the point; Morty *wasn't* a good fit for me, and therefore I should endeavor to chill a little. Lean into the chemistry, instead of stressing over the possibility of a compatible partnership.

"So, your burlesque photos look like such a blast," I attempted. "I didn't realize there was even a scene here. I love anything like that, especially with a cosplay element. Kind of grew up with it."

His eyebrows ticked up at that, as if he were shocked that a sad stick-in-the-mud like me could appreciate any form of risqué or creative entertainment.

"There isn't, really," he replied. "I stick to Carbondale for that. They have plenty of theaters and clubs that do cabaret nights. I think they host some events over at Castle Camelot, too. But fuck if I'd ever set foot on Blackmoore property, much less give those tools my money."

I tried to keep my face schooled in the same expression of polite interest, even though my blood pressure felt like it had shot up to press against the underside of my skull.

"And why is that?" I said, clearing my throat, my fingers twitching around my glass.

"Because they're a bunch of outrageous, entitled chucklefucks," he spat, jaw tightening, his face settling into harsh lines I wouldn't have expected to ever see on such elfin features. "Who can't take no for a fucking answer. The oldest one especially—that sublime shithead Gareth—rolls into the Shamrock all the time like some kind of *lordling*. Like he owns *my* place. They tried to buy it out from under me and my pops a dozen times over the past year or so, no matter how often we shut them down. Just kept grinding at it, even after he . . ."

He swallowed whatever he'd been about to say and shook his head instead, mouth curling in disgust. "Some people have no limits, you know? No basic decency."

I dug my nails even deeper into my palms, trying to keep my lips from quivering—because in this instance, "some people" was me.

Since we lost the Gauntlet of the Grove, along with the magical boost in fortune that the Victor's Wreath provided, the profitability of our holdings had taken a significant hit. We'd lost a good chunk of the seasonal tourist horde to the Avramovs' Arcane Emporium and haunted house, and the Thorns' orchards with their enchanted hedge maze and sunflower field. In response, my mother had wanted to expand our presence into Castle Camelot–themed stores and bars in downtown Thistle Grove, where they'd be even more readily accessible to strolling visitors. And there had been a particularly promising row of commercial real estate on Myrtle Street, just off the main drag, Yarrow, that lent itself easily to that kind of conversion.

And it wasn't just her; we were all excited about the idea, this new chance to do more, become bigger. Feel relevant again, central to this town the way we'd historically been.

The Shamrock Cauldron had been the only one of the venues that hadn't agreed to sell to us, no matter how we sweet-talked them, or how much pressure we applied behind the scenes. I knew, because I'd been the one drafting increasingly insistent letters of intent addressed to Armando Gutierrez and Mortimer Gutierrez, co-owners of the Shamrock Cauldron. That was why I'd remembered the name in the first place.

Because it was the bar that belonged to the Mortimer Gutierrez now sitting in front of me, fire blazing in his eyes at the mere mention of my family.

In my (admittedly biased) opinion, we hadn't done anything that your standard deal-driven businessperson wouldn't do; certainly nothing unsavory, or even borderline immoral. They'd said no to us repeatedly, yes, so we'd tried different tacks, searching for a mutually viable solution—because that was how negotiations *worked*. From what I remembered, we'd ended by offering a significant lump sum, well above the Shamrock Cauldron's market value, and they still hadn't bitten. So it wasn't like we'd been turning the screws on them.

Somehow, I didn't think we'd be seeing eye to eye on that.

"I am very sorry to hear you think so," I said through tingling lips. I was used to—and even relished—a certain kind of confrontation. But that was in my work life, when I was safely ensconced inside the chilly sheath of professionalism and my impeccably tailored business suit. This felt more like an ambush or a trap, even if an unintentional one. Like I'd found myself thrashing in eel-infested waters when I'd thought I was just going for a relaxing, balmy dip. "Especially because that happens to be my family you're bad-mouthing."

"Holy shit," Morty said slowly, jaw dropping as the pieces clicked into place, narrowed eyes glinting icy blue with even more concentrated dislike. "'Nineve Blackmoore, Esquire.' Fuck me, that's *you*, isn't it? You're *that* Nina."

"I am that Nina," I agreed, forcibly quelling any tremble in my voice, pushing back my chair before I could hear more about what he thought of me, specifically. "And now, I think I'm going to go."

At least, I thought, as I shrugged into my parka and hightailed it out of the bar before Morty could respond, as far as silver linings went—Jessa owed me *so many* pigs in blankets (and hot succubi) for this debacle.

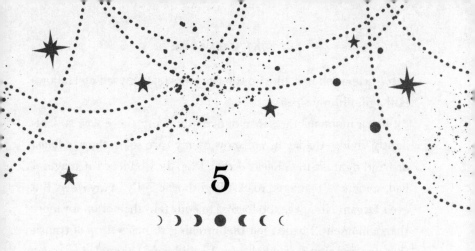

5

The Lady of the Lake

BACK HOME ON my couch, tucked under an angora throw in my underwear while more snow pinwheeled against the dark beyond the floor-to-ceiling picture window, I proceeded to get pity-drunk by myself. At least my wine fridge served the kind of delicious and expensive red that only theoretically shared a name with whatever swill they poured at the Moon and Scythe. And instead of football gibberish and shouted conversation, I got to wallow in the most tragic parts of the *Battlestar Galactica* score on repeat.

Overall, an undeniable improvement in setting if not mood.

Trapped in that obnoxiously maudlin "I will never love again" wasteland that apparently came with tannins, I dragged myself to bed only once I'd started dozing off between weeps. I didn't usually dream anything at all when drunk. But tonight, almost as soon as my head hit the pillow, I found myself back on the lake's snow-heaped shores, like I'd somehow portaled myself up Hallows Hill again in my sleep.

For a moment, the sense of actually being there was so brilliantly vivid—the icy fire of snow on my bare soles, the sandblast of wind against my cheeks—that I hazily wondered if maybe I had, somehow, managed to cast Lightborne Folly in my sleep. But even Dream Nina was too logical to entertain the notion for more than a moment. I hadn't felt that lurching stomach drop of transition, for one thing, and not even I could have channeled as much will as a portal passage demanded without sensing it, especially not asleep.

And that was the other thing—I *knew* that I was dreaming, in that lucid sense that felt both divorced from reality and utterly real. Yet a part of me also couldn't shake the pervasive conviction that I *was* really here, with the emerald fronds of the aurora borealis rippling above my head, the stalactite points of frozen stars shimmering coldly against the night.

But I wasn't here; I couldn't be. Not only because there was no magic I knew of that could have whisked me here but also because, above me, the stars had begun to fall.

Another perk of Thistle Grove—we got many more stars to wish on than should have been our due. But this . . . this shower was unlike anything I'd ever seen. Silver streaks rained furiously from above, striking the lake's black surface like molten arrows without disturbing it. They fell all around me, too, pinpricks that tingled without quite stinging where they struck my skin, melting into me like sparks cast off from an icy fire. The ones that fell on my hair caught and tangled in it like captive snowflakes, a spangle of blinding glitter in the edges of my vision.

It reminded me of earlier, when I really had stood up here, that vast and shimmering explosion that had detonated beneath the lake. As if what was happening now had happened then—only this time, I was seeing it from above.

Then the lake called my name.

NINEVE CLIODHNA BLACKMOORE
NINEVE, MY VERY OWN
NINA, MY NINA, COME NOW, MY NINA

I felt the summons rather than hearing it; a thrumming tremor that buzzed down to my marrow, rattling through my bones in the most compelling way.

"I hie to you, my Lady," I responded, my voice resonating with doubled harmonics, like some powerful instrument. My mouth shaped the words of its own accord, a colossal swell of awe expanding in my chest until it strained against the confines of my ribs, coupled with a knowing like déjà vu.

I'd been here and done this many, many times before—and then I'd forgotten.

But I remembered now.

Without thinking twice, I took one step, followed by another—leaving searing footprints in my wake, as if my soles had gone red-hot, turned closer to flame—and then I broke into a headlong run toward the lake. Once I reached the edge, I pushed off my toes and simply jumped, sparing just the slightest panicky thought for the hypothermic rush that awaited me on the other end.

And by the triple goddess, it was fucking *cold*.

Freezing water fractured around me like shards, bitter blades of cold pressed against every inch of my skin, flooding down my throat when I gasped at it. For a moment, I thought with sheer, terrified conviction that I was going to drown and die, frigid water stopping up my lungs. My limbs turning numb and leaden as that all-consuming cold leached all the warm life from my blood.

And then, it was over. The cold abruptly fled, rushing off as if it had been sucked away, a pleasant flush of heat stealing in to cover me in its place. I had a niggling sense that something like this had always been a part of it; a painful test that I had to pass, to be granted access to whatever came next.

For a moment, I floated without any effort, the water holding me suspended like a buoy. My hair writhed around my head like a pale corona, those plunging stars still falling all around me in a shimmering underwater cascade. I could still feel that invading water inside my mouth, the press of it against my open eyes and cheeks—but I could also breathe without any trouble. As if I'd spent my whole life with secret gills, waiting to be deployed at a moment like this.

Then I began a slow, tugged descent toward the bottom of the lake.

It was a drifting plunge that felt a little bit like flying, as if something deep down in those fathoms were magnetized, and I was just a tiny iron filing. I could feel the pressure of the water building, pressing down on my head as I sank deeper and farther, the dazzle of that star shower lighting my way through the liquid dark. Some of the weirder fauna that lived in the lake nosed curiously up to me, drawn by the light; vast translucent jellyfish filled with silvery squiggles like coiled springs, deep purple squid that watched me with glittering black eyes. But none of them ventured too close to me.

I *should* have been afraid. Though Thistle Grove witches (and the few bolder normies of Morty's persuasion) swam freely in Lady's Lake—and had probably dived in it, too, over the years—no one knew how deep it was. How far it tunneled down into the mountaintop.

How far I had to go, until I reached whatever it was that waited for me at the bottom.

But I wasn't afraid, or in any rush. The descent felt timeless, as in, lifted entirely out of time; like something I'd been doing forever, or possibly just the last ten seconds, without any distinction between the two possibilities. When the bottom began looming into sight, I was faintly surprised, like I'd been ready for a much longer trip.

The lake bed held nothing of what you'd expect to find, not tumbled rocks or kelp or tattered shipwrecks, nor the odd sea monster curled up in its den. Instead, there were coins; whole legions of them, heaped on top of one another like the glitter of a dragon's treasure chest. And as I watched those infinite stars fall around me, I saw each bounce as it hit the bottom, turning into the shimmer of a spun coin in slow motion before it settled into the sediment.

I shouldn't have been able to see their legends; I was still too high up for that. But still, I could tell that each one was inscribed with an eight-pointed star, drawn around a woman's face. And I knew, without understanding how I knew it, that this was *her*. The Lady, the one who called to me so insistently.

The Lady who presided over this lake.

Then I drifted even farther down, borne like a tiny barge on my own private current, and the statue finally hovered into view.

She was carved from some glowing alabaster stone, bright and pale as a star's own heart. A tall and lovely woman lying naked on a plinth, long coils of her hair ribboning all around her, the oval face they framed such a painful perfection it made you want to cry.

A rush of pure adoration filled me, a love above and beyond any other love. I sank to the lake bed by her feet, disturbed silt drifting around my knees. I knew this Lady with my whole heart; I'd *always* known her. She'd been calling to me in my dreams since I was a little girl, and I'd been swimming down to meet her for all these years, to pay my respects and simply see her, spend some time.

And then forgetting each visit with her, as soon as the night was done.

Head bowed, I reached up to the plinth and pressed my palms to the pale stone. It glowed with heat like a forge, as if it existed somewhere far from even the concept of winter. As soon as I touched it, a pulse of deep approval shimmered through me, and *O HOW I'VE MISSED YOU, MY NINA, WELCOME BACK TO ME* clamored through my bones.

"I've missed you, too," I whispered back, my voice distorted with those resonant harmonics even underwater. And apparently, even this far below the water's surface, Dream Nina could still cry. Grateful tears sprang to my eyes as I pressed my forehead to the Lady's plinth, feeling a warm current rush through my veins like electricity, like a slew of sunshine buried fathoms deep.

My Lady was not only a lady of the water, but also one of fire and light.

Now that I remembered her, and all the other times I'd come here in my sleep, I knew—this time was different. There'd never been all these stars before, or the coins that they'd become. There'd been only light and water and solace; the loving silence of me and her in our private communion.

COME, NINA, pressed against my mind, a vibrating summons that had me rising to my feet before its echo even trailed off. *COME FOR THE REQUESTED BLESSING.*

I drifted over by her side, until I reached her face. And slowly, so slowly, over a span of seconds and minutes and sprawling eons, the Lady did what she had never done before.

She turned her implacable stone head toward me, and opened her eyes.

They were huge and honey colored, a crystalline amber like a cat's. And they shone with a riotous overflow of life, a ferocious, knee-trembling love of a magnitude far beyond human comprehension.

Shock surged through me like grounded lightning; even now that I remembered all the times I'd sat down here with her, I knew it hadn't been like this. I'd always felt, from the weight of her awareness, her massive regard, that some small part of her was here with me. But all those times she'd been frozen, unmoving, a true statue of stone. Not a living being, a goddess in situ, but only the avatar of one.

I had a sudden revelation, like a knowing dropped directly into my mind, that this statue wasn't *really* the Lady herself. That in another lake very like this one, the two of them inextricably entwined—though the other existed somewhere far away, in this world or possibly some other—the actual goddess incarnate slept an endless sleep.

O COME, MY NINA, COME NEARER STILL
AND LEAVE NO ROOM FOR FEAR

She gave a slow blink, her eyes narrowing as if she were trying to smile at me. I smiled back, a huge and wobbling and delirious grin, beside myself with happiness. The pull toward her grew even stronger, a humming compulsion I couldn't have resisted even if I'd wanted to, and no part of me felt any inclination to resist. Her summons had a distinctive sound to it, a warbling waver that traveled between us like a single plucked note carried by the water.

I let my own face fall forward, closer and closer yet to hers, until I could see every bold line of those beautiful features—every eyelash and cleft and sweetheart dimple—imperfectly rendered though they were.

Wherever this Lady really slept, she was infinitely lovelier than even this lovely stone could convey.

O KISS ME, NINA, MY NINA

I obeyed, my star-studded hair swirling around both our faces, my mouth just grazing hers, the stone turning to a supple, living softness beneath my lips . . .

And then—

6

The Starstruck Coin

IWOKE WITH A shearing gasp, feeling like my lungs were splitting in two.

I sat bolt upright in bed, my teeth chattering with the memory of a terrible, consuming cold; even as a heat like melted butter still warmed the pit of my stomach, trickling in warm runnels through my bones.

"What the *hell*," I whispered shakily to myself, pressing a fist to my chest. My heart battered so hard against my sternum I could feel its shudder against my hand. Memories flooded me, of plunging deep into the frozen lake, drifting down and down for some unknown eternity, to meet the glowing goddess who waited for me on the other end of the descent.

Now that I wasn't dreaming, the idea of that plunge, all that awful, crushing water above my head and all around me, filled me with jangling panic, a volcanic terror. Not even the thought of the goddess herself—the ferocious sweetness of her, the luminosity of all that inexplicable love she somehow had for me—could cut the fear. I could have drowned. I *should* have drowned. Even in a dream, you weren't damn well supposed to go without breathing for that long, like some free diver plunging for pearls.

"It was just a dream," I told myself, squeezing my eyes shut hard, trying to rein in the furious gallop of my breath. *"Just a dream*, Nina. You're here, in your own bed—and see, you're not even wet. It was just—"

Then I felt something cutting into my palm, something wedged tight inside the knot of my fist. A fine tremble racing through me, I lowered my hand into my lap, holding my breath as I slowly peeled my fingers back.

A coin sat on my palm, as if it had been pressed into my hand like a token. Golden and shimmering, an octagram inscribed around the cameo of a familiar, gorgeous face. It felt warm against my skin, like an oath; a promise that this time, I would not only remember—this time, I would *know* beyond the whisper of a doubt that it had really happened.

Somehow, I had really been down there with her.

I dropped the coin as if it had caught fire, leaping from my bed as it vanished into the tangled nest of my sheets with a final glimmer like a wink. Arms wrapped around myself, I paced back and forth across my chilly marble floor, predawn light sifting through my windows like a frosty film, trying desperately to keep my extremely tenuous shit together.

Because this, whatever was happening to me—even by Thistle Grove standards—this was very, very far from normal.

Yes, I was a witch of ancient lineage, living in an objectively enchanted town; it wasn't as though I didn't *believe* in goddesses and gods, or doubted the magic that rolled like a reliable tide through my own veins. And all the families held specific beliefs of their own, often faiths that included divine pantheons. Even the branches we all traced our family trees back through sank their roots deep into old and venerable magic. My own name was one of the variations of Nimue and Vivien—names for either one enchantress or several, who'd variously seduced Merlin, given Excalibur to Arthur, and raised Lancelot, in different iterations of the Arthurian tale.

But even Morgan le Fay, the infamous Blackmoore ancestress—she'd lived, what, a solid thousand years ago? Maybe in *her* time there'd been sleeping goddesses lurking in every random body of water, and no one gave it so much as a second thought when they got summoned down for an impromptu dive by one of them.

But this was the twenty-first century, and these days we didn't have deities traipsing all over Thistle Grove. I couldn't remember a single story told during a Sabbat or Esbat circle, not even during one of the eight Wheel of the Year holidays, about a Thistle Grove witch encountering an actual goddess in either the flesh or the stone. Up until last night, none of us had even known what fueled the magic of the lake.

The idea that only I knew what was really down there—not the elders or the Harlow historians; not even Emmeline Harlow herself, the living Voice of Thistle Grove and the current Victor of the Wreath—made me want to melt into a puddle of stunned disbelief.

I buried my hands in my hair, nearly tripping over Nadja of Antipaxos as she twined between my ankles with an anxious purr. My sweet (and profoundly unstable) tabby familiar preferred to live under my bed rather than sleep in it with me, and I usually saw her only when I needed her help for spellwork, or in one of her rare bouts of manic love. The fact that she seemed legitimately worried about me now only amplified my distress; when Nadja bothered to make an appearance, that meant shit was getting real.

And why was this happening to me? Even for a witch, I was too damn *average* for divine visitations. Yes, I'd spent my much of my adult life savoring rewatches of *Supernatural* and *Torchwood* and *The Magicians* alongside my many sci-fi favorites—but I was also a lawyer, a planner, an arguably overly enthusiastic spreadsheet maker. Hell, I wore suits nearly every day of my life and relished it. I was a grounded, competent, mundane person, someone who thrived on rules and stability.

What I wasn't, was equipped to process the existence of an entire goddess—or a sentient statue of one, or whatever implausible thing it was that lived inside our lake.

"Screw it," I muttered, bending over to scratch Nadja between the ears as she worry-purred. "This is just not gonna work for me today."

I tried not to go into the office on Sundays, so I could at least maintain the semidelusional pretense of work-life balance. But now I desperately needed—scratch that, *craved*—the normalcy of my two-screen desktop, the extensive list of contractual law and employment issues that were on my agenda for next week. I even had a court appearance coming up for a labor dispute, an atypical and exciting challenge for me. It would be so easy, so satisfying, to shift my attention to that instead of dwelling on . . . *this*.

I knew, logically, that I should go to my mother with what had happened, first thing. Lyonesse was the Blackmoore matriarch, and had been since my grandmother had stepped down as elder following the Avramov-Harlow joint Gauntlet win last Samhain.

But my mother could be . . . challenging, and I wasn't sure if I could handle any further emotional escalation at this moment. And it wasn't like the *stone statue in the lake* wasn't going to keep for another day or two, after however many centuries—or hell, millennia, who knew—it'd been languishing in there.

Mind made up, I took a long shower, then picked out my outfit while my five-step skincare routine seeped into whichever dermal layers it was supposed to be targeting. By the time I'd blown out my hair and finished an understated no-makeup look, it was kind of demoralizing to see how clearly hungover I still looked. Dull and red-rimmed eyes, violet half-moons beneath them that even La Mer concealer couldn't quite cover. That general listless quality that somehow sucked all the volume from your freshly washed hair.

But this, at least, I could fix.

In front of the bathroom mirror, I closed my eyes, bringing both hands above my head with my fingers steepled. I didn't usually resort to glamour spells; unless you were doing them for some particularly worthy reason, they always felt a little bit like cheating.

But maybe, today of all days, I could give myself some grace.

Murmuring the incantation, I brought my hands down over my face, tapping a dainty, precise pattern against my skin with my fingertips. Magic surged up my arms and bloomed in my hands, all swirling heat and liquid honey, the usual exhilarating rush— but *much* zestier than normal, like someone had sprinkled some unexpected Carolina Reaper into the special sauce.

I opened my eyes, and gasped so hard at my reflection that I nearly inhaled my own tongue.

I'd intended the spell to just perk me up a little; erase those bruised circles, infuse a little bounce into my hair and glisten in my eyes. Instead, the glamour had not only understood the assignment, but racked up several thousand bonus points.

My dark brown eyes had turned a lustrous black that shone with refracted color, golden and ruby glints reflecting from my irises like gems. My eyelashes curled so extravagantly long and dark they looked like a doll's, and my eyebrows, which had been perfectly fine before, now looked like the After picture at a very upscale microblading salon that catered exclusively to Beyoncé and Rihanna and other actual queens.

I tilted my face back and forth, inspecting my reflection with a slack jaw. My skin shimmered in a strange, glassy way, as if it had been airbrushed and then lightly dusted with crushed diamonds. My hair all but billowed around me, drifting in a nonexistent breeze, absurdly thick and glossy and nearly four-dimensional in color, as if my highlights reflected more light spectra than the rest of me.

I looked like some uncanny fairy princess, nowhere near the slightly improved version of myself that I'd been shooting for.

It was so overblown and ridiculous that once I got over the sheer shock of it, I actually laughed aloud. Even my voice emerged in a crystalline chime, like a host of delicate cymbals ringing, an entire chorus of Disney princesses tittering together in harmony.

"Okay, well, that was bizarre," I muttered through helpless giggles, lifting my steepled hands back under my chin to reverse the spell. "Hard pass on this whole . . . *look*, however."

I closed my eyes again, murmuring the charm that would undo the glamour, ticking my fingertips back up over my face as another giddying, full-blooded rush of power whipped through my hands.

When I opened them again, the residual smile slipped completely off my face.

The charm hadn't just reversed the glamour. It had, once again, risen far above and beyond my intent—stripping my face completely free of both makeup and moisturizer, even undoing the volume I'd achieved with my blow-dryer and round brush alone. I looked like I'd just rolled out of bed after a sleepless night, and when I experimentally rubbed my fingers over my skin, they came away completely clean. The cosmetics and creams really *were* gone, whisked away by the magic.

The charm had somehow undone not just the glamour, but all the mundane effort I'd put into my makeup and hair.

A chill blew through my belly, sending a flurry of tingles up my spine—because this wasn't supposed to happen. Blackmoores were elementalists and illusionists both, flip sides of the same coin. But an illusion-based spell like the one I'd used wasn't meant to be able to affect the underlying matter this way. It was one of the natural limitations on illusion magic; unlike elemental magic, it could only *mimic* the effect you wanted. But it couldn't transmute, couldn't make any true changes to the base elements.

"What in the actual hell," I said to my reflection as I met my own eyes in the mirror, dull and bloodshot once again, "is happening here?"

7

A Play of Ice and Fire

AN HOUR LATER, I arrived at Castle Camelot looking as close to a normal person as I could manage. Rather than risk any more demented glamour whiplash, I'd just swiped on some concealer and rosy lip balm, coiled my hair into a simple bun, and called it a day. As I stepped from the drawbridge through Castle Camelot's massive wooden double doors, twin onyx-and-gold pennants rippling on either side against a gunmetal sky that presaged yet more endless snow, I was still feeling rattled to the core.

But just the first breath of its familiar air—stone dust, fried carnival food, and the distinctive claylike smell of the cosmetics the face painters used—put me more at ease. Much more than Tintagel, my family's ancestral demesne, Camelot felt like home.

I'd been pelting through these winding corridors of polished flagstones, French braids flying behind me, since I was tiny. Here, I'd eaten myself sick on blooming onions and turkey legs; had my face painted into dragons and tigers and fairy queens; watched knights joust in the courtyard while the reigning court of royal cosplayers cheered and booed them, sometimes letting me play the princess role. When I got older, I often celebrated professional accomplishments with a six-course dinner at the Avalon, an up-scale restaurant marooned on the artificial island in the moat, to which you had to be rowed. And the times I'd gotten tipsy with my brothers in the countless secret places tucked into the towers and battlements practically went without saying.

To me, Camelot wasn't just the cheesiest jewel in the Black-moore crown, the way I knew so many of the town's witches saw it, for sour-grapes reasons or more legitimate ones. It was the cherished place that had shaped me, molded my internal topogra-phy in ways that were often invisible to anyone else. The space in which I'd grown into myself, for better or worse. Even now, though I could easily have moved to some fancier locale downtown much better suited to a legal office, I still preferred to work out of the castle proper simply because I loved being here every day.

In the Great Hall, only a dozen or so tourists were milling around, examining the empty throne and the looming suits of armor guarding the corners, craning their necks at the winged gargoyles clinging to the ceiling, the "medieval" tapestries draped over the stone walls. I'd come at an in-between time, when every-one was either enjoying the matinee, watching the joust, or seated at one of the taverns and snack bars for early lunch. One of the visitors—a burly lumberjack-looking guy, with a tiny, sheepish partner in tow—was jamming his fingers into a suit of armor's visor and yanking it up and down, despite the roughly one thou-sand placards asking tourists not to touch the exhibits.

It sent a bolt of pure rage through me to see it, this blatant disregard for the rules that applied to everyone else, as if he were somehow above them just by existing.

Before I had the chance to do anything about it, one of the squires who served as ushers and attendants bustled toward him, clearly intending to intervene. Still fuming, I headed toward the hidden staircase that would take me the six flights up to my office, directly above the Grand Theatre—where, despite the extra insulation, I could often hear fine strains of music weaving through the stones, the appreciative rumble of applause—when the air turned . . . brittle.

I could feel the change against my skin immediately, all the fine hairs on my neck standing at attention. It was a weird texture thing at first, as if all the humidity had been sucked away. Then the temperature dropped, a frigid plummet so abrupt and unexpected it stole the breath from my lungs.

The tourists felt it, too; they stilled, heads cocked, hugging themselves as they glanced around uneasily.

"Did their heat for real just go bust out of nowhere?" Lumberjackhole muttered to his unfortunate partner, in the peevish tones of someone already composing a pissy Yelp review in their mind. "Because I didn't pay out the wazoo for these tickets just to freeze my ass off."

"I'm sure they'll fix it, honey," his companion said with a conciliatory pat to his arm, as if her Womanly Responsibilities included perennially talking this dipshit down. "It *is* pretty cold outside . . . maybe a pipe just blew or something?"

"They better have those refunds primed and ready, is all I'm saying."

Then a silvery mist came creeping down the hall that led to

the Grand Theatre, and the background music that I'd been hearing filtering from the matinee simply cut off.

"What the shit is that?" Lumberjackhole demanded, spotting the mist at the same time as I did. "Holy fuck, is that—Britt, does that look like *snow*?"

Suck though he did, he wasn't wrong. The mist was indeed coalescing into crystalline snowflakes, small but so perfectly rendered they looked like flakes trapped under a microscope; minute, symmetrical wonders of points and spires, sparkling almost viciously bright, like the edges of keenly whetted blades.

As I watched in mounting horror—because this was most definitely *not* part of *Yvain: The Knight of the Lion* performance that had screeched to such a weirdly silent halt behind the theater's gilded double doors—more and more snowflakes emerged from the mist, an entire lashing flurry of them.

A proper blizzard, except inside the castle.

"The hell is going on out here, Nina?" Gareth said, appearing beside me without warning; slightly out of breath, as if he'd run here at full sprint.

My older brother had been cleaning up his tiresome "rakish scion" act as of late, and part of this personal renaissance included spending more weekends working in his own office, a few doors down from mine. His management of our financial portfolio often intersected with my legal work, so he liked to have me nearby to yank in for help whenever a thornier issue presented itself. He must have sensed the abrupt and ominous shift in atmosphere, too, and followed it down here.

"Why is there a *storm* happening indoors?" he demanded. "Man, Gav had better not be on some other shit again."

"I really don't think it's his . . ." I started to say, but the words withered in my mouth before I could finish.

The snowflakes had begun gathering, swirling around each other in unnervingly intentional little maelstroms, as if they were forming something with a distinctive shape. Something that emerged humanoid but crystalline, with elegant, spindly spikes in place of limbs, and long vulpine faces with eyes of faceted ice, distant ruby lights glimmering in their depths. The mist swathed around it like layers of tulle or gathering robes, as if the thing was wrapping chill air around itself like a garment.

Fear rimed my belly, a spreading frost. This was a creature that I recognized, though I'd heard of them only in stories—and as dire warnings about getting too cocky with your magic.

"Ice wraiths?" Gareth gasped beside me, blanching under his unlikely winter tan. "Are you shitting me right now?"

Ice wraiths were an elemental manifestation, one of the ways Blackmoore magic could go disastrously wrong if pushed too far, manipulated with too much force and too little finesse. When an elemental spell, even a simple one, got pumped too full of magical juice, it had an alarming tendency to go rogue—turning halfway sentient, occasionally even conjuring full creatures that identified closely with that element. Some were relatively benign, like chill-sprites and snowbirds.

Others, like ice wraiths, not so much.

The *Yvain* musical production did feature a gorgeous winter scene, one of the few instances of magic embedded into its otherwise mundane but stunning special effects. It was precise and large-scale enough that usually my own little brother, Gawain—our musical director—cast it himself when it was time, rather than delegating it to another of the Blackmoores who worked with conjuring magical backdrops.

But this show had already run dozens of times this season, and Gawain had never fumbled it like this before. Why today? Why now?

It *had* to be connected to what had happened to me last night.

As Gareth and I stared, appalled, a second wraith appeared, followed by another, and another. They started vocalizing to each other like a hunting pack, in a litany of spine-chilling, high-pitched howls, like a gale whistling between alpine mountain peaks. The tourists had, at this point, twigged to the fact that something uncool—or, possibly *too* cool, so to speak—was transpiring in front of them. Something so uncanny, so divorced from the buxom wenches and chivalrous knights they'd been very reasonably expecting, that they weren't totally sure yet how horrified they should even be. They began slowly backing away from the corridor where the wraiths advanced, about a second away from turning heel and running.

Then one of the ice wraiths rushed at a tourist in a whirl of scything claws—it gunned straight for the Lumberjackhole, as fate would rightly have it—and blew right through him like a winter wind. Leaving him frozen, encased in a thin, glittering shell of ice, his eyes behind it still alive but wide and unblinking.

"Oh, *no*," Gareth exhaled beside me. I nodded mutely, still unable to speak.

So that was why the *Yvain* music had died. There were probably ice wraiths in there, too, along with a whole theater now stacked with aisles of ice-pop people. Including my own annoying, overly sensitive, beloved little brother.

The only way this could possibly be worse would be if our mother were here to witness this catastrophe.

The shock abruptly shattered, falling off me in a fractured sheet, the way it always did when an imminent crisis beckoned. My brain thawed in an instant and then hardened, into something swift and dauntless and capable.

"Gareth," I barked at him, reaching for his hand. Assuming command the way I always did with both my brothers. "Uriel's Flame, in three!"

My brother stared for one more second, slack-jawed and dazed. Then he grasped my hand with a curt nod, interlacing our fingers, grim conviction snapping over his clean-cut face like a knight's visor. My brother might have been the epitome of messy in other areas of life, but he was handy as hell in a crisis. Not like I was—not to plan or lead—but he could fall in line whenever needed. Never a commander, but the best lieutenant you could ask for to stand by your side.

I closed my eyes and took a breath, counted down from three, and began chanting the words in tandem with Gareth, drawing the power sigil of angelfire in the air with my left hand. This elemental spell conjured a benign, angelic fire; one that would conquer cold even in its physical manifestations—and also burn to a crisp those who meant you harm. But it would part harmlessly around those who didn't, would leave any living and innocent thing untouched.

It was a demanding working, best cast in circle, though I could have pulled off a minor iteration even on my own. But since Gareth was here anyway, a mini Blackmoore circle composed of just the two of us would be even more powerful.

As soon as Gareth and I spoke the final, bellowed *ignis* together, the power that whipped up to meet me was monumental—vast and searing, like a vengeful dragon that had been locked inside me for decades was now death-metal raging its way out. Its scalding wings beating inside my own chest as if I'd become its prison, its claws raking at the bars of my ribs. I actually screamed like a harpy with the force of it—a triumphant, resonating shriek, half ecstasy, half pain, that echoed off the walls and probably scared the tourists just as much as the ice wraiths had.

Then a ceiling-high curtain of flame blistered to life in front of me and Gareth, leaping scarlet and gold, giving off a dazzling refracted light that reflected everywhere like a flaming disco ball.

It was colossal, tremendous, so much bigger than it could or should have been. Uriel's Flame usually manifested as an isolated sphere of angelfire, which then traveled to wherever it was guided by the igniter's will. This was . . . not that. *This* was a fearsome tower of flame, a fiery colossus whole scales of magnitude larger than what the spell had called for, and what I'd intended.

And I knew, from the way the magic had roared through me with barely an effort, that I hadn't even needed Gareth's help at all. I could have cast this Godzilla version of the spell, Uriel on All the Steroids, entirely on my own.

Crackling with fury, it surged forward like a towering, infernal wave, burning off the icy mist and dissolving the wraiths as it met them. They melted instantly into harmless wisps of mist, their howls dialing down into fading hisses. As the angelfire seared mercilessly past them, it lapped much more gently over the trapped tourist, thawing him in an instant even as it parted around his shrieking, terrified partner, not even singeing her skin.

Lumberjackhole tumbled to the stones like a sack of stupid potatoes, his companion dropping to her knees beside him, running her hands frantically over his face. I had to admit she seemed genuinely concerned about him; maybe he wasn't always such a high-key ass.

While the rest of the tourists spilled around us in a confused panic, torn between the oblivion glamour already manipulating their short-term memory and the visceral sense that something was Very Wrong Here, the angelfire kept surging down the hallway, licking up and down the walls without damaging them, throwing its strange refracting light up into the gargoyles' peaked faces, making them seem alive. Then it flamed right through the wooden doors, again without leaving so much as a scorch mark—blazing right into the theater, where it would lay waste to the remaining wraiths and set free the audience of frozen spectators.

As if on cue, we could hear a slow, growing commotion kick up from within the theater, a milling churn of fear followed by bewilderment as the ice spell broke. At least our aggravating little brother would live to overemote another day, I thought with a wash of deep relief, nearly sagging with it.

"So," Gareth said conversationally, knuckling back his ash-blond hair, a mixture of awe and trepidation flickering across his face as he turned to eye me with considerable caution. "You and I should probably have us a little chat, then, huh?"

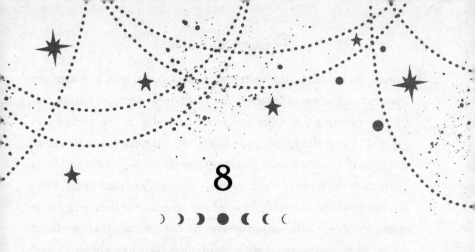

8

What Did You Do to Me?

As it happened, we didn't have much time to talk.

An entire horde of befuddled (and toasty) normies soon came rushing out of the theater, in the thrall of the oblivion glamour that had—clearly very forcefully—erased their memories of the megawatt production they hadn't bought tickets for.

"Do you feel like . . . like you even know what that show was *about*, though?" I heard one groggily murmur to another as they streamed around us, sounding like they'd just woken up from deep sleep or gotten way too high. Apparently the oblivion glamour had had to channel some extra effort to erase the memory of something so epic as a showdown between ice and fire.

I hoped they all still remembered their own middle names and social security numbers.

Then Gawain himself came tumbling out in typically severe emotional distress, mostly on the topic of his show having been ruined, just *ruined*, and what abject blackguard was to blame for this travesty, anyway? Gareth and I had only managed to talk him into flouncing off to take the rest of the day to "re-center and ground" when the missive spell arrived, winging through one of the arched windows with a muted screech.

It took the form of a snowy owl conjuration—part of the Harlow family emblem—which folded and rearranged itself in a series of improbable, Escheresque geometric conversions that produced an envelope, wax-sealed with Emmeline Harlow's personal sigil as both Victor of the Wreath and Voice of Thistle Grove.

"Was all that really necessary?" I asked a little dryly, lifting an eyebrow as the envelope floated over into Gareth's hands.

Gareth rolled his eyes almost fondly, shaking his head. "Nah, it's just Emmy dunking on me again. Fair play, sort of, don't worry about it. Let's see . . ." He slit the envelope open with a thumbnail, then read the paper inside, eyebrows lifting.

"What is it?" I asked, stomach churning with apprehension.

"She's calling an emergency quorum at Harlow House, right now," he said, looking a little stunned as he met my eyes. "Apparently she somehow sensed what happened here today."

"I . . . didn't know she could do that," I said faintly, a tendril of foreboding slithering through my chest as I considered what this might mean for my experience at the lake. Had Emmy felt that, too, that massive disturbance in power? Did she know, somehow, that I'd been there, too?

"Neither did I," Gareth responded with a shrug. "But we've never had a double-threat Victor before, have we?"

That was true. Having traditionally served as Arbiters rather than combatants in the Gauntlet of the Grove—the spellcasting tournament that determined which family scion would govern Thistle Grove's magical community for a generation—the Harlows had never even had a chance to win before. Apparently, this had been by design. Elias Harlow, the founder of their house, had been the first to discover the primal power of Lady's Lake; something about his family's particular brand of magic served as a funnel, allowing the rest of us to tap safely into the lake's vast reservoir of power ourselves. The Harlows were functionally the power plants of the town, filtering and distilling the wild onslaught of magic that flooded from the lake. As the Voice of Thistle Grove, their reigning elder also enjoyed some strange, personal communion with the town itself.

That role had originally belonged to James Harlow, Emmy's father and our head recordkeeper. It had transitioned to Emmy upon her participation in the Gauntlet as both Arbiter and combatant, once she'd stepped in as champion for House Avramov when its scion, Natalia, was hurt.

The Harlows' tremendous boon to the town had been kept under wraps for centuries, due to Elias Harlow's bizarrely skewed notions of honor and equitability—but in her new dual role, Emmy wasn't handling it like that. Her first formal act as Victor had been to educate the witch community about what it meant to be the Voice, and the great service the Harlows rendered unto the rest of us. Even as it left them capable of casting only minor spellwork of their own as the heavy toll.

From the tone she'd taken with that message, we'd been lucky that she hadn't seen fit to impose a tithe on the rest of us, to even out the scales a little.

"She also says there was an incident of some kind at the lake last night. A large-scale magical fluctuation," Gareth continued, his eyes skipping over the rest of the letter. My fledgling chill expanded into full-blown frost, creeping down my belly as my suspicions were confirmed: so Emmy *had* felt that disturbance, too. But if I wasn't being summoned to appear before the emergency quorum, maybe she didn't know I'd been a witness to it. "She wants to discuss how the events might be connected, and then talk about next steps."

"Got it," I said faintly, pressing my lips together. "So I guess you have to run now, Scion Blackmoore, and go collect Mother as well. And Father, if she's planning on taking him along this time."

"Yes, but I'll be back," Gareth said, with more steel to his voice than normal. "And then we *are* gonna talk, Nina. Because what you did back there, with that Supersize Uriel's Flame—don't even try to tell me that was some kind of fluke. You blew right the hell past me, sis; you didn't even bring me in at all. I know your magic packs a wallop, but I've never even *felt* anything like that before, and I'm supposed to be the scion here. The least you owe me is an explanation for how you pulled that off."

I nodded briskly, lowering my eyes. Even though we did it as a matter of course when it came to managing our parents and our little brother, Gareth and I didn't, as a rule, keep secrets from each other. For all that he could be an undeniably flaky fly-by-night, in many ways my polar opposite, my big brother had done a lot of (very belated) growing up recently.

And he'd never let me down before.

I could use his take, his counsel on whatever was happening to me now.

"Go," I said shortly, giving him a little push. "And then we'll talk, I promise."

IN THE MEANTIME, I took myself to the Avalon, my favorite of our on-site restaurants. I'd always loved its "luxurious monastery" aesthetic: graceful stonemasonry, a soaring double-vaulted cathedral ceiling, Moorish peak windows, azure stained glass reflecting the flames of the candles held by the silver candelabra chandeliers. The reflection of the water from the moat flung rippling light through the windows, dappling their colors across the stone and lending the interior an ethereal air, as if you were in an underwater chapel.

There, I proceeded to order just about everything on the menu.

I was *starving*, in a way that felt completely unfamiliar. I was no stranger to carb-loading, or the ravenous frenzy that often set in postmarathon, but this was an entirely different level of "stranded in the desert for a week" hunger. I ordered three appetizers, followed by two entrees and a dessert, asking the (slightly scandalized and clearly confounded) server to please bring out everything as soon as it was ready, and not worry too much about any kind of "order."

As I devoured hamachi ceviche served over ice, truffled poutine fries, and the slow-simmered French onion soup that made me weak in the knees even when I was just normal hungry, it occurred to me that even though I was more voracious than I'd ever been, I didn't actually feel depleted or weak. Instead, I felt *wonderful*, aglow with a pervasive sense of well-being and serenity, as if casting that spell had burned away the last remnants of my hangover, scoured through me like some purging flame. Stranger still, I felt like after a solid lunch, I would be completely game for doing it again.

I was diving into the surf and turf with scalloped cheesy potatoes when Morty found me.

I paused midchew, so surprised to see him here that for a moment I thought I must be imagining him; maybe some kind of hallucinatory aftereffect of having channeled the strongest spell I'd ever cast in my life. He was wearing heavy, Soviet-looking boots and a vintage sheepskin duster that nearly brushed the floor, a dusting of snow sparkling in his windblown ruff of hair. Those ridiculous gemstone eyes skimmed over the tables that were almost entirely empty save for me in my banquette; the Avalon did serve all day, but this was off-peak, too late for lunch and not quite dinnertime. There was only one other couple, huddled over their drinks, too engaged in what was clearly an intense conversation to pay mind to anyone else.

As soon as he spotted me, Morty made a beeline in my direction, radiating a very disconcerting vibe as he slid into the seat opposite me without even bothering to dust off the snow from his collar.

"Uh, hello," I ventured, forcing down my bite as I eyed him warily. "I don't mean to come off rude, but what the hell are you doing here?"

He shrugged off the duster in one smooth motion, tossing it off his shoulders and bundling it behind him. Then he flicked his head to the side to clear snow-spangled hair from his eyes, in a gesture that was, despite everything, infuriatingly attractive. Fixing me with a brilliant blue glare, he held both hands above the table, palms up.

"I'm here because I woke up this morning," he said through his teeth, his voice an unnerving mixture of furious and terrified, "being able to do *this*."

Brow knitting, he gazed down at his blurry tattooed palms—where a dancing shimmer of gold suddenly sprang to life above each. Twin swirling globes of witchlight.

A baby illusionist spell, one of the first that Blackmoore witches learned to do.

My jaw dropped open, and I found myself struck speechless for what was possibly the first time in my entire life. I was a lot of things, but "lacking in words" did not tend to be one of them. How in the triple goddess's name could a normie, and Mortimer Gutierrez of all people, suddenly cast a working—and one that was such traditionally Blackmoore magic?

I glanced back up at his face, my gaze shifting between his eyes as I waited, without much real hope, for the oblivion glamour to set in. But no such luck; his eyes remained clear and steady, completely unmuddled, blazing with that electric heart-of-flame blue. The unsettling mixture of fear and rage in them tugged at me again in a way I didn't like, plucking on my heartstrings.

Angry as he clearly was, he also looked . . . vulnerable.

"So, you're really gonna just sit there and stare at me, pretend like you don't have the first clue about this?" he demanded. "Is that the play here?"

I drew my lips through my teeth, thinking furiously. "I'm not sure what it is you want me to say," I replied carefully. "I don't understand how you're doing that, whatever *that* even is. What am I seeing here?"

"Kindly cut the shit, Nina," he hissed through his teeth as he leaned forward across the table, the witchlights casting flickering glimmers over his face. "I know you know something about this. And you know why? Because I've seen *your* people do this—this sparkly crap before. That fuckweasel Gareth—"

"Do you feel like calling my brother a fuckweasel is conducive to this conversation?" I asked him, as calmly as I could, my fingers curling around the table's lip so hard that splinters threatened.

Morty cut himself off, closing his eyes and taking two ragged breaths.

"Okay," he muttered, more to himself than me. When he opened his eyes, they were the slightest bit steadier, more distraught than angry, and that damn inconvenient sympathy reared back up in me again. "Alright. Maybe I'm coming in a little hot, yeah. I don't—this isn't me, you know? I don't do toxic man-rage, that's not my style. I'm just, like, extremely thrown over here? I got a little too deep into the drinks last night after you left, because, full disclosure, I felt kind of shitty about how things went down between us—"

"Thanks for that," I murmured, thinking how sad-funny it was that we'd both been doing the same thing, in our separate ways.

"Yeah. I mean, definitely a topic for another time, but anyway." He took another shuddering breath, gave himself a little shake. "So I slept in this morning, and when I got up I was late to . . . to a thing I really needed to be on time for, so. Then the fucking light in my bathroom died, because of course, why not. So I was just thinking to myself, 'Really wish I had some goddamn light to shave' . . . and then, *bam!*"

He gave a harried, half-hysterical little laugh, staring down at the witchlights still flickering sinuously above his palms.

"And then this happened," he finished, curling his fingers around them to extinguish them. It was such a natural way to huff out that particular spell that it threw me a little; it didn't look like something a beginner would have done. The instinct to blow the lights out like candle flames tended to be a strong one. "And I suddenly—I just *remembered* out of the blue, all these times that fu—your brother Gareth used to come into my bar. Do flashy shit like this like a magic trick, to pull some tourist for the night."

I exhaled, clenching my jaw, because this tracked, unfortunately. Even with the townwide oblivion glamour in place, we weren't supposed to cast in public, but that didn't mean all of us always complied with the prohibition.

And my brother really could be the most spectacular fuckweasel that way.

"But I always forgot," he said, confusion brewing in his face. "All those other times, I just *forgot* about it, somehow, almost as soon as it happened. Until this morning. This morning, I remembered everything—and now, I can apparently even do it! So. That's why I'm here."

"How did you know where to find me?" I asked, a coal lump of dread landing in my belly with a sickening thud. Because I was starting to get a profoundly unfortunate inkling of what the answer to that might be, something I very much did not want to be the case.

"I don't even know!" he exclaimed, with another shrill half laugh. "I could just . . . tell where you were? *Feel* you, somehow? That's when I got really spooked, like, am I losing my entire mind right now? Do I have a brain tumor or something, am I fucking hallucinating this whole deal? How is that possible—how is *any* of this possible or real? I didn't even believe it until I got here, and here you were. Exactly where I thought you'd be. Where I *knew* I'd find you."

I took an unsteady breath myself, splaying my hands flat on the table to find some badly needed purchase as panic rolled through me like an avalanche. Because there *was* a way that some normies were able to come into magic even if they weren't born into it. There was a way they could come to feel the presence of a certain special witch even from a distance.

It just couldn't possibly be happening right now, and definitely not to the two of us.

It *couldn't* be.

"Nina," Morty said, half pleading, leaning over the table with distress etched into every fine line of his face. "Just tell me, okay? I won't even be mad, I swear, I just need to understand. What is this paranormal activity shit? What did you *do* to me?"

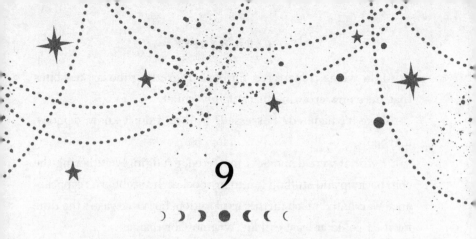

9

The Starstruck Coin, Again

BEFORE I COULD reply, something small abruptly warmed in my back jeans pocket, like a lodged ember flaring back to life. Frowning, I wiggled around in my seat until I could wedge my fingers into it, my chest clamping down like a vise as my fingers closed around hot metal, familiarly ridged edges.

"No. Goddess-damned. Way," I breathed, fishing the object out and dropping it on the tabletop. The lake coin—the same one I'd flung into my bed this morning, and definitely left abandoned somewhere inside my sheets—had turned back up in my pocket. It spun on the table for a moment like a top, even though I hadn't meant to spin it, before it settled onto the wood with a final, feisty glimmer.

So underwater goddesses had jokes, apparently. How *whimsical*.

"Nina?" Morty said, sounding, if possible, even more beleaguered. "What is it? Why are you staring at that coin like that?"

"Like what?" I managed, furiously regretting the last few bites that were now crowding back up my gullet.

"Like it's haunted? Possessed? Full of, I don't know, demons, maybe?"

"I wish it were demons," I muttered, grudgingly gathering the coin back up and stuffing it into my pocket. Its stubborn reappearance warranted much further exploration, but now wasn't the time for it. "I could at least call an Avramov for that."

"Like Talia or Issa, you mean?" Morty's brow crinkled, his face swarming with even more hopeless confusion. "Or Micah? What do *they* have to do with any of this?"

Oh, this poor, sweet summer child.

"It's—look, it's very complicated," I said, drawing a breath. "This town . . . you grew up here, too, right? So you think you know it? But you don't, trust me. There's a lot going on under the surface here, things people like you couldn't possibly understand."

"'People like me,'" he mimicked in a deadpan tone, his face darkening. "And what category of woefully ignorant folk would I fall into, exactly, according to you? Please do educate me on what you mean by that, besides some kind of elitist shade."

I huffed out a weak laugh, shaking my head. "Nothing like that, no. How do I even begin? It's . . ."

I trailed off, catching sight of Gareth emerging through the restaurant's doorway, velvet-curtained against the cold. He gestured to the maître d', then caught sight of me in my banquette and changed direction, heading my way. By the time he reached the table, confusion had replaced the grim determination on his face, his eyes flicking between me and Morty.

"Uh, Nina, why is the Shamrock *bartender* here?" he asked, scrunching his nose in an expression between bewilderment and distaste, and it became abruptly clear to me why my brother in-spired such a specific sense of loathing in Morty. Across the table from me, I could practically feel his hackles rise in response, his entire demeanor skewing toward pissed-off cat. "Wait. *Wait.* Are you guys, like—"

"No!" Morty and I half shouted in unison, and despite myself I felt a little miffed by the vehemence in Morty's own denial, even though I'd echoed it. He didn't have to sound quite so *not if we were the last two people on earth* about it.

"No, we're not," I told Gareth, clearing my throat, widening my eyes at Morty in emphatic *I'm aware he's being a fuckweasel, but please do take it down a notch yourself* fashion. "Morty just . . . had some questions for me."

"Still do," Morty muttered, glaring daggers at my brother. "In case anyone's wondering."

"Hey, is he bothering you, Nina?" Gareth asked in an entirely different tone, belligerence lighting in his eyes, choosing the very worst path as he was so often wont to do. "Because if he is, I'd be happy to—"

"Step away and give us a minute?" I asked pointedly, trans-ferring my stare to him. "Because that's what I need you to do, please. We'll catch up as soon as Morty and I are done, okay?"

Gareth shifted his weight from foot to foot like a streetfighter, mulling this over. Then whatever semblance of reason he possessed thankfully prevailed, and he gave me a reluctant nod, sidling over to the empty bar.

"Sorry about that," I said to Morty, suppressing a wince. "He can be a little . . ."

"Oh, I know what the *lordling* can be like, trust me," he said, more coldly than he'd spoken to me since he arrived. Gareth's appearance had clearly snuffed any slow-budding rapport between us, and given the way Gareth had spoken to him—as though even here, Morty was just the hired help, like that was some kind of intrinsic quality a person carried around with them—I couldn't really blame Morty for that. "I'm not here to discuss his failings, so spare me. Just tell me what's going on here, make it stop, and I'll get right the fuck out of y'all's hair. Leave you to go swim laps in your vault of coins, or whatever else you do with your Sundays."

I stiffened, squaring my shoulders. "That was uncalled-for, but you're having a rough day, clearly, so I'll let it pass." So was I, for that matter, but at least I wasn't utterly at sea the way he was. "I can explain . . . some of it, anyway. But it's going to take a minute, and Gareth and I need to discuss some things first. Can I meet you tonight, to talk? Wherever you like. I'll come to your bar, even, if you want."

Morty stared at me a little balefully, plucking at his lower lip with a thumb in a way that would, under different circumstances, have been very distracting.

"Okay, fine," he finally said, shrugging into that annoyingly attractive Captain Jack Harkness duster and standing in another of those seamless motions, his eyes still chilly. "I'm not exactly dying to keep sharing space with His Majesty the Scum King, so I'll be waiting for you at eight at the Shamrock. And if you don't show, Nina, I'll just come find you again. Ruin your extremely fine ambiance with these pungent riffraff vibes."

"That's not . . ." I hissed in a breath, nostrils flaring. "That isn't fair. I'm not like that."

"Whatever you say, milady," he retorted, sliding out of the banquette with a scornful glance tossed over his shoulder. "See you tonight."

I was still stewing by the time Gareth made his way over, tumbler of scotch in tow.

"No way is that fucking dude gonna be my brother-in-law," he informed me, wrinkling his nose. "Just so we're clear on that from the jump."

I glared at him so stonily that he flushed, his ears pinking.

"Okay, so, maybe I overshot that one," he said, in lieu of an apology. "Not telling you who to date. Though, in my defense, he doesn't seem like your type. Like, *at all.*"

"Squarely trespassing in Not-Your-Damn-Business territory over here, brother," I shot back. "Probably you should beware."

"I just—I don't love that guy, okay?" Gareth said, with a finicky shudder. "He always acts like I'm some kind of sloppy shit-for-brains quarterback or something when I go drink at his bar. Like he thinks I'm being a date rapist just by default. Meanwhile he's this bleeding-edge 'ooooh, check me out, y'all, I'm so hip and fluid and all about that sweet-ass consent' hero."

"Maybe he *wouldn't* think that about you," I said edgily, "if you hadn't been using *his* bar for your pickup artist garbage, especially by shock-and-awing his customers with spells to entice them home. I mean, seriously, Gareth? What is the *matter* with you? That's not just horribly gross and wrong, it's embarrassing as hell."

Gareth flushed a full, mottled crimson at that; in this, at least, we were very much alike.

"Okay," he allowed, looking genuinely chastened as he took a deep pull of his scotch. "So maybe I've pulled a slightly sketchy flex or two there, not gonna lie. But I'm really not about that anymore. You believe that, right, Nina? You know I'm working on myself, trying to do a lot better."

"Then why not *do* better, instead of trying?" I suggested, not even bothering to dilute the acid in my tone. "Starting now. I promise, it's not that hard once you commit. No more snotty talk about Morty will be permitted, for starters. Are we clear on this?"

"Crystal," he allowed, working his jaw from side to side. "So, you gonna tell me what he was doing here?"

"We went on a date last night," I admitted, feeling heat rise like steam in my own cheeks. "It was a silly dare from Jessa, basically, as one would expect. And it went about as terribly as one would also expect."

"'Cause he sucks," Gareth mumbled, skimming an appraising scavenger's eye over my food. "And isn't your type."

I made a pinching "zip it" motion at him with my hand. "*But*, something else happened last night, something very weird. And I think it's having some . . . lingering repercussions."

I filled him in on everything, from the spectacular display at the lake to my later underwater visitation, to the way even my minor spells this morning had been almost comically super-powered.

"Back up," Gareth said, scrubbing a hand over his face. "You're telling me there's a—there's a *sentient goddess statue* in Lady's Lake? And you've, like, been having girls' nights with her your whole life?"

"Apparently so. Though I never remembered any of them until now."

"What's she like?" he said, a tinge of awestruck wonder momentarily displacing the shock. "A whole goddess, damn. I can't believe it. That's wild, even for Thistle Grove."

"I mean, I suppose we can't be positive that's what she is," I replied, though truthfully I hadn't even really considered any other possibility; I knew what she felt like, what she *had* to be. Even now, with a little bit of distance from the encounter, there was no true doubt in my mind. "But I'm fairly sure she's it. The thing that, somehow, makes Lady's Lake what it is. And Thistle Grove what it is, too."

"And you're besties with her, eyyyyyy!" He held out his fist for a bump and grinned at me when I bumped back, he looked dimpled and sweet, a flash of the deeply people-pleasing kid he'd once been—and still often was even as an adult, when he managed to cast all the other encumbering crap our family had saddled us with aside. "That's pretty badass."

I looked down, a smile twitching at my own lips—until I remembered that every wondrous moment that had transpired last night had also somehow initiated an ice wraith manifestation.

"I have to go to the quorum with this, right?" I asked Gareth. "To report it? I can't just keep a bombshell like this secret; the entire community needs to know. Just think how mindblown the Harlows are going to be over this kind of revelation. And it must be connected to what happened today. It has to be, don't you think?"

"Yeah, most likely," he replied, a more analytical expression sifting over his face. Contrary to popular opinion, my brother was far from a simple thinker; just intellectually lazy, in the absence of the right motivation. He wasn't going to strain himself unless the moment really called for it. "As far as the quorum is concerned, something distorted Gawain's snowfall spell—you know, the one he uses for the winter wonderland scene in *Yvain*. Some random, huge power flux, essentially. Emmy felt it happen, but doesn't know what it was."

"It was me, somehow," I mused, thinking aloud. "It had to be. Everything was running smoothly at Camelot until I got here."

"Probably, yeah," Gareth agreed. "Which is why I'd suggest you not say anything about it right now. Nothing at all, to anyone but me."

I straightened, every quantum particle of lawful good in my body rebelling against this suggestion. "What do you mean? It's my responsibility to report something like this! It would be *anyone's* responsibility!"

"I hear you, and I get it. But think about it for a second, Nina," Gareth reasoned, tipping his head. "Ever since the Gauntlet, we've been stuck in the doghouse, right? Our whole family. Everyone turning against us, nothing going our way. How could it possibly do us any favors, admitting that one of us might have had something to do with a calamity like this, even if unintentionally? A spell going rogue like that? Normies possibly getting hurt?"

"No one got hurt," I objected, but only mildly, because that was true by sheer technicality. And I could already see where he was going with this.

"Yeah, because you were there to save everyone's ass," Gareth countered. "But if you hadn't managed to swing a Uriel like that so quick, who knows what could have happened. If there'd been injuries, real ones, possibly even deaths? There's only so much the oblivion glamour can erase. It's not intended to tamper with normie minds to that severe a degree. And if it came out that we were behind something like that?"

I gave a grudging nod, hating absolutely everything about this. But Gareth had a point; we couldn't afford this kind of negative attention, not right now. Especially not as we were considering expanding Camelot again, trying to restore some of the lost dignity to our family name.

"So, what do you suggest? I keep quiet on this for a minute, but how long? And in the meantime, what, do I even tell Lyonesse?"

Gareth physically balked at the mention of our mother, taking a swig of scotch to fortify himself.

"Uh, *no*, have you met our esteemed lady mother?" he demanded. "I can't even predict which way she'd flip her shit over this, so let's not inflict that grief on ourselves just yet. I say we just sit on it for a while. That's what the quorum agreed on, anyway—watchful waiting, no further action for the moment. Emmy doesn't love it; she'd rather lock in precautionary measures right now. But everyone else wasn't having it."

I nodded, unsurprised. Thistle Grove witches thrived on our magic, our connection with the lake and the town. I couldn't see anyone, not even the seasoned elders, leaping on the idea of restricting our spellwork when things had gone awry only once. We all loved it too much for that.

"And in the meantime," I said slowly, "I could try to get to the bottom of this on my own. See if I can figure out what even happened, somehow reverse it."

"We," Gareth corrected. "I'm in this with you now, sis. A Blackmoore team effort. Deal?"

"Deal," I said, a smile reluctantly tugging at my mouth. I'd never thrown my lot in with my brother's before, at least not willingly—but this time, he wasn't just stepping up in some symbolic way. He was making actual, logical sense. I could see how this might be the correct path to take, at least for now. The one least likely to harm our family, among other significant considerations.

"Sick," he said, reaching out to grab my fork and spear a remaining clump of poutine fries. "So now that we're decided, back to that guy. The bartender."

"Play nice, brother," I warned. "You *know* his name."

"Right, right." He shoved the pilfered fries in his mouth and chewed contemplatively, brow creasing. "Why was Morty, Bartender-by-Profession-but-*So*-Much-More-than-That-in-Spirit, here with you? What'd he want, anyway?"

"Well," I said, drawing a deep breath. "I think whatever happened at the lake had another unintended effect. I think he and I . . . I'm fairly sure we're witchbound, now."

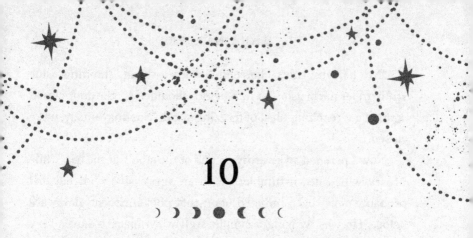

10

Definitely Not Just a Lawyer

THE SHAMROCK CAULDRON looked like it had been designed to serve as a preview of my own personal hell.

For one thing, I hadn't been prepared to be the only person there, besides Morty himself; I'd figured there'd be at least a few customers around, enough to disperse the tension between us, bleed off some of the nervous energy I was bringing to the table. But I'd arrived to find the shamrock-shaped neon CLOSED sign glaring at me in the window in what felt like a personal affront, the door locked until Morty appeared to unbolt it at my tentative knock.

"Aren't you usually open on Sunday nights?" I'd asked, as if this banality really mattered—though I did dimly remember my brother heading here to top off one of his rager weekends a time or two, with his usual obnoxious retinue of cousins and various hangers-on.

"My bar, my rules," he replied with a shrug, standing aside stiffly to let me brush past him before shouldering the door closed against a wrenching blast of freezing wind. "So, this Sunday, we're closed."

Now I perched awkwardly on one of the stools at the bar, while Morty wiped down tumblers with an aggressive zeal that had probably never been inflicted upon that poor innocent glassware before. He was wearing a simple, well-worn black tee over very tight ripped jeans and work boots, and even this pared-down look was distressingly attractive on his lean frame. No eyeliner tonight, either, just that brilliant blue glare. I was trying my level best to keep my gaze locked on my own reflection in the mirror behind the staggered shelves, to avoid the twin downfalls of staring at him and becoming shell-shocked by the psychedelic decor. The walls were an unruly carnival of clashing color and glitter, plastered with sparkling shamrocks and neon signs, while Halloween bat-and-pumpkin string lights looped above the bar in chaotic whirls, flashing in patterns seemingly designed to incite seizures. There was even some unholy Travesty of Tackiness sprawling in one corner: what looked like a plastic science skeleton sporting a jauntily tipped leprechaun's top hat, purple Mardi Gras beads, and a *ukulele* on its lap.

I couldn't bring myself to believe people came here on purpose, and yet. On the upside, at least it didn't smell like stale beer. More like cinnamon and orange peel, surprisingly festive and appetizing.

"I take it milady doesn't wholly approve of my establishment," Morty said, flicking a challenging glance in my direction, accompanied by a sarcastic little head wag. "Shocker."

"No, it's—no," I said hastily, trying to rearrange my face out of whatever expression I'd been unwittingly making. "It's just extremely . . . colorful? Quite a lot happening, everywhere?"

"Oh, feel free to hate it, milady," he said with another shrug. "No skin off this humble servant's nose, believe me."

I peered around, ticking my fingertips nervously against the bar top. "What exactly is this motif supposed to be, anyway?"

"Like I said before, my mom's Irish. Well, Welsh and Irish, but born in Glengarriff."

"Oh, my family's Welsh, too!" I broke in, surprised by this congruence. "Though, quite a few generations back."

We probably didn't need to begin the primer on Thistle Grove with the fact that my family traced our lineage all the way back to Morgan le Fay; the reality of twelfth-century sorceresses seemed like something I needed to ease Morty into slowly.

"So, my pops is first-generation Portuguese, met her when they both moved here within a few years of each other. This place . . ." He waved a hand around at the Shamrock's questionable glory, fondness skimming over his delicately chiseled features. "He opened it kind of tongue-in-cheek in her honor; the plan was he'd do the bartending, she'd take care of the books. She likes 'a bit o' flash,' as she'd happily tell you, so he did everything up very kitsch Irish as an inside joke to begin with, crossed with a little witchy shit to go with the town's history."

"Right," I said, eyeing the flickering bat-and-pumpkin lights above my head. "I can see that. Very, um, authentic."

"But then she loved it for real, so, here we are, almost twenty-five years later. There've been a lot of tweaks over the years, of course," he added, jerking his chin toward the skeletal travesty. "Proud to say that Dead Frederick over there was my contribution. But the spirit is the same."

"This place has been around for that long?" I asked, marveling, even as a part of my brain noted that of course the whacked-out skeleton had been Morty's brainchild. "I had no idea it was such a Thistle Grove institution. You must be really proud."

"I am. As a matter of fact, it predates Ye Castle Cornballfest," he said, raising a sharp dark eyebrow like a fencing blade parry. "So maybe you can see why we might've been averse to letting your Dread Empire buy it out from under us to assimilate into the collective."

I chewed on my lower lip, barely restraining myself from twisting a lock of my hair around my finger, lest he think I was trying to flirt instead of defusing mounting anger.

"Look, I'm aware our past interactions have been less than ideal, given the circumstances in which we now find ourselves," I said, summoning up as much cool and poise as I could, though my skin felt like it was buzzing with irritation. "And you've been decidedly unambiguous about how much you hate my brother. But I'm *not* Gareth, clearly, as you can see."

He waggled his head back and forth, lips pursed, as if this point were somehow debatable.

"And the stuff that happened with your bar?" I went on, my cheeks burning. "That was just me doing my job, protecting my family's business interests like I'm *paid* to do. And I'm not exactly dying to be here, either, but I still showed up tonight like I said I would. Because having this conversation was the right thing to do. So can we tone down this whole 'Blackmoores are the spawn of Palpatine, and/or the Borg' energy?"

This time both eyebrows shot up, and he rested his inked forearms on the bar top, leaning over them. I did my best to ignore the way the tendons shifted under his ink with the movement, the way those watercolor tattoos flowed over them. I'd never wanted tattoos of my own, but I loved the look of them on others.

And I always was the very worst sucker for a beautifully sculpted forearm.

"*Star Wars* plus *Star Trek* references seen and raised, no shit. Wouldn't have pegged Nineve Blackmoore, Esquire, for the type to hang with all that."

"Oh, I'm sorry, do only nerdboy edgelords get to enjoy such cool-kid stuff as sci-fi classics?" I snapped, losing the remainder of my patience. "Did I not understand the assignment about what girls like me were supposed to like, to your personal satisfaction? Maybe *you* can just tell me which references are in my lane, so I know to stick to them. Am I a Kardashians devotee, perhaps? Housewives of Somewhere, possibly? Seriously, you tell me. I'll wait."

He stared at me for a moment, taken aback, then gave a slow, acknowledging nod.

"You know what," he said, straightening up from the bar and running a hand through the tousle of his hair. It fell right back over his forehead, unfazed by the interruption. "You're right. All the other shit aside, I actually *am* the asshole here, in this moment. My bad, okay? I'm sorry. My family's in kind of a complicated situation right now, and . . . well, even if that weren't the case, I'm not always the best with bygones. So, truce? For this evening, at least?"

He held out a hand across the bar, his dark hair flickering with the white and orange reflections of the string lights, eyebrow cocked.

I stared at him for a moment, my nervous system still buzzing like a disturbed beehive, a little uncertain how to take this unexpected apology. In my family, moments of high conflict didn't tend to resolve like this, with so little bloodshed and drama, and in such a short span of time to boot. Even Sydney had been part of that ingrained pattern, instigating and then elongating arguments until they felt like you'd become trapped in a Möbius strip of time that would possibly outlast the universe itself. Sydney also faithfully subscribed to the "don't go to bed angry" maxim, mostly because you weren't *ever* going to get to sleep, not on the night of a fight with her.

As a result, my body didn't quite know how to process this rapid turnaround, nor the seemingly genuine offer of a cease-fire.

"Okay, sure," I said slowly, trying to wrestle my fight-or-flight response down as I took his hand. His was warm against my own cool palm, his grip firm and reassuring, the tiniest bit electric when he squeezed mine back. "Yes, we are now operating strictly under truce terms. Do you think we could maybe . . . toast to that, or something? I don't know about you, but I'm feeling like I could use a drink."

He broke into a crooked smile at that, dazzling and completely unexpected, and I felt the high color in my cheeks transmute into another type of alchemical reaction entirely.

"Dang, I should've been the one to suggest that," he said, shaking his head. "Where are my manners? Peace always deserves a toast, right? Will you have a malbec? Gin martini?"

"You remembered," I said, absurdly pleased he'd been paying attention at the Moon and Scythe, before everything went haywire between us.

"Another occupational hazard. I never forget a drink order.

Especially when—" He cut himself off, giving himself a little shake. If I looked closely, I *thought* I could detect the slightest rise of color in his own clean-shaven cheeks, which was . . . curious. "Never mind. Which will it be?"

"Gin martini, please," I said, wondering what he'd been about to say.

"Solid. I believe I'll join you."

By the time he slid my martini in front of me, the chilled glass already sweating, I'd coaxed myself back into some modicum of calm using the mantra Sassy Sue had taught me many sessions ago. *You're in no danger from this person. He holds no power over you, nor any license to do you harm.*

You are who you are, and his opinion of you is not dispositive of anything.

It didn't always help, but tonight it had, especially when boosted by the fact that Morty had actually already apologized. When he lifted his own glass and said, "To peace," I caught myself smiling back at him as I clinked my rim against his. The martini was flawless, icy and dry, and I felt myself relax incrementally more as soon as it hit my tongue.

Then I realized, as we both finished our sips, let out matching little sighs, and set our glasses back onto the bar, that Morty and I were unintentionally moving in perfect tandem.

"Oh, what *now*," Morty said, noticing my expression. "Whatever it is, seems like it can't be good."

"It isn't," I said shortly, picking my glass right back up and taking another swig. "But we'll get to that part. Let's start with . . . hell, I don't even know. The basics. The very beginning, maybe. You're familiar with the tale of the founders, correct? The four people who established Thistle Grove?"

"Well, yeah, sure," he said, in the tone of an adult indulging a child. "Caelia Blackmoore, Alastair Thorn, Elias Harlow, and Margarita Avramov. The 'witches' who founded the town because the lake was special somehow. Cute story for the tourists. Shades of Salem right here in Illinois, except without any of the burning at stake, or the grotesque misogyny."

"So, for starters, you can ditch the finger quotes, because the founders *were* real witches. And Lady's Lake *is* a magical font." I twitched my chin at his hands. "That light you can summon out of nowhere? It's called witchlight. It's a beginner's working, one of the easiest spells in the Grimoire—which is the book that holds all the spells the four families share between them."

"The Grimoire," he repeated, staring at me slack-jawed, disbelief stamped across his face. "Okay, setting aside the fact that we are apparently now living in *Wicked: The Musical*—"

"*That* book was called the Grimmerie, actually," I corrected, wrinkling my nose. "Weird take on the spelling, wasn't a fan. The soundtrack mostly slaps, though."

Morty huffed an incredulous laugh, shaking his head. "Cool, let's table the crucial discussion of the merits of 'Defying Gravity' versus 'As Long As You're Mine.' But you're—you're seriously saying that the story is real? *All* of it?"

"All of it," I said firmly, spreading my hands. "My own ancestress, Caelia Blackmoore, was descended from Morgan le Fay. You might've heard of her—legendary sorceress, twelfth-ish century, generally considered King Arthur's half sister?"

"I know who she is," he said, in the leaden, seminumb tones of someone whose reality was spiraling away from them with disturbing speed. "I've seen *The Mists of Avalon*. And *Camelot*. And *Merlin*. And the BBC *Merlin* reboot."

I tipped my head, unable to resist a jab. "For someone who rags on Castle Camelot with such regularity, you certainly seem familiar with the underlying lore."

He let out a strangled little laugh, dropping his head into his hands, elbows propped on the bar. "I truly cannot believe we're having this tripped-out conversation. And that you just casually dropped the term 'lore' on me."

"Like I said. Attorney by day, profound nerd by night," I replied, with a shrug of my own. I was starting to perversely enjoy myself a little, seeing Morty thrown this way. It made me feel like maybe I could actually regain the upper hand. "Never seen an episode of any *Housewives* in my life, not that I judge anyone who has."

"Why should I believe you?" he demanded, drawing up his spine. "Why should I believe *any* of this wild bullshit? Maybe the thing I can do with my hands is some kind of, I don't know, weird-ass fluke. Saint Elmo's fire or something. A freak accident of physics that might have a scientific explanation, something that isn't magic."

"I guess that could be true," I said equably, lifting up my own hands. "But even if that were the case . . . what do you think you'd call this?"

Closing my eyes, I summoned up witchlights of my own, letting them flare above my palms. Pulsing and expanding, shifting in color from warm amber to dazzling platinum, melting into sapphire blue followed by rose gold. Then I opened my eyes and murmured the incantation for Phoenix Rising, an illusionist spell we sometimes used in the shows.

The globes of witchlight spun themselves up into whirling helices, then expanded into delicately drawn avian silhouettes, graceful as calligraphy. Radiant birds built entirely of light, rendered in perfect detail to their outstretched downy wings and the swooping fronds of their tail feathers.

They rose to hover above each of my shoulders, wings softly fluttering. This was where the spell usually drew to a halt, the firebirds shining like bright beacons before fading away. But I'd forgotten that I was now supercharged, and that Phoenix Rising had no intention of phasing out at any reasonable stopping point. Instead, the birds grew larger and brighter with every beat of their wings, blazing so radiant that the entire bar drowned in their pulsing light, iridescence bouncing off every reflective surface.

The inside of the Shamrock looked like it'd been swallowed by a rising newborn sun, a shimmering dawn confined to these four walls.

Morty threw up a hand to shield his eyes from the glare, just as a shower of sparks began to fall from the firebirds' crested wingtips, a golden flurry that swooped into a whirl above our heads before bursting into miniature fireworks as the birds winked out of existence.

"Oh, shit," Morty breathed as he slowly lowered his hand, staring at me with something between sheer terror and awestruck amazement. "Fuck *me*. You . . . you had *fire* in your eyes, Nina."

Had I? Well, *that* was not customary.

Luminous specks were still drifting down to coat every surface, glimmering like phoenix dust. Some of them landed in the dark ruck of Morty's hair, and sprinkled onto the bridge of his dainty nose; I felt the insane urge to reach out across the bar and brush them away.

"You are definitely not just a lawyer, are you?" he said, gaping at me, still teetering on the dividing line between aghast and wonderstruck. "You're a . . . a goddess or something. Or, like, an actual fucking superhero."

"No," I said simply, lowering my hands and folding them primly on the bar, even though on the inside I still felt like a gorgeous, raging maelstrom, like the blaze that now lived inside me had guttered but far from died. "Believe me, I definitely am a lawyer—and I'm *also* a witch. And what you just saw? That was magic. Not Saint Elmo's fire, not some physics freak show. *Real* magic, the kind they tell stories about."

"Why don't you wait right here, please," Morty said abruptly, turning to dash toward the door behind the bar. "I'm gonna need a minute to go breathe into a paper bag and handle my shit."

By the time he returned, I'd drained my martini and the phoenix dust had evanesced, leaving the Shamrock speckled only in its own gaudy and entirely mundane glitter. With an air of restrained, buzzing energy, Morty silently shook us another martini each—a double this time, by the looks of it.

"Alright," he said, tossing back half of his, still blinking a little rapidly. "That was, uh, very impressive, yeah. And convincing as fuck, tell you what. You're a witch, everyone is witches, no further proof necessary! Are they all . . . is everyone else like you? That crazy strong?"

"Not exactly. Blackmoores are the most powerful of the lot of us," I said, leaving out my own recent indeterminate power surge. "But the rest of the families have different talents, their own mythologies. The Avramovs, for example, are Baba Yaga's descendants, necromancers from—"

Morty's head shot up. "The fuck you say! Baba Yaga? Necromancers? You're—you're telling me Micah, Talia, and Issa, all of them . . . they raise the *dead*?"

"Well, not exactly," I hedged, tilting my head back and forth. "I mean, I believe they could if they wanted to, but resurrecting the deceased is *severely* frowned upon. They incline more toward divination, communing with spirits, working with ectoplasm. The more benign aspects of being speakers to the dead."

And occasionally, one of their restless dead possessed a living Avramov and wreaked utter hexing havoc upon the rest of us— but based on Morty's reactions, I was getting the sense that such a story was out-of-bounds for this preliminary conversation.

Morty gave a tortured little moan, nostrils flaring as he took deliberate breaths through his nose. "Ectoplasm. Like the shit they talk about in *Ghostbusters?*"

"Well, it's not exactly like that, but same general principle, yes. Spirit stuff. Ghostly matter."

"They work with ectoplasm," Morty repeated to himself, looking haunted. "Hell, I used to date Micah, a little while back . . ."

This little nugget of information gave me an indistinct, pulsing pang of discomfort, something I probably needed to address for myself at a later time.

"Went to The Bitters for a few of his parties, even," he continued, shaking his head. "And yeah, it was goth as fuck in there, but I figured that was just their vibe. Didn't look like the house had any chicken legs or anything. And wouldn't you know it, he never thought to mention anything about ectoplasm!"

"That's because we're not allowed to tell normies about the magic," I clarified. "It's part of the rules the Grimoire sets out, for the witch community of Thistle Grove. Only long-term partners get to hear about it, and are able to retain the information. Know about it without forgetting."

His face darkened as he considered this. "Yeah, what's that

about, anyway? Why couldn't I remember Gareth slinging sparks around all those times?"

"It's because of something called an oblivion glamour," I explained, feeling a strange, creeping hint of embarrassment. "A large-scale forgetting spell cast over the town's normie population, for our safety. So, you know, you don't realize you're living side by side with a host of tremendously powerful witches, whom you might then be moved to burn. Or send to fringe-science government facilities as specimens."

He stared at me for a moment, silent, azure eyes shifting between mine.

"So, you keep us hypnotized, basically," he finally said, delicate features stony. "Just living in the dark, like a bunch of thralls. No idea what this town really is. What all of *you* really are."

"It's for our safety," I argued, though that flare of embarrassment sparked again, stronger this time. He had a point; I knew that much and always had. Otherwise I wouldn't feel as guilt-sick as I often did, keeping so much of the truth of my life from Jessa.

I just didn't *want* to know it.

"What about *our* safety?" he challenged. "Not to mention our agency or autonomy. You know, all those minor concerns that could ostensibly be considered human rights. How do we not get any say in this equation? What if some of us wouldn't even want to live here, knowing what you are? What if we figured, hey, building our lives next to a whole mess of wildly powerful witches might possibly be dangerous?"

"I know it's not a perfect solution," I said, looking down at my hands. They seemed so innocent curled up on the bar top with their nude manicure, the one simple silver ring set with a tiny ruby on my right index finger. So deceptively harmless. And yet, those were the same hands that had called down Uriel's Flame to counter a pack of ice wraiths that had probably manifested because of me in the first place.

None of the normies who'd visited Castle Camelot for some light Sunday entertainment had consented to *any* of that.

"And morally, yes, maybe a little gray," I went on, trying not to sound as defensive as I felt. "But it was the best the founders could come up with, for protecting themselves and their descendants."

"Then maybe it's time for you all to put your arcane little heads together," he said testily, taking another sharp swallow of his martini like a shot, "and come up with something better—not to mention more ethical. I assume you do have some kind of leader, right? Some manner of government. Not like any *normie* law could really touch you, not if you can whip out Jedi mind tricks without breaking a sweat."

I winced at the vicious twist he gave the word, making it sound like the slur that, admittedly, it often was. "We do. There's a quorum of us, charged with making decisions that affect the community as a whole. And we have a position called a Victor of the Wreath, too. Essentially the person who calls the shots."

"And who might that be?" He huffed out a laugh, rolling his eyes. "Someone else I've dated?"

"Right now, it's Emmeline Harlow. Not sure if you know her."

"Emmy! Get out, she's a witch, too?" His face brightened annoyingly at the mention of her name, as if we couldn't *all* be bad, not if Emmy Harlow was one of us. "I do know her, yeah, we went to school together. She's good people."

Swallowing down my irritation, I gave him a brief rundown of Emmy's family and the dual role she played for the town, followed

by an introduction to the Thorns, our green magicians and heal-
ers. By this point, he'd transitioned to a kind of rapt, awed
acceptance—a radiant wonder at the notion that magic was real,
and here, right in front of him.

An unlikely myth he was now living in.

"So how do I play into all of this?" he asked, fixing me with a
keen blue stare. "Why am I suddenly a Padawan witch? Isn't that
shit supposed to happen on your sixteenth birthday, or some other
milestone moment? As opposed to out of the blue on a random
morning, when you were just trying to shave?"

"Ah, no," I said, feeling the heat pooling into my cheeks
again—because this was where things were going to get tricky.
"As far as we know, there are only two ways to become a Thistle
Grove witch. One, you're simply born into one of the four families,
part of a magical bloodline."

"That one's definitely not me," he said, with a decisive shake of
the head. "My parents are for absolute sure my real parents, no
shady dalliances there. All you have to do is look at them. What's
the other way?"

I cleared my throat, twisting my ring around my finger. "You
fall in love with one of us, and become our long-term partner. It's
called being witchbound. Usually there's, um, a formal ceremony.
It's actually quite ritualized."

He stared at me, comprehension dawning on his face. "So
you're saying . . . you and I . . . ?"

I nodded, taking a deep breath. "Yes. I deeply regret to inform
you that we are, apparently, witch married to each other now."

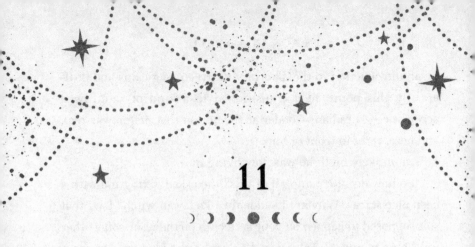

11

A Crashing and Spectacular Chaos

EN MINUTES LATER, Morty and I were still wallowing in a silence so deeply and excruciatingly awkward it was probably breaking some kind of world record on pregnant pauses.

"Sorry," Morty said, flicking a glance up at me. "I'm really—I'm just trying to process all this. Take it in, if that's even possible."

"Believe me, I get it," I said, fiddling with my martini stem. "It's uncanny to me, as well. And this is my world we're talking about."

"But . . . how?" he said, spreading his hands. "I mean, we haven't even—we didn't even kiss the other night. Exactly *how* are you my witch wife now?"

I vented a sigh through my lips, wondering how deep I needed to go here. But, in for a penny, in for a pound; given the enduring nature of witch bonds, Morty and I were going to be in this together for quite some time, stuck with each other. He had a right to the information that I had at my disposal, anything that might help both of us understand how we could've wound up here.

"Something major happened to me the other night," I told him, catching his gaze with an effort. It really was difficult to maintain eye contact with someone whose eyes were that brilliant of a color, and so unflinching to boot. Everyone in my family was blue-eyed, besides me; none of them had eyes remotely as magnetic as his. "And I think it must have triggered this as well, somehow."

As simply as I could, I explained my dream descent to the bottom of the lake, the goddess who lived down there, the ramifications for the rest of the town.

"There's a statue of a goddess in the lake?" he said, slack-jawed. "A statue that *moves*, that can call you down to it, that can somehow transport you to the bottom? That is—Nina, that's insane. That is absolutely nutbag bonkers, even compared to everything else."

"Trust me, I know. But she's there, alright; and whatever she did, it seems to have affected me," I finished, spreading my hands. "Dialed up all my natural talent to colossal levels. And I think you got caught up in the undertow, somehow. The magic mistook you for my partner—that's why you're no longer subject to the oblivion glamour. It appears to have triggered the creation of a witch bond without any of the, uh, consensual requirements that typically need to be met. Or the lakeside rituals."

"The magical version of getting blackout drunk and eloping in Vegas, basically," he quipped, twisting the cleaning cloth in his hands, winding it around his knuckles like a boxer. "So, how do we . . . I don't know, get a witch divorce? A witch annulment? I'm assuming that's what you want, too."

"Oh, yes," I assured him hastily, giving a frantic nod. "Definitely on the same page there. The thing is, I've never actually heard of that happening. Even if a witchbound couple does choose to separate, the bond remains in place, forever. You only get the one, and you get it for life. Those are the lake's rules for it. There are no ways to reverse or break it that I know of."

"But what if the couple breaks up? That must happen sometimes."

"It does, but it's very rare. I personally don't know of any witchbound couple that's split up. The bond . . ." I frowned, trying to articulate it properly. "It doesn't only instill magic in the other partner, in the event that they're not already a witch. It also comes with other qualities. You've already noticed one of them—the fact that you can feel wherever I am, if you're looking for me."

"And can you do the same for me?" he asked, his face tightening. "Just locate me anywhere I happen to be? Drop a pin on me?"

"Yes, if I tried," I said, tucking in my lips behind my teeth. "You have to specifically think about your partner, focus on where they are. But I assumed you wouldn't want me invading your privacy that way. So I haven't done it."

"Thanks for that," he said shortly. "So, what's the rest of it? What else does it do?"

"It, um, boosts empathy," I said, licking my lips. This was where things were about to get extremely up close and personal. "That's partly why witchbound couples rarely leave each other. Sinking into the bond allows you to experience the other person's emotions. And their physical sensations, even, if you want. Their pain. Their, uh, their pleasure."

"I don't get it," he said, though the complex flurry of emotions—fear, discomfort, and something curiously like intrigue—drifting across his face suggested that he did, in fact, have an inkling of how this might work. "You're telling me I could feel you? Literally feel something you were experiencing? A *Pacific Rim*–style neural handshake?"

"You're lucky I happen to love that glorious trashfire of a film, and therefore get such an obscure analogue, but yes," I said, as a flush that was two parts mortification, one part something else altogether, traveled up my throat like paint spiraling through water. "You and I could officially pilot a mech together, congratulations to us. And from what I know, partners can also create a positive feedback loop, if they want. If they're the ones touching each other."

This time, he couldn't conceal the flare of interest sparking in those vivid eyes. He moved closer to the bar, leaning across it again—but this time the way he extended his hand to me was slower, more languid, his eyes latched on mine. The atmosphere between us seemed to thicken into something darker but softer, as if the air were gaining material substance, gathering like swagged velvet around us.

"Will you show me?" he said, a huskier note whispering into his tone.

Even with all the martini flooding my blood like a buffer, my heartbeat kicked up, ratcheting into a thrum that I could feel in all my pulse points. For all the awkwardness and mistrust between us, that initial spark of attraction, the intense jolt I'd felt back at the Moon and Scythe when we'd first hugged, clearly hadn't been snuffed out.

I slowly rolled up my sweater sleeve and rested my bare forearm on the bar, palm up. I'd worn an ivory angora sweater that slipped invitingly off one shoulder—which was, now that I allowed myself to consider it, more the kind of thing you'd wear for a second date than a difficult, mind-bending conversation about magic.

Maybe my witchbound subconscious had already been entertaining other . . . notions.

"When you touch me," I said, looking up at him, my cheeks pulsing with heat. "Think about me. Think about what I'm feeling, too. And while you do that, I'll be doing the same thing, but with you."

He nodded, swallowing so hard I could see his Adam's apple bob beneath his jaw. Then, without breaking that hypnotic eye contact, he stroked his fingertips up the inside of my arm, tracing a light, shivery path to my inner elbow.

It was a soft touch, silken and skilled, and it would have given me tingles all on its own. But as I thought about him touching me, focusing on the idea, I could suddenly also feel the satiny texture of my own skin under his fingertips—and I could feel him feeling *me* in return. The bright tingle of pleasure his touch had sent surging up my arm, the sudden quickening of my breath. And below that, I could feel the instant spike of lust this sensory overload induced in him, at every level; the pleasure of my skin under his, his thrill at feeling what I felt, both on my skin and in my response to him.

It was shocking, a delicious deluge of sensory information far beyond what I'd expected, even if I theoretically knew what being witchbound meant.

"Damn," he whispered almost reverently, lips parting, eyelids lowered. Even in the dim light, I could see how his pupils had flared, engulfing the blue in black. "That's . . . that is *intense*."

"Yes," I whispered back, biting my lip hard as he continued that trailing stroke, up and down the inside of my arm, up and down, until my head swam. I could feel what seeing my teeth sunk into my lower lip did to him, combined with the sensation of feeling him experience that sharp nip as if it were happening to him.

"Do you . . . want me to stop?" he asked, in a ragged, breathless tone that I liked far, far too much. Because I could feel the hard flare of his lust beneath it, the outsize and immediate surge of his desire for me; how fast this situation was spinning outside both of our control.

And he already knew full well that I didn't want him to stop, but I liked that he asked, anyway.

"No," I said, more an exhale than a word. "Don't."

With a wordless sound of approval, he slid his hand up my arm; his touch firmer now, fingertips sinking into the toned outline of my biceps under the sweater's soft fabric. He swept his hand over my bare collarbone and up the column of my neck, sliding his palm up under my hair to cup my nape, all the while never breaking our gaze.

I was breathing so hard it was almost a pant, completely overwhelmed by the pounding intensity of my response. I liked sex a lot, and had had plenty of it in my time—many different flavors of it, in fact, and it had been particularly passionate with Sydney—but I'd never reacted to anyone like this before, especially not before we'd so much as kissed. I hadn't even thought I was remotely capable of this kind of need. The sudden, hot ache between my thighs felt like a vacuum, like some crucial part of me was missing, and I wanted, *needed* to slot it back into place.

I wondered, for one totally absurd moment, whether anyone had ever actually died from wanting to fuck someone this badly.

Morty gave a soft, pained groan, feeling exactly what I felt, multiplied and then *Inception*'ed several times over by our shared sensations. He leaned across the bar and covered my mouth with his, hand tightening around my nape. His lips were plush and perfect, his tongue skimming over mine with the light flicker I liked best—and I felt my own mouth open against his, the delicate outline of my own thinner lips, the slick, silky heat of my answering kiss.

It was just a kiss, not even a very deep one; and still it felt infinitely better, more thoroughly intoxicating, than anything I'd ever done before.

Shit, no wonder witchbound couples stuck together, if even basic contact like this edged so close to bliss.

"Fuck," Morty gasped against my mouth. "Just, wait just a minute."

He pulled back—which felt, quite honestly, like some devastating loss, a tragedy I wasn't equipped to handle—and rested a hand on the bar, vaulting over it in a lithe, almost feline motion to land next to me. Then he stepped in front of me and hoisted me up onto the bar top, standing wedged between my knees, his hands clasped tight around my waist.

"Nina," he whispered, his eyes shifting between mine, glassy with a need that I felt as if it were my own, curling right alongside my desire. This time my name sounded like a prayer, a supplication.

And somehow that felt exactly right to me, like the natural order of things.

"Kiss me," I ordered—and there was a new note in my own voice, too, a strange undercurrent of command that I'd never heard myself make before.

Licking his lips, he leaned forward, and this time the kiss was feral, a spontaneous combustion. A full-blown, transporting fire that enveloped both of us completely.

He drew my bottom lip through his teeth, nipping it hard

enough to hurt—because he knew already that this was what I liked—and the surge of our tongues together, his hands running up and down my back, sinking into my hair, felt like some gorgeous chaos. Like wheeling together through a star-riddled expanse of space veined with whole jeweled galaxies, the rest of the world fallen completely away from us.

I could feel how hard he was against me, and I slid my hand down the taut line of his belly to fondle the bulge of him pressed between us. He slipped my sweater entirely off my shoulder, letting it slide down my arm, sinking his mouth into the curve between my throat and shoulder, lips and tongue and teeth flickering against that hypersensitive juncture before he bit down on me. He was cupping one of my breasts, rolling my nipple between his fingers in that firm, deft way that felt like a stream of liquid fire, a vibrating silver thread drawn straight from nipple to clit.

I could hear myself moan, in a high, helpless pitch—and I could *feel* the effect it had on him, as if that separate sensation were also my own. The utter frenzy of desire it stoked him into to hear and feel me want him, even as the squeeze of my hand between his legs urged him on.

Holding me close with an arm wound tight around my waist, he unbuttoned my leather pants with his other hand, slipping his fingers past my panties and then farther down, grazing against my wetness and heat.

"Ahh, fuck me," he groaned against my neck, fingertips circling my clit, strumming over and around it. I could feel the bright, keen pleasure beckoning already, so close—*way* too close, given how long we'd been doing this—and he felt me feel it, in a way that made his breath hitch against my skin. "Fuck, Nina, you're so wet, you feel so good—"

"Take off your pants," I said, again in that weirdly commanding, bell-like tone—and I *liked* it, liked hearing myself this way, in such control. It felt like me—the way I'd once been, with everything else—though that had never carried over into sex before. "And mine, too."

Damn, Nina, not even a "please"? And yet tacking that on hadn't even occurred to me.

He pulled away from me with a raw moan, shoving a hand into his back pocket to pull out a condom packet and set it beside me on the bar. Then he pulled his T-shirt over his head and tossed it over his shoulder, and unzipped and slid out of his jeans with impressive efficiency; apparently he hadn't bothered to wear anything underneath.

My eyes flicking down, I caught a sharp breath at the size and breadth of him; very different and extremely *more* than I'd been expecting. The handful of men I'd slept with had *not* been this manner of equipped.

He glanced up at me for a moment from under black lashes, and I could feel the ripple of his amusement, that distinctly male undercurrent of pride, as if he were somehow responsible for his own size.

"This gonna be okay for you?" he asked, eyebrow lifted, a corner of his pretty mouth curling.

"I don't know," I admitted, but the surge of pure desire and thrill that reared up in me at the thought of trying swept all concerns aside. "But trust me, we're going to give it a shot."

He bent to yank off each work boot and step out of them, tossing both jeans and shoes haphazardly to the side. Rising smoothly, he helped me slip my sweater over my head and tug off my own pants. I leaned back and propped myself up on my hands, lifting my ass to let him peel them down my legs. He even got to his knees to gently slip off each of my boots, setting them down with much more care than he'd given his own shoes.

Like he was worshipping me, with that same reverence he'd spoken my name with before.

When he rose back up to meet me, I'd already ripped the condom open, reaching down for him.

"You really sure about this?" he asked again, exhaling sharply against my mouth as I pulled him closer, hand wrapped around his heat, then unrolled the condom over him. I was very out of practice, and it was far from a smooth maneuver, but even that level of clumsy contact left both of us shuddering with need.

"You know I am," I murmured, winding my arms around his neck. "Come here."

He did, mouth covering mine, positioning himself against me. I gasped sharply at even the gentle, tentative first nudge; even such careful pressure felt a little overwhelming. Responding to my hesitation, he moved to pull back—but I wrapped my legs around his hips, urged him closer with my heels dug into the backs of his thighs.

"No, no, don't stop," I whispered against his mouth. "Just, need a minute."

He nodded, exhaling a ragged breath against my lips. I could feel his caution and the swell of desire jostling against it, as if both feelings were mine—and that respect for me, combined with the blazing want, only made *me* want him more.

"Okay," I whispered, grazing my mouth over his. "Again."

Slowly, with the utmost care, he moved against me, pressing a little deeper. This time, I relaxed into it as deeply as I could, lifting my hips to meet him, trusting that he'd stop exactly when and if I needed him to.

"Oh, *fuck*," he moaned against my mouth, dragging my lower lip sharply through his teeth. A wave of giddiness swept through me like a high, as I *felt* myself slide against the straining length of him; the taut heat of me, surrounding and engulfing and all-encompassing. His arms locked around my waist, my mouth caught in that snaring, shared-breath kiss, he began to move in long, sure thrusts, each one a bright, explosive sensation of fullness like something I'd never experienced, never even craved this way before.

Pleasure swept back and forth between us in nebulous waves, part mine, part his, until the boundaries melted away, the heat building much faster and harder than it should have. He nipped at me as I moaned against his mouth with each stroke. Every kiss melting into the next, neither of us wanting the intensity of it to end.

I usually had too much self-consciousness, a tendency to overthink even in moments of peak passion, for an orgasm to build with this kind of barreling speed. But now I could barely think at all, much less criticize and overanalyze myself; how I was moving, what expressions I might be making that could be less than flattering.

Now, there was only this, this crashing and spectacular chaos, Morty's pleasure building until it outpaced even mine, me feeling its every vibrating peak and valley. Every veneer melted away, all barriers between us stripped.

"Nina," he groaned against my mouth, the whole of him shuddering against me as he fought the tide. "I'm gonna come, I'm sorry, I can't—"

"No, don't be sorry," I whispered, letting my head fall back. "I want you to. I really, *really* want you to. Right now."

With a raw, high groan, he bucked against me, all that keen pleasure spilling into me as if it belonged to both of us. It was a high-pitched sensation like the one I had when I came; but still differently contoured somehow, not quite shaped the same as mine. Unfamiliar enough that it drove me wild, tipped me over the edge myself.

I pitched back against the bar, flinging my hands behind me to support myself as my back arched, needling currents of pleasure unfurling in my core, spiraling down my legs all the way to my toes. It came in pulsing waves with almost no space in between, a furious tightening unlike any I'd experienced before. I could hear Morty gasp as the force of it crashed over him, too, shaking us both like some massive seismic event confined to the two of us.

As it faded, with agonizing slowness, I propped myself back up on quivering arms to drop my head on Morty's shoulder. He drew me gently against him, making no move to separate us, as content as I was to linger in this moment. There would probably be awkwardness later; whole oceans of it, most likely, given that we were essentially two strangers who had just enjoyed life-altering sex in an extremely tacky bar.

But right now we were still too close, too deeply entwined. There wasn't any space between us yet, for discomfort or second-guessing.

"Well," Morty finally breathed into my hair with a soft half laugh, reaching up to idly stroke my head. "Guess we consummated the hell out of this witch marriage."

I sputtered a little laugh into the warm crook of his neck, the smell of his skin drifting up with each inhale. Every person I'd been with had a distinctive skin scent; his was surprisingly sweet, a desserty almond smell like marzipan.

"Ten/ten, five-star consummation, yes. Maybe not the venue I'd have picked, to be fair."

"Thread count less than optimal, huh? Not enough scattered rose petals for milady?" This time, the salty nickname felt like a true pet name. Genuinely affectionate, without any malice.

"More like, thread count entirely and tragically absent. But turns out, I can be somewhat flexible." I shifted against him, taking another deep breath. "Also, you smell like cake."

"Do I?" I could feel his amusement, curling up against mine like a wisp of smoke. "Never heard that one before. Feels like you think that's a good thing, though."

"I do," I assured him, nestling closer. "I *love* cake."

He held me like that for another minute, until I started feeling a little too warm and sticky for comfort. As soon as my restiveness reached him, he eased away, slipping free of me. Both of us gasped in tandem, then laughed in sync.

"Fuck, this is so weird," he said, shaking his head, pretty lips curling. "But, maybe, the brand of weird I'm partial to? Either way, gotta admit, didn't think this was where tonight was headed."

"Me neither," I admitted, shimmying off the bar in pursuit of my abandoned clothes. "I—look, this is not something I normally do. Kind of the opposite of what I normally do, in fact."

"I very much believe you. Second-date sex doesn't seem your speed at all." He flicked me another amused look as he pulled his jeans back on. "Not that this was even supposed to *be* a date."

"But I'm . . ." I swallowed a surge of shyness, surprised by how easily it went. "This is so strange to say, but I'm glad this happened."

He smiled fully at that, bending to scoop up his T-shirt, dark hair falling into his face. "Same. So, what now? I completely get it if you'd like to head out. But my place is just upstairs, if you'd rather stay the night. Or I could make you something first in the kitchen down here, if you're hungry? I'm not much of a pastry chef, if you're really fiending for that cake, but I do kind of kill at anything savory."

I paused, pulling my sweater over my head. A small part of me clamored that I should leave, that this was all entirely nuts, the sort of situation no reasonable person should desire to prolong.

The rest of me—most of me—wanted nothing more than to stay put, keep on being close to him. And it helped that I could feel that Morty felt the same; was actively dreading the idea of seeing me vanish into the cold winter night outside when I could stay here, safe and warm with him instead. Plus, no one had ever offered to postcoitally cook for me before, and the new Boss Nina who'd taken up residence inside me apparently really dug the idea.

"Actually, I *am* hungry," I told him, tugging my sweater back over my head. It was true, too; I was still ravenous, as if I hadn't eaten Avalon out of all their backroom stores not even that long ago. "So that sounds wonderful."

"Amazing." He grinned at me, running a hand through that mess of hair. "Anything in particular you feel like you could go for? You know what—let me just get a menu for you."

12

My Forever Kenzi

"SO LOWKEYLOKI *COOKED* for you," Jessa said, in tones of such rapturous and unapologetic "I told you so" glee that I almost threw a pastry at her, before deciding that would be a waste. "And then you spent. *The. Night.*"

"You don't have to say it all smug like that," I groused, sinking farther into her overstuffed couch.

Everything in Jessa's spacious living room was designed to foster comfort: a huge, plush modular sofa that you could re-arrange into a lounge nest for watching TV, a slew of pillows in peacock blue and teal, five different throws in a variety of soft fabrics, a tall, curved lamp that swooped over the couch to shed warm light on us. It was the opposite of my own minimalist aesthetic, which tended more to cool Nordic without too much distracting hygge. Lots of clean, stark silhouettes, thoughtful art, and muted colors.

Soothing and lovely, but less than ideal for a binge-watch session, which was why Tuesday TV nights usually happened at Jessa's condo.

As per her house rules, we were both wearing the matching fleece-lined adult onesies patterned with flannel-clad penguins she'd gotten us one holiday season, which I pretended to hate but secretly adored. Her pup, a massive black labradoodle who lived to crowd you with affection, was a huge draw, too. I wasn't the kind of person who ever wanted to experience the questionable joys of dog ownership, but I loved getting to borrow other people's. Jake was currently sprawled next to me with his head in my lap, staring up at my unattainable snack with desperate hope and yearning.

"What other way is there to say it?" Jessa asked, finger to her chin, making a faux pensive moue. "Operation Doggy Paddle was a spectacular success by any standard. You got hella laid, then you got fed—by a sexy-ass individual who cooked for you, no less—and then you got the lovely snugs."

"I did get the snugs," I agreed, remembering the languid comfort of sleeping tucked up against Morty, the witch bond open between us even as we dreamed. There'd been no more mind-blowing sex, but that was only because he'd made us crispy honey brussels sprouts and buffalo chicken enchiladas. I'd eaten so much that any type of strenuous activity had not been a viable option, even if the spirit was more than willing. "All those things were, admittedly, very good."

"And now here I am, rewarding you for losing your own bet," Jessa pointed out, gesturing at the still-warm pigs in blankets nestled on a tray in front of us, one of my favorite episodes of *Lost Girl* playing on her massive screen.

"Technically, it was *your* bet. That I didn't even want any part of in the first place."

"And yet, here you are, winning on every front. The good dick *and* the pastries, because I'm just that proud of both Operation Doggy Paddle and my own bestie's prowess. All things considered, you're really the one making out like a bandit here."

"It's true, you spoil me," I agreed, reaching for another pastry, teeth sinking into flaky crust followed by caramelized onion, melted Gruyère, and the bougie kind of tiny cocktail sausage. Jessa's pigs in blankets were a whole culinary event. "But I'm still having trouble getting over the fact that I banged a near-stranger in a bar. *On* a bar, to be precise, in full view of a plastic skeleton in a leprechaun hat. Sassy Sue's going to have a field day helping me process that, if I can even bring myself to tell her."

Jessa sat up, pausing the show.

"The thing that's really getting me, though, is that you don't actually *sound* all that bugged about it," she said, canting her head and fixing me with that Machiavellian gaze, so out of place on her soft features. "Like, I get it, Nina's getting her groove back with a vengeance. But two dates in a row? *Bar-top* sex, on the *second* date, followed by a sleepover? No hint of any real mortification at having thrown caution to the passionate zephyrs?"

"Why does it suddenly feel like you're judging me a little?"

"Sweetheart, don't get me wrong, I am beyond stoked you're living your best life. But this doesn't sound like you at all."

I heaved a sigh, sinking back into the nest of pillows. I'd known this was going to be a tricky conversation to navigate, without being able to tell Jessa about the witch bond—the way it had enabled me to lean into the attraction, leap into the sizzling moment.

Be the right kind of heedless for once in my life, while still feeling like I had both hands firmly on the wheel.

How was I going to express any of that to her, or to properly explain that I was still reeling from the best sex I'd ever had? That I'd thought about nothing but Morty, the marzipan scent of his skin, his soft mouth and clever hands, the way he felt inside me—the way his *feelings* felt inside me, too—for the past two days? Before I left the next morning, we'd agreed to keep the witch bond shut down when we were apart, since we were still so new to each other, so unsure of how we wanted to proceed with *any* of this.

But I'd missed him since, almost painfully. And I'd be willing to bet much more than snacks and an evening of comfort shows that the missing was mutual.

"I'm not sure myself," I said slowly, the lie sour in my mouth even as I reached for a way to better describe the situation for her without revealing anything off-limits. "It just feels . . . different, with him. Everything feels different. He's not what I usually go for, not at all—again, why you picked him for me in the first place. But it was, ugh, *so hot*, Jessa. I think maybe that's why it all happened so fast? Like, possibly neither of us was prepared for that kind of out-of-control chemistry? So it's making us, um, more receptive to each other on other levels, too."

"That does happen sometimes," she said, still dubious, but willing to take my word for it—because why wouldn't she believe her own best friend? She trusted me to tell her my truth, the whole of it. And here I was, hiding in my walled-off, secret magic garden. Keeping most of it concealed from her. "Like with me and Steven. It's just balls-to-the-wall every time we fuck. And there's, like, *emotions* threatening to happen. Entire feeeeeelings, dude. Some-times, Nina, I swear, we're actually almost making love."

I burst out laughing at the revolted face she made at this, as though she could imagine literally nothing worse than an emo-tionally charged sexual connection.

"You are such a die-hard fuckboi," I informed her, still chuck-ling. "I mean, I love you for it, you know that. But you really need to own it."

"Oh, I own it with pride and dedication," she said with a shrug, unpausing the show. "Throw me a fuckboi parade any old day. Hence why it's baffling to me when one of the rotation actually wriggles under my skin like this. Like, I have you and my man Jake to tend to my emotional needs, I'm all set on that."

"It's okay to like them, you know," I said softly, running my fingers over Jake's warm curls until he gave a contented huff against my leg.

Jessa made an ambiguous sound, eyes fixed on the TV, where Bo and Kenzi sprawled on the floor together, Bo writhing with laughter at some joke Kenzi had just cracked. I always loved the episodes that highlighted how pure their friendship was, the way Kenzi accepted her succubus bestie without any fear or reluctance, no barriers or judgment between them. And I'd never wished more that there was no minefield of secrets between me and Jessa, either. That I could tell her what it had truly been like with Morty; to feel what really lay under someone else's skin, to crack a door open into their mind and have them do the same to you.

"To let them in a little," I added. "Sometimes, that can even be really nice."

"You know my deal with that," she said, twisting a stray curl around her finger and drawing it taut, before letting it spring back into its corkscrew shape. "I'm not doing Allison all over again. That isn't how my life plays out."

I did know. Jessa's dad had walked out on them when she was only a baby, and her single mother had proceeded to run an entire gauntlet of turbulent relationships, dragging Jessa through all the ensuing emotional carnage. Constantly seeking male validation— or "chasing dick," as Jessa so delicately put it, even though the turn of phrase made me shudder each time—and doing whatever it took to secure it, stability be damned. In turn, Jessa was hell-bent on overcorrecting by never desperately running after love the way her mother had, especially at the expense of a child.

To be fair, Allison had gotten her act together. In her fifties, she'd married Jessa's stepfather, Daniel, who by all accounts seemed like a wonderful, decent man—so committed to his new little family he'd actually talked Jessa's mother into moving to Thistle Grove, too, so they could be closer to her.

"I hear you," I said, treading as carefully as I could. "You know I just want you to be happy. And it sounds like, *just maybe*, this guy has the potential to do that for you."

"Perhaps!" she said, a shade too brightly. "I'm not planning on holding my breath. And it's not like I'm some kind of commitment-phobe, dude. I came all the way to these here Illinois boonies for you, didn't I? I know a solid life partner when I meet one—even if I don't happen to be dating them."

Another throb of guilt lurched through me at this reminder. Jessa enjoyed her Thistle Grove life so much, fit here so seamlessly, that sometimes I forgot she hadn't grown up here like I had. We'd met at Columbia Law in New York, and she'd lived in New Jersey before that. We'd become roommates our second year, not that I'd needed one to afford the penthouse I lived in, while almost everyone else in our class shared matchbox apartments with four other people; I'd always refused to let Jessa pay any part of the rent when the money could go to her savings instead. We'd just loved each other's company, cohabitated with absolute ease and comfort. Been family to each other without ever having been blood.

After hearing me rhapsodize about Thistle Grove for years—and coming back with me to visit for holidays more than a few times—she'd decided to follow me here after school. Get barred in Illinois and hang out her own shingle close to the one person who mattered to her more than the parade of seemingly interchangeable lovers who never lasted more than a few months.

She'd come here for me, and I'd never even told her what this town really was. What I was.

"And how successful would you say I've been at that?" I asked, in the same carefully lighthearted tone. "The whole platonic life partner thing, I mean."

She paused the show again at that, catching the underlying current of gravity in my voice. "What do you mean, sweetheart?" she said, brow furrowing. "You know you're my forever Kenzi."

"Okay, well, I'd say it's fairly debatable which one of us is which. I just mean . . ." I trailed off, trying to understand what I even wanted to ask her. "Do you feel like I'm available enough to you? Open enough?"

She rubbed her lips together, still clearly a little thrown. "Well, if we're really going to talk about this . . . I do find it just the *slightest* bit achy that I never get to spend time with your family. Like, they throw a literal shit ton of parties and galas and whatever else fancy, that's their main thing. Yet I've been over at Tintagel for dinner, what, maybe twice since I moved here?"

"But that's because they're obnoxious!" I argued, with such zest that Jake stirred against my leg, disgruntled. "Both my family and all those overblown affairs themselves, for the most part. I only go to those things because I have to."

This was only partly true. The real reason Jessa didn't get to enjoy Tintagel festivities with me was because they tended to be witch-community-centric events, featuring the kind of magical displays that would trigger the oblivion glamour. Even our more "casual" family dinners often entailed spellwork, just because it was so natural to all of us to rely on magic, to work it almost thoughtlessly. I could ask my family members to refrain on Jessa's behalf, but I couldn't be positive that everyone would remember the restriction, or bother to take that extra care. My family didn't exactly excel at being that kind of considerate, especially when it came to normies.

Even back when she'd come to Thistle Grove with me for holidays, I'd always insisted we share an Airbnb, ostensibly because I didn't like being that close to my family for protracted periods of time—in truth, because I didn't trust them to behave around her.

"I know, I get that. Difficult mom over here, too, remember?" She shrugged a shoulder, smiling a little ruefully. "But you do really love your brothers, even if they're kind of shitheads. And it would be nice for me to get a chance to know them better, too."

"I didn't know you felt left out that way," I said, the space behind my sternum constricting. "I'm sorry, Jess."

"It's really not *that* big of a deal," she said, reaching over to squeeze my socked foot and give it a little shake. The unruly mop of curls perched on her head in the loosest approximation of a bun quivered with the motion. "I would've mentioned it if it was. Like I said, only the *slightest* bit achy. Same deal for how you won't come over for Seder even though I all but send you an engraved invitation every year. And it hits a little weird that you always have plans, are somehow always busy those specific times."

I hung my head, letting my hair curtain my face. That one, I *had* known bothered her. Seder was meant to be a family gathering, and I knew Jessa considered me family, the sister neither of us had ever had. But for me, it was the flip side of the same coin. Even though, technically, I knew Jewish people could be Wiccans, too, it felt dishonest and disrespectful to not inform someone hosting a sacred religious meal that they were breaking bread with a real-life witch.

I didn't feel like I had the right or permission to be there, because I had no way to ask for it.

Still, maybe that had just been selfishness. A cowardly projection of my own guilt for all I'd been holding back from my best friend, who'd happily arranged her entire life so she could be closer to me. It wasn't like the Seder food was going to burst into flames if a Blackmoore witch dared eat it or something.

At least, to the best of my knowledge it wouldn't.

"I'll come next year," I said, girding my resolve. "Okay, Jess? And that's a promise."

"You sure?" She smiled at that, more fully this time, a sweet brightening that warmed me, too, made that sharp sternum pressure abate a little. "Because I'm gonna hold you to that one, Kenz."

"Dude. *I'm* Bo. I am obviously Bo."

She snorted, picking up the remote and shaking her head. "In literally no world are you Bo, sweetheart. But whatever gets you through the day."

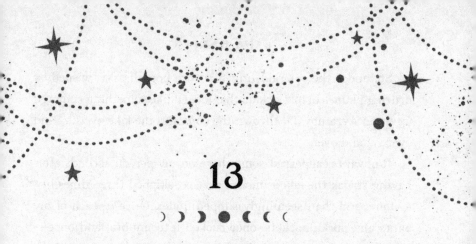

13

Why Won't You Just Melt

"AND YOU'RE *SURE* you being here won't screw with this?" Gareth asked, for approximately the tenth time.

"Of course I'm not sure, Gareth," I snapped, already running plenty short of patience. "But seeing as the damn thing won't tolerate being out of my sight, does it seem like we have a choice?"

After work the previous day, I'd portaled back up to the lake with the wild idea that maybe, just maybe, I could break what I'd taken to calling the Goddess Spell by simply chucking the coin back into the water. It seemed fairly self-evident that the octa-grammed coin was a talisman, an emblematic representation of the mysterious casting itself. My thinking had been, if I just returned it to its source—rejected it by a symbolic act—possibly that would be enough to break the spell. In any case, it would be worth a try.

So, under the emerald-tinged aurora borealis sky, wisped by drifting plumes of black cloud that looked like something conjured up by an Avramov, I'd thrown the coin into the lake over . . . and over . . . and over.

It always reappeared somewhere on my person seconds after having struck the lake's smooth surface, skipped three times like a stone, and then seemingly slipped under. Once in each of my pants and parka pockets, once tucked into my bra, and once—shockingly—in my mouth, hot like an ember on my tongue. Like something between a magician's trick and a caution.

O WOULDST THOU CEASE SCREWING WITH ME, NINA, MY NINA, I imagined the luminous statue under the lake belling in my head, those bright golden eyes narrowing with disapproval. *ALL IS AS I WILLED IT, AND WHO ARE YOU TO OBJECT?*

I'd tried changing my intentions with each throw, intoned different mantras, even attempted keeping my mind carefully and completely blank. Nothing made the slightest bit of difference.

The coin was clearly sticking with me to the bitter end of whatever this even was.

Goddess-willed or no, the entire experience had severely pissed me off. I hadn't *asked* to be saddled with this extra power, along with the accompanying danger of triggering another cataclysmic event like the one that had happened at Castle Camelot. Not having attended oracle or priestess school—or whatever degree of education was required to divine an underwater goddess's intent—I couldn't understand why such a radiant and seemingly benevolent being would be playing with me like this. *Toying* with me. Treating me, frankly, like the same kind of entertaining plaything on a string that Sydney had sometimes used me as.

But I did know that whatever was happening to me was happening without my consent, and that wasn't something I could tolerate. So now, Gareth and I were taking another, more aggressive tack.

We stood in a vast, windowless, completely empty room at the Tintagel estate, the ceiling so high it almost disappeared above us, the stone floor and walls bare and featureless. This was the Cell: not a prison, despite its foreboding name, but the massively warded haven where Blackmoores learned to wield the more destructive spells in our elementalists' arsenal. The Cell was its own enclosure, a freestanding structure like a barracks set a healthy distance away from the manor proper. Just for an extra bit of buffer should anything go awry—not that it ever had, in the nearly three centuries we'd been using it as a teaching arena.

Every surface in the room was threaded through with hugely powerful wards; if I narrowed my eyes and brought my focus to bear on them, I could *see* them glimmering, like a complex web of golden wire or metallic filaments. A crisscrossing matrix of potent spells that would ensure that nothing dangerous could escape this space, and that no harm would come to those within it. The idea was, Gareth would fling destructive castings at the coin—out of the three of us, my brother had always excelled in elemental demolition—to try to physically, literally break the spell by destroying its talisman.

It wasn't the safest—and certainly not the smartest—idea either of us had ever had. But this *was* the most secure place to try that kind of gamble.

"It's still risky, I agree," I said to Gareth, making a conscious effort to soften my tone when I saw him flinch. Sometimes I forgot how sensitive he could be, when I sounded even remotely like our mother. "Because, yes, theoretically just my being here might render anything you cast way more explosive. But the wards should be able to take it; diffuse and bleed off even that added burst of energy. I mean, that's the entire point of them."

These wards were centuries old, designed by Caelia Blackmoore herself for this purpose; Lyonesse and Igraine personally tended to them on a weekly basis so the youngest generation of Blackmoores could freely practice here.

"And you *definitely* want to do this?" he pressed. "Aggressively fuck with something a goddess gave you? I mean, shit, you know I'm all about those power moves. But this . . . this is next level, Nina. Just want us both to be clear on that."

I gave a helpless, angry shrug, flinging up my hands. "Honestly, brother, at this point I can't do *nothing*—and this is all I can think to try. If you're still game, that is."

Gareth nodded, squaring his shoulders and twisting his neck to each side. "For you, of course I am. Let's do this. Take one, your basic smash."

He took a bracing stance and lifted his hands, murmuring an incantation under his breath. I could feel the kinetic energy building around us as raw magic rushed toward him, gathering in vast, thickening folds. Funneling toward the spot right above where the coin glimmered—somehow saucily, as if it were always winking just at me—on one of the flagstones.

The air above it darkened, grew in density and substance; the faceted outline of a massive boulder appearing in the air like some huge architectural sketch, its rough lines slowly taking on depth and texture.

Until suddenly, with a massive, thunderous crack, a gigantic hunk of stone hung suspended in the air, slowly rotating.

It was a rough-hewn sphere, shot through with cracks and what looked like streaks of moss and lichen, which made me wonder if Gareth had actually built it from raw elemental material or simply transported it from elsewhere, whisked it here from Hallows Hill or some other rocky outcropping in the vicinity. Telekinetic spells like this weren't my forte—I wasn't even sure which one he'd chosen to use—but Gareth was a pro at this kind of brute strength display. When I glanced over at him, his boyish face was completely relaxed and serene, as if he were meditating instead of levitating a several-ton boulder fifteen feet up in the air by arcane strength alone.

Lack of nuance aside, sometimes my brother's magic *could* be kind of badass.

"Really?" I said, flicking him a doubtful glance. "You think smashing it with a *rock* is going to do the trick?"

"Won't know until we try! Impact in three," he announced, more out of habit than anything else. Normally we'd both summon shields for something like this, but such precautions weren't necessary in the Cell.

As soon as the boulder began to drop, a glimmering sheath of webbed gold sprang up around both of us, encasing us each in a shield designed to deflect any amount of shrapnel or air displacement that might happen, anything that could hurt us.

Which was excellent, because upon impact with the coin, the boulder *exploded*.

It didn't just crumble, or shatter, or fracture; as soon as it hit the ground, it pulverized itself completely. A burst of tiny shards like vicious arrows fired in every direction, fine needling projectiles that would have shredded both Gareth and me if the Cell hadn't been shielding us. We both swiveled away out of pure instinct, flinging up our arms to guard our faces. I could hear the cacophony of bursts, pops, and sizzles as the shields incinerated each separate fragment, but every impulse in my mammalian brain shrieked at me to take cover, and I couldn't bring myself to crack my eyes open and see what was happening.

By the time silence had settled back over the room, and Gareth and I turned back to where the boulder had fallen, there was nothing left of it. Not even dust.

Just the coin glittering maddeningly at us, shiny and undinged, light glinting off it in that taunting way.

"So, that was ballistic as shit," Gareth remarked, with such uncharacteristic dryness that it startled a real, slightly shrill laugh out of me. "Like, yeah, it probably wasn't going to work in the first place, but that was way out of bounds. What the hell is that coin *made* of, anyway? Adamantium? Unobtainium? Kryptonite? I don't even get how something so small could have triggered that intense a disintegration."

"Was that a real boulder from somewhere?" I asked, my own thoughts tumbling over each other. "Or did you build it?"

Sometimes magically conjured constructs—even if they were, for all intents and purposes, indistinguishable from their natural counterparts—were slightly more unstable than the real thing. Or considerably more so, depending on the strength and skill of the caster, but Gareth was such a top-tier elementalist that it shouldn't have made this much of a difference in any case.

"Jacked it from an abandoned quarry a couple miles outside town," he replied, shaking his head. "Don't worry, no one was gonna miss it. So, not even construct weakness as a contributing factor, if that's what you were thinking."

"So the coin doesn't respond to that kind of pressure," I mused out loud. "What about a temperature change? Deep freeze? Most metals shatter if they get cold enough, right?"

Gareth nodded briskly, rubbing his palms together. "Yeah, but you have to drop really far below zero for a lot of the hardier ones to go from ductile to brittle. I can swing it, though, no problem, if that's what you want to try."

"Might as well give it a shot, since we're here," I said, hands on my hips. "Especially because it always feels so warm to the touch. So a cold snap may actually do the trick."

With a nod, Gareth brought both hands in front of his sternum, palms together, then rotated them, until one faced up, the other down, elbows out at his sides.

"Try your best not to invite any ice wraiths to come party today, okay?" he tossed to me over his shoulder. "And for the record, that's, like, only half a joke."

"Fair enough. I don't think that could happen in here, though. Too much warding in the floor and walls."

Gareth took a long, deep breath, holding it as he rotated his hands through a series of precise, minute positions like compass needles quivering between the four cardinal points. When he exhaled, a sparkling purl of chill swirled on his breath, expanding and brightening, filling the room with white. I recognized this working; a Welsh frost spell, used to restore Wheel of the Year order by ushering in winter when it lagged so far behind it threatened to disrupt the natural balance.

Why anyone would ever want to go chasing winter was beyond me, but likely that was precisely why I hadn't been born a Welsh village sage.

As ice crystals shimmered to life around us—like a host of tiny snowflakes, a flurry of floating crushed diamonds—the Cell's shields snapped into place again, this time to keep our body heat safely sealed in. Unlike at Castle Camelot, I couldn't feel the plummet in temperature; but I could see frost riming the walls, even the floor smoothing into milky glass as what little moisture the room contained turned to a brittle skin of ice. A pale fog swirled all around us, curtains of wavering white like gathered gauze.

"How cold is it now?" I asked Gareth a few moments later, squinting through the fog as I peered at the coin. It sat in a prim little circle of bare stone, the encroaching scrim of ice unable to so much as touch it. A small, dense ball of dread began to form in the pit of my stomach; the boulder might have been an obvious fool's errand, but a temperature drop like this should at least have been able to *faze* the coin.

"I b-believe the m-most offensive take would be, 'as a w-witch's tits,'" my brother replied tersely, through chattering teeth. This spell *was* wearing on him, even though during last year's Gauntlet of the Grove, he'd summoned up entire glaciers from Lady's Lake without seeming to break a sweat. So that gave me some indication of just how unearthly a cold he was channeling. "P-pardon my French. Or, outer-space cold. Cold as fuck. T-take your pick."

"Can you go any colder?" I urged, still glaring furiously at the goddess-damned coin, as if I could will that tauntingly untouched protective circle into diminishing. How could a coin look like it was flipping you the bird just by sitting there? I'd never seen an object with quite so much attitude.

"N-not safely," Gareth gasped, his voice so hoarse my gaze snapped to him—his lips were blue, and a clammy sheen of sweat stood out on his brow, despite the heat his own Cell-provided shield was surely lending him. That would go only so far, though, when it was his body being used as a temporary conduit for this cold. "S-sorry, N-N-Nina. This—far as I can go."

I hissed in frustration, feeling like a monumental asshole even as he released the frost spell and the Cell began inching back toward a more normal, human-friendly temperature.

"No, Gare," I said, reaching out to squeeze his shoulder when the heat shields finally winked out around both of us, the last of that swathing white fog melting away. "*I'm* sorry. I didn't mean to push too hard. You're—I know you're doing me a solid here."

He threw me a faintly disgusted look, like, *duh*, even as he wiped the chill sweat from his temples. "In this together, remember? I'm only doing it because you'd probably blow both of us into smithereens if you tried to cast even a starter-pack spell. You're like a magical nuclear reactor right now, and kind of a helpless kitten at the same time. Can you *imagine* how awesome it is for me, being the responsible, capable one for once?"

I chuckled, shaking my head. "I'm glad you're finding your joy here, brother. Really love that for you."

He flashed a smile at me over his shoulder, the rakish grin I knew had an entirely different effect on people not blood-related to him. "I realize you're being a dick, but I know such trifles as my happiness actually *do* matter to you, sis. Kind of a rarity, in this family."

He turned away before I could even fully register the gut punch of that sentiment, and the fact that he clearly meant it.

"So, what do you think, time to try killing it with fire?" he asked, rolling up his shirtsleeves as he shifted his gaze back to the coin. "You know I'm up for that."

I nodded, chewing on the inside of my cheek as emotion prickled in my nose. There'd be time to talk to Gareth about what he'd said later—if either of us could bring ourselves to do it. Admitting and navigating emotional vulnerability wasn't exactly a prized Blackmoore family skill; what little I knew of it myself had emerged out of my friendship with Jessa, and many, many painful sessions with Sassy Sue. And it was still far from one of my favorite activities.

"Let's do it," I said instead, pressing my lips together. "Maybe Gofannon's Blaze?"

The Welsh metalsmith god's fire was the most powerful incendiary charm in the elementalist workings contained in the Grimoire, and, unlike Uriel's flame, indiscriminately destructive. If it couldn't melt this stubborn little fucker of a coin, then nothing would.

The nugget of dread shifted nauseatingly in my stomach, because what if this *didn't* work? Did that mean I'd be stuck with this spell for the foreseeable future—maybe even forever? The idea that my magic might become permanently unstable, a volatile element I wasn't allowed to access if I wanted to keep the people around me safe, made me want to double over and retch.

"That's what I was thinking," Gareth said, licking his lips. He lifted his arms, fists clenched in front of him, wrists up. Slowly, he swept them in ever-widening circular motions, speaking the Welsh incantation first under his breath and then aloud, the unfamiliar words gaining force and cadence until they rose into a yell—a powerful, commanding bellow that carried with it the tolling timbre of my brother's own considerable will.

Then Gareth opened his fists, and pure, brilliant fire bloomed out of them.

Twin gouts of it gushed from his palms; an inferno of liquid gold and orange, veined with scarlet strains. The streams converged halfway between Gareth and where the coin sat on the floor, ten feet away from us. At that midway point, they braided together into a single entwined stream, a blinding jet of flame that struck the coin head-on.

And it *did* strike—I could see the coin skid slightly to the left as Gofannon's Blaze met it, though it moved much less than something so small should have beneath such a pummel of force. Still, even that slight judder gave me a bright, dizzying rush of hope; so it *was* possible to impact the coin, then.

As soon as the contact was made, the temperature of the entire room ratcheted up, enough to trigger the Cell's shields back into place around us, this time to preserve pockets of cool air around our bodies. I could see the coin heating, turning a dangerously hot white where it ate all that concentrated flame. But its edges didn't soften, didn't even begin to lose shape. If anything, the scorching white only made the octagram glow more brightly defined, honed the exquisite lines of that cameo profile of the goddess's face.

For whatever reason, the sight of this particular resistance enraged me where the boulder and freeze failures hadn't managed to, tipped my mounting dread and frustration into full-blown rage.

"You shitty little motherfucker!" I shrieked at the coin, my hands clenching into helpless, furious fists by my sides. That trapped dragon inside me reared up again, scaly wings rasping at my lungs, its vast length battering against the scaffold of my ribs. "Why won't you just *melt*? Why won't you just be *gone* and let me be?"

"Uh, Nina?" Gareth said, a new, sharp note of panic to his voice. "Nina, what—"

The streams of flame flowing from his hands doubled, and

then tripled—and then magnified so many times over that any measure of their scope lost meaning altogether.

They spread across the room like an infernal brush fire, engulfing everything but us. The tiny piece of me that wasn't entirely raging registered a slight concern that I could now feel an uncomfortable rising heat—as though the shield surrounding me might be weakening at the onslaught.

All around us, I could see the overwhelmed web of wards flickering wildly in the blazing walls. Working overtime, frantically channeling magical energy away to keep that conflagration from bringing the entire structure down. But there was so much fire around us, so much. *Too* much. I could smell it now, the stench seeping even through the shield, its acrid scorch triggering a scrabbling, atavistic fear of being burned alive. I could hear Gareth screaming my name in genuine terror, tinged with something that wasn't quite pain but dangerously close. My own skin suddenly warmed even further, the fine hairs on my arms and neck sizzling with new heat.

And then with a terrible, blinding flare, a roaring *whoomp* like a gale all around us, everything went white.

14

An Echo of Morgan Herself

WE SURVIVED.

The Cell did not.

Fortunately, it had expended its last warding efforts into making sure the shields stayed put around me and Gareth, enough to protect us from the tumbling, fiery wreckage of the building's collapse. From what we'd gathered after—even with the wards' last-ditch efforts to protect us, both Gareth and I had passed out from sheer shock and the impact of that final implosion—Lyonesse and Igraine had portaled over and put the fire out in short order between the two of them. Together with some of the rest of the family, they'd easily levitated the charred ruins out of the way and excavated our sorry selves.

And by that time, Gareth and I were feeling *extremely* sorry about our recent life choices.

"Starting to think it might've been easier if we'd actually bought it," Gareth muttered under his breath beside me, as if reading my mind. A scrawl of soot like some deathly rune unscrolled from his forehead all the way down to his jaw; his hair was a ridiculous ruckus, sticking up in a nest of ashen and blond spikes. Lyonesse hadn't even given us time to clean up before marching us over to Tintagel's War Room for a "debriefing" that had all the classical hallmarks of an interrogation. "'Cause this has the makings of a colossal cluster."

"Did you have something to say, Gareth Aurelius?" our mother inquired witheringly, perching her chin on one palm. She and our grandmother sat across from us, on the other side of the massive oak round table that dominated the room. Bas-reliefs of knights on horseback galloped across the walls around us, while four massive Corinthian columns surrounded the table, each entwined with a circling dragon, their roaring heads coming together at the dome-vaulted ceiling to breathe painted fire into the burning-sky fresco overhead.

The War Room always *did* give such casual, low-key vibes.

With their near-identical tasteful pantsuits and blond chignons—Igraine's just a touch frostier—our mother and grandmother looked like two beautifully kept and extremely sinister modern Fates. They hadn't even bothered to include our father in what was sure to be an epic dressing-down; as far as our mother was concerned, Merritt was more window dressing than person. The human equivalent of a tasteful set piece that had the good sense to yield to her opinions and otherwise stay out of her way. He was probably spending the afternoon in the stable with his beloved Thoroughbreds, which, frankly, sounded like where I'd rather be myself. And I didn't even care for horses, not since one of his prize stallions bit me when I was five. I still had the scar on the inside of my left forearm.

Still. Preferable.

"You must be terribly hoarse from all the smoke inhalation, my darling, as I didn't quite manage to catch that," Lyonesse added, pursing shell-pink lips and tilting her head delicately to the side. That porcelain finish of hers could be so deceptive; she didn't look half as dangerous as she was.

"No, Mother," Gareth replied, ducking his head, his throat working as he swallowed hard. "I don't have anything to say."

We'd often found ourselves in this exact scenario throughout our childhood, but back then he used to reach for my hand under the table for courage, confident that I'd be able to tow him safely through to the other side. This time, neither of us was quite so sure. We'd never, between the two of us, managed to bring down an entire bastion of Blackmoore architectural and magical history before. There wasn't really a precedent for this kind of catastrophic screwup.

"Just, uh, clearing my throat," he finished, his jaw clenching.

With an answering roil in my own stomach, I knew just how he felt; the humiliation and the instinctual fear our mother could instill in both of us just by taking that frigid tone. The unpredictable precursor to anything from a flaying-by-emotional-scalpel to a full-fledged explosion.

Gareth sometimes referred to this experience, only half jokingly, as playing Lyonesse Roulette.

"Of course you were, son. When *has* Gareth Aurelius had anything of particular import to say for himself, scion or no?" she mused, each word dripping contempt, those piercing blue eyes shifting to me. "Not in recent memory, anyway."

I could practically feel my brother cave in on himself, that inner shrivel Lyonesse was so deft at provoking. While we were growing up, Gareth had been the relatively cosseted eldest; the one who'd always had it the easiest out of the three of us, often told how handsome he was, how talented and special. At the time, the difference in treatment had stung, but I'd learned what he hadn't: how to manage expectations and set boundaries, how rules would protect me.

And it was much easier to see now, as an adult, that he hadn't emerged from the familial battleground anything like unscathed.

"Why don't we start with you instead, Nineve?" our mother said, sliding that heavy gaze onto me. I could practically feel it land on my shoulders, like a millstone around my neck. "I have to imagine that whatever bloody disaster you just brought down upon both your heads—perhaps all of ours—you were the likelier mastermind. The much more competent, at the very least."

I gritted my teeth, swallowing my annoyance at the anglicized phrasing that the entire older generation of our family affected for no good reason. It wasn't enough that Tintagel looked like the *American Horror Story* version of Downton Abbey, all loomingly ornate wooden paneling; overwrought gilding; art featuring fox hunts and sallow, prissy aristocrats; and ceilings coffered, frescoed, or vaulted to within an inch of their unfortunate lives. Unlike Castle Camelot, which I'd always loved for its endearingly intentional kitsch and whimsy, I'd hated our family demesne and its overbearing decadence my whole life. And then on top of it, the boomers all had to sound like ersatz peerage, too.

For a wild moment, I debated lying to my mother, but what would I have said? What possible explanation could I have come up with in the spur of the moment, for why and how my brother and I had managed to level a centuries-old structure that was not only a wonder of Blackmoore magic, but had been *created* to withstand magical assaults?

So I told her and Igraine the truth, beginning with my night at the lake. Lyonesse's platinum eyebrows only barely flicked up at the revelation of a goddess statue at the bottom of Lady's Lake; so exactly our mother's blasé way, as if news of an underwater deity hit the bottom of her list of priorities when she had adult children to berate. I walked them through my waking with the coin clutched in my hand, the way my own spells were now superpowered even when I didn't intend them to be.

But I left out my witch bond with Morty. It didn't seem directly relevant to what had happened, and I had the absurd impulse to protect it—to protect *him*—from their scrutiny.

"And it seems to be my emotional state that triggers the additional fluctuation. The unpredictable influx of power into someone else's otherwise normal spell," I explained, something I'd only just realized myself at the Cell. "My temper flaring, specifically. That's what happened with Gawain's snow spell at Castle Camelot, the one he uses in *Yvain*. When the ice wraiths manifested, I'd been feeling angry at one of the tourists, for . . . touching things he shouldn't have been."

"Oh, impertinence, of course. As fine a reason as any to conjure up a pack of elemental creatures on a Sunday afternoon," my mother remarked, rolling her eyes with extravagant scorn. "And what were you feeling *angry* about *this* afternoon, that deserved wreaking fiery cataclysm on our own estate?"

"The coin wouldn't melt," I said shortly, my own sooty cheeks flaming. Because when she put it that way, it sounded impossibly stupid, beyond mortifying to have lost control over myself for something like that. "We were attempting to destroy it; it's clearly a talisman, a locus point tied to the spell itself. I'd tried throwing it back into the lake already, but that failed to make an observable impact."

"The true question is, why didn't you come to us with all this immediately?" Igraine broke in for the first time, her aquiline nose flaring with aggrieved disdain. "A sleeping goddess statue in the lake—the heretofore unknown root of this town's power—and one whose notice *you* somehow warrant? A deity who has made you the focus of a divine spell? Oh, you absolute *idiot* child, what could you have been thinking? We should have been your very first port of call!"

Gareth twitched beside me, his knee jerking in secondhand reaction to the harshness of the reprimand. Sometimes our grandmother made our mother seemed downright benevolent.

It was, at least, helpful for maintaining perspective.

"We . . . thought you might feel obligated to go to Emmeline Harlow with it immediately," I said, improvising. "Which, Gareth and I both agreed, would be unwise. Considering our family's current standing, our precarious position with the other families."

"So you *have* managed to demonstrate some modicum of sense," Lyonesse replied, Igraine giving an austere nod of agreement beside her. A tiny bubble of relief expanded in my throat; I had been right to think this might be the (appealingly treacherous) tack to take. "Of course the Victor shouldn't be told, given the way it implicates us. Though why in the triple goddess's name would you have thought *I* would go to her with this news, put us all at risk like that?"

"Gareth and I were unsure how the responsibilities of the elders to the Victor are governed by the Grimoire, Mother," I said, the height of (deceptive) decorum. "I thought you might be magically obligated in some way, as with the Arbiter's Mantle. Bound to honesty."

Igraine and Lyonesse snorted in tandem. "As if Caelia would ever have agreed to such overreaching terms," Igraine scoffed, rapping her long pearly nails on the table's polished mahogany. "Standing as she did for blood above all else. And do you not remember our family's creed?"

When both their blue gazes turned sharply expectant, Gareth and I realized this was supposed to be a call-and-response moment that we were about to fumble.

"By wit or by might, we take what is ours," we both recited, in clumsy duet. I hated the motto, always had, and suspected that deep down at least, my older brother felt more or less the same. It made us sound like awful playground bullies by edict, stomping around wrenching candy out of other children's hands. Maybe Morty hadn't been far off at all, to feel so personally offended that we'd had our eye on his property.

Maybe *everyone* in this whole damn town wasn't that far off about us.

"And a silver lining worth noting," Lyonesse said, interlacing her hands and sliding them onto the table. "Unlike the manifestation at Castle Camelot, the Victor doesn't appear to have detected this fluctuation on our grounds. If she had, we'd have received her summons by now, and nothing's come from Harlow House. I suspect it was because the Cell's wards shielded most of the flare before they collapsed in such spectacular fashion. So she has no reason to know this even happened, or that we—or rather, you, Nineve—might be in the thick of it again."

I expelled an involuntary sigh, grateful that I at least hadn't mucked up an even worse mess for us.

"That being the case," she continued smoothly, "Igraine and I agree that you and Gareth should continue investigating this casting. Discover exactly what is happening, why it's focused on you."

"And of course," Igraine interjected, a crafty look sparking in her hooded eyes. "How it might be turned into something very much to our family's benefit. Once you know what manner of working this is, Nineve, you should be able to learn how to control it, to make it your own. And what could be better for us, more welcome, than an infusion of a sudden new strength like this? The appearance of an unparalleled Blackmoore sorceress, like an echo of Morgan le Fay herself?"

A bone-rattling chill blew down my spine like an icy wind breathed down my collar, because this—this, I hadn't even remotely foreseen. The possibility that my family could look at this affliction, this unwanted surplus of power, and see it as a blessing, an indication that we'd somehow been *chosen* for some dubious greatness. And yet how could I not have immediately jumped to that possibility, knowing them the way I did?

"Just consider, Nineve," Lyonesse said, fixing her pale blue gaze on mine. "That this goddess might have chosen you for a *reason*, to usher in a new era for our family—a new epoch for Thistle Grove itself. Not just a return to grace for us, but an elevation to unprecedented heights."

"And in the meantime," Igraine added, steel girding her voice, "until you have a better understanding of what transpires here . . . by no means should you let a single word of this slip to anyone else. Particularly not to the Victor herself."

For a single furious moment, I wanted to stand up, argue,

shriek "NO!" directly into my grandmother's insufferable, compla-cent face. No, I would not go traipsing off to become some kind of demented conquering sorceress, a new Blackmoore queen rising to wrest Thistle Grove away from Emmy Harlow, or whatever it was she and my mother were conspiring to do.

No, if I managed to break this spell, Gareth and I would never even let them know how it had been done.

And above all, no, I would not keep this from Emmy for a sec-ond longer.

No, no, *no*.

"Understood," I said instead, biting down on the inside of my cheek until I nearly tasted metal—because this was what Black-moores did, when our elders ordered it. We came to heel, and did as we were told. "Thank you for your counsel, Grandmother."

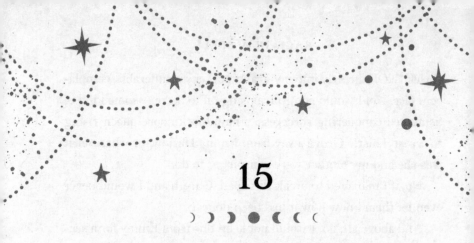

15

Sometimes You Have to Roll the Hard Six

GARETH AND I spent the rest of the week immersed in our mundane work; ours weren't the kinds of jobs you could just neglect for days on end while you embarked on a magical wild-goose chase or hero's journey, whichever one this even turned out to be. I had the usual stack of vendor and employee contracts and legal HR issues to review, while he had our ever-shifting portfolio to oversee.

And even if that hadn't been the case, both of us were still smarting from our encounter with our mother and grandmother. We needed time to lick our wounds separately, grapple with the usual muddle of conflicting emotions, before we went out and just did Lyonesse and Igraine's bidding, like we always did in the end.

When Saturday finally rolled around, I went to see Morty instead.

I'd barely restrained myself from reaching out to him all week; even muffled by the shielding, the witch bond tugged at me almost painfully, like a fine line of fishing wire attached just behind my solar plexus, drawing me inexorably toward him. The night before, I'd asked him to meet me at the Thistle Grove cemetery for his first magical lesson this morning. No matter what happened with the Goddess Spell, I had no idea if the gift of magic granted by the witch bond was a permanent one for him. He had to learn how to navigate it, at least for his own safety if nothing else. As long as I kept my wits—and my temper—about me while he practiced casting, I assumed that teaching him some basics should be safe enough for both of us.

Now, the sight of him standing among the gravestones and crypts in that sweeping sheepskin duster, snow falling so light and slow around him you could practically count the flakes as they drifted from the blue of the late morning sky, gave me a completely unexpected flush of joy.

"Hey," he said, turning at my approach, even though the snow-lined ground dampened the click of my bootheels.

He felt me, too, the same way I felt him; through the shielded bond, I could sense the barest hint of his own pleasure at seeing me even before he broke into a beautiful lopsided smile, those eyeliner-smudged jeweled eyes glittering above cold-flushed cheeks. I'd somehow forgotten just how pretty he was, the fine lines of his face and that sharp jaw, the softly made mouth bracketed by a shadow of dark stubble. And there was still no trace of awkwardness between us, even with everything that had happened the last time we'd been together.

"Hi, yourself," I said, stepping into his arms without even questioning whether I should, as though I'd been doing it for years already, my face tilted for a kiss.

It was light and warm, a bare grazing of those plush lips against mine, his cologne sharp and distinctive even against the chill and woodsmoke of the air. Soft as the kiss was, it still sent a purl of pure heat coiling down my throat and into my chest.

We lingered in it for a moment, relishing the closeness of the bond pulsing contentedly between us, until the kiss threatened to grow into something more than just hello. I stepped back first, clearing my throat and rubbing my gloved hands over my upper arms. "Sorry," I said, tucking my lips behind my teeth. "I didn't mean to be so abrupt. I was just, uh, starting to have non-cemetery-appropriate feelings."

He gave a soft breath of a chuckle, shaking his head, then twitching it in that achingly sexy, graceful way to clear fallen hair from his eyes. "Believe me, I get it. And it's not even open between us, not like it was the other night. Yet still distracting as all hell. How do witch-married people ever get shit *done*, walking around all fired up like this?"

"I have to assume you get used to it," I said with a shrug. My own parents were witchbound, and they certainly seemed to have no trouble *not* being completely consumed with each other; maybe it wasn't the same for everyone. Or maybe with time, you learned to manage it better. "That level of intensity must fade eventually."

His gaze snared mine, so keenly blue it was nearly painful to hold. "I'll believe that when I feel it fading."

"Well, ideally, you won't have to wait that long," I said, turning away from him with an effort and starting down one of the meandering little paths that wound through the cemetery, between snow-topped statues of angels and gleaming black obelisks.

The Thistle Grove cemetery was a strange and beautiful space, as much a daily haven for the living as a resting place for the town's dead. It sprawled languidly across almost a hundred acres, enclosed by a fleur-de-lis-tipped wrought-iron fence, lovingly landscaped and tended to in the rural cemetery style even though many of its tombs were aboveground crypts. The kind of neoclassical, Gothic, Romanesque, and Egyptian Revival mausoleums you rarely saw outside of places like New Orleans. All of the Thistle Grove founders except for Alastair Thorn were interred in their crypts here; only the Thorn founder had insisted on being buried at Honeycake Orchards, in the family's private cemetery.

In the summer, a luxuriant profusion of the now-bare trees and shrubbery overhung the graves, lending shade to the scattered congregations of statues and sculptures. Besides your more standard angels, there was a massive marble stag with huge, branching antlers that supported a series of globes like planets; an armillary sphere, worked in a shining metal that seemed like it might be actual platinum; and in one of the tucked-away corners at the end of a path, a sculpture of a crowned lamia sat on a towering throne, wrists crossed in front of her chest, a scepter in one hand and a skull in the other.

Town legend had it that some of the statues came and went at whim, old ones disappearing overnight to be replaced by new ones that had never been seen before. I couldn't have said one way or the other; when I came to visit, my own favorites were always exactly where I'd left them.

"That's what Gareth and I are trying to do," I went on, as

Morty fell into step beside me. We were still moving in that lock-step we'd fallen into at the Shamrock Cauldron, an organic tandem that somehow looked and felt completely natural. I kept having to resist the urge to hold his hand; the desire to initiate contact with him felt almost like a compulsion. "Figure out how to break this spell, or whatever it is. I assume when it goes, the witch bond will, too."

Even through the locked-down bond, I could feel little runnels of mutual dissatisfaction sluicing back and forth between us at the idea. Bizarre as this whole thing was—unwanted and foisted upon us as the bond had been—it seemed neither of us was completely sure we even wanted it gone.

"Right," Morty said a little hoarsely, clearly suppressing the same preemptive pang of loss. "And how has that been going?"

"Poorly," I said, so dryly that he chuckled again. "Catastrophically, actually. We, uh, kind of burned down part of the estate, trying to get rid of that damn coin. Suffice it to say that our mother was not best pleased with the fallout."

The flare of pain that lit inside me at the thought of her—a comet blaze of ache streaking across my chest—was so strong that it made Morty stumble, then draw up short on the path.

"Nina," he breathed, reaching out to take my hand like I'd wanted to do only moments before. "Hold up, just wait a minute here. You're *hurting.*"

"So what if I am?" I said roughly, though tears were already prickling in my nose. "Nina's hurting, must be Tuesday! It doesn't *matter* what I feel. We're here for your lesson. Not for me."

"Of course it matters," he insisted, gently but indomitably, as if the importance of my feelings were a fact as incontrovertible as the direction of the rising sun. He reached for my other hand, then pulled me in until I faced him, our joined hands clasped between our chests. "Let me feel it, Nina. Let me help."

I ducked my head, my lips trembling. "You don't want to feel this," I said, in a quavery near-whisper. "I promise you don't."

He tilted his forehead against mine, his breath steaming like a small, contained fog between our faces. "Yeah, I do. And believe me, I can handle it. Whatever's going on with you, I assure you I've walked through the Valley of the Shadow of Steaming Piles of Shit this past year, too. So I'm about as prepped as you can get."

That startled a fractured little laugh out of me. Feeble and unsteady, but genuine just the same.

"Okay, then," I said softly, closing my eyes, tears pressing against my lashes. "If you're sure. I'm going to drop the shield now, so, be ready."

Biting my lip, I lowered the defensive barrier I'd erected between us—and let everything pour out in a miserable cascade.

A torrent that didn't just break down the dam I'd constructed between myself and the world, but wrecked it to ruin, thoroughly demolished it. First came a rush of the pure, raw pain of how my mother treated me—and not just me, but Gareth and Gawain, too, and all the ways I'd failed to protect them from being trampled by her and Igraine over the years, even though I'd always been the strongest—followed by the duller but no less powerful ache of the way loving Sydney had undone me. The way she'd cast me off and abandoned me the moment I no longer suited her.

The way I'd started to feel like joy, or even simple contentment, had never been meant for someone rigid and bitter and broken like me.

"My god, Nina," Morty whispered, his voice breaking, staggering in place. When I opened my eyes, the dazzling blue of his was glossed with tears, unabashed sympathy etched onto every line of his face. "Oh, lady, come here."

I all but flung myself into his embrace, arms locking around his neck as his wound tight around my waist, folding me perfectly against him. Then I turned my face into his woolen collar and cried without reservation, the way I rarely let myself. Not my usual pathetic dribble of tears, but open and ugly and hard, in wrenching, heaving sobs that felt like they might crack my ribs open and let spill some crucial marrow. I could feel Morty's chest hitch against mine as he wept quietly for my own feelings, sieved my pain readily through himself.

And somehow that feedback loop between us, me feeling my own pain mirrored and felt and affirmed by someone else, *helped* instead of making it worse.

We stood there for so long and so unmoving that a flock of hopeful birds landed around us; the ones that didn't head south for winter, and were clearly accustomed to bread crumb feasts courtesy of cemetery regulars. Amid the ruffle of their wings and the soft chorus of their cooing, I clung to Morty until the flood of agony abated, withdrawing like a slow tide.

Leaving behind something closer to peace than I'd felt in a very long time. Longer than I could remember.

"All that," Morty marveled against me, making no move to let me go, the wealth of his free-flowing empathy surging inside me like a balm. A tincture for the soul, like something the Thorns might know how to brew. "So much pain, and you just keep it locked up inside like a fucking soldier, marching on. And shit, *I* thought *I'd* had it tough."

"You know what they say," I managed thickly, through the residual tears. "Sometimes you have to roll the hard six."

This time his amusement bubbled up inside me, too, fizzing like a swallow of Moët. "Oh, of course you'd randomly be a *Battlestar* nerd, too. How could you not be?"

"Blame Kara Thrace slash Katee Sackhoff," I admitted with a little shrug. "My first and most beloved TV wife."

"Fair enough." I could feel him smile. "I was more Team Lee Adama myself, but yeah, I could definitely see that Starbuck appeal."

"Apollo was too much of a bro for me," I murmured against his neck, feeling both slightly ridiculous and ridiculously happy that we'd somehow meandered into this conversation. "Like that super-stiff lantern jaw all the time, no thanks. Can we compromise on Athena, though? Because if memory serves, she was so completely fine."

"Oh, *entirely*." Another soft laugh into my hair, before he reached up to run a hand over it, then cup my cheek. Unlike me, he wasn't wearing gloves, but his palm was still warm and the slightest bit scratchy against my skin; calluses, probably, from the silks. "Do you want to sit down with me for a minute, talk a little? Or will you be too cold?"

It suddenly occurred to me that I hadn't *really* been cold—not the way I normally got in winter, the relentless, bone-deep chill I could never shake—since my underwater foray. I wondered what that might mean, if it had any bearing on or connection to the spell. The bizarre hunger had continued, too. I was putting away more than twice my normal amount of food per day without gaining weight, and I still felt peckish most of the time, like there could never really be enough snacks to tide me over to the next meal.

"That sounds nice," I said, pulling back a little and tilting my head toward one of the nearby benches that sat along the paths. "And I'll be fine. Unexpected upside of whatever's happening to me, apparently winter doesn't get under my skin anymore."

When we reached the bench, I set a hand on one of the slats, sending the gentlest possible pulse of elemental heat through it. Even with as much restraint as I could manage, the wood momentarily glowed red, its sparkling crust of snow not just melting into a dribble but sizzling like water splattered onto coals before it steamed off into the air. It was so smoldering hot we had to wait a few moments for the wood and iron to cool to a reasonable temperature, and even then residual heat seeped through all our layers when we sat down.

"Dang, this is actually quite pleasant," Morty remarked. "A luxury seat-warmer bench experience. Like a spa for your ass."

I gave a little mock bow, complete with a courtier's flourish of the hand. "Uncontainable surplus of magic, at your service. Though I am planning on teaching you a few of the more normal spells like this today."

"Before we do that . . ." He reached out and took one of my hands, folded it between both of his own, and rested it on his lap, like he couldn't bear not touching me any more than I could. "Want to share what some of all that was? What you've been grappling with? I mean, that first soul-crushing rush alone . . ." He whistled under his breath, eyes darkening. "That is not an acceptable way to walk through life."

"Welcome to being a Blackmoore," I said, with a bitter half shrug. "That was you feeling how my mother has made me feel, pretty much since I can remember. And my brothers, too. Like we're never quite meeting her exacting standards. Like even at our best, we're some level of defective or mediocre, or vaguely disappointing for reasons indeterminate. Sometimes, we get frozen out; other times, things get very loud. You can never really tell what you're going to get, when it comes to Lyonesse. Worst ever box of chocolates."

"That's fucking terrible," he said, jaw setting. "Why even have children, if you're going to emotionally abuse them like that?"

I swallowed hard at that word, though I knew that this was what my brothers and I had endured, even while we'd been showered like royalty with every possible creature comfort, shown every material indulgence. Sassy Sue had never minced words when it came to naming it, either. But I still had a hard time hearing any mention of abuse spoken aloud, a part of my brain instinctively rejecting it as a silly overreaction.

The same part of my brain that had been drilled since childhood that this was simply how things were, and who was I to rail against it?

"Part of it is generational, I think. She was raised that way, too; our grandmother is actually worse. Stricter, less tolerant, even more demanding. And the worst part is . . ." I heaved a shuddering sigh, leaning back against the bench. "Sometimes, when you least expect it, my mother can be *wonderful.* Hilarious, warm, supportive. Willing to stay up all night drinking wine and listening to your ruminations on life, or sharing behind-the-scenes gossip about the Blackmoore dynasty, the wild magic she saw growing up. My brothers and I . . . we all have these amazing memories of her, of shining moments like that. But you never know how long you'll get. When that inevitable gate is going to come slamming back down, and you're stranded back outside in the cold."

"You're right," Morty said, an even harsher undertone to his voice, his hands tightening on mine. "That *is* worse. That's how they make rats lose their minds in conditioning experiments, did you know that? Give them unpredictable positive reinforcement, so they never know what's coming. Deconstruct their egos. Break down their little souls."

"That's what my therapist says, too." I took another breath, struggling to explain the next bit. "She . . . she thinks Lyonesse might be a narcissist. A clinical one, I mean."

"Sounds like it. And sorry if this comes off harsh, but I'm not one to accept any diagnosis as a blanket excuse for damaging other people. Whatever her own shit, that doesn't entitle her to dump toxic waste on you and your siblings your whole life." He tilted his head, peering at me with narrowed eyes, though nothing about this close scrutiny felt unkind. "And you and your brothers, none of you ever thought to just cut ties? Leave all that trash behind?"

"Where would we go?" I said, with a helpless shrug. "Who would we be? Even if we were okay with being cut off from the family fortune—which, believe me, all of us have seriously considered at one point or another—that's only half the point. If we move away from here permanently, we lose our magic; that's how it works in Thistle Grove. And none of us would ever do that willingly."

"Fuck me," Morty muttered. "So that's the dilemma. It's bend the knee, or lose pretty much everything."

"That about sums it up," I agreed, despondent. "So then I . . . I think when I was picking partners, I chose one who seemed completely different on the surface. Charming, spontaneous, open. All the things Lyonesse isn't. All the things *I'm* not."

"You think you aren't charming?" Morty said, genuinely baffled. "Admittedly, I haven't known you very long at all, but,

Nina—I already know you're *adorable*. Weird as hell, in the most endearing and surprising way. You must know that."

"Oh, sure, I'm plenty awesome," I replied wryly, "if you love rules and structure and a quasi-pathological need for stability. Along with an endless stream of nerdy references. To be fair, Sydney—that's my ex-fiancée—she and I did have other things in common. She liked having and enjoying beautiful things, like I do; we shared a certain aesthetic. And she wanted to be part of a family like mine. You know, the prestige by association."

"A gold-digging star fucker!" Morty exclaimed, in such a sing-song, upbeat tone that I burst out laughing. "Oh, *yeah*. She sounds straight-up spectacular. Fucking catch of the year right there."

"My best friend, Jessa, would really be enjoying this conversation," I noted. "She was, likewise, not a fan. Especially when Sydney changed her mind about marrying me, fairly last minute. Very apropos of her spontaneous approach to much of life—including, apparently, major commitments. She decided basically overnight that I was too suffocating to live with. And she . . ."

I ducked my head and nibbled at my lips, my insides quaking. I hadn't told anyone the full extent of what Sydney had said about me; most of the time, I didn't even let myself remember it. And I had been far from mentally prepared to admit it today—much less to Morty, of all people.

"You don't have to say it," he said gently, skimming his thumb over my knuckles. "Not if you don't want to."

"I do," I said, more fiercely than I expected, my gaze flicking up to his. Beneath all that sadness, there was a rage I'd never fully faced, a livid fury I'd been too afraid to give space to grow—and now it reared up inside me, fully ablaze. Because I wasn't just feeling devastated and empty and unmoored. I was fucking *pissed*, and had been for a long time now, deep down in that dark oubliette where I stored my most ungovernable feelings. "She said that I was like some kind of robotic protocol. A human algorithm. Joyless and predictable and . . . *boring*."

I felt a flare of answering anger in Morty, entwining protectively around mine like a shower of sparks.

"Idiot," he said simply, as if he couldn't be bothered to spare more creative invective for Sydney. "You couldn't be boring if you tried. Having rules and boundaries doesn't make you dull, Nina. From the sound of it, it's what's helped you survive the kind of family you have. And even if it hadn't, there's nothing wrong with governing yourself. Setting rules for what you will and won't accept."

"You sure thought there was when we first met," I pointed out, flicking up an eyebrow. "Case in point, I've never felt so judged for having strong opinions about not running outside in winter."

"Well, I was pretty intentionally being a dick that time," he admitted, holding my gaze easily, eyes clear as water. "Even before the whole Blackmoore thing came out, I misjudged you, thought you were only what you looked like. A basic chick looking for a little fling, a run on the wild side with someone like me before you settled down with somebody . . . *respectable*. Normally, I might not have reacted quite that rudely, but I'd been having a rough time myself. And the idea of being someone for you to play with . . . let's say it brought out the not-inconsiderable jackass in me."

"A basic chick," I repeated, grimacing a little. "Okay, ouch, I felt that one."

"A *beautiful* basic chick," he amended, with a tiny smirk. "Absolutely hot as shit. Any better?"

"Not completely, but I'll own it. Self-delusion *not* being one of my things." I glanced down wryly at the high gloss of my Moncler parka, my maroon Fairfax & Favor boots. "Not like I can claim to be any kind of alternative."

"What about the rest of it?" he challenged. "You're gonna tell me you *weren't* looking for a joyride with me?"

I opened my mouth to deny it before remembering that, in fact, this had been Jessa's precise plan.

"I was," I admitted, a little guiltily. "It's complicated. It had been a year since my breakup, and my best friend was just trying to help get me unstuck. Dating after Sydney was some fresh hell, and you seemed, maybe, like someone who wouldn't psych me out too much—because we were so different, and it seemed so clear we wouldn't be a match. But I . . . I'm sorry. You're a person, not some edgy toy, obviously. I never intended for you to feel that way."

He tugged me close, for a quick, soft kiss on the cheek. I loved being kissed on the cheek, the casual, easy affection of it; it wasn't something Sydney had ever done with me, or a habit my family subscribed to. Of course.

"Nah, it's okay. You weren't doing it on purpose—that reaction was on me. How were you supposed to know that was a sore spot?" He paused for a moment, eyes distant, as if mulling what he wanted to tell me.

Then he gave a little nod to himself, meeting my gaze head-on again.

"The thing is, I've played around plenty, right?" he said. "Been poly with a million partners, been open with one, run the whole gamut of relationship anarchy. And don't get me wrong, I'm probably never going to be down for anything totally conventional.

But turns out, I *do* want one steady partner who also wants me. Someone who's always there; someone who knows all of me. Who's rock-solid, not going anywhere. I *need* that kind of stability. Maybe I always did, but especially now."

"Why?" I said, shifting closer to him on the bench until we sat thigh pressed against thigh, sensing that he wanted me even nearer. "What's changed?"

"My dad has MS," he said, a muscle flickering in his fine jaw. "We found out definitively about six months ago, though he'd been sick for a good while before; we just didn't know what it was. That was why he retired early in the first place, passed on the Shamrock to me for the day-to-day. He got the formal diagnosis right around the same time your family started gunning for the bar. And it just felt like, damn, being at war all the time. A different battle to fight every day."

"Oh, no," I breathed, guilt lashing painfully at my insides, even as I felt the electric twinging of Morty's own fresh pain. "I'm . . . Morty, I am so, *so* sorry!"

"You couldn't have known." He flicked up a shoulder, glanced up at the sky. "And like you said, you were just doing your job."

"Well, yes, and High Queen Lyonesse's cruel bidding," I said with a sour twist, though I knew full well that was only part of the truth. Damaged as we all were, the entire family took pride in our holdings and the idea of expanding them; they were the one thing binding us together. It was very possible I'd been more forceful and dogged than another attorney might have been, because I'd bought so heavily into the idea, too. "And to be honest, it's never just business with Blackmoores. You're right about us; everyone is. My family does feel a certain entitlement toward this town, after so many centuries of all but running it."

"I *have* met your brother," Morty reminded me, but gently. "Though now that I know what's up behind the scenes, I may have to permanently retire 'fuckweasel.'"

"Many thanks," I said dryly. "But I really am sorry, for bringing even more of a burden to your family."

"On the upside, my pops is doing much better these days," he said, slinging an arm around my shoulders and tugging me closer. "The meds have helped in slowing the progression, and he's in physical therapy, too. I always go with him, for moral support. That's where I was supposed to be, actually, when my hands turned radioactive the morning after our date."

"Also courtesy of me," I muttered. "Along with immaculate timing, I really do give the best gifts."

"You do, though. I'm really not *that* averse to developing sudden superpowers," he said with a wink, clearly unwilling to dwell on heavier subjects. "Didn't even have to get bit by a mutagenic spider or anything! Nor am I against very memorable non-cemetery-appropriate activities. So maybe we can call it even for the moment."

"Speaking of the superpowers," I said, getting up and extending a hand to him. "Want to go break yours in a little?"

16

Ice Swans and Silver Mulberry Bushes

I'D BROUGHT MORTY to the cemetery because, in typically (and macabrely) charming Thistle Grove fashion, this was where the town held its annual ice sculpture contest.

Over by the frozen pond that glittered beneath the circle of weeping willows near the center of the graveyard, Morty and I wandered through open space filled with row upon row of sparkling creations. Swans and peacocks, horse-drawn carriages and rings of fairies, lounging mermaids and whales spouting water, frozen archways so elaborate and fantastical they looked like they might lead to realms unknown. There was even an old-timey locomotive exhaling icy smoke, big enough for little kids to sit in. And subzero as it was, there was no one around admiring the sculptures today; perfect for my purposes.

BACK IN A SPELL

Why the town chose to hold the contest here rather than in the Thistle Grove square, on the common, or even up by Lady's Lake was unclear—but there was no question the sculptures looked particularly stunning here, set against the ice-crackled pond and the bare black flourishes of the overhanging trees, the snow-shimmered crypts rising in the distance.

"We're going to start with animation," I said, leading Morty over to the swan sculpture. I'd chosen to kick things off with one of the first spells Blackmoores learned; visually impressive, but deceptively simple to execute compared to some of our other elemental castings. "Turning inanimate matter into something that mimics life, without actually being sentient."

"Holy shit, no way!" Morty said, breaking into a boyishly delighted grin, practically bouncing from boot to boot with excitement. "We talking, like, *Fantasia*? Dancing brooms and all that jazz?"

"Actually, yes," I said, grinning back, feeling the pure rush of his delight surge through the bond as if it were my own. "But honestly, even better. I'm not going to demonstrate for you, because goddess only knows what would happen if I tried. Probably I'd raise an army of ice statues to march on Thistle Grove, or something even worse. And I'm trying my best to keep today's forecast clear of any cataclysmic occurrences."

His brow wrinkled. "Then how will I learn it?"

"Start by thinking about how you summoned witchlight the other day," I directed. "Both in the morning on your own, and later at the Avalon. You began with a wish, right? A clear desire, a willful thought. It was probably a very strong one, too; any witch can manifest a witchlight even without using the most common spell for it, but it's generally much harder to do without the incantation. So, gold star to you, you're already ahead of the class."

He yanked down a victory fist for himself, giving a mock-smug nod. "I may not look the part, but you're checking out a Thistle Grove High salutatorian over here. Would've been valedictorian, too, if it hadn't been for Emmy's overachieving ass salting my GPA."

"Good thing you weren't my year," I said, flicking a strand of hair coyly over my shoulder. "Or I'd be the one catching that shade right now."

He flashed me a defiant blue look, a corner of that delicate mouth curling with amusement. "Isn't *someone* cocky. You never know, milady, I was quite the scholar in my youth. I might've given you a run for your money, too."

"Doubtful," I said, suppressing a grin as I turned back toward the swan.

It peered at us with transparent eyes, its graceful neck a curving swoop like a bass clef, wings tucked against its sides. It was gorgeous work, delicately rendered to the finest detail, each distinct feather already an almost-living marvel. "Today, you're going to be using the Animating Charm. And while you speak the words, I want you to hold an image in your mind—this swan coming to life, as detailed as you can imagine it. Head turning, wings lifting, feathers ruffling. Whatever you'd like to see it do."

"Piece of cake," he said cheerfully, tucking his hands into his duster pockets. "Let's hear those words."

"Really?" I said, skeptical. "Imagining an entire ice swan moving sounds *that* easy to you?"

"I'll have you know that my meditation practice is on point," he informed me. "Courtesy of aforementioned emotional hellscape, mostly. So, silver linings, I can now visualize the shit out of just about anything."

"Ah, that would explain the facility, then," I said, nodding to myself. "A lot of our foundational magical training comes down to the same basic groundwork as meditation. So you'll want to hold that image in your mind as firmly as you can, while you speak the words."

I leaned close and whispered the couplets into his ear—feeling, through the bond, the frisson of tingle that spiraled down his arm at the warmth of my exhale—just in case actually saying the words aloud myself got us into some kind of trouble.

"You can say them as many times as you need to," I instructed, moving back. "You'll feel it when it starts to happen and the magic rushes in; it's unmistakable. You should already know what it feels like, from summoning the witchlights. And before it happens, there'll be something like a . . . a mental *click*. A knowing, a certainty that you've gotten it right."

He nodded once, then turned to the swan.

"Got it," he said, closing his eyes. There was something infinitely endearing, almost tender, about his earnestness. How seriously he was taking this lesson, like the most avid student. I wouldn't have expected teaching him to feel so . . . pure.

To be fair, I'd never taught *anyone* spellwork; it was a specialization within the magical community, with a certain number of members of each family training to be teachers for the next generation—a profession funded by contributions from the witch community at large, as set out in the Grimoire. So maybe it was always satisfying to impart this kind of knowledge, even if I didn't really know whether I was doing it right.

Somehow, I doubted teaching baby witches felt like this, quite so warmly compelling.

"Should I, uh, be doing something with my hands?" he asked, sneaking a glance at me from the corner of one eye. "Or, hell, is that a stupid question?"

"It's not, at all," I assured him. "Some spells are much easier if you guide them along with motions; others actually demand physical shaping, like playing an instrument. But for this one, it isn't necessary, unless you feel it helps you hold fast to the visualization in your mind."

"Maybe I'll mess around a little, then." He slid his hands out of his pockets and held them loosely lifted in front of him, black-polished fingertips twitching, clearly a little self-conscious.

Then I could see the concentration slide like a mask over his face, jostling away the uncertainty as he began to chant the words over and over, like I'd told him.

The spell took a while to manifest. At least a few minutes, much longer than it would have taken me—but also much faster than it generally took a young witch. When the working fell into place, I could feel it happen through the bond, almost as if I were the one casting. The heady, shimmering rush of magic welling just beneath the skin in sparkling streams, like sweetness singing through your veins; that infinitely gratifying feeling of the casting's shape falling into place, impressing itself upon the parchment of the world like a wax seal.

The swan began to stir, ever so slowly, twitching its icy head from side to side in awkward, brittle movements.

"Whoaaaa," Morty exhaled, breathing out a little laugh of pure delight. "Fuck me, there it is. It's actually *working*."

"It is," I assured him, reaching out to squeeze his arm. "But don't lose focus. Keep at it."

The swan's tentative movements gained elegance as Morty found more purchase, a deeper confidence in his own casting. Then, the bird stretched that sinuous neck toward us, lifting its wings in a gentle flutter. Extending its head as far as it could reach, to peck the icy, avian equivalent of a kiss onto my cheek.

"Morty!" I gasped, sputtering laughter as the ice swan continued to sway its neck from side to side, pressing more kisses onto my face with its sharp little bill like some overfamiliar European relative. It even reached its glittering wings out toward me, as if for a hug. "Are you serious right now?"

"Whaaaaaat?" he drawled, widening his eyes at me. "I nailed the charm, did I not? And please, you like it, you know you do. *I* know you do."

"Maybe just a little," I admitted, through helpless giggles. The swan would not quit getting in my face no matter how I dodged its parries, and there was something both completely darling and desperately comical about its efforts to plant another smooch on me. "Now let's see if I can teach you the Disanimating Charm, before you make this bird try to elope with me."

ONCE MORTY HAD both the Animating Charm and its opposite down pat, I walked him through the rank and file of sculptures, having him animate and then release larger, more difficult shapes, ones that took even more focus and imagination. I also ran him through our complement of basic elemental conjuring and transmutation spells as well: heating and cooling, summoning up gusts of wind, turning one substance into another.

For whatever reason, transmutation delighted him the most,

and he took to it the most readily. We spent over an hour with a mulberry bush, turning its branches to silver and back again, until beads of sweat stood out on Morty's brow despite the cold.

"You need a break, Padawan," I said, gently guiding him away from the shrub. "It's not safe to push yourself this hard when you've just started learning."

"Are you kidding?" he demanded, sheer joy blazing on his face; he really was a natural at it, stronger than many of the Blackmoore witches I knew who'd been born to the blood. "I could do this all day. Shit, I could do this *forever*, fuck everything else. This is goddamn amazing, Nina! I just . . . I had no idea it would feel this way, to have that kind of power. To feel the magic rushing inside you like that."

"Believe me, I know," I said quietly, feeling a little twist of chill that had nothing to do with the weather. "There's nothing more intoxicating. Why do you think my family are the way they are, at least in part? Because we've been like *this*, this kind of strong, for centuries. It's hard not to let it get to you, to keep things in perspective, when you feel a little like you could rule the world. Like the world should submit and *let* you rule it."

"I could see that," he said, face going solemn. "I really could. And to know I'm nowhere even close to the things you can do . . ."

"You could be, though," I said. "I was just thinking about that. Your latent ability is impressive. You're stronger than a lot of natural-born Blackmoore witches I know, the ones I grew up learning with. I don't see any reason why you couldn't learn to do everything I can."

"So let's keep going!" he demanded, bouncing from foot to foot again. "I'm not that tired, for real."

I skimmed an appraising eye over him, noting the slight pallor against the flush of his cheeks, the overbright glaze in his eyes, then shook my head.

"Enough for today. I mean it, Morty. You can really hurt yourself like that, overexerting your talent. I'm not completely sure about this, but I think that especially holds true for someone who's only just stepped into their magic."

Morty blew an exaggerated sigh through his lips, mock sulking. "Fair enough, I *suppose*. Wouldn't want to get hurt on your watch, Obi-Wan. So what else do you have on today? Wanna come hang with me at the Shamrock for a while? It'll be pretty packed in there, but I can offer gin martinis on the house, along with whatever assorted bar snacks might tempt milady."

"I can't," I said, with real regret. Another few hours in Morty's company sounded delightfully enticing, and I couldn't lie—the sorts of bar snacks he was likely to whip up for me were of almost equal appeal, as was the fact that his apartment *was* right upstairs, should we be inclined to visit it. "I'd love to, but I'm drowning in work. I'll be playing catch-up for the rest of this afternoon, at least. Likely well into the evening, if I'm being realistic."

"What about tomorrow? It's Sunday lunch over at Casa Gutierrez. A potluck, basically; my sister and I come hang with our parents every week, and my sister—Meg—brings my niece, Marisol, too, when she's not with her dad." He glanced up at me through his lashes, almost bashful. "Maybe you'd want to come? Delicious food, excellent sangria, generally civil and typically uproarious conversation. It's a good time, promise."

"I'm sure it would be, but a family lunch?" I asked, balking. "With *your* family? I realize you probably don't need reminders on this front, but you do recall I'm still a Blackmoore, right? Do you really think they'd want me there, under their roof, given . . . well, everything?"

Morty cupped my face with gloved hands, leaning in just enough to brush his nose lightly over mine. "You're not some rando Blackmoore. You're *Nina*."

"But that's kind of the point, isn't it?" I insisted, though even as I argued against it, I realized how much I did want this, to steal a glimpse into this piece of his life that sounded nothing like mine. "You won't be able to tell them about you and me. What I really am. Won't that bother you? Won't you hate it, keeping them in the dark like that?"

"Oh, it'll bother me, no question," he admitted with a shrug. "But it'll also be worth it, for you to get to know them."

"And you don't . . . you don't feel like it's too soon for that?"

He made a face like, *What even* is *time*, which, given our circumstances, felt fair enough as an assessment. "I don't think any particular timeline applies to this, do you? To us? And it's no pressure, really. But if you *do* want to come, I'd be stoked to have you there."

"Well, okay, then," I said softly, a warm, happy flush stealing into my cheeks. That he would invite me to something like that, despite the harm my family had done to his; that he'd draw such a clear dividing line between who I was and who I'd come from. "I'll think about it. But, let's go with a tentative yes."

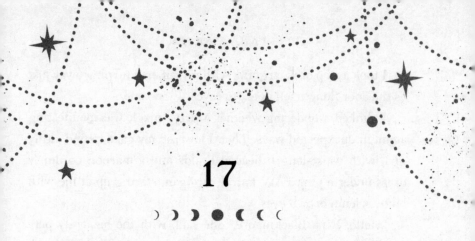

17

Offerings of Flowers and Cake

STANDING ON THE Gutierrezes' welcome mat the next day, with a gigantic orchid arrangement under one arm and a string-tied bakery box of Camelot's fanciest caramel apple cake under the other, I wondered what in the unknowable cosmos had possessed me to agree to come.

Maybe the Goddess Spell included a mind-addling element that had only just begun to express itself, or possibly—and more likely—I hadn't given Morty's considerable charisma and powers of persuasion the full credit they deserved. Because what else could explain my having shown up here of my own free will, to what was functionally enemy territory, about to present offerings of flowers and cake to people who believed my family had been actively trying to encroach on their livelihood? Even if Morty *did* want me here, how could it be respectful or appropriate to impose on his parents that way?

I took a step back, arguing with myself, half turning away just as the door flung itself open, to reveal . . . no one.

I blinked, wondering whether Morty's magic was manifesting again in unexpected ways. Then I lowered my gaze to find a tiny girl, with waist-length beaded braids and a maroon corduroy dress under a pink PAW Patrol cardigan, staring up at me with huge, solemn brown eyes.

"Hello, Nina Blackmoore," she said, with the bizarrely perfect diction of a tiny herald instead of an ostensible five-year-old. "My uncle Morty said you'd be coming today. I saw you from the window, but you looked like you were leaving."

"Ahhh . . ." I flailed under that unflinching brown gaze, desperately trying to exude the impression that *of course* I'd been planning to do no such ignominious thing as flee before I even knocked. "Nope, no, here to stay! I brought some presents, too . . . I hope you like caramel apple cake!"

A pearly, baby-toothed smile transformed that serious little face, a deep thumbprint dimple denting one round, light brown cheek.

"I *love* cake," she informed me in a conspiratorial whisper, shooting a furtive look over her shoulder like a secret agent. "I'm going to eat a whole bunch of it. Don't tell my mommy, okay? She's only that demented about not letting me have sugar."

The faint brogue that stole into her piping voice made me think she'd heard that expression from someone else—possibly an Irish grandmother less averse to doling out sugary treats, if I had to guess.

"Got it," I whispered back, giving her a grave nod. "It'll stay between us."

Morty appeared behind his little niece, setting a hand on her shoulder. He wore unripped jeans, and a green cable-knit sweater much more conventional than anything I'd seen him in before—along with zero makeup, his fingernails were stripped clean of the chipped dark polish I was so used to seeing on him. Even his hair seemed somehow less unruly. I remembered him mentioning how he made concessions around his mother when it came to gender expression, and ironically, the fact that he also had to accommodate one of his parents gave me a little confidence boost.

If there was one thing I understood, it was having to walk on eggshells, tiptoe around another person's needs. Maybe things weren't *that* different in this household.

"Let's let Nina in, Sol, okay?" he said, winking at me as he squeezed her little shoulder. "And keep all the heat in while we're at it."

"Okay!" She whipped around, braids clicking against each other as she skipped back into the house. "Mommyyyy, Nina Blackmoore said I could have a whole cake! And she's our guest so you have to let me, that's the rules!"

Her mother's response drifted in from the next room, not quite audible but in a distinctly unamused in tone.

Morty and I winced at each other as I stepped in, both of us biting back laughter. My first impression of his parents' home was a balmy heat almost completely alien to me when it came to interiors; I kept my loft at a reasonable seventy-two degrees or so, but I'd grown up in the drafty, chilly palace of Tintagel, which never rose above the low sixties, like we all might melt into some unacceptable softness if we weren't always kept on ice. The Gutierrezes, on the other hand, clearly believed in having their thermostat set to summer. The warmth only enhanced the savory aromas drifting into the foyer, of simmered tomatoes and garlic and the rich, yeasty smell of home-baked sourdough.

"For the record," I told Morty, handing my packages over to him so I could squirm out of my parka and hook it on an already heavily laden coat tree, "that is *not* what I said."

"Oh, I'm sure. Marisol doesn't exactly believe in nuance." He pulled a grimace, widening his eyes. "Neither does Meghan—only in the other direction, kind of. So at least Sol comes by it honestly."

"Wonderful," I muttered, reaching out to take back the flowers and the cake box—if I was already in the doghouse, I might as well make a more formal gesture out of my offerings. "Already getting off on a fantastic foot with your family."

"Oh, it's gonna be great," he assured me, leaning in for a light hello kiss. I could feel that warm, blithe confidence lapping at me reassuringly through the bond; he definitely *believed* his own optimism, at any rate, enough to ease my misgivings just a touch. "You'll see."

I trudged after him through a comfortable family room, featuring a huge flat-screen TV displaying an atmospheric crackling fireplace—presumably since lighting a real fire at the current ambient temperature would have melted everyone's skin off—well-loved brown leather furniture, pastoral landscapes, and an array of thriving houseplants clustered beneath the windows and suspended from the ceiling. Someone in the family had a green thumb, and gravitated toward the kind of sturdy, leafy plants that had very little in common with the dainty and demanding flowers I'd brought.

Down the narrow hallway, I spotted a home office off to one side, likely where Morty's mother kept the books for the bar, a tiny guest-bedroom-cum-library to the other. Sometimes I managed to forget that other people—the vast majority of people, in fact—lived in normal houses like this, with narrow corridors, zero picture windows, and ceilings that didn't soar theatrically above your head, to the extent that the lack of space seemed a little shocking to me, almost claustrophobic.

This particular knee-jerk reaction was not one of my favorite things about myself.

"Used to be my bedroom," Morty remarked as we passed the guest bedroom, waggling his eyebrows at me. "Teenage kid's dream, pretty much. First floor, easy access to both the front and back doors, window that opened into the yard. Perfect for sneaking out to engage in questionable activities . . . should one be so inclined."

"Something Teen You never even contemplated, I'm sure."

"Of course not, do you even know me?" he retorted, fluttering a hand to his chest in mock outrage. "I was an *exemplary* youth in every respect."

"Right. Super circumspect."

As we walked, I also noted that every door we passed was flung open, as if even the concepts of privacy, secrets, and solitude were foreign to this house.

Morty led me to the open-plan kitchen and dining room, where everyone was already gathered, with the kind of comfortably familiar energy that indicated that this was the true heart of the house, the room where the most time was spent. The massive, clearly heirloom dining table was loaded with food: a shepherd's pie topped with creamy mounds of potato, a steaming Instant Pot of chili responsible for the pervasive savory aroma, a glass bowl of what looked like Greek salad, a tray of empanadas with sauces on the side, and a gorgeously crusty loaf of sourdough presiding over the center of the table, slices already missing. There was no rhyme, reason, or general theme to the dishes, besides the fact that they all looked mouthwatering.

A ponytailed brunette with a striking, strong-jawed face, her flannel shirt unbuttoned over a white tank and low-slung jeans, was lifting Marisol onto a booster chair—so this was Meghan, Morty's older sister. At the head of the table sat a burly man with graying dark hair, with the same heavily dramatic bone structure as his daughter but with Morty's magnetic azure eyes under bushy, white-flecked brows; Morty's dad, Armando. A cane rested against the table next to him, within easy reach.

On his other side sat Morty's mother, Fiona; bird-boned and slim, her light brown hair pulled back into a low bun, her delicate features reminiscent of Morty's in a resemblance so pronounced it was almost jarring.

I could see what Morty had meant, back at the Shamrock, when he told me there was no way his parents weren't his parents. He looked like the clearest possible amalgam of the two of them, with the balance tipping toward his mother. The way that I was unmistakably my father's daughter, at least when it came to looks.

Yet another faux pas for which Lyonesse had never quite forgiven me.

"Why don't we wait until after you've had something healthy to eat first, huh, baby?" Meghan was saying to Marisol, in the kind of strained tone I associated with parents reaching the outer limits of "gentle parenting." "Then we can discuss how much cake you really need in your life."

"All of it!" Marisol insisted, thumping the table with an emphatic little fist. "I need *all* of it, Mommy! Apples are healthy, anyway, and Nina Blackmoore *said* I could!"

Gritting my teeth, I paused in the hallway behind Morty as Meghan's face tightened, wondering if it was officially too late to beat a retreat—and, alternatively, whether Marisol would feel obligated to call me by my full name every single time she mentioned me, just in case anyone might forget who I was.

Given children in general, and my luck of late, chances were solid that this trend would continue.

"Meggie, sweetie," Morty's father said, his *s*'s just the slighted bit slurred. I'd stayed up late last night reading up on MS, and I knew it could affect speech as well as movement during flare-ups; other times, it was all but invisible, a malevolent lurker hiding in the nervous system, preparing to mount its next guerrilla offensive. "It's just *cake*. She's not *really* going to eat—"

"Boundaries, Pops," Meg replied, just a little testily, like this was territory that had been trod many times before. "We're learning them, remember, and I'm the one who sets them? That's how this parenting thing is supposed to work?"

Morty's mother pursed her lips in amusement, flicking her eyes skyward when her daughter turned away. "Right you are, darlin'," she said, very seriously, the suppressed playfulness even starker against the lovely lilt of her brogue. "And in this house, we respect *boundaries* above all else."

Meghan cracked a grudging smile, rolling her own eyes. "You're both impossible, you know that? I cannot even handle either of you."

"Can ye imagine, Armando, if only we'd known of this 'setting of boundaries' when we were raising the likes of our two misfits?"

Morty's mother went on, thumping her husband on the shoulder for emphasis. "Instead of more like, 'Set that down right this very instant or I'll whack ye with a wooden spoon'?"

Marisol's smooth forehead wrinkled, lips parting in pure astonishment. "Gram, you used to whack Mommy with a spoon? Made of *wood*? But hitting's wrong!"

"Don't worry, sunshine, Gram did not ever whack anyone with spoons of any kind," Morty interjected, taking the opportunity to walk us both into his family's line of sight, me slinking in behind him like a stray. "Gram just likes to talk a big game, doesn't she? For real, Ma, don't even pretend you were some kind of old-school disciplinarian. I've been respectfully ushering spiders out of the house for you since I was seven because you wouldn't smush one to save your life."

All eyes turned to us, the lively conversation cutting out so abruptly at the sight of me that it was as if a dial had been twisted, shutting off the natural channel of conversation and tuning us all into a painfully awkward new frequency.

"Family, this is Nina," Morty said, eyebrows raised as he swept a pointed gaze over them. "Can you all say hello to Nina, family?"

The "like we agreed" was so implicit I could feel my cheeks throbbing with heat, practically imagine the angry splotch mottling my skin.

"Thank you so much for having me!" I jumped in, before any of them could muster a reluctant reply. Taking the conversational burden onto myself, brandishing my orchid arrangement like a shield. "Your home is beautiful. I, uh, could unwrap these for you, if you like? And I brought cake as well, for after."

"Cake, how lovely," Fiona commented with deceptive mildness, eyebrows lifting, though the subterranean antagonism that emanated from her was almost palpable, a solid 4 on the Richter scale. "So you bake, then, Nina? Wouldn't have thought it."

The subtext of "Don't your lot have people for that?" was so deliberate it might as well have been scrawled directly into the air in hovering, sparkly letters, like a conjuration missive spell.

I swallowed hard, wondering why I'd thought gaudy orchids and purchased dessert would absolve me of my name here, where everything was clearly both homespun and made with love. I could feel Morty sense my guilt pulsing through our bond, shot through with mortification, along with the answering flare of protectiveness my emotions elicited in him. He was ready to defend me from his own family; people whom he clearly adored, and who hadn't actually done anything wrong by me, besides being rightfully wary of my presence in their home.

I'd be damned if I was going to put him in the position of having to act as my champion here. Not when I could do that for myself, come what may.

"No, I don't bake," I admitted, twitching one shoulder. "It isn't one of my strengths. But this is caramel apple cake, from my favorite vendor at Castle Camelot, and it—it really melts in your mouth, especially when warmed up. They've been making it the same way for almost twenty years; I remember eating it as a kid. So I thought, well. If you're being so kind as to offer me a place at your table today, the least I could do was bring you my very favorite thing from home."

Fiona's gaze softened at that; even Armando seemed to relax a little, though his gruffer face gave less away. Only Meghan's energy stayed steely, completely reserved, her bold face shuttered. She wasn't at all sure where I stood with her yet, and until that judgment changed, she wasn't inclined to pretend, either.

I could appreciate that kind of integrity.

"Come sit, Nina," Armando said after a moment, motioning to the table. "Eat with us, before everything gets cold."

"And I'm after putting that cake in the oven now," Fiona said, pushing back from the table to come take the box from my hands. "It'll keep lovely. And thank you for the flowers, Nina. I do always love orchids."

SUNDAY LUNCH AT Casa Gutierrez was beautiful.

It wasn't just that everything tasted sublime, though it did. The sangria was tart and rich, the sourdough round somehow both fluffy and chewy, and the chili had an intense umami note to it, which—Morty slyly revealed, after much badgering by both me and Meghan—came down to generous dollops of peanut butter. It was also the way that the Gutierrezes treated each other, the currents of easy affection that flowed between and around them as warm as the air in the house itself. Everyone catered to Armando, refreshing his water and sangria glasses, refilling his plate for him with seconds and then thirds. The banter between Meghan and her mother maintained a teasing timbre that never tilted into anything remotely cruel. At some point, Morty and his father even got into a gentle argument about the possibility of getting a service dog for Armando.

"It's that I don't *need* that yet, son," Morty's father insisted, holding up a staying hand. "When I do, you'll be the first to know, I guarantee it."

"But you've been saying that for months now, Pops," Morty pointed out, head tilted. "And remember what the therapist told us. It might stabilize you even better than the cane. I've got a bunch of articles about the benefits . . . will you at least look through those? For me, Pops? I can send you the links."

"I'll keep thinking about it," Armando replied equably, giving a measured nod. "And of course I'll give your articles a read, son. Send them anytime."

Morty nodded, seemingly appeased. I'd been so steeled for an explosion, or an icing-over between them, that it was absolutely stunning to me when none came. The discussion was simply, peaceably put away, tabled for another time, and no trace of bitterness lingered.

Compared to the household in which I'd grown up, it was like witnessing a miracle.

When it came to me, it wasn't like the tension was absent, conveniently sluiced away. All was not forgiven; what had happened between our families wasn't going to be written off as water under the bridge just because I'd brought orchids and apple cake and their son suddenly—inexplicably—found me so compelling. Meghan, particularly, maintained her reserve, made sure I was clear on where I stood with her as a Blackmoore avatar, though she didn't do it in any cutting way. And it wasn't like she was fundamentally incorrect to be on the defensive with me, given that I'd been thinking the worst kind of elitist thoughts about the size of her family's home not two hours before.

And they were all bemused by me, I could tell, beyond my family name. I was clearly nothing like anyone Morty had brought home before, and they simply weren't sure what to make of me as a potential partner for him.

But they tried. For Morty, they *tried* in a way my parents had never done for me, in any situation I could think of. They made an effort to engage me in conversation whenever it was natural and unforced. I had a lovely little chat with Fiona, when we discovered that we'd visited many of the same beautiful places in North Wales. When I admired the gorgeous dining table, it turned out that it was an heirloom just like I'd thought, from the Welsh side of her family; it'd crossed the ocean with Fiona thirty years ago. And for once, my forced familiarity with the FIFA World Cup, courtesy of Gareth's obsession with soccer, came in handy—Armando seemed genuinely thrilled that someone besides him was conversant with the Portuguese national team's various challenges this season.

Even Meghan warmed to me the slightest bit when I complimented how wonderful and patient she was with Sol, how clearly precocious her daughter was. The kind of daughter I hoped I'd have, one day.

"You want kids, really?" she said, wrinkling her long nose, so genuinely taken aback I wondered if maybe she thought we Blackmoores somehow outsourced procreation in addition to our baking. (To be fair, I did have a cousin who'd had all three of hers by surrogate, and in my mind there wasn't anything particularly wrong with that, either.)

"Yup," I confirmed, fortified by enough sangria in my bloodstream to feel both relaxed and candid, and to not take offense where none was probably meant. "I've always known I did, maybe just because I wanted to do things so differently from my parents. My mother and father . . . well, they didn't set a superlative example of what it means to parent well, to build your children up. Make them feel loved, give them a soft place to land."

"That must've been hard, growing up like that," she murmured, and I could see she meant it from the tentative flicker of sympathy in her dark eyes, along with the acknowledgment that it probably wasn't easy for someone like me to admit this to someone like her. A person secure in the knowledge that her parents adored her.

"It was," I said, with a half shrug. "But there are so many other, infinitely better ways to do it. The way you are with Sol, for instance. So completely present and kind. Even if allegedly stingy on the sugar."

"Well, thank you for that," she said with a little laugh, her olive cheeks pinking. "It sure feels like I'm failing hard, a whole lot of the time. And this is supposed to be my most important job. So, you know, that's not great."

"You aren't failing," I assured her, wishing I was the type of touchy person who squeezed people's arms for emphasis. "You're doing a *wonderful* job with her, it's obvious. That's what I'd want to be as a mother—exactly the way you are with her."

And it was true. I wanted *all* of this for myself. I wanted the thoughtful way Meg talked to and played with her daughter; the bottomless love and consideration, the clear effort she was expending into being a parent. I wanted the mellow way Morty and Meg coexisted, the sense that they'd never been pitted against each other as siblings like some torturous rite of passage, or otherwise expected to vie for their parents' affection. And most of all I wanted the way Fiona and Armando treated each other; the casual, fond touches passed between them like little gifts, so unlike the frosty tolerance between my own parents, the way my father barely existed as a person outside of my mother's overbearing influence.

I wanted everything about these family dynamics, these painless ways to love your blood that I hadn't even fully believed existed in real life.

"You liked them," Morty said as he walked me out hours later, my arms heavy with the bags of leftovers Fiona had pressed on me—not that I'd protested overmuch. Behind us, the Gutierrez windows glowed like cutout squares of light suspended against the wintry afternoon darkness of the sky. I could feel Morty's pleasure radiating through the bond, luminous in itself, the gratification of having had everything play out exactly as he'd hoped. "And they liked you, too, I could tell."

"Despite themselves," I pointed out. "But they did seem to, yes. I do think the caramel apple cake helped the cause."

"That cake could facilitate world peace, given the chance. Excellent call." He held up his fist for a bump, and I laughingly met it with my shoulder, my arms too laden with bags. "And for real, you didn't even need the boost. Ma told me to tell you she'd love to have you back, and she's not one to extend invitations for courtesy's sake. She and Meg, they're cut from the same cloth when it comes to stuff like that. Neither of them waste much time on anything just to be polite."

"In that case, please thank both your parents for me, and tell them that I'd be more than happy to come by again. Obviously, I'll send them a thank-you note, too." I tipped my head to the side, gave him a little closed-lip smile. "And thank *you*, for inviting me—I really loved being with them. They're exactly as wonderful as you said. More so, even, which is kind of wild."

"Maybe next time, you'll even stay for movie night."

"Let's not rush it. In the meantime, how's Wednesday for your next session, Padawan? I can take a half day, if that's good for you. Things should be a little calmer by then at work."

"That's perfect for me," he murmured, leaning forward to close the distance between us in a lingering kiss that made me wish I hadn't set the date for three days from now. "Can't wait, Obi-Wan."

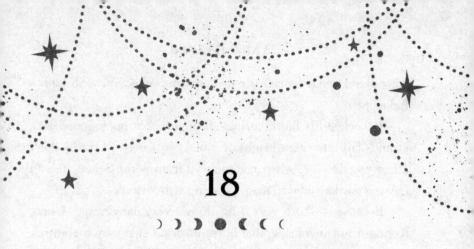

18

The One Who's in Charge

WHAT WOULD YOU say is the most badass thing?" Morty asked. We'd been in the graveyard for three hours, practicing his magic under a cloudless cobalt sky so pure and brilliant with cold it looked somehow transparent. Morty had refused all breaks, afire with enthusiasm, drunk on his own new abilities—and infinitely adorable in his infatuation. "The spell you like the most, the one that feels both the hardest and coolest to pull off?"

"Portal magic," I replied, barely even having to consider it. "Folding space and time to create a gateway for yourself, transport from one place to another almost instantly."

His jaw hinged open. "Are you . . . you can *do* that? Like, teleportation? You can go anywhere with it?"

"Exactly like that, yes. That's why I never lost my magic, even when I went to school in New York. I just portaled back here whenever I needed a refresh, to keep my connection with Lady's Lake open."

He cocked his head, curious, in a way that made loose dark strands fall into those bright eyes most enticingly. "So why don't all of you do that, when you're away from here? Seems like an obvious workaround to magic waning with distance."

"Because it's both very difficult and very dangerous," I said, feeling a not-inconsiderable burst of pride at my own abilities, even pre–magical surplus. "To my knowledge, only Blackmoores are strong enough to cast a portal at all—and just a handful of us, at that. My grandmother and mother can both portal. So can Gareth, but he's garbage at it, so he barely ever tries. And like with any other skill, you only get better with practice."

"But *you* can do it, right?" he said, and the sheer confidence in his voice—the absolute lack of doubt in me—warmed me all the way through.

"I can," I agreed, ducking my head to hide my spreading blush. "I'm, uh, actually fairly proficient at it."

"Will you show me?" he said, awash in eagerness, his eyes so keen on mine when I looked back up that I felt myself go a little breathless. "Because, damn, I would give almost anything to see that. A kidney? A firstborn? Name your price."

"We don't have to go full Rumpelstiltskin over it," I said, laughing. "It's more safety that's my concern."

"Just so we're clear, I'm willing to take whatever risk to experience something like that," he said, with a devil-may-care shrug.

"Sounds like something lowkeyloki would say," I teased.

He scrunched up his pert nose, tossing me a rakish smirk. "Chose that handle for a reason, right? I'm dead serious, though. As long as you're not the one who might get hurt, I'm absolutely game."

I nibbled at my lip, mulling it over. On the one hand, casting anything at all seemed like an untenably huge risk right now, when I was so volatile; that was why I'd been holding back, not trying to teach Morty anything by example. On the other, unlike the havoc I'd wreaked on Gawain's and Gareth's spells with my flares of temper, my own castings had only ever been much stronger in my current state—unpredictably stronger, yes, but stable in their tremendously enhanced power. Portaling was demanding enough at the best of times, and if I was going to try taking Morty with me . . . maybe this was close to the perfect time to attempt it. When I was so overstuffed with magic that I felt confident I could portal myself with barely any effort, and transport the both of us with only slightly more exertion.

Even stranger, the thought of it—of throwing caution to the winds that way, embracing the knowledge of my own power— brought a flood of sweet thrill, like molten sugar coursing through my blood. I *wanted* to do this; I *wanted* to flex a little, both for Morty and for myself. And the more I considered it, the more confident I felt. Bold, both in a way I'd never experienced and in a way that reminded me of how I used to be back in the day, before Sydney had dismantled me so thoroughly.

When I'd known what it was to feel in control, at the top of my game.

"If you're down for it," I decided, taking a step toward him, "then so am I. All you need to do is hold on to me, tight. And do *not* let go, not for anything. It's going to make you dizzy as shit, and queasy, too. Like you're falling in place, being pulled in too many directions at once."

"I'm the one who does aerial silks, remember?" he said, with a wry arch of an eyebrow. "I promise my proprioception has been extensively fucked with before, and I've never even fallen once." He considered this a beat longer, head canted. "Well, okay, maybe one time, but that was more Matteo's fault than mine. And I didn't even break any bones."

"That's my point: partner acts are harder by definition," I replied. "So, like I said. Trust that I'm in charge, and that I'll get us there. And hold on tight."

"Don't have to tell me twice, milady," he said as I stepped into his arms again, fitting myself against him as closely as I could. "Wait, though, Nina . . . where are we even going?"

"I'm the one who's in charge, *remember*?" I echoed into his ear, grinning into his collar. "We're going where I'm taking us."

"But I—"

Without waiting for him to finish the question, I flung a portal open and whirled us both inside.

ALL THE OTHER times I'd portaled before, I'd never thought to open my eyes.

It was such a disorienting endeavor—a part of me had been afraid each time, even while wresting my will into the monumental effort it took to portal—that I always kept my eyes tightly shut. Focused fiercely on the spell, and the need to keep myself knit tightly together even as cosmic forces acted upon me, tried to wrench me apart. Those other times had seemed to take only seconds, too, though even that could feel unbearably long.

This time was different.

For one, I could *feel* the rabbit hole of the portal unfolding open around us like some architectural flower, a complex schema full of self-contradicting lines and angles; as if I'd developed some extradimensional sense, a fresh perception I'd never been privy to before. As I flung us into the gateway, time itself seemed to grow slow and somehow languid, dripping like honey around our passage through space even as I burrowed through it for us.

I could hear Morty scream-laughing against me, his voice ringing in distorted slow motion, as if he were on the most awful and amazing roller-coaster ride.

That by itself was curious enough; I'd never made a sound of my own before while portaling, never thought the fabric of this space could even *carry* sound. It made me want to see, to look at what was around us—and so I opened my eyes. Expecting nothing but black, an infinite wall of impenetrable dark.

And there *was* darkness. A great unending swath of it, like a universe of black velvet expanding around the plummeting fall of our tiny selves. But there were also streaks of something like stars, dazzling and multicolored, like traveling through the bloom of a firework even as it exploded soundlessly around you. A little like the way some of my favorite shows depicted tunneling through hyperspace, traveling faster than light.

Except it was more beautiful, more breathtaking, more brilliant than even exploding stars.

And it wasn't empty, far from it. Great luminous shapes in a jeweled array of colors moved alongside us, both near and far, breaching through the dark like unearthly sea creatures. Silhouettes that drifted alone or in small clusters, side by side. I could feel their intrigue, their surprise, their curiosity—and in some cases, their sharp and distinct disapproval—and abruptly I understood that some of the discomfort I'd previously experienced while portaling had nothing to do with distorting the rules of physics, with piercing the fabric of space and time.

Instead, I somehow knew down to my marrow, with fire-forged certainty, that this in-between space we traveled through belonged to the gods.

All of the many gods worshipped by the witches of Thistle Grove—and not only us, but everyone else who had ever prayed to or wished for or summoned something Greater Than. The deities that had been here all along, that predated humanity and would long outlive the brief and fiery contrail of our existence as it blazed across the heavens before we faded altogether out.

This in-between space was *theirs*, not ours—and some of them didn't appreciate human trespassers, even if they happened to be witches. For a split second, I had the terrible thought that maybe that was what had happened to all the witches who'd portaled unsuccessfully, never to be seen again.

Possibly they'd snared the wrong kind of attention here, been erased by some fearsome regard. If there were gods, it was entirely possible some of them were more of the dread persuasion than others.

Even more confusingly, what disapproval there was seemed concentrated on Morty, not on me. As if I had a celestial hall pass, some special permission. A temporary allowance to move through here with impunity, just as they did.

Before I could consider this mystery any further, time snapped back into place with a jarring shudder. We both stumbled, arms still locked tight around each other, as the portal unceremoniously deposited us where I'd aimed it to arrive—one of Castle Camelot's topmost towers, with one of the gold-and-onyx Blackmoore banners hanging above the castle's doors snapping in the wind many feet below us.

Due to an architectural quirk—or possibly just shoddy workmanship, never to be ruled out—there was no internal access point to this tower rampart. No way to get up here without portaling or scaling the castle walls. It was possible I was the only one who'd ever come up here before, to sit alone with a contraband bottle of wine—or whatever else I'd been able to pilfer as an angsty teen—look over Thistle Grove, and think too much.

"God." Morty was gasp-laughing against me, shivering so hard under his thick duster that I could feel the quaking translate into my own body. And I could feel the rolling depth of his wonder, too, the vast expanse of sheer awe shot through with terror that I'd been too busy to sense through the bond before. "Oh, my entire fucking Christ, Nina! You could have *warned* me, don't you think?!"

"I did warn you," I said, just as unsteadily, still processing my own revelations about our journey. How could none of us have known what we were doing, what manner of realm we were passing through while portaling? The portal spells mentioned nothing about what I'd just felt and seen. And why did I suddenly understand it so much better, as though it should always have been obvious to me?

"What a fucking ride. I really—I really thought maybe I wasn't going to make it for a second there. And there were things, Nina, weren't there?" he breathed, pulling back to stare at me with wide, enthralled eyes. "Things that could *see* us."

"Wait, you saw them, too?" I said, taken aback.

"No, no, I was shitting myself *much* too hard to look. Fuck if I was going to open my eyes, when it felt like all my cells were trying to tallyho in different directions. I just . . . I felt them, somehow? Through you?"

"What do you mean?"

"I could feel you notice them, and then once you did, I could sense they were there, too. And something about them . . ." He drew a shuddering breath, drawing back to look at me with the first semblance of real fear I'd ever seen in him. "This is gonna sound insane, okay, but something about them felt like *you*. Like the way you feel to me, through our bond."

"That doesn't make any sense," I whispered, pulling fully away from him, wrapping my arms around my chest as I went to lean against the ramparts. Letting chill, woodsmoke-scented air blow into my face, its bracing cold welcome for once.

"What were they?" Morty asked, coming to lean next to me, arms draped over and through the crenellations. Kudos to him, he seemed to have recovered from our trip with remarkable resilience; if anything, he appeared less thrown than I was.

Maybe I needed to look into his meditation practice.

"I'm not sure." That transcendental certainty I'd felt had begun to fade a little, like waking from a dream, and now I wasn't positive what I'd seen. "It's never been like that, before. I think I thought . . . that they were gods. And that we were tearing through their space, like intruders."

"Maybe they were," Morty said, with an easy shrug. "And maybe we were."

"You say that like it's nothing. No big deal."

"I mean, why should it be? There's a goddess statue under the lake, right? Hell, *you're* damn near a goddess yourself, from what I've seen you do. And you know what they say, about there being more to heaven and earth than is dreamt of in our philosophy."

"Don't butcher Shakespeare at me, Padawan," I said, elbowing him in the ribs. "I'm supposed to be the sage one here."

"We're both grown, we can take sageness turns." He looked

out into the distance, the sun setting over Thistle Grove, already dipping below the crest of Hallows Hill. We'd whiled the short winter afternoon away at the cemetery practicing Morty's casting, and now the sky looked like crème brûlée, all smooth cream and gold-torched at the edges. You could see the rolling Thorn orchards from here, bare and spindly with winter, a charcoal sketch of their summer glory. The Witch Woods loomed beyond, too, their evergreens a deep and somehow sinister emerald against the black snarls of the leafless deciduous trees.

And snow everywhere, blindingly luminous, the glow of the setting sun sheeting off of it in sparks. Like light itself made dense and cold.

"It's gorgeous up here, by the way," Morty remarked, smiling at the view. "But I thought you were supposed to be afraid of heights."

"I would be, if I were dangling from a ceiling by a bunch of flimsy fabric, without magic or a safety net below," I pointed out tartly. "It's situational. I love being up high, as long as there's something solid between the ground and me. And this is my favorite secret spot."

"Classic superhero move," he said, slipping an arm around my waist. "You're aware of that, right? Taking your impressionable, awestruck love interest up to your special aerie."

"What can I say?" I quipped, leaning against him. That electricity surged between us again; the fire that now lived split between us and the bond. "I'm a walking nerd girl cliché, so sue me. In my defense, you're the only person I've ever brought up here. I wouldn't have had the guts to try portaling anyone else before, anyway. And even if I had, the only person I'd have wanted up here with me to see this is my best friend. Which wouldn't be allowed."

"Why not?"

"Oblivion glamour, remember?" I reminded him. "First she'd be terrified out of her wits, and then she'd forget it all. I love Jessa. Why would I want to do that to her?"

"And you couldn't just tweak it?" he asked, looking over at me with those ridiculous, bluer-than-sky eyes, still rimmed in dark liner. I wondered when they'd stop feeling like such a sucker punch; part of me hoped they never would. "It's set in stone, somehow? You can't carve out exceptions? Or cast, like, a counterspell on her, something that would allow her to experience magic and not forget it?"

I thought about this, taken aback. The oblivion glamour *wasn't* completely black-and-white; for instance, when we used magic to enhance our musicals, the audience didn't forget what they'd seen, because they had no reason to think that what they had witnessed was anything but mundane theatrical artistry. I wasn't actually sure whether the glamour had been designed that way originally, or whether some artistic Blackmoore had fiddled with it at some point, to facilitate our use of magic in the Camelot shows.

But if such a loophole already existed, why couldn't others be made to exist?

"Well, I suppose there might be," I said slowly. "We just . . . it's forbidden by the Grimoire to let normies see magic, unless they're partners. Likely-to-be-witchbound partners, who are on the path to becoming witches themselves. That's how it's always been."

"Seems like a silly distinction to me. Arbitrary. I get you all fear that burning mob, which is entirely legit, all things considered. But chosen family is still family, romantic interest or no." He tilted his head from side to side, pensive. "Shit, I'd argue some friendships are more solid and enduring than romances. Many, even."

"Case in point, my ex-fiancée," I said, jaw clenching. "She knew about magic, and it was absolutely wasted on her. For someone as deliberately whimsical as she was, you'd be surprised how little she cared about that piece of things. I've never even seen the oblivion glamour work that quickly on someone so previously immersed. She forgot every witch thing she'd ever seen like two days after breaking off our engagement."

"Probably a lesson in there somewhere," Morty said, with a slantwise little glance. "Maybe something about not trying to marry people lacking in a sense of childlike wonder. Or respect for you."

"One lesson of many, when it came to her," I said with a sigh. "That I should have learned much earlier."

"We all have our blind spots," Morty said, drawing me against him until my head rested on his shoulder. "Believe me, I've gone astray many a time in my own dating life. Mistook a bunch of red flags for a carnival, as they say—and by 'they,' I obviously mean the relevant memes. My philosophy tends to be, as long as you learn *something* from it, there's not much point to regretting anything. Or anyone."

"You and my best friend are *really* going to hit it off," I noted again. As if to underscore my point, my stomach grumbled so loudly it was audible even above the wind whipping at the ramparts. Morty chuckled, not even bothering to pretend he hadn't heard it.

"Maybe we should feed you, before you cause a cosmic rift or something with your hunger pangs," he said. "And I mean that very fondly. I'm actually starving, too."

"Well, if you're willing to suffer being fed on Blackmoore grounds," I pulled away to glance over at him, just a little challenging, "I could give you a tour-de-force sampler of Camelot's culinary offerings?"

"I accept, milady," he said, soft mouth curling. "But only because it's you offering."

ONCE MORTY CAME around to the fact that Castle Camelot was, in fact, ridiculously fun when you leaned into its intentional camp, we did much more than just eat.

As I drew Morty from the tavern where they peddled ale and actually delicious turkey legs, to the snack bar with the fried dough smothered in powdered sugar and drizzled with chocolate syrup, to the little bar hidden in one of the towers where you could get "medieval" sliders and other themed apps and cocktails, we somehow wound up getting our faces painted, too; Morty's idea, but one I wasn't even a little averse to. I went with a phoenix, its blazing wings curling around my left eye like a mask, while its glitter-strewn tail swept down my cheek all the way to my jawline. Morty chose an abstract, cosmic purple-and-silver medley that somehow managed to evoke both Prince and David Bowie, and set off his eyes to an almost unnerving degree.

"That is literally *exactly* what I was going for," he said gleefully, when I informed him as much. "So, maybe you're a little bit right about Camelot. This place . . . not terrible."

"Since you're feeling more open to things," I said, looping my arm through his, "could I interest you in a joust?"

"Turns out I can't say no to you." He waggled his eyebrows. "And lance-slinging gentlemen knights don't sound like the worst, either."

"Wow, medieval dick jokes!" I marveled. "We're really reaching new heights here."

"Gotta aim for those stars, babe."

In the summertime, the jousts were held in the courtyard, but in the winter, we moved them to the indoor amphitheater, where you could also enjoy a prix fixe dinner while you cheered on your knights of choice. So we ate yet again, because I was somehow still intrigued by the notion of roast Cornish hen, crispy new potatoes, and mini bread puddings even after everything we'd already sampled.

"It is so strange to me how much you like this," Morty mused as I yelled myself hoarse for Sir Agravain and his fine steed, looking at me with a mixture of awe and tenderness that I could feel stirring in my own solar plexus. "Just absolutely baffling."

"Why would it be strange? I *did* grow up here. Those are my people out there—literally, I know and am friends with half our 'royal court.' This is, functionally, my home. And you know it vibes with lots of other things I like. I don't think, for instance, that anyone's ever accused *Gene Roddenberry's Andromeda* of being a classy show—and yet, here we are, with it one of my forever favorites."

"But you're so polished," he said, with a vague wave in my general direction. "So completely smooth, and obviously averse to tackiness in other contexts. And all this is so . . ."

"Cheesy?" I offered, just a little edgily. "Campy? Utterly ludicrous, in the best of ways? I *can* do both, you know. Be both. Be complicated, like anybody worth knowing. It's not like we Blackmoores are some entirely different, one-dimensional species of human."

"I know. Of course, I know that." I could feel the sincerity of the remorse surging through the bond, almost a little comical against the backdrop of blaring trumpets and whinnying horses. "And I know *you* . . . or at least, I'm slowly getting there. I really don't mean for it to offend. Honestly, what I'm trying to say—very poorly—is that I'm more impressed than anything."

"By what?" I asked, smiling a little at the flattery, because I could feel that it was genuine.

"By you," he said simply, his eyes shifting between mine. A glowing wonder in them unlike anything I'd ever seen when someone looked at me. As if he could peer inside me somehow, and had discovered in me an entire unexpected galaxy, full of new stars. "That you can be so many things. And be them all so well, so gracefully. Not everyone is like that, you know. Some people are straightforward, simple all the way through—what you see on top is exactly what you get, nothing unusual below the surface. Which is fine, but it's never been my thing."

"I get that," I said, feeling a giddy swirl rush up from somewhere right below my rib cage. I did get it—and what was more, I recognized this feeling, what was happening here between us.

It was falling in love; the dizzying, almost vertiginous drop of it, that initial and absolute enchantment with another person. But with the witch bond in play, the way it conveyed and facilitated emotions—the way it made it impossible to obfuscate or lie—it was not only falling, but falling far too quickly, in helpless fast-forward.

And triple goddess help me, I couldn't seem to make myself mind.

"I feel the same about you," I added softly, reaching out to trace a swoop of silver glitter on his cheekbone. "And I want to know much more. I want . . . Morty, I want to know *everything* about you."

I could feel the soft brush of my own fingertips on his face through the bond, the intense way he responded to it, everything in him surging to a single point, focusing in on that light touch.

The heat of it blew through me, too, so headily intense it made me a little dizzy.

It seemed impossible that we should want each other this way, especially somewhere as cacophonous and unromantic as this amphitheater. And yet there was no question that I'd never responded to anyone else quite like this, not even in that very first blush of new emotion.

"Would you like to come home with me tonight?" I asked, holding his eyes. Not like there was any space for bullshit or pretense between us, anyhow; nowhere to hide. "Because I would really like that."

"Yes," he said instantly, covering my hand with his, curling his fingers around mine even as he turned his cheek into my palm. "Yes, I'd like that very much. Especially if we could, maybe, take a car this time."

19

So Full of Stars

"**T**HIS IS MORE the Nina I had in mind," Morty said, wandering over to the wall-to-ceiling picture window of my soaring loft, pressing a palm against the cold glass. "You know?"

"Oh, I'm aware," I said, moving to slip my arms around his waist from behind, dipping my head to rest my cheek between his shoulder blades. It seemed beyond strange that it had been only a week and a half since I'd been curled up on my couch pity-drinking, staring at whirling snow through this same window because he'd upset me so much. It was almost as if the Morty I'd met that night at the Moon and Scythe had nothing to do with this one, the person I was coming to know.

People were like that, sometimes. Like nesting dolls.

"And the Nina you had in mind," I murmured against him, "would *love* it if you didn't leave handprints all over her clean, pretty window."

"Touché," he said with a low laugh, immediately lifting his hand away. "My bad. Who can blame me, though? Your place is almost too perfect; it makes me *yearn* to touch it all over, like some miscreant running wild in a museum. Must be like living in an ice palace, but in the good way. Maybe I just wanted to see if a pleb like me could even leave a mark."

"You can't," I informed him, pressing a kiss against the warm back of his neck. "I was merely fucking with you; the glass is be-spelled to stay pristine. It's actually kind of a tricky casting, and it takes a ton of maintenance, but honestly? Worth the effort. I mean, behold that flawless view. *So pure.*"

"See, that's exactly what I'm talking about!" he exclaimed, turning around in my arms, the light of the dozens of candles I had lit around my living room reflecting in his eyes. I was a hope-less sucker for bougie scented candles, the same as for perfumes. My loft smelled like the Neiman Marcus cosmetics floor, exactly the way I liked it. "On the one hand, ravages a turkey leg and blooming onions like there's no tomorrow. On the other, requires her windows so pristine she resorts to magic. It's *confounding.*"

"I mean, I washed my hands very thoroughly after the turkey leg and the onion," I said with a shrug. "I really don't see the problem."

"But if you were to imagine the opposite of Castle Camelot, this would be it," he said, twitching his chin toward my cool-toned, low-profile furniture, the angular glass cabinets and sil-vered console tables, the mirrored wall hangings that shimmered like artfully arranged shards, reflecting the night outside. Even the variety of wineglasses hanging above my bar looked like a thoughtful installation. "You have to admit, it's a little dissonant."

"Castle Camelot is its own thing. I like my personal spaces

clean and open," I replied. "And I like a lot of light. In Manhattan, I actually lived in a penthouse, and it was . . . well. Spectacular."

I thought about describing it further for him, but I wasn't even sure I could properly articulate those memories. Cars like beads of light threading through the streets far below; my own reflection in the glass hovering in the dark beyond, like a ghost projected onto the light-pricked night. As much as I'd missed Thistle Grove and Lady's Lake, I'd adored that penthouse, felt like the essence of myself there, streamlined and distilled.

This loft was the closest I could come to approximating that feeling, that sense of pervasive airiness and light that felt the most like home to me.

"I could see the sky all the time," I said, giving it a shot. "And I really loved that. It was like watching a constantly moving Rorschach blot, right outside your windows. Getting to see cloud patterns changing all day, sieving through each other. Swirling like vapor, reconfiguring into other shapes, like something alive. It made me think, you know, *of course* the ancients saw gods and devils and monsters up there. It's an ever-shifting canvas."

More than that, even. The sky was like the world's constant dream, never settling, never waking up.

"Mmm, weren't you supposed to be studying or something, instead of sky gazing? Cracking those law books?"

I shoved him a little against the window, none too gently. The bespelled glass could take it. "I'm poetically rendering my penthouse experience for you here, and you're going to be a dick? That's your move?"

His mouth twitched. "I'm sorry, you're right. If I was going to bust your stones about it, obviously some kind of eat-the-rich joke would have been the superior play."

"Not to put too fine a point on it," I said, and I could hear the sudden sizzle of invitation in my tone, feel that beautiful, unfamiliar brazenness stealing over me again, the flicker of that inner fire. "But if eating the rich is what you're aiming to do . . . well, I'm right here. Not sure what you're waiting on."

"You know what?" he said, his voice dipping a little lower. "I'm going to take that as a very literal invitation."

"Good. Because that was how I meant it."

The next thing I knew, we'd stumbled our way over to my couch—me banging my shin hard on the coffee table as we staggered past it entangled with each other, because real-life passion didn't come with stage blocking or choreography—and I was on top of him. Straddling his lap with my arms wound around his neck, his hands buried in the fall of my hair. I'd somehow forgotten what a perfect kisser he was, exactly what I liked. All soft lips and little nibbles and the light but searing graze of tongues, intense and intimate without being too deep or too much.

But the free-flowing, back-and-forth current of sensation was just like it had been in the bar, keenly overwhelming. Feeling every touch mirrored back, the rising surge of lust growing alongside mine, as if I had two people's worth of desire inside me at once.

Then he was unbuttoning my cream blouse, letting it slip off my shoulders, his gaze roaming my snow-white-and-gold Agent Provocateur bra, a gorgeous, flimsy thing with way too many tiny straps, and a little halter that wound around my neck but hadn't been visible under my demure Peter Pan collar. I could feel the swell of his admiration, the rush of heat that pooled at his middle. The way he went rock-hard under me as he saw me blush under the intensity of his gaze.

Or saw my chest and neck flush, in any case; both of us still had our face paint on. Neither of us had been particularly moved to wash it off when we got to my place, and now the uncanniness of his galactic swirls and my phoenix mask felt weirdly sexy, compelling instead of ridiculous. As if we weren't just Nina and Morty, but something different, rarely seen roaming this realm.

A pair of unusual, quixotic creatures, magical and untamed.

"Jesus fucking Christ," he murmured on a breath, trailing a hand down my neck, over the hollow at my throat, before reaching down to cup both my breasts with his palms. I let my head fall back at the warmth of his touch, the insistence of it as he squeezed and stroked my nipples through the thin fabric, attuned to the flare of my every reaction. "Look at you. I don't remember you wearing anything like *this* last time."

"I wasn't planning on fucking you last time, was I?" I said, eyes still closed, feeling the silken course of my own long hair down my back, sensing the way he felt it, too—a sensation completely unfamiliar to him. I'd also deliberately used the word I knew would provoke the strongest reaction from him, turn him on even more.

Among many other things, Morty Gutierrez *really* liked it when I swore.

"And this time, you were?" he asked, hoarse and low, a smile in his voice.

I lifted my head, met his eyes, a slow smile spreading over my lips. "I absolutely was, yes," I confirmed. "Unless you object?"

"I do *not*," he said, so fervently it startled a bright little bubble of a laugh out of me. In one deft instant, he reached behind me and unhooked my bra with one hand, faster than I could normally even do it for myself.

"Ooh, skills," I murmured, goose bumps prickling my bare skin as he slipped it off me entirely and set it on the couch beside us, with that same care he showed all of my belongings, that sweet semireverence. Like anything that touched my skin must be precious by association. Then he looped an arm around my waist and tugged me closer, his other hand winding in my hair and tugging, just enough to arch my back a little.

"And a wealth of natural talent," he informed me, flicking a devilish blue glance up at me as his mouth hovered right over my sternum, lips so close I could feel the heat of his breath. "Pretty sure magic isn't my only forte."

Then his mouth settled on me, and anything I'd been about to say wisped out of my head like dispersing fog burned off by the sun.

I clung on to his neck like I needed it for support, stroking the soft close-shorn hair at his nape, twining my fingers through the longer fall of it above. He lingered over my breasts with agonizing slowness, pressing a slow stream of grazing kisses around each nipple until my whole chest felt engulfed with heat, a slow simmer like hot springs bubbling under my skin, his fingertips feathering over my upper arms.

When he finally closed his mouth over a nipple, I let out a needy little high-pitched sound, between a moan and a sigh. The tug and heat of his mouth, the silken lap of his tongue, the way I twitched when he nipped me hard, just a little more painful than was comfortable—like he'd remembered that I liked, from last time—all melded together into a single sensation of utter overwhelm.

And the fact that I could feel every moment of how much he liked it, too, the taste of my skin and the soft feel of me, the sway of my hips as I ground against him on his lap . . . It made me feel like I was going to explode, spontaneously combust, burst into an actual phoenix right on top of him.

"You, too," I said, fumbling with his own shirt—one of his blousy Byronic affairs that somehow still had too many finicky damn buttons—my fingers trembling and clumsy with need. "Now."

"I love that, you know," he whispered, helping me along, shrugging out of the shirt in one sleek movement that bared that finely lean, muscle-carved torso, his gleaming inked shoulders, those watercolor tattoos flickering in the candlelight. "That you don't say 'please' to me when you want something in bed."

"I don't know why I don't," I admitted, taking a beat to just look at him. The impossible, almost feline beauty of that lithe and gorgeous body; the dazzling, dark-smudged eyes; the hair I'd disheveled myself. His face paint was hopelessly smeared in purple and silver, a mess from rubbing against mine, the way my own no doubt was, too. Somehow, this only felt sexier. "I always used to, before. Does it bother you?"

"Not at all. It suits you like this," he said, running his hands up and down my sides, sinking his fingertips hard into my flanks. "Being in charge."

"We can both be in charge," I whispered, leaning down for a long, clinging kiss that left us both out of breath, gasping against each other's lips. "If you want."

"I want what *you* want, Nina," he said, eyes heavy-lidded, hands still grasping tight to my hips. "If you want to be the boss, then here, with me, you are. And that's the way I like it, too."

"Then this is what I want," I said, shimmying off his lap until I knelt between his legs, wriggling out of my vintage jeans leg by leg and tossing them somewhere behind me, the marble tiles a sudden and shocking cold under my knees after all that heat.

Leaning forward, I trailed a line of slow, hot kisses of my own down the hard planes of his belly; he was tattooed there, too, a gorgeously geometric rendering of a black-and-white beehive and a bee below his left rib cage, an ouroboros circling his right hip bone. I alternated the kisses with little nibbles that made him hiss, curl a hand around the back of my neck to keep me in place. I ran my lips over the outer edges of his torso, where I knew—and felt—that his skin would be even more sensitive. Nuzzling my cheek against him, letting my hair trail after in a caressing stroke.

"Ah, Nina," he groaned, head falling back against the couch. "You're going to—fuck, you're going to make me lose my mind with this."

"Fine by me," I purred against his skin. "But I think you can take it."

Every hitching breath spurred me on further as I dipped lower, then unbuttoned his jeans—thank the goddess he wasn't wearing a belt, because I was so giddy with want that I'd have been woefully inadequate to deal with it. He lifted his hips to let me tug them off him, boxers coming with. I slid my hands up his thighs, stroking the smooth muscle of them, reaching between to cup him. Then I dipped my head and took as much of him as I could manage in my mouth, in a long, languid slide that drew an unsteady moan from deep in his throat.

"Oh, babe," he breathed, rocking his head from side to side. "Oh, *please.*"

Apparently I liked "please" just fine, I thought with a spike of lust, as long as he was the one saying it to me.

I couldn't even remember the last time I'd gone down on a

man, but apparently you didn't lose that particular muscle memory. I moved slow and steady, with control and intention, even though I could feel every high-pitched sensation scorching through me, too, as though his own hand and mouth and tongue were between my legs.

It felt *phenomenal*, better than just good. A rising ecstasy like a fierce spiral that kept tightening on itself, clamping down.

I didn't draw back until I felt like both of us might legitimately die of overstimulation, our hearts hammering furiously in tandem, his moans a delicious clamor in my ears. Both of us dizzy and drowning, adrift together in a sea of desperately urgent need.

"Condom?" I demanded thickly, reaching behind me for his discarded jeans.

"Back pocket," he directed, gritting his teeth. "Oh, fuck, hurry."

I fished around in his pockets until I found it and passed it up to him—then clambered back up on top, all unsteady, trembling limbs, to straddle him again. Foreheads tilted together, mouths a breath apart, I slowly lowered myself on him; catching my breath hard at the sudden intense pressure, the sharply compelling sweetness of his girth inside me.

"Okay?" he asked, catching my lower lip in a sucking kiss.

"Oh, yes," I assured him, sweeping both hands through his hair, taking long breaths. "Just need a beat."

I paused for a second, let myself acclimate, then slowly bore down the rest of the way. Leaving him buried deep inside me, the length of my upper body pressed against his.

When I began to move against him, in long, slow rolls of the hips, the colossal shared pleasure of it, both of us feeling not just our own sensations but also the other's, felt almost like a separate entity. Something that lived between us, bright and molten. A fire we'd kindled together that now roared like something sentient and ravenous, a self-sustaining blaze of light and heat.

And it wasn't even just sensations, this time. This time, I could feel Morty's wonder that this was even happening, his admiration and enjoyment of me not just as a sexual partner but as a human being. A wondrous and fascinating and precious person he was only beginning to understand.

When I drew back enough to look at him, my hands laced behind his neck, I could see that tender gaze again. The one that made me feel like I was overflowing with light, maybe even made of it.

It felt incredible to be seen like that, after everything; after the way being with Sydney had eroded me, torn me down, terraformed me into something that I was never meant to be. But Morty felt and already knew me, better than any other partner ever had—and still looked at me in that awestruck way, like I was blindingly bright, so full of stars. Exquisitely flawed and flawless just the way I was, with all my rules and hang-ups and confounding contradictions.

Perfect nonetheless, the way I'd come to him.

It felt so deeply good and right that it nearly brought me to the sweetest kind of tears, and I was *not* the sort of person who cried during sex.

And I could feel how much he wanted to tell me that he loved me as I moved faster against him, that relentless pleasure bucking between us; the same wild, unreasonable urge uncoiled inside me, too, straining hard against the confinement of my ribs. It was much too soon, and we both knew it, no matter our unusual circumstances. It wouldn't mean as much as it might one day in the future, when the enchantment wore off a little, and we could decide how much we meant it.

How real it actually was, without magic ushering it in.

So neither of us said it, though I could practically feel the words jostling against one another in my mouth, overeager to be released. Instead we stared into each other's eyes until the crest of the pleasure came to break over us, never unlocking our gaze— until I started to feel like I'd never even *really* looked at anyone before, seen them the way I was now seeing him.

I still didn't understand why any of this was happening; why my power had grown by such orders of magnitude, why the witch bond had ensnared us without either of us agreeing to it. But as I writhed in his arms, head flung back, caught up in a keener ecstasy than anything I'd known I could experience, I felt an equally immense surge of gratitude, accompanied by new understanding.

Whatever else Morty was going to be to me, I suddenly knew his presence in my life—his mind and heart braided with mine through the bond, his body ensconced in me—was intended to be a gift. Something to enhance, to protect, to bring joy.

Something meant to heal.

And maybe, if I let myself, I could be the same for him.

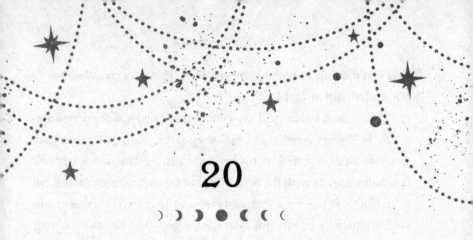

20

A Deity's Favor

"WELL, *YOU'RE USELESS* today," Gareth proclaimed, petulantly shoving a book away, sending it sailing across the polished table toward me. "You're not even really reading any of that, are you? Just pointing your eyes at it, occasionally."

He wasn't wrong. Technically speaking, I *was* reading the words, but none of them were even close to sticking. Instead, I was dreamily dwelling on the afterglow of Morty lounging diagonally across my bed last night, his head propped up on my lower belly, my fingers running through his hair while we told each other stories about ourselves.

"I want to know something weird about you," he'd said, smiling up at me. By then, we'd both washed our faces, but stubborn specks of glitter were still adhering to his eyebrows, shimmering at his temples as they caught the cold moonlight streaming through my bedroom window. "I mean, even weirder than the fact that you'd admit to having enjoyed *Gene Roddenberry's Andromeda* not under pain of torture."

"To be clear, I didn't just say I enjoyed it. I said it was my *favorite*."

So he'd discovered that I had very large pupils, and that they were significantly different sizes—something that always shook ophthalmologists with the certainty that I was stroking out, instead of having just been made that way—and that I couldn't eat sushi with chopsticks to save my life. I'd learned that he was a strong swimmer but had a phobia of drowning, and a fear of geese from having nearly lost a finger to one when he was a kid. He'd also told me more about how Marisol was one of his favorite people in the world; she'd been the one to paint his face in the picture I'd seen in his dating profile. Before Sol was born, he'd been convinced he didn't want children of his own, but seeing her grow up was slowly turning him on to the idea, though he still wasn't sure he was cut out for it.

"How does that work, anyway?" he'd asked me. "When your bloodlines mix, and you have, say, Blackmoore-Harlow kids? What kind of magic does the kid inherit?"

"It's unpredictable," I'd replied. "No one knows exactly how those genetics work. The new witch's magic will incline one way or the other of its own volition—and then they'll take that last name, even if they're part of both lines. Cleaner that way, though it still leads to kind of a messy family tree for all of us."

At some point, we'd gotten out of bed for long-past-midnight snacks, which we'd eaten standing at my counter, torn hunks of baguette dipped in olive oil and shaved Parmesan. I'd even played him some of our favorite songs from various musicals and the *Battlestar* score on my baby grand, because we were both apparently fine with being *that* insufferable couple.

My bed had still smelled like him this morning; a mix of that distinctive cologne, the sweeter, almost floral product he used on his hair, and the natural marzipan scent of his skin. It was a minor miracle I'd even managed to unravel myself from those tantalizingly Morty-smelling sheets at all to go to work. If he hadn't had plans with his father today, we might very well have spent the rest of the day tangled up together, perfectly content to see how deep we could dive into the bond, explore the contours of it.

The vibe had been so inviting that even Nadja of Antipaxos had emerged from her antisocial underbed lair to curl up by our feet—another minor miracle, as far as I was concerned.

Now, Gareth and I were in the Tintagel library, in a thus-far completely useless effort to dig up any information on the goddess statue in the lake and what she might possibly want with me.

"I'm sorry," I said, closing my own tome with a sigh. It was a comprehensive dictionary of Celtic deities compiled by some long-ago Blackmoore with an unusually scholarly bent. Our family wasn't famous for our contributions to magical literature; we tended to be more interested in just doing the damn thing with a lot of pizzazz and flair, instead of fussily writing about it after the fact. When it came to a penchant for books and academics, I was definitely an outlier. "You're right. I'm just tired, is all. And a little distracted, maybe."

"So I take it you were with him last night," Gareth said dryly, in tones of profound resignation and mild disgust, presumably at the notion of his sister with anyone. "Your inexplicably witch-bound bartender."

This time, I only had to glare to bring him up short.

"Okay, okay, *Mortyyyyy*," he corrected himself, wincing at my expression. At least he was capable of learning. "Though for real, I have no idea what his last name is."

"It's Gutierrez. As you should know, considering we tried to buy his family's bar out from under them in the none-too-distant past. Part of Lyonesse's Camelot expansion project."

"Oh, shit!" His eyebrows soared. "I *definitely* should have put that together—it was my idea, actually. I've been to that bar enough to know how much foot traffic that area gets; pretty sure I suggested it to our lady mother, back when she was still in the planning stages. I like the spot, don't get me wrong. But I kinda figured we could do something cooler with it."

"Ughhh." I dropped my head in my hands, massaging my temples. "Well, that's extra terrible. Yet another reason for you and Morty to hate each other's guts."

"And this matters to you now?" Gareth said, with one of his rare but piercing flashes of insight. "That he and I get along?"

I lifted my head, rested my chin wearily in the cup of my palm.

"It does, actually," I admitted. "You're my brother. And he's, well. Witch bond aside, I'm really starting to like him, quite a lot. And before you rip into me with the mockery, I understand we're not the most obvious of pairings, at least surface-level. But he's . . . let's just say he's more than he seems. In a way I really enjoy, turns out."

"Come on, Nina, I'm *not* that much of a dick. I wasn't going to say anything like that," he said quietly, uncharacteristically restrained. "I understand what it's like, you know."

I cocked my head, puzzled. "What do you mean?"

"When the feelings get scary real, that quickly," he clarified. It shook me a little to see genuine pain surface in his eyes, an old, deep ache that he obviously kept firmly buried the rest of the time. "That's where I was with Linden, before I fucked shit up egregiously, as is now a matter of Thistle Grove canon. I was . . . man, I was so in love with her, even if I hadn't said it yet. That was what made me panic, mess with Talia when I shouldn't have; I figured Lin would find me out any minute, discover what trash I was on the inside. So why not at least deserve the judgment, when it finally happened?"

He shook his head, disgusted with himself. "And whatever Lin might say about me now, I remember how she looked at me then. Before. Like I was good. Like I was *wonderful*."

"I'm sorry," I murmured, aching for him—even if it had been wholly his fault, exactly like he said. "I hadn't realized you were . . ."

I trailed off, unsure how to finish without presuming.

"*Still* in love with her?" he said, arch. "Totally fucking destroyed, more than a year later? Yeah, well. Did it to myself, didn't I? Literally have no one else to blame."

"And there's no way for you two to talk about it, at least? Does she even know you still feel like this?"

"Please." Gareth barked a sharp half laugh, giving a brusque shake of his head. "She won't even be in the same room with me, not that I blame her. Nah, sis. I'm never getting another shot with her, and frankly, I don't deserve one, no matter what I might've done in the meantime. Growth, personal development, all that mess . . . it doesn't really count. Yeah, I genuinely want to be the kind of man who's worthy of someone like her—but that's who it'll have to be. Someone *like* Lin. Not her, not ever again."

For a moment, we just sat in a gelid pool of silence, neither of us sure of what to say.

"Sorry, Nina," Gareth said automatically, swiping a hand over his mouth. He'd done that constantly, growing up, forever apologizing for his feelings. Another lovely heirloom from our mother and grandmother. "Didn't mean to whine."

"You don't have to be, I'm glad you told me. But I *am* sorry, Gare," I said wishing we were the kind of family who hugged, knew how to offer each other meaningful comfort. "I'm sorry things fell out that way. I don't know what else to say."

"There's nothing to say," he replied roughly. "Point being, I get where you are with Morty, no matter my personal feelings about him. And if you care—really care—then I'm not going to be the one to harsh it for you, not when things are going well."

"Thank you for that," I said, even more surprised to see this mature, well-intentioned reaction from him. He really *had* taken the time to grow over the last year and change; this wasn't the brother I remembered, incapable of so much as articulating his own emotions. "He just . . . seems to *see* me. And he's perceptive, kind, without judgment. I've been able to share things with him that I've never told anyone else. About Sydney, for one. And about Lyonesse, Igraine. What growing up with them was like."

Gareth's blue eyes chilled at that, his brow knitting together. "Wait, wait. You're letting him in on family shit already? Our actual private stuff? Seriously, Nina?"

"And why wouldn't I?" I challenged, my back stiffening. "Because we need to keep the rampant ugly under wraps at all times, just keep it in the family like our dirty little secret? So we can continue as we've been, stay completely fucked up like all of us are?"

He clenched his jaw, discomfort emanating off him. "I just . . . it doesn't seem right, that's all, telling an outsider about that. Spreading it around. That's *our* business."

"Oh, just *look* at us, Gareth!" I snapped, my patience fraying, that flame leaping to life in me again. "Really look at us. There's Gav, the clingiest, most melodramatic borderline personality you'll ever meet. There's me, the perfect pillar of ice, the one who has to white-knuckle her way through life just so she can feel worthy of being loved. Look at our father, Tintagel's own ghost, basically haunting this place instead of living in it."

I focused on him hard, eyes blazing, my shoulders heaving with emotion. "And there's you. Given what you just told me, do you even need me to break down what's wrong with you? Because it seems like you've got a solid handle on it already."

"And you want to blame Lyonesse and Igraine for all our varied shit?" he shot back, flattening his palms on the table with a smack. "Like we had no say in any of this, no agency in who we are? Who we've become?"

"Of course not," I said, shaking my head, subsiding just a little. "That's not how a reckoning works. Like you said, we're adults—which means everyone takes their share of responsibility. But I won't pretend anymore that this family is anything like perfect. Anything like normal. Anything like *good*."

Gareth rocked back in his chair, crossing his arms over his chest. "Fine, Nina. That's your prerogative. And what do you intend to do with it, exactly? This newfound revelation about how much we blow, as a family?"

"First of all," I said, laying my own hands flat on the table and leveling a gaze at him. "I'm going to admit to myself that you and I aren't going to get anywhere with this endeavor. Not without outside help."

EVEN THOUGH IT had been one of my favorite Thistle Grove haunts as a child, I hadn't been to Tomes & Omens in years.

The Harlow occult bookstore—though it billed itself to tourists and collectors more as an indie bookseller, specializing in rare and antiquarian finds—sat on Yarrow, the town's picturesque main drag, right across from the Wicked Sweet Fudge Shoppe, which wreathed the entire snow-strewn street with the melting fragrance of sugar and chocolate and caramel popcorn. As Gareth opened the door for us, the little brass bell above the jamb sang out our entrance; I could feel the tiny spurt of a spell it triggered. An alert charm, likely keyed to whichever Harlow was in charge of the storefront today, notifying them of a new visitor.

"Smells like incense crossed with one hundred years of grime in here," Gareth groused at me, muffling a sneeze into the elbow of his peacoat. He'd agreed to accompany me with extreme prejudice, more out of sibling solidarity than anything else, but we were still feeling prickly with each other from the night before. "You'd think they'd bother to dust, like, once a decade or so."

"Stunningly, some of us actually have to work for a living," a low, tart voice responded from somewhere within the warren of shelves that wound through the dim space like a hedge maze of books. "*Without* the luxury of a no-doubt pert and buxom cleaning staff at our perpetual beck and call."

Then Delilah Harlow herself emerged from somewhere between the shelves—even though I hadn't noticed so much as an opening there before—with a precarious pile of books stacked haphazardly in her arms. Emmy's oldest first cousin and James Harlow's understudy, the Harlow witch who would one day inherit his title of master recordkeeper.

Her dark brown gaze shifted flatly between the two of us, from beneath full, lowered brows. As accustomed as I was to difficult people, Delilah still always struck me as the proud owner of one of the surliest dispositions I'd ever encountered—incongruously matched with a sweet, open face like a fawn's. Heart shaped, with huge, uptilted dark brown eyes fringed by thick lashes, a tiny ski-slope nose dusted with a faint smatter of freckles, a rosebud mouth now pursed with displeasure at our unannounced appearance in her domain. Light brown hair spilled over her traditional dove-gray-and-white Harlow family robes—whatever she wore beneath them, I'd never seen Delilah less than fully decked out in witch attire—its loose waves glittering with suspended crystals and tiny talismans.

The fact was, Delilah Harlow was remarkably beautiful, like the saltiest of Disney princesses. She would have been hugely appealing to me under different circumstances, had she not been one of the few people outside of my own family I found legitimately intimidating.

"We're sorry to bother you, Ms. Harlow," I interjected hastily, hoping a little well-timed groveling might smooth our road. "But we have . . . an inquiry that we were hoping you might be able to shed some light on, concerning a magical artifact. We were wondering if you might examine it for us. Give us your professional opinion, as a Harlow recordkeeper and magical historian."

She paused, shifting a little to accommodate the weight of her wobbly book pile, dark eyes lighting with a grudging flare of interest.

"What kind of artifact?" she said through an impressive scowl, not bothering to offer up the use of her first name instead.

As with everyone else in town, there was little love lost between most Harlows and Blackmoores, especially considering what had happened between Gareth and Emmy Harlow. Though to be fair, James Harlow had only ever been kind to me, back when

I used to come creeping in here as a book-hungry shadow of a kid to spend hours roaming his shelves, ravenous for words.

And at least I knew for a fact that my brother hadn't slept with *this* Harlow, or royally fucked her over in any way, shape, or form. To the best of my knowledge—which was extensive, given how relatively small Thistle Grove's witchy dating pool was—Delilah dated only women, and certainly not ones affiliated with my family.

"A coin," I said, producing it from my pocket. It glimmered warmly on my palm, reflecting a shimmering waver from no obvious source, given how dark it was in the store. Only the faintest of winter light filtered through the dust-furred storefront windows, the wall sconces glowing like dim afterthoughts.

Delilah stared at the coin almost hungrily, eyes narrowing, as if she could sense the magic emanating from it even from where she stood.

"Interesting," she muttered, turning on her heel and disappearing back into the shelves. "Follow me."

I darted in after her, followed by a visibly long-suffering Gareth, grumbling under his breath. "Would you quit your bitching," I hissed at him through my teeth once she was out of earshot. "If we're polite, she might actually *help* us!"

"Or sell us poisoned ink or some shit," he groused back. "She was looking at us like she'd rather we both drop dead than keep screwing with her day."

"It's not about us, it's about the coin. And that, she's clearly into."

I followed Delilah's swirl of robes through tunnels of books, the towering shelves nearly grazing the double-height ceiling overhead, magic swarming against my skin. The buckling book-shelves were layered with complex strata of protection spells: anti-theft, anti-fire, anti-defacement, anti–generally malicious or nefarious activity. It was quite an impressive accumulated casting, no doubt the handiwork of generations of Harlows who took both book husbandry and their role as Thistle Grove's magical record-keepers very, very seriously. Surely no single Harlow could have managed this on their own, relatively weak as they were compared to the other families, even with the magical boost Emmy's Victory of the Wreath had given them.

Slipping behind the cluttered counter, Delilah set down her teetering stack and slid it carefully to one side, next to a banker's lamp, presumably for later sorting. Then she simply held out an expectant hand to me, palm up.

I hesitated, suddenly beset by a bizarre impulse to keep the coin on my person, protected. As if I hadn't spent hours last week with Gareth trying to smash/freeze/burn the thing into smith-ereens.

Apparently, when I wasn't looking, my feelings about it had changed.

"Can't do a whole lot of professional examining," Delilah said, her tone dripping with sarcasm, "unless you let me *see* the ar-tifact."

I cleared my throat, feeling my cheeks flush. "Right. Of course."

With an effort, I reached out and dropped the coin into her waiting hand, feeling an absurd little pang of loss. *She's not going to steal it from you, weirdo*, I chided myself. *She couldn't even if she tried. Get a grip.*

"A profile within an octagram," Delilah murmured to herself, tilting her palm this way and that, her little nose furrowing with concentration as she peered closely at the coin. "And too warm by half for this alloy. Unusual. Where, exactly, did you find this?"

Gareth and I exchanged furtive glances. We'd concocted a passable story between us, since even I wasn't ready to fully defy my mother and grandmother by letting Delilah know how I'd come to be in possession of the coin.

"By Lady's Lake," I said smoothly. "I go up there sometimes, to think. Meditate. It was right by the lakeside, sitting on top of one of the snowdrifts. I saw it catch the light, went over, picked it up."

"And how do you know for certain that it's a magical artifact?" she said, flicking a keen little dart of a glance up at me, serrated with suspicion. "And not something that fell out of, say, a coin collector's pocket?"

Whatever else she was, Delilah Harlow wasn't anybody's fool. Now came the tricky part, even sooner than I'd anticipated.

"Well, besides the warmth and the fact that I found it by the lake, it won't be parted from me; if I try to leave it behind, throw it away, it just reappears on my person. And I've been having strange dreams ever since I found it," I added, licking my lips, trying to hew as close to the truth as I could without giving myself completely away, like Gareth and I had agreed. "Very realistic ones, about a statue of a goddess. That's what I think she is, anyway. And she's underwater, in my, uh, my dreams. Surrounded by something like shooting stars, which turn into coins. Coins exactly like this one."

Delilah's eyes lit fully at that, a bright, intrigued gleam all the more gorgeous for how unexpected it was. This was clearly the sort of fresh discovery she thrived on, and I didn't imagine she had much opportunity to indulge it here, surrounded by these old, static books.

"That sounds *beautiful*," she said, unable to dampen her enthusiasm. "A goddess of light, then, most likely. And a patron of bodies of water, too, if you get the sense that's where she is in your dreams. But, that all holds only if this little buddy really is a deity's favor."

"What does that mean?" I asked softly, even as my chest heated with a warm bloom of certainty—because I knew, I *felt*, that this was right. That Delilah was onto something. "A deity's favor?"

"The symbol of some kind of granted blessing," she explained. "Like a token of divine favor, bestowed upon a supplicant judged particularly worthy."

I abruptly remembered what I'd heard in my mind, when I'd been summoned down to the lake, as the star coins were falling all around us, right before the statue had kissed me.

COME, NINA—like a thunder quaking against my mind— *COME FOR THE REQUESTED BLESSING.*

Whatever the goddess had given me—the surging surplus of power, the new, fiery brashness that lit inside me like a brazier whenever I experienced strong emotion, maybe even the witch bond with Morty—she'd thought I *wanted* it. Had been asking her for it, even, as a supplicant.

But *why?*

"So you either found a deity's favor intended for someone else," Delilah continued, ticking the possibilities off on her fingers, "or it was yours to begin with. Meant for you. That seems the much likelier supposition, considering that it's attached to your person and that it's gifting you dreams. Have you noticed any other effects?"

"Such as?" I asked, stalling.

Delilah cut me an irritated look. *"Such as* any noteworthy changes in yourself or your life since you found the coin. If you were the supplicant, then presumably this favor was meant to *give* you something, something you were previously lacking. The way favors and/or blessings are generally known to work."

"I haven't noticed much of a change," I said, lying through my teeth, my belly churning with discomfort. I really did despise lying, any sort of deception, and I'd been forced into far too much of it recently. "I will say, I've been . . . more emotional, maybe, since I found it. Does that count?"

"That could be part of it," she said with a slow nod, tapping a finger to her chin. I could see that murky drift of suspicion in her eyes again; Delilah was sharp to begin with, and part of her work at Tomes was likely assessing collectors' intentions and financial capabilities, bargaining with them during rare book sales and acquisitions.

Right now, she wasn't buying what I was selling, and I absolutely could not blame her for it.

"Another angle to consider," she went on. "If you are indeed the supplicant, then you wanted this, whatever it is you've received. It may not have arrived in the form you were expecting; divine blessings rarely do, since deities don't tend to think in human modalities. But it's still the answer to your original question. The fulfillment of *your* wish. So, before you found the coin, can you remember what you were thinking? What you were hoping for?"

I crossed my arms tightly over my chest, considering. Before the coin had appeared in my bed after my underwater sojourn, I couldn't remember wishing for anything in my dream—but I'd been up at the lake earlier that night, too, before my date with Morty. That was when the star shower had originally happened, only from within the lake.

When the beginning of the spell, ostensibly, had taken hold.

I could remember standing up there in the blasting wind, the emerald frills of the aurora flicking above me like twitched petticoats, the stars like crystal points against the black of the sky. I'd wrapped my arms around myself, closed my eyes, feeling momentarily content; a fleeting instant of serenity that the lake always inspired in me. I thought I might have wished to feel so untroubled all the time. And I knew I'd wished myself different and stronger, better somehow. I could even remember yearning for *everything* to be different, but in a way that would let me make some badly needed peace with myself.

I hadn't realized that I'd been asking—wanting, supplicating— nor had I consciously known there was anyone *to* ask. Though some dim, deep part of me must have understood she was down there, from all those years of forgotten visits.

That was when the wind had died, and the lake flared white.

I nearly staggered in place as the glittering rush of pieces finally came flying together, snapping into a clear mosaic of a conclusion. I'd wished for power, strength, comfort—and the goddess had granted it, by giving me the most literal version of what I'd asked for. The most obvious and dramatic way she knew for someone as damaged and unsteady as I was to step back into her power.

She'd enhanced my magic, flung open the doors to the hurricane cellar in which I kept all my locked-down emotions, and bound me to a partner who could hold me as I passed through such a blistering transformation. Given me someone to guide through an awakening of their own new magic, even as he guided me through my own feelings.

It would have been nice if she'd consulted either of us on whether we wanted to be bound to each other in the first place, and why she'd chosen Morty was probably beyond my ken, or anyone's. Maybe it had only been proximity; or maybe there was something tender and accepting in him, something she'd felt would resonate with me. Given what his family was like—in many ways, the polar opposite of mine—this was a distinct possibility. And like Delilah said, goddesses didn't roll in obvious ways, especially not when they thought they knew best.

But even this revelation still begged the question of why. Why me? Why grant *me* this power, why heed any of my needs? Why call me in particular down to the bottom of the lake to sit with her?

"Nina?" Delilah prodded, a slight edge to her voice. "*Do* you remember wishing for anything?"

"I . . . no. I might have, but I really don't recall. Even if I did, why would a goddess listen to some random supplicant?" I asked, my heart pounding almost painfully. "Especially one who didn't even *know* she was making a supplication. I mean, many people must be needy, right? And Lady's Lake is an obvious place for a Thistle Grove witch to visit, when she's in any kind of need or distress. Hard to believe no one else has ever made a lakeside wish."

"For all we know, someone might have—and theirs might have come true, too. But maybe *they* didn't feel the need to be forthcoming about what had happened to them," she replied, eyes glittering with bright mistrust.

She *knew* I was concealing something from her, I could tell; she could sense the hidden contours of everything I wasn't saying, but couldn't think of how to push me harder without directly accusing me of lying. A line she clearly didn't yet want to cross.

"You're right, though, in thinking that it's unusual," she went on. "What I've read about this indicates that typically, your average mortal doesn't earn divine favor no matter how stirringly they beg or plead. It's usually the god- or goddess-touched who end up with a blessing."

"What does that mean, to be goddess-touched?" I asked her, trying to keep my tone steady as a sharp chill trickled down my spine. "And how would you know if you were?"

Besides being summoned down to the bottom of a lake for communion dates, for instance.

"Sometimes deities play favorites with us," Delilah said with a shrug. "For unfathomable reasons, usually. If you did happen to be one, it could be because something in you, your fundamental nature, aligns with the goddess's own aspects."

"Like we *vibe* with each other," I said, barely able to contain the sarcasm.

"Sounds a little silly, maybe, but yes," Delilah countered. "We're talking deities, energetic beings that spend most of their time existing in incomprehensible planes. *Vibrations* matter, even if you choose to be snarky about them."

And maybe the sort of person I'd been while growing up had played into it, too, I mused to myself. The fiercely protective way the goddess statue had seemed to love me suggested she responded to a certain kind of craving—and I'd been a hurt and lonely child so often, the kind that yearned for some benevolent patron and protector.

Maybe, combined with whatever nature I had in common with her, she'd felt the clarion call of all that need.

"Names, too, can be another important thing, an intrinsic source of power and alignment," Delilah continued. "What's yours? Your full name?"

"Nineve Cliodhna of House Blackmoore," I said, my back straightening automatically. I'd been reeling my formal name off since I was a child, at Camelot and other witch functions, so often that I was basically my own herald.

Delilah tilted her head, thinking, clicking her nails against the counter in a complicated rhythm. Her nails were longer—coffin shaped, and polished a bright teal with various interesting nail art adornments—than I'd have expected from someone who worked with books and delicate parchment and scrolls all day. Maybe there was just the teeniest slice of whimsy to her, after all, and it did play well with her ornamented hair.

"If we're talking a goddess with water associations, you already have several," she finally said. "Your family descends from Morgan le Fay, for one thing, one of the Ladies of the Lake in Arthurian myth. And Nineve is a name in the Vivien/Nimue tradition, as you likely already know. The line of enchantresses linked to Avalon, all considered Ladies of the Lake in their own right. If I'm remembering right, Cliodhna is a Celtic sea goddess of passion and prosperity, possibly beauty, too."

She waved an irritable hand, scrunching up her nose. "That or a fairy queen, the lore is ambivalent on the specifics. But the sea always makes an appearance, one way or another."

"Let's say all this is true. I'm goddess-touched, and in divine favor. What if it turns out you don't want the blessing?" I asked, though my throat tightened ridiculously at the thought. "How would you get rid of it?"

Delilah tossed me a bluntly uncomprehending look, like maybe I was certifiably insane. "Uh, not a common complaint in the books, I must say. In the literature, most supplicants are, you know, overwhelmed and giddy with gratitude. The first step, I'd imagine, would be discovering who bestowed it in the first place. What deity it is that you're dealing with."

"Do you think you could help with that?" I asked, trying to keep my tone even. "I know we've already taken a good bit of your time."

"Consider it my honor," she said dryly, though her tone was more like, *Oh, by all means* do *keep imposing on me, it's my* favorite. But she still hadn't returned the coin to me; there was genuine professional curiosity in play here. And she probably wanted to get to the bottom of me, too, figure out what I was keeping from her.

"The coin is a helpful start. We have the octagram, which is a fairly broad symbol, but still, promising. We know it can mean salvation, resurrection, new beginnings, abundance. Sometimes it also corresponds with chaos magic, though I doubt that's the case here."

Given my newfound power, those attributes sounded more like what the goddess had been intending to give to me than what she necessarily stood for, but that wasn't something I could share with Delilah.

"But the fact that it's warm," she murmured, passing it from hand to hand, a fine wrinkle knitting her brow, "and that it shines like this . . . I'd say we *must* be talking a light deity, as well as one with water correspondences. That narrows it down for me somewhat, at least."

She clicked her fingers on the counter again in that complicated tattoo. Then she nodded to herself, leaned over to drop the coin back into my palm, and took off toward the spiraling metal stairs in the bookstore's back in that brisk march, like some kind of soldier of knowledge.

"Wait there," she ordered over her shoulder. "I have an idea—just need to gather some things."

21

Not Just Goddess-Touched

WE SHOULD GET the fuck out of here, Nina," Gareth hissed into my ear as soon as Delilah's pounding footsteps faded. "Did you see how she was looking at you? She *knows* something's off. That we're not exactly laying our cards on the table for her perusal here."

"Leave, and *then* what?" I challenged, pulling away from him. "We've barely learned anything we can actually use! I know what's happening to me now—I'm goddess-touched, for whatever reason, and because of it, the Lady in the lake gave me a gift. And even that much, we wouldn't have learned without Delilah's help. But who is this goddess? What do I do with her blessing? What if I don't want to keep it? We need much more information here."

"I'm just saying," Gareth replied tightly, rocking his head from side to side, a vein pounding at his temple. "I have a bad feeling about this, okay? The more Delilah knows, the more detail you give her . . . it's risky for us. It's not how Lyonesse and Igraine wanted you and me to handle this, and you know that."

"Are you really *that* afraid of them?" I demanded, halfway pleased to see him cringe at the accusation. "That even us being here, the slightest bit out of pocket, makes you this uncomfortable? *They're* the ones who want us to understand what's happening to me, remember? So just focus on that, why don't you, and leave the rest to me."

We were still glowering at each other when Delilah returned, ten minutes later. She glanced briefly between me and Gareth, flicking one eyebrow up at the obvious tension curdling the air between us, but refrained from any comment.

"These are some of the artifacts in our safekeeping," she said, delicately unfolding a black velvet cloth on the counter, pulling the corners smooth. A cracked-open, creamy pink shell sat tucked inside, with a tiny pearl glimmering within it, next to a miniature stone carving of a cow, and what looked like a small, flat river rock polished to an almost mirror gleam. "That have made their way to us, over the centuries. Each one of these is said to have belonged to a particular goddess, or been touched by one with intention— and they *are* true magical artifacts. Talismans of pure power. I want to see how you react to them."

"Which goddesses?" I asked, my gaze drifting over them. I could *feel* the magic she'd described; the air above them nearly wavered with it, pulsing like a slow heartbeat. "How did you pick these?"

Delilah shook her head, holding up a finger. "I don't want to bias you with any prior knowledge. Just touch them, handle them a little. Let's see if any of them speak to you."

I reached out, let my fingers hover over the trinity. It was hard to tell if any of them drew me, when the warble of magic was so powerful in all of them, creating that collective, compelling thrum. On impulse, I reached for the shell—probably only because it was so pretty—curling my fingers around it. It felt cool and slick, somehow *watery*, even though it didn't look at all wet. I could hear a rushing in my head as I held it, like the swishing give-and-take of the tide, along with the hiss of sea-foam and the crash of cresting waves.

But there was nothing beyond that, no particular resonance with me.

"It feels like the sea," I said to Delilah, setting it back down on the velvet. "But I don't sense any personal connection to it."

"So not Cliodhna, then," Delilah said with a nod. "That one seemed like an obvious possibility, given your name. And since we happen to have one of her wishing shells, I thought, why not?" She jerked her pointed little chin back toward the items. "Try again."

I went for the cow this time, again for no particular reason other than that I found it kind of cute. I felt water from it, too; but more like the snaking wind of rivers cutting their serpentine paths through soil, the stir of submerged cattails growing near their banks, the marshy, saltless smell of river water drifting in the air. And there was a sense of pervasive relief to this one, too—a feeling that it abhorred any kind of pain.

"Water, again," I told Delilah, when I opened my eyes. "But riverine, this time. And . . . healing, maybe? Something to do with alleviating pain, at any rate."

"Yes!" she exclaimed, her mouth twitching into a tiny smile, like a prickly teacher grudgingly pleased with a student's progress. "This one is a figurine sanctified by Damona, who appears in both the Celtic and Gallic pantheons. She's associated with rivers, and with healing. And cows, apparently."

Nodding, I set the cow back down and reached for the river rock, expecting to experience nothing of any greater intensity.

Instead, as soon as my fingers wrapped around it, I became a living star.

The heat that filled me was searing, scorching, yet somehow not painful at all. A sense of liquid light rushing through me, streams of flame being poured into my mouth and ears and nose, roaring like a fierce yet benign flash fire through my veins. I could see myself begin to glow, shedding a light so dazzling that both Gareth and Delilah cried out, flinging their arms up to shield their eyes.

"WHAT THE FUCK?!" I gasped, and my voice emerged tripled with harmonics, wavering as if it were being filtered through water. *"WHAT—"*

A cascade of water abruptly crashed over my head, as if a waterfall had opened in the ceiling just for me.

Lake water, to be exact, drawn specifically from Lady's Lake. I knew what it was, could sense the precise difference between this water and the sense that I'd gleaned from the other two artifacts.

As if their sources were different, on both a magical and a molecular level.

"My books!" Delilah was shrieking in a full-blown panic, frantically casting some sort of protective working. I realized I could *see* the skeins of magic as they rippled out from her, clicked into place like keys sliding into locks, fitting into the workings already encasing the shelves. She was triggering the anti-damage wards that shielded the books, specifically the ones that guarded against water.

Well, *that* was also new, I considered dimly, as if from a great distance from myself, so caught up in the euphoric blaze of elation that I could barely think. Non-Blackmoore spells had never been visible to me before, magic itself never made manifest like this.

"Put it *down*, Nina!" Gareth was shouting, one hand still flung up to guard his eyes. I was glowing even through my personal deluge, like some underwater beacon, my skin shedding a furious, fiery light as the water coursed over me. "Just drop the fucking rock!"

I let that terrible, tremendous, ecstatic feeling flood through me for a moment longer—the idea of losing it felt unbearable, the worst kind of devastation—and then I reluctantly managed to pry my fingers loose of the stone, letting it fall to the floor.

The waterworks above me cut out, as if someone had swiftly turned a faucet off. Meanwhile, the molten light inside me began to subside, ever so slowly, the fire leaching out of me in wisps, smoking off my drenched hair and clothes. I dried out in an instant, and the water that was puddled around my feet disappeared in the blink of an eye, as if it hadn't even been there at all. Even the water that had splashed Gareth and Delilah and the counter vanished in a breath.

Suddenly deprived of that torrent of power, as if I'd been forcibly unplugged from it, I sagged over the counter, propping my arms against its edge to bolster myself as I drew ragged breaths. I could still feel the bright little ember lodged inside me, the glowing seed of power the goddess had left buried in the deepest soil of my own core—but touching her stone had been like touching the source of the power itself. The original foundry.

I wanted it *back*, worse and more than I'd ever wanted anything.

"Nina!" Gareth burst out, coming up behind me to wrap firm hands around both my upper arms, steady me against him as I hyperventilated. "You okay? What the entire fucking hell was *that*?"

"A little miracle, is what," Delilah breathed, laser-focused on me again now that her precious books were safe from harm. "So, not just goddess-touched by Belisama, then. *Much* more than that."

"Wh-what?" I gasped, swinging my heavy head up in an effort to meet her gaze. "And, who?"

"Belisama," she repeated, her face bright with the satisfaction of having uncovered the answer, delved down to the mystery's tangled root. "Gaulish theonym, most likely meaning 'the Very Bright.' A goddess of fire and light, as well as lakes and rivers, but fairly obscure. We know very little about her, at least definitively. But I'd bet *you* know more than most of us do, don't you, Nina? Considering she's made you into a demigoddess in her own image. Turned you semidivine."

I gaped at her, reeling, trying to force the words into some semblance of sense. *Belisama*. The name rang in my head like a struck bell, resonant with truth. And when I remembered how the goddess had glowed beneath the water, her statue carved of that pale, radiant stone, calling her the Very Bright seemed almost insufficient, the wannest representation of her luminous truth.

But the notion that she hadn't just chosen me and lent me her favor, but elevated me to a mythical status, to something none of us thought still existed in this world . . . My brain wouldn't wrap around it, accept it as even remotely possible.

Things like this just didn't *happen*, not even in Thistle Grove.

Yet there was no denying what I'd looked like just now, like a human star trapped under a flood of utterly miraculous water. And the spells I'd cast most spectacularly since all this had begun had tended almost exclusively toward light and flame. I remembered my own ravenous hunger, too, the way I'd been eating much more than it took to sustain myself—my normal *human* self.

And then it occurred to me in a flash that maybe *this* was also why portaling had felt so different, when I'd transported Morty and myself up to the Camelot ramparts. Because that typically terrifying midspace, the essential fabric through which portals burrowed when they opened, belonged to the gods—and if I really was a little bit of one myself now, that might be why they'd looked upon me more kindly than on Morty, accepted my presence in their realm.

As if I had permission to be there. As if I were one of them, at least in part. Even Morty himself had told me that I felt like one of them to him, through the bond.

"Goddess," I mumbled to myself on a shaky exhale. "Fuck. *Me.*"

"It's true, isn't it? Oh, I *knew* you were full of shit!" Delilah announced, pounding a triumphant little fist against the counter. "So, what else can you do? Because you were lying, weren't you, about the favor not having changed you. Even without holding one of her artifacts, your spells must be *galvanic* right now. The kind of power the rest of us can't even . . ."

She trailed off, her rosy lips parted as her eyes flicked rapidly back and forth, thoughts chasing each other across her face like storm clouds.

"It's *you*," she said slowly, face clearing as some internal puzzle clicked into place for her. "You're the one causing the distortion!"

"What distortion?" Gareth snapped, slinging a protective arm around my shoulders. "The hell are you talking about?"

Delilah glanced over at him with vague annoyance, as if she'd halfway forgotten he was even here and would have preferred to keep him well out of mind.

"Spells are malfunctioning all over town," she said, with a sweeping gesture. "Little ones, big ones; the scale doesn't seem to matter. They're just . . . sputtering out, even when cast by seasoned practitioners. As if the caster can't quite draw enough magic from the lake to see them through."

I tilted my head back to look up at Gareth, exchanging baffled looks. That was the opposite of what had happened at both Camelot and the Cell, when my temper had gotten the best of me.

"Then why haven't we heard anything about this?" Gareth demanded. "As scion, I should have been notified. Not to mention my mother."

"You weren't notified because the Blackmoores are the only family that haven't reported any such weakening among their ranks," Delilah cut in, eyes narrowing. "Rather suspect, no? And of course you haven't—because you have *her*. Your very own demigoddess, channeling extra fuel for you. She must be something like a lightning rod right now; the magic of the lake focused on her, drawn to her. Which means there's less for the rest of us."

And we wouldn't even have heard of it by way of rumor, I thought hopelessly, because so few of the others talked to our family if they could help it.

"We've all been banging our heads against the wall, trying to get to the bottom of it," Delilah muttered, shooting me a viciously indignant glare. "Emmy, most of all. And here you are. Here you've *been*, this whole time, keeping the answer to yourself. Selfish and greedy and heedless of anything that doesn't benefit you, like every last Blackmoore that ever lived."

"I didn't realize," I protested weakly, shaking my head. "I didn't know . . ."

"Well, now you do. And more importantly, now *I* do," she snapped, reaching for a parchment scroll from beneath the counter, an owl's-feather quill floating to her hand from the stacks behind her. "And as a Harlow recordkeeper, it's my duty to report what I've discovered to the Victor—and more importantly, to the Voice of Thistle Grove."

"Nina," Gareth muttered into my ear, hand clamping down harder around my arm as Delilah bent over the parchment and wrote in a furious scrawl, sparks billowing around the scratching tip of her nib. A basic missive spell, one that would likely appear in Emmy's hands in moments once Delilah was done composing her letter. "You can't let her do this. You *can't.*"

I could hear the wavering discord of panic in his voice, feel the way it set the wick of my own alight. If I allowed Delilah to share this knowledge with Emmy, what kind of disaster would it bring down on our family's heads? And what would the Victor do with me?

Would she force me to give up this magic—this blessing—now that I'd only just tasted the full extent of it?

She would, *of course* she would. Emmy would never allow one Blackmoore's strength to outstrip that of the entire town, not on her watch. She'd see me as a looming threat to her flock and its magic, a danger to the community she was bound to protect and serve and lead. And yet, with Belisama's rock, I could become what my mother and grandmother wanted me to be—more, even, than they could ever have expected. More than any of us could have dreamed, when it came to restoring Blackmoore glory within our lifetimes.

If that was what I chose to do with it.

At the very least, I needed time, the chance to think clearly about this. I couldn't allow Delilah to strip me of that control, to take even that choice away from me.

"Gareth," I said, drawing up my spine, making a split-second decision so instantaneous it felt more like reflex or instinct. "Take the stone. I can't touch it right now; I don't know what else might happen if I do."

"Excuse me?" Delilah hissed, head snapping up from the parchment. "You will *not* steal—"

"Forget," I began, lifting my hands to cast the oblivion glamour. The words that actually emerged from my mouth sounded more like some savage echo catapulting around a mountain range, shrieking, *OBLIVION.*

I'd never cast any version of the oblivion glamour before; had never needed to, given the mega version of it already cast over the entire town, specifically geared toward managing normie exposure to magic. And memory-tampering spells were strictly prohibited by the Grimoire when it came to witches using them on each other. I should know; back when Igraine had been the Victor, I'd sat on her tribunal a few times myself, to determine punishment for those who'd violated that precept. The consequences had never been pleasant for the caster, and I could remember my own righteousness, the moral certainty that they'd done grievous wrong.

But model student of the Grimoire that I was, I knew the incantation—and I didn't have a choice. I couldn't let Delilah render me helpless this way, take the decision out of my hands by alerting Emmy now.

I *needed* her to forget that Gareth and I had been here, talked about this. I *needed* that time alone, to decide what I was going to do, chart my own course.

Boosted by demigoddess magic, the oblivion glamour struck Delilah like something physical. A supersonic boom, a wave made of air. I could see her hair fly back as if in a whooshing gust of wind, her entire head rocking back so hard it must have jarred her spine. Then her face went disturbingly, awfully slack, her eyes emptying like an upended hourglass sifted free of sand. The hand clutching the quill drifted aimlessly back down to the parchment in slow motion, like a sparrow drifting on a wind current.

When her fingers uncurled, it dropped out of her hand, rolling off the desk and landing soundlessly on the floorboards.

"What?" she whispered blankly, blinking as if to clear her eyes, struggling to focus on us. "Who . . ."

I clapped my hand to my mouth to stifle a moan, engulfed in a wild, sickening regret that rose up in my throat like bile, threatening to choke me. This was beyond wrong. This was *terrible*. I had hurt Delilah, erased her memory, possibly caused damage not even yet perceptible. And I'd done it anyway; for myself, my family, in one semi-unthinking instant. For something I wasn't even sure I wanted, much less deserved.

And the superpowered glamour hadn't even stopped with Delilah.

Too strong to contain, or to spend itself entirely in her, it unfurled away—leaping along her still-open connection to the many Harlow wards that wreathed the bookshelves. Even though it had already wiped her memory clean, it still brimmed with too much power, far too much. So much of it that it rattled the floor under our feet, made the shelves themselves tremble with its force like a minor earthquake, books shuddering against each other.

Then, layer by layer, it began to *peel* away the wards themselves, like stripping wallpaper in great curls. Making the spells themselves forget what they had been cast for, what it was their duty to protect. What generations of painstaking Harlows had intended as their purpose.

"Oh, no," I moaned, reaching out frantically to call it back, unable to so much as budge it now that it had set its course. *"No."*

"Shit," Gareth muttered tightly beside me, jaw clenched so hard the muscles strained under his tanned skin, though he could see only Delilah's distress and confusion, not what was happening to the bookstore. "Oh, this is very fucking bad."

But the casting was beyond my control, a column of force all its own. A chain reaction that couldn't be contained once it had been catalyzed by so much magic. I could only stand back helplessly and watch as it blew the centuries of careful wards into literal oblivion, leaving the books naked and defenseless while Delilah still sat sluggish behind the counter, blinking owlishly as she struggled to regain her bearings. Barely aware of our presence, much less of what was happening around her.

I ached at the thought of how she'd feel once she realized what was wrong with Tomes & Omens—and that she, its sacred guardian, couldn't even remember how it had happened.

"We have to go," Gareth was saying as he snatched up the stone and dragged me back toward the doors. *"Now,* Nina. Before she gets it together. Before anybody comes."

And like the most abysmal of cowards, I went with him.

22

The Right Thing

WHEN MORTY FOUND me that night, I was curled up on my sofa with my knees pressed to my chest, trembling so hard my teeth chattered.

Gareth had left me with strict instructions to do nothing, say nothing, until I heard from him. His assumption was that Emmy would have sensed the massive collapse of the wards at Tomes & Omens, recognized it as another magical fluctuation. But with Delilah's memory erased, there was nothing to connect us—or any Blackmoore—to the incident. So we'd lie low, at least until the inevitable storm rolled in.

That was how my mind was insisting on referring to what had happened. *The incident*, in a stunted attempt to distance me from it as much as possible, diminish my responsibility. But it hadn't been an incident, something that implied accident, a lack of fault. It had been a catastrophe, a tragedy of my own making.

The worst thing I'd ever done.

Worse yet, I missed Belisama's stone with an ache that bordered on craving. I'd urged Gareth to take it with him, afraid I wouldn't be able to resist the impulse to pick it up again, feel that gorgeous inferno crackle through me. Heedless, just like Delilah had said, of whatever might happen to the rest of Thistle Grove's magic as a consequence of my own selfishness.

"Nina, what *happened* to you?" Morty said as he sat beside me, his face drawn with concern. "What's wrong?"

"H-how did you g-get in here?" I managed through the clatter of my teeth, tugging my quilt closer to my chin, though even just his nearness comforted me a little, lent me a sliver of relief.

"Your door was unlocked. That would've tipped me off that something had gone very badly fucked, even if I hadn't already known as much from afar." He stared down at me, those brilliant eyes clouded with fear. "Nina, I felt it, through the bond—this . . . *blaze.* This wild euphoria from you. And then, just, terror. Remorse. Guilt."

"It was me," I whispered, biting down on the inside of my cheek until the pain became too sharp to withstand. I could feel tears leaking down my face, but I couldn't even summon up the will to wipe them. My cheeks were already salty anyway, crusted from hours of silent crying. "I did . . . Morty, I did something *awful.* Something so, so bad."

Moving slowly, with utmost gentleness, he reached down and pulled me upright, slipping an arm around my shoulders and letting me rest against him. I burrowed my cheek into his collar, inhaling the cologne-and-almond smell of him, the floral scent of his hair.

It beggared belief, the way he already smelled like home to me, when we'd barely even had a month of knowing each other.

"Will you tell me about it?" he asked, resting his cheek on the top of my head.

"Yes," I said, shutting my eyes hard. "But I think . . . I'm pretty sure it's going to make you hate me."

"Impossible." I could feel him shake his head against me, his arm tightening. "I could never. I know you, remember? I can *feel* you. Whatever you did, whatever mistake you made, you couldn't regret it more. And that's what counts, right, when it comes to fixing things."

I took a shuddering breath, gathered myself a little. Then I told him, in dribbling bits and pieces, exactly what had happened at Tomes. What we'd learned from Delilah about me, what it had been like touching Belisama's stone. What Delilah had concluded about my newfound power sucking magic away from the rest of the witches of Thistle Grove.

"But I could still cast," Morty broke in. "You even said I was strong, for a beginner."

"Because you're a Blackmoore by affiliation," I explained. "Thanks to your witch bond with me. Blackmoores seem to be exempt from the drainage, probably because they're of my blood— things like that matter when it comes to magic. And to the lake, apparently. I'd assume being witchbound to a newly minted demigoddess might have something to do with it, too."

"I wish I could've seen it," he said, voice hushed with wonder. "You like a star, under all that water. That must have been epic. Colossal."

"It was," I whispered, my voice tear-blurred again. "That's— that was the problem. I *loved* it. It felt beyond wonderful, better than anything ever has. But Delilah was going to go to Emmy with it, report me. Which I understand, of course. She's a Harlow, and the next master recordkeeper to boot. It's her duty, her responsibility. But I . . . I couldn't. I couldn't just let her take it away from me like that, without even giving me time to think."

I could feel a slight stiffening in Morty's body where I pressed against it, followed by a slow nod. "Okay. So what did you do, Nina? How did you talk her out of it?"

"I didn't. I made her forget," I forced out, through numb lips. Little bits of me had been going numb and then tingly since I'd gotten home; I was starting to wonder if I was in shock. "I used an oblivion glamour, like the one cast over the town. But I needed her to forget everything that had happened—having seen me and Gareth, having found out about me and Belisama. Having given me the stone to touch."

"Oh, Nina." This time there was something like dread in his voice, a terrible resignation. "You didn't."

"I did. And the glamour . . . it was much stronger than it should have been, because of what I am now." I licked my lips, swallowed through a throat that felt like corn husks. "I don't know how much she's forgotten, what else she might have lost. And it didn't stop with her, either; it affected the entire store. All the wards the Harlows had cast over it for centuries are gone now. Like they *forgot* themselves. I didn't even know spells could do that."

We lapsed into silence for a moment, breathing together in that uncanny witchbound tandem. With the bond open between us, I could feel his reaction as it developed, track it in real time. Fear for me, profound sadness for the Harlows, followed by judgment, censure, even a touch of revulsion. Though the bond wasn't telepathic, I could piece his thoughts together. He understood how and why it had happened, because he felt it, could trace the contours of my own motivations—and he didn't hate me, like he'd promised me.

But he was also furious with me for what I'd done, and he believed with unshakable certainty that I should turn myself in. Take responsibility.

All the things I'd been afraid I'd sense from him, knowing how revolted he was by even the basic version of the oblivion glamour, and the notion that normies should be constantly plied with it.

"You know what you have to do, right?" he said. "There's only one way out here."

"Morty—" I began, seeing where this was going.

"No." He cut me off, every muscle in his lean torso going rigid against me. "No, Nina. You need to go to Emmy, immediately. Right now. Return the stone, tell her what happened, do what you can to help her fix Delilah and the wards. And figure out a way to reverse this blessing, give back what isn't yours."

"But the Lady *gave* me her favor," I argued, drawing away from him. "And the lake is hers, isn't it, along with its magic? And the town, too, by extension. Maybe she *wants* me to have this. To . . . to be this."

"At the expense of every other witch in Thistle Grove?" he challenged, fixing me with such a severe, unflinching stare that I wanted to disappear, melt into the couch. "*Is* that who you want to be, Nina? A demigoddess, powerful beyond reckoning, while everyone else—people you know, people in your own community—lose what they had? How would you feel if someone else did that to you?"

I sagged back against the couch, crossing my arms tightly around myself.

"No," I said finally. "I don't want to cause that kind of loss. But . . . there's my family to consider, too. What this would mean for them. We were Victors for hundreds of years, like Emmy is now. Whatever everyone else might think about us, we *shaped* this town, made it what it is—and we could have it back. I could be something different, something new. Something like the Victor and the Voice of Thistle Grove rolled into one, but even greater."

"Yeah, you could be a fucking righteous megalomaniac," Morty snapped, his tone so harsh I flinched at it, even as he pushed up from the couch in one lithe, furious motion. "Thistle Grove's very own supervillain in residence. Because that's what you're really saying here, when you get down to brass tacks. Isn't something like that your family motto, anyway? 'As long as we prosper, everyone else can go merrily fuck themselves'?"

"That's reductive and unfair, and you know it," I argued. "I know my family's faults more, better, than anyone. But I . . . I'm still *one* of them, Morty. I might hate them sometimes—more often than not, even—but they're still *mine*. My blood. This isn't just about me. I have to factor their best interests in, too."

"Like hell you do," he shot back, rounding on me. "The very last thing you *have* to do in this life is pander to toxic people. Keep catering to them even as they do their very best to damage you, keep you small and controlled. Caged in the box they built for you. You can certainly choose to do that, but, Nina, listen—this is not you. It's not who you are, what you stand for. From everything I've seen of you, I know you're better than this. Stronger, wiser. So much kinder and more compassionate."

"I'm just saying I need time to think," I mumbled, dropping my chin. Hating myself for how weak I sounded, how obviously ambivalent. "I'm not—I'm not saying I won't do it. Come clean with Emmy. But not right now. Not tonight. It's too soon."

"Fine," Morty ground out, stalking over to the chair where he'd slung his scarf and heavy duster. "Do you, milady. Whatever that even means to you."

"Are you . . . are you going to tell Emmy?" I asked, my heart beating so hard it felt like it was quaking against my rib cage. "If I don't?"

He shot me a bleak, revolted look over his shoulder. "Am I going to narc on you, you mean?" he bit off, every word edged with acid. "No, I won't be ratting you out, never fear. Wouldn't you just hit me with a nice dose of oblivion, anyway, if I even tried?"

"I would never do that to you," I whispered, drowning in shame.

"Oh, is that right?" he shot back. "I think your record speaks for itself there. Besides, this is your mess, your problem—and *your* decision. I'm not going to be the one to take that away from you, the way your precious family is so happy to."

"Thank you," I breathed, closing my eyes at the notion of this temporary reprieve.

"But I also won't be part of this," he added, thrusting an arm into his coat. "Involved in any way. I want you to shield the bond; I don't want to feel any more of you, not until you've sorted your shit out. Decided who it is you actually want to be. And I don't know how to muffle it myself."

I pressed my lips together, appalled at how gutted, how desolate and lonely, the idea of closing the bond down made me feel.

"Please don't ask me to do that," I whispered, feeling like he was threatening to cut a lifeline, the only tether I had to hold on to.

I need you, I wanted to say, but didn't.

Don't leave me like this.

Please stay.

"Like I said." He looped the scarf around his neck, fixedly not looking at me. "This is your decision. Not mine. And not one I have any desire to live through vicariously, tell you what. So if you do the right thing, you know where to find me."

"And if I don't?" I managed. "Do the right thing, according to you?"

"Then we're going to have to figure out how to break this bond." He met my eyes then, unwavering, a painful, lancing spike of blue. "Because you won't be the kind of person I want to be tied to in any way."

23

To Duel or Not to Duel

As it was, I didn't have long to marinate in my misery.
Emmy Harlow came to me, just three days later.

I was sitting at my desk at the Camelot office when one of the "squire" attendants announced her, my head spinning from lack of sleep. I'd gotten barely any rest the past few nights, tossing and turning in an anxious haze; caught up in the torment of my decision, what Morty had said to me. What was I going to do? Who did I want to be? Was I Nineve Cliodhna Blackmoore, daughter of the Blackmoore elder and sister to the scion, a faithful avatar of the family? Or was I Nina, Jessamyn Singer's best friend and confidante, the Bo to her Kenzi? The real and complicated and ostensibly appealing person Morty had begun to care for, before I'd screwed things up with him so royally?

Somehow I still didn't have the first fucking clue, and attempting to line-edit contracts while the letters swam in front of me hadn't helped a bit.

"Good morning, Victor Harlow," I said carefully as the squire ushered Emmy in, motioning her toward the leather chairs in front of my glass slab of a desk. Keeping my face carefully smooth, as though my heart wasn't pounding in my ears, my hands trembling in my lap. "What a surprise to see you here."

"'Emmy' will be fine," she said, shooting a brief smile at me as she sat, shrugging off her textured black faux fur coat and folding it across her lap.

When she'd returned from Chicago, her hair had been cut in a sleek, asymmetrical bob, but she'd grown it out some since returning to Thistle Grove for good. Now it was longer, lighter, and wavier, closer to Delilah's shade; a pretty, striated mix of browns that complemented her dark green eyes well. More like what I remembered from when we'd gone to school together, though not quite as leonine. Both looks had suited her, but this softer middle ground felt somehow more authentic, truer to her.

There was nothing soft, though, about her outfit. She was wearing an angular cowl-necked sweater and slick, snakeskin-patterned leggings, as well as thigh-high boots with a heel that clicked sharply against my rose-veined marble floor as she recrossed her legs. All black, I noted to myself. Even her lip gloss was a deep plum, darker than normal. As if she'd come dressed (stylishly) for war, or someone's funeral.

The energy was strongly of the "Cersei comes to burn the Sept" persuasion, at any rate.

"Of course. Emmy." I tilted my head, the picture of outward composure, my stomach roiling beneath it. "And please, call me Nina, too. How can I help?"

"I'm here about Tomes & Omens," she said, her pretty face falling into grim, almost dangerous lines. "We had a magical assault there three days ago. Delilah—my cousin—was struck with an oblivion glamour. One that seems to have somehow undone most of the wards that protected our books, as well."

"I see," I said, trying to keep my breathing even. "And how do you think we might assist you with that?"

Emmy recrossed her legs again, leaning forward slightly over her thighs. Somehow the change in posture instantly lent her more gravitas, an almost frightening amount of authority; she clearly wasn't trying to disarm me anymore. A faint blue light had begun glowing in her eyes, something I'd seen happen sometimes during ceremonies. It was part of her connection with Thistle Grove, the magical energy that ran through her and connected her to the town itself.

"Nina, I know you were there," she said quietly, and I could hear that magical thrum in her voice, too, laced with a hint of unmistakable threat. "You and Gareth both. There's an alert spell on the door, but it does more than notify the storekeeper—it also records visitors, keeps track of them. A safeguard, in the event of situations like this one. It was one of the few spells to escape erasure, due to its placement, probably. Far enough away from the heart of the store where the worst of the damage was done."

I froze, unwilling to confirm or deny, uncertain what to even say.

"I *know* you were there," she repeated, raising an eyebrow, "and that's why I'm coming to you first, instead of raising hell with Lyonesse—as I'll admit was my first instinct. From everything I've heard about you, you're the bulwark here, the reliable one. The reasonable one. And I need to understand what happened, Nina.

What Gareth did, and why in the world he'd ever have done something like that."

I choked down a semihysterical laugh, because *of course* Emmy would think that whatever had befallen her cousin and the store, it must have been Gareth's fault. Given their history—and to be fair, his reputation—it was a rational enough assumption.

"Is she alright?" I said, unable to help myself. "Delilah? How . . . how is she doing?"

"She'll recover her memory, in time," Emmy said, her tone still even, though I could see a dark new glimmer of suspicion in her green gaze as she reconsidered me. Her eyes narrowed further as she appraised me more closely; maybe she could sense some hint of that goddess ember, even if it lay dormant when I wasn't casting anything.

The starstruck coin glowed even hotter in my pocket than normal—as if it could feel her, too, was responding to her scrutiny.

"She's still groggy, no recollections of the day," Emmy continued. "Fortunately, all Harlow recordkeepers are imbued with an anti-oblivion charm when they begin working at Tomes. Again, it's to safeguard against situations exactly like this. The possibility of someone ill-intentioned breaking in to steal a powerful book or an artifact. *If* that's what we're dealing with here."

I hadn't known this, obviously, but it made sense. Of course the Harlows would have protective fail-safes in place, when they'd been in charge of keeping our history for centuries.

"That's the puzzling thing—an oblivion glamour of any kind shouldn't have worked on her in the first place," she continued in that whetted tone, glinting with careful menace. I didn't remember Emmy Harlow as being quite so terrifying, but that was before she'd become both Victor and Voice, the first ever such mingling in our history. "It would have had to be a tremendously strong casting, far beyond what Gareth's working with, even as a Blackmoore. So, how? And again, *why* lash out at Delilah like this? What could she possibly have done to him?"

I sat for a moment, like a statue myself, mind whirling at what felt like the speed of light. This was it, the moment of truth. There was no way to stall, nowhere to run. Nowhere to hide.

My clock had run out. It was time to decide.

I remembered Morty's passion, the gleam of conviction in those radiant eyes. *This is not you,* he'd insisted. *It's not who you are, what you stand for. You're better than this. Stronger, wiser. So much kinder and more compassionate.*

Whether this was true, I wasn't sure. But I did know that I wanted it to be.

And if I did, I needed to start now. Take that first step toward a different me.

"Gareth didn't do anything," I said, almost surprised at how steady my voice emerged. Not Nineve Blackmoore, Esquire's frostily competent tone—but not Nina's wavering uncertainty, either. Something entirely new; something in between. "It was me. I cast the oblivion glamour. I erased Delilah's memory. The damage to the wards . . . that was an accident. I didn't realize anything like that could even happen."

Emmy rocked back in her chair, nostrils flaring, something between shock and vindication flashing across her face. The blue glow in her eyes intensified—maybe she was readying some defensive magic as well, drawing on her connection with Thistle Grove in case I turned on her—but beyond the way her knuckles paled as she curled her fingers tighter around the chair's arms, she didn't betray any further reaction.

"Why would you do something like that, Nina?" she said, much gentler and more tempered than I'd been expecting. "I might not even be surprised, if it had been someone else in your house. But *you*? Help me understand, here."

I closed my eyes for a moment, letting myself sink into the surprising relief of my admission, tinged with pure terror at what I was doing. Because this was a line I could never uncross; there'd be no coming back from here. This was the sort of treason my mother and grandmother could never forgive.

But maybe their forgiveness—their acceptance and approval—wasn't something I needed anymore.

"There's a statue of a goddess in the lake," I said, meeting Emmy's eyes as calmly as I could. "Delilah thinks it's the statue of a deity named Belisama, and that I have a special connection with her. Goddess-touched, she called me. She wasn't sure why; because of my ancestry, possibly, the connection to Morgan le Fay. Or maybe something about the way I naturally align with this particular deity, or even my given names. It wasn't entirely clear to her."

"A goddess in the lake," Emmy repeated, eyes flaring wide. "Nina, that's . . . are you *sure*?"

"Positive," I said, with a tight little nod. "Not the true goddess herself, but a sentient emblem of her. The real goddess—she's somewhere else, I think. But a significant, meaningful part of her lives down there in the statue, too. It's what makes the lake as magical as it is. It's what fuels all of us, I think."

"How long have you known?" Emmy whispered, still awash in astonishment. "And how?"

"She calls me down to her, to the lake bed. It's been going on for years; since I was little, probably. I don't know how that's possible, but that's goddess magic for you, I suppose. I didn't have any memories of it, not until one night about a month ago. I made a wish that night, without knowing what I was doing. And Belisama . . . she granted it. She gave me power. Forged me into a demigoddess in her image, according to Delilah."

Again, I left out Morty and the witch bond. That part of the favor had nothing to do with Emmy or Thistle Grove—and whatever the outcome would be here for me, I didn't want to expose Morty to any repercussions yet, not until I knew more about what they'd be.

The very least I could do was protect him.

Emmy nodded, her eyes flicking back and forth as she made the connections, as quickly as her cousin had done at Tomes. "So it's you, then, causing all the magical fluctuations. The odd power fluxes, the weakening in everyone else's magic."

"That's what Delilah thought—that I'd become kind of a lightning rod for the lake's magic. A power suck, a center of increased gravity. She tested me, too, with various goddess-imbued artifacts. The one I responded to was Belisama's, a river stone."

I described what had happened, the water and the fiery glow, what Delilah had called a little miracle. Emmy stared at me, rapt, nodding along.

"I felt it, when that happened," she said. "It rippled all through Thistle Grove; I'd never sensed anything like it before. Not even when I wore the Arbiter's Mantle for the Gauntlet, and that's the biggest, oldest magic I've ever known."

"I've never felt anything like it, either. And it was spectacular," I admitted. "I couldn't have imagined it, being that strong."

Emmy's face hardened a little, but she nodded again, watching me with wary speculation.

"I can imagine," she said. Still cautious, but understanding where I was coming from. "It's intoxicating, right, having something that powerful flowing through you? Like a drug. I still dream about wearing the mantle, sometimes. Even what I have now as Victor, and as the Voice . . . it still pales in comparison. Which begs the obvious question, of course."

"You want to know if I'm willing to give it up," I said, holding her eyes.

"Yes," Emmy replied simply, tilting her head. "You're a Blackmoore, after all. And believe me, I understand exactly what kind of golden opportunity this must seem like, to someone as ambitious as you. And to Lyonesse and Igraine, the sheer potential of it. Of having a *demigoddess* in the family. Not to mention that you erased Delilah's memory of her conversation with you, ostensibly so you could steal that stone. And it's been weeks since this all began for you, which means you actively chose to withhold this information from me. I assume that was a family decision?"

I chewed on the inside of my cheek, because this was another tipping point. I could shoulder the full responsibility, keep my family out of it entirely. But I didn't owe them that kind of sacrifice; they'd done nothing to earn that sort of loyalty. That also wasn't who I wanted to be, not anymore.

"I cast the oblivion glamour of my own volition," I said, tipping my head. "Lyonesse and Igraine didn't even know I was going to Delilah for help. But they knew about my power surplus, the statue in the lake. And they were adamant that we keep everyone else out of it, and that I say nothing to you. The plan was for me to understand this new power, seize it fully—and then, possibly, plan a coup. Wrest the town from you, if we could."

A ripple of pure fury wavered across Emmy's face, her eyes flashing a searing sapphire. "A Blackmoore queen, to reign over

Thistle Grove," she bit off, her delicate jaw tight. "No matter the cost. How very Targaryen of them."

"In their defense, we didn't know about any of the other consequences," I added. "As you know, we haven't been experiencing any loss of power, unlike the other families—due to the blood connection with me, I'm assuming. So that wasn't part of it."

"Do you honestly believe knowing the cost would have made any difference to them?" Emmy demanded flatly. "Stripping everyone else of almost all their power, so you—and the two of them, of course—could finally rule the roost again? Doesn't sound like the kind of thing they'd consider much of an obstacle, in my opinion, or particularly morally problematic. Possibly even preferable, to have everyone else left weak. Fewer pretenders to the throne."

"It's true," I said, with the same equanimity. "I know my family—or, at least, the two of them who lead us. But we're not . . . we aren't all like that. Gareth isn't, or at the very least, he's trying his best not to be. Though I'll be the first to admit, he still fails with unfortunate frequency."

"Unsurprising," Emmy said, with a crisp half shrug. "But I'm glad to hear some efforts are being made. That's a new development."

"And *I'm* not like that," I went on. "Or I wouldn't be sitting here, telling you all of this."

"No, you wouldn't, would you," she said wryly, a faint smile curling her plum-glossed lips. "You'd be challenging me to a duel. The Great British Sorcery-Off. One that you'd probably win, by the sound of it."

"But I don't *want* to win," I said with a little twitch of a shrug, and the truth of it melted warmly through my veins. Nothing near as headily sweet as that scorching goddess fire, but real and sustaining all the same. "Not at everyone else's expense. Not if it means I have to fight you for Thistle Grove. I can't live with that; I don't want that for this town. Or for either of us."

Emmy's piercing gaze shifted between my eyes as she assessed my sincerity, the blue in it dimming noticeably, her hands knitting more loosely in her lap.

"And I'm . . . Emmy, I am *so* sorry about Delilah and the wards," I continued, my voice fracturing, my lips trembling with the effort of holding back tears.

A different me would have hated that, such an admission of weakness in front of a member of a rival family. But I didn't feel any self-castigation, not a hint of regret. If anything, I was glad Emmy could hear my remorse, see that I truly meant what I said.

"That was a terrible mistake, the worst choice I've ever made," I continued, wresting myself back under control. "I can't undo it, or make any excuses for myself. And I know, I understand, that there'll have to be consequences for me. I accept that, whatever they end up being—along with whatever kind of restitution I can offer."

"I'm really glad to hear that, Nina," Emmy said, that little smile widening into something more genuine. "So. What shall we do, the two of us, instead of dueling?"

24

Fire in the Sky

I STOOD IN FRONT of Morty's door for almost five minutes before I summoned the courage to knock. I knew he could feel me out here on the threshold; even through the shielded bond, being this close to him felt like standing at the outermost periphery of a bonfire, its warmth enticingly close but just out of reach. And if I could feel him inside, that meant he could feel me, too—and he wasn't opening the door for me.

What if he couldn't forgive me, even though I'd done the right thing? What if he decided that I'd taken too long with my decision, that someone who struggled so hard with what they wanted, who couldn't immediately choose honor and nobility, wasn't a person he wanted in his life?

Only one way to find out, I guessed.

My stomach lurching with preemptive, aching nausea, I rapped my fist against the peeling wood.

He opened on the second knock—so he *had* been waiting for me to make the move. His hair was wet from a recent shower, and he stood barefoot, in a black tank that bared his collarbones and those corded, watercolored arms, ripped jeans that clung low to his hips. We stared at each other for a moment, long enough for him to prop a forearm against the doorjamb, shift his weight into it in a feline way that made my insides flutter despite everything.

"Well?" he said, carefully neutral, jeweled eyes shifting between mine. "Did you have something to say to me?"

"Yes," I replied, swallowing. "I do. Could I—do you think I could come in, to talk?"

He licked his lips, considering. I couldn't quite feel his uncertainty through the shielded bond, but I could speculate what he felt; a deep ambivalence about letting me in, in case what I had to tell him meant that we'd never be seeing each other again. The kind of emotions you wouldn't want seeping into your apartment walls, tainting them with the memory.

"Sure," he said finally, shifting sideways to let me move past him. He smelled even more strongly than normal of almond skin and floral hair product, and I had a dual lurch of sensation as the pit of my stomach tightened with both instant desire and fear of rejection.

Morty's living room was cozily dim, soft lamplight falling across the plush scarlet beanbags and blue velvet couch, the Turkish rug draped over the floorboards somehow managing not to clash with the rest of the eclectic decor. Old-school framed movie posters hung all over the walls, from *Indiana Jones* and *Star Wars* to *Blade Runner*, alongside Vampire Weekend and Ratatat concert flyers. I didn't remember having seen the collapsible silks rig in the corner by the window, its tip taller than the dormer windows; maybe he'd been practicing before his shower.

I followed him to the couch, sitting down primly with legs crossed, unsure how close to him I was allowed to be. He took the other end of the couch, establishing a firm buffer zone between us, though even at that distance his proximity made my head swim a little, heat rising to my cheeks.

Triple goddess, it was so fucking awkward to be this turned on by someone who might be chucking you out of their place in a matter of minutes.

He cocked his head, eyebrows raised. "Well? It's your show, Nina. Tell me what's up."

"Emmy came to see me yesterday," I began, twisting my hands nervously in my lap. "She knew—she'd found out that Gareth and I were there, that one of us had glamoured Delilah. She, ha, thought it was Gareth. So she was starting her inquiry with me, instead. The reasonable Blackmoore."

Morty's jaw tightened at the mention of Gareth's name, but he didn't respond, watching me silently. So he'd meant it literally; this was my solo show. He wasn't going to make it any easier for me by participating in this conversation.

"I came clean with her," I continued, lacing my fingers so tightly the knobs of my knuckles pressed painfully against each other. "Told her everything. About the goddess, my deity's favor, the stone. What my family had wanted me to do with it."

At that, I thought I could detect a glimmer of shock in those azure eyes, as if implicating my family was a different tack than he'd been expecting. But he kept his face schooled into near-perfect neutrality, not so much as a twitch at the corner of his mouth.

"She thought maybe I wanted to duel with her," I said, with a rueful little laugh. "The Great British Sorcery-Off, she called it, which, actually funny. But I said—I said no. I told her I didn't want to be Thistle Grove's supervillain-in-residence, or her enemy, to take what belongs to her and to all the other witches in this town. And that I was sorry for what I'd done to Delilah, and willing to do whatever it took to make things right with her."

"So you're going to give back the stone?" he said, and I could feel a hot, bright pulse of *something* even through the shielded bond. "And what, your family's just gonna let you do that?"

"I won't be asking them for permission," I replied, swallowing down a piercing pang of pain at the thought of letting the stone go, losing that dazzling conflagration, that celestial fire gone from me forever. "I'll have to talk to Gareth about it, of course, since he's keeping it for me—but he'll do the right thing, too. I know it."

"But will that be enough? Just returning the stone? You were distorting power channels before you even had it."

"I'm going to return the deity's favor to Belisama, too," I said, unable to keep my eyes from surging hot with tears at the thought of the loss. "I think . . . I'm pretty sure I know how to do that, now. What she wants to hear from me before she'll accept the return. That's why I came here tonight, actually—I'll be going to the lake tomorrow night to do it, with Emmy. And I was hoping . . . I was really hoping you'd want to be there, too."

He took a long, shuddering inhale, closing his eyes tight. When he opened them, they shimmered bright with tears, the cooler counterpart to mine.

"*Of course* I'll come with you," he said, sliding across the couch to pull me against him. The wave of relief that broke over me was so sweet and tremendous that I laughed a little, so absolutely thrilled to be touching him. "Oh, thank fucking baby Jesus you made the right call. You have *no* idea how scared I was that you'd go dark side, and I'd have to let you leave without ever kissing you again."

"So . . . you *do* want to kiss me, then, is what I'm hearing," I said, just a little coy, my heart racing even harder.

"I want to kiss you, and I am so goddamn proud of you, and I also want to do much more than kiss you," he said, bringing his lips close to mine without quite touching. "How's that plan sound?"

"Fabulous," I assured him, brushing the tip of my nose against his. "Flawless, in fact."

"Dope. I also really want you to drop that shielding right now, please." His arms tightened around my waist. "Because I want to feel you again."

He did not have to ask me twice.

The shield dissolved with a single concentrated thought from me, and as his emotions collided with mine, I gasped aloud at the force of them—he *was* proud of me, bursting with pride and awe commingled with delight, along with a profound respect and understanding for how difficult the decision must have been for me. And I could feel just how impressed he was that I'd managed to choose against my lifelong conditioning, how strong and brave and bold he thought that made me.

A forever-demigoddess in the soul, even when I was no longer one in the flesh.

It stripped away any of my lingering doubts about whether I'd done the right thing. Washed me clean of them entirely, like a cool, welcome tide.

"I don't think I'm as amazing as you think I am," I whispered into the space between our lips. "But thank you anyway, for thinking it."

"You're right," he whispered back. "What you are is even better than that."

And he meant it, I could feel how much. Because with him, I didn't have to be perfect, or anywhere even near it. I just had to be good, and that was more than enough.

His mouth melted against mine, and in an instant his tank was tugged over his head, my sweater pulled off and tossed on the floor as I climbed onto his lap. The feel of his skin against mine as his emotions surged inside me was delicious, intoxicating, an elevation of arousal that made me feel something close to high. I pulled back to look at him, the utter, improbable beauty of that delicately etched face and dazzling eyes, the luminous way he watched me as I wove my fingers through his damp hair. I might be readying to give up all the borrowed light and fire I'd been given, but he himself *was* light.

Maybe that was the answer, why the goddess had bound the two of us together. Because here was a fire that I could keep for myself, something that was meant to be mine.

"Why do you always do that?" He exhaled on a light laugh, eyes heavy-lidded with pleasure as I ran my palms down his cheeks, the sides of his neck, the firm lines of his chest.

"Because I like to look at you," I told him, leaning forward to nuzzle my cheek against his. "It makes me happy."

Dipping my head, I ran my lips down his neck, then sank my teeth into the defined curve of his shoulder, like I wanted to do whenever I saw it bare. I bit down hard, hard enough for him to feel a bright sting of pain that made his hips buck against mine, a low groan tearing from his throat.

Moving slowly, deliberately, teeth followed by lips and tongue, I bit him from the outer curve of his shoulder to his throat, leaving a series of imprints on his skin, little crescents that marked him as mine. His hands roamed over my back, fingertips digging hard into the tuck of my waist, palms sweeping up to cup my breasts and squeeze them through my bra.

"Bedroom," I whispered to him, nipping at his ear. "Now."

By the time we made it to his bed, we'd both somehow managed to shed pants and underwear with impressive efficiency, leaving a messy trail of discarded clothing behind us. Then there was only skin and heat, the length of him against me as he pressed me into the comforter, trailing kisses down my ribs and stomach, nipping at the insides of my thighs until I thought I might pass out from breathing so hard. His mouth moved between my legs, the slick heat of his tongue sliding deftly against me as his lips fit around my clit, making me cry out. I could feel the intensity of his reaction to my own wetness and warmth, the way sucking and licking me made him feel the same kind of out-of-control lust.

And he felt mine, the pleasure building in me to that sweet, piercing crescendo, so hard and fast it took all I had to keep it at bay.

"Fuck, you taste so perfect, Nina," he breathed against me, trembles racing up my legs at his exhale. "I could do this all damn night."

"Some other time," I promised, pressing my head back into his pillows. "Tonight, I want you inside me. Right now."

He slid up my body, bolstering himself on his forearms, hands cupped warmly around my face. We were kissing deep as he slid slowly, carefully inside me, me gasping into his mouth as my head arched back.

"Like that?" he asked, a low chuckle in his voice.

"Like that," I confirmed shakily, biting back another gasp.

He rocked against me; not the full length of him, just enough to drive me wild with the promise of much more. It felt like the most agonizing sweetness, a delicious, tantalizing tease that made me swear into his mouth. He drew back enough to smile at me, and for a moment we grinned at each other, purely delighted that we were here together, so entwined and vulnerable.

"Stop teasing me, Gutierrez," I demanded, reaching up to snare his lips in a biting kiss. "And show me some things."

"If you insist."

"And don't be careful with me, you know I want this. I want to feel everything."

With a shuddering groan, he thrust fully into me, in deep and forceful strokes that made me press my palms against his head-board to steady myself, take perverse pleasure in how hard it smacked against the wall. I wasn't sure if Morty had neighbors on this side, but if he did, they weren't going to be at all confused about what was happening tonight. I shifted to sling both legs over his shoulders, wanting even more; more impact, more pressure, simply more of everything.

The resulting angle was so deep that my moans pitched up into little shrieks, and I slid a hand between us, so caught up in my own pleasure and Morty's own spiraling lust that I couldn't wait to come.

"Almost there," I moaned into his mouth, tangling one hand tight into his hair. "So close."

"I know," he gasped against me, running his tongue along my lower lip. "Me too."

When I came, it was with the kind of clenching, seismic spasm that felt like it echoed through my body, melting down my legs and curling my toes—stronger than something should ever be and still leave you alive after it. But it was doubled, tripled, then raised to an impossible degree by Morty's own orgasm, fitting into the seams that mine left behind, drenching us both with a shocking flood of pleasure. I could hear myself screaming as if from a tunnel's length away, in a raw, stripped cadence that sounded like it belonged to someone else but felt entirely mine— and hearing Morty, too, the helpless pitch of his own cries, only leveled everything up.

The pleasure felt like it took much longer than it should to subside, furious aftershocks that sent reverberating ripples through us both. When it finally receded, Morty lowered himself onto me with shaking arms, his heart beating so furiously through his chest I could feel it hammering against mine.

"Could I just chill here for a minute," he panted, "or am I too heavy? Because if I move right now, I might straight die."

"Oh, don't die, please." I wrapped my arms and legs around him, cheek pressed against his, his hair damp and cool against my temple. "You stay right where you are, and take your time."

LATER, LYING NESTLED against his chest with my skin still teeming with warmth, a twinging, unexpected sadness snuck over me. "What's wrong, babe?" Morty murmured sleepily. He'd been drowsing while I listened to the calming cadence of his breath and thought myself in circles; I rarely got to enjoy a mellow orgasmic afterglow, "Not today, peace," being my brain's staunchest slogan.

"It's just . . ." I swallowed hard, wishing I felt differently, not wanting to ruin this oasis of serenity for either of us. "I'm going to miss it so much, being this strong. Having this much magic living inside of me."

Morty stayed silent for a moment, but I could feel the surge of his sympathy through the bond.

"Why don't we say goodbye to it, then?" he suggested, kissing the top of my head. "In a formal way. Have a private little ceremony for you, together?"

"What do you mean?"

He sat up slowly against the headboard, drawing me up with him. "This building has a roof deck. And it's late as hell, and cold to boot . . . so there won't be anyone outside to see."

"See what?" I said, forehead wrinkling as I peered up at him in the dark.

"You, silly, in all your glory. Come on, let's throw on some clothes and I'll tell you what I mean."

Fifteen minutes later, we stood bundled under a night sky so glassy and brilliant it looked like a fissured black mirror laid over some gigantic source of light, like the chaos of stars was shining not from but through it. A waxing half-moon hung among them, like a pale and heavy-lidded eye. Ghosts of our breath tumbled up and away from us as we stood next to each other, watching the dark, distant outline of Hallows Hill against the horizon; the few glimmering lights still on at Yarrow a few streets over; the more distant, deeper black of the Witch Woods that appeared somehow matte, cut from a darker bolt of velvet than the night.

It was past three, and a near-absolute hush had settled over the town, not so much as the distant rumble of a car engine gunning to disturb it. Just the whistle of the wind past the rooftops, the chill density of the air itself pressing into our ears. The night smelled of sharp cold and woodsmoke, so purely wintry it made even me a bit nostalgic about how soon we'd be meeting the winter solstice, the world pivoting back toward spring.

"This is your chance," Morty murmured to me, pressing his still-warm cheek against mine. "Cast away; cast anything you want. Make some big ol' fireworks. Nobody's awake to see, and even if they are, the glamour'll take care of it."

"I thought we were Team Anti-Glamour here," I said, even as the craving reared up in me to make some magic, tap into that radiant internal heat.

"This one time, I think we can put the moral compasses down for a minute." His gloved fingers tightened around mine, giving me a squeeze. "You're doing a hard, hard thing here, Nina. And you deserve this; one last night to let go. To just give in to what you want."

"Maybe you're right," I whispered back, taking a few steps away from him into the center of the shoveled-off roof deck, the weathered floorboards creaking under my boots. I closed my eyes and lifted my hands, sifting through my mental repertoire of spells that drew on light and fire; the ones that Belisama's favor would take to best. "Here we go."

Then I flung a parade of spells up into the star-prickled black canvas of the sky.

One after another, not even pausing for the buffer of a breath in between them, because I didn't need it. I was a furnace, a forge, a human Promethean fire, and the spells rolled out of me like I'd been born to cast them exactly like this, blazing and spectacular, one final, glorious time. A blinding deluge of cosmic fireworks that burst so high I could imagine they must be visible even in the stratosphere, to the gods or anyone else who happened to be peering down at us.

I started with Phoenix Rising, the birds' golden plumage melting immediately into Polaris's Ascent—a tremendous, pulsing, platinum star like a diamond mined from ice and light, that went soaring up into the darkness as if to join its natural sisters. After that came Brigid's Primordial Spark, followed by Spears of Dying Sun, Apollo's Radiant Quiver, Moonlight Grazing Water, and the Infinite Aurora. With each new spell, the seed of fire inside me burned hotter rather than guttering, those dragon wings beating against the constraints of my ribs in a wild, triumphant euphoria.

I could only imagine how monumental this would feel if I were holding Belisama's stone, and for a moment I felt like I was falling, into an all-consuming abyss of sadness at the idea that I was letting the stone go. Could I go through with it, after all? Was it too late to reconsider whether I should keep what felt so rightfully mine?

Then I glanced over my shoulder to see Morty's face, rapt and delighted, flickering with my own magic-made light as he laughed into the sky. And I knew that I couldn't possibly do anything that would compromise that pride, risk losing that faith and joy in me.

The person I'd become if I kept this temporary gift wouldn't be one that either of us could love.

So I kept casting and casting and casting into the sky for what felt like hours, until the twinned joy and grief overwhelmed me, closed over my heart like stage curtains drawing shut. And when I dropped to my knees on the cold floorboards, sobbing like my heart would break with the immensity of everything I'd never feel again, Morty was there to catch me, to pull me against him and hold me tight. To feel and share the firestorm inside me until it subsided, and left mostly peace behind.

25

Say Goodbye to Fire, Farewell to Light

THE FOUR OF us stood by the lake, under a starstruck sky veined by the wavering emerald of the northern lights. There was no snow tonight, only the black mirror of the winter night; hushed, this time, somehow expectant. As if it knew that soon, there'd be something to see below.

Morty and I were in the middle, gloved hands joined. Gareth stood to my left, Belisama's stone in his hands. I'd gone to him earlier today to tell him what I'd decided, give him the chance to make his own choice. He could stand with me on this, or he could decide to go to Lyonesse and Igraine, pick blood and mindless loyalty over the dignity and power of doing the right thing.

I'd known—or at least hoped—that he would choose me. Choose the right kind of change, for both of us. And he had,

LANA HARPER

though I also knew that as scion, his betrayal would be considered even greater than mine, the strain on him more than anything he'd ever had to withstand before. Obedience and family fealty were ingrained powerfully in the both of us, down to the bone; but he'd always bought into it with more gusto than I did, and less critical thinking. It would be even harder for him to rebuild himself after this, discover who he was in his own right without the stamp of the Blackmoore name on him.

Emmy stood on the other end, to Morty's right. I didn't think her presence would be necessary, at least not magically, but I wanted her to bear witness. To know that I meant this sacrifice fully, was committed to staying this course. She caught my eye as I looked over at her, gave me a small, solemn nod of respect.

"It's difficult," she said, tears glimmering in her eyes—and I knew she must be remembering the mantle, and ceding it to Delilah for the final round of the Gauntlet that Samhain, before she stepped in as Natalia Avramov's champion. "Believe me, I know. And you're brave, so brave, to do it."

"Thank you," I said, biting the inside of my lip. "That means a lot coming from you, Victor and Voice."

I closed my eyes, let the icy breeze ruffle my hair, listening to it whisper through the pine needles of the trees that ringed the lake.

"You ready, milady?" Morty whispered to me, squeezing my hand.

"As I'll ever be," I murmured back, leaning over to brush a kiss over his cheek before turning back to the lake; focusing on that heat inside me, the glowing ember. The goddess's gift.

"Lady," I started, in a whisper. "Belisama, if that's a name you like. I came to thank you for your favor. I know, now, what you did for me. And I . . . I think I know why you did it, too."

A thread of light raced through the lake, just the slightest glimmer, before vanishing. Nothing like the storm of fallen stars that had greeted me the last time. This was more of an acknowledgment, a subtle tip of the head; a sign that deep beneath fathoms upon fathoms of black water, she was listening.

"I needed power," I said, my voice gaining in strength and volume. "I needed control—but not the kind I had before. The suffocating kind that wrapped around my neck, and wouldn't let me breathe or live or *be*. So you gave me fire; you lent me light; you gifted me the kind of love I didn't think existed. Or at least a taste of it. The promise of what could be, if I was brave enough."

The light flared again, and this time the breeze through the trees sounded almost like a voice, the whispering breath of a low, sweet chuckle.

"You gave me *everything* I needed to find my own strength," I said, my voice trembling now, tears prickling in my nose. "To step into the right kind of power. But I don't think you intended for me to keep it forever, did you? Not if it meant that everyone but my family had to lose power of their own. Not if it meant Emmy losing what's hers by right—because if she's the Voice, that must mean you know her, too. That she's also yours, even if she isn't touched by you like I am."

Another flare of light, an approving sigh from the trees, as if to say, *Go on.*

"This was just a push for me, a nudge in the right direction. A stepping-stone. And to really accept what you've given me, to complete that transformation . . . this last bit is part of it, too. I'm so grateful—so deeply thankful—for having had it. But I have to let it go now. Give it back to you."

I turned to Gareth, offering him my palm. "The stone, brother," I said, trying to keep my voice from quaking as I swallowed back tears.

"One last time," he said, low, his eyes catching the pale glint of the waxing half-moon above. "I have to ask . . . are you sure?"

"I'm sure," I said. And I was, even if my voice fractured, even if I felt like I might cry for days once the deed was done.

Then the stone was in my hand, my mind and body suffused in liquid fire, ecstatic power surging through every fiber of me. Illuminating me until I felt like I was no longer even flesh and blood, but something purely wrought of light. There was no ceiling waterfall this time, but the lake itself began a shimmering ripple, lapping toward me, creeping over the frozen edge like a personalized tide.

I clutched the stone tight, willing the seeded goddess ember inside me to meld with that flood of light, to rejoin it. And when I wound my arm back and flung the stone into the water, I could feel it leave me in a dizzying, forceful rush; all of it as one, including the little spark that had been the root of the favor. The coin disappeared from my pants pocket in the same instant; I could feel it vanish, huff out into nothing. If Morty hadn't been holding my other hand so tightly, I would have sagged where I stood, fallen to my knees like I had the previous night, pressed my forehead to the frozen ground and wailed like some tragic Shakespearean figure.

Because it *hurt* to lose that ferocious power, to feel it tear out of me like a thorn. To say goodbye to fire, farewell to light. To know nothing would ever be so fiercely bright and warm inside of me again, not after tonight.

As soon as the stone hit the lake's surface, the whole of the water turned a scintillating, blazing white, dancing with pearly effervescence, little bubbles of silver rising to the top. The air seemed to warm around us, dispelling some of the wintry frost. And I could *hear* the goddess in my mind again, though I didn't think she'd spoken aloud—at any rate, none of the others seemed to register the enormity of her belling voice, caught up instead with the blinding dazzle of the lake.

> O MY NINA
> MY VERY CLEVER NINA
> I KNEW THAT YOU WOULD FIND YOUR
>   WAY TO UNDERSTANDING
> AND WHAT OF YOUR NEW LOVE . . . WOULD
>   YOU BOTH KEEP IT, OR RETURN THAT,
>   TOO?

I turned to Morty, tears shimmering hot in my eyes.

"She wants to know . . ." I began, my throat tightening, "if we want to keep the bond, or break it. If we break it, I don't think you'll get to keep the magic; that isn't how that works. But if we keep it . . ."

"Then I stay a witch, but we're bound forever," he said gently, his delicate face luminous in the flood of light shining from the lake. "No matter what. Even if we decide we aren't for each other, right?"

"Yes. It would make conscious uncoupling kind of tricky, at the very least. And you and I . . . you know how different we are. Who knows if we're going to want the same kind of life?"

He huffed a laugh, brought my gloved knuckles to his lips for a grazing kiss. "I mean, does *anyone* ever know that for sure, when it comes to another person? What I do know is, I'm willing to take that risk if you are. So, what do you think?"

"I think that *yes*," I whispered fiercely, leaning in to press my forehead against his. "I think that out of all of this, you were the best gift by far. And I think we see where it takes us."

The light in the lake flickered once, twice, and then three times, as if in acknowledgment. Then it winked out, leaving us all engulfed in the chill mountaintop night.

26

A New Era for Us All

AFTER EVERYTHING, IT seemed profoundly strange that the Wheel of the Year continued to turn as it always did—leading inexorably to Yule, the return of the light after winter's deepest darkness. But that was the point, and the comfort of it, too; no matter the weight of your pain or loss, the world only ever knew how to move on.

And so did you, even if you'd lost something like a goddess ember, even if you were only just a witch again.

One who possibly no longer even had a family, depending on how things shook out. In the week since I'd relinquished my power, nothing had happened yet with Lyonesse and Igraine; Gareth and I were still waiting for the other shoe to drop. Emmy hadn't made any move to impose sanctions on us, either, for the way we'd kept things from her—but that, I suspected, was just a matter of time, too.

And what better time to lay down the law than when we all gathered for the Winter Solstice ball.

This year, the Thorns were taking their turn to host at Honeycake Orchards. I'd always loved a good Thorn Yule; rather than hosting inside Honeycake Cottage, their demesne proper, they liked to erect what was functionally a greenhouse made of magic. A vast weatherproofing spell yielded a transparent dome to keep out the cold and snow, trellised by a network of living plants shoring up the casting. This kind of elemental working fell more squarely within my family's wheelhouse than the Thorns' affinity for green magic—so they tweaked it, relied on their facility with flora to boost the elemental spell itself.

This year, the dome looked slightly different than I remembered from previous Yules. I could see fine skeins of wispy darkness lacing through the green, as though ectoplasm had also been braided through the casting for even more stability. A nod, most likely, to the unexpected new alliance between the Thorn and Avramov families—Isidora Avramov and Rowan Thorn, partnered since last Beltane, had probably cast this dome between the two of them.

The end result was like standing under a smoky glass bell full of plants; curling ivy and flowers creeping up an invisible curvature, upon which also hung mistletoe, holly, and pine-needle wreaths with clusters of candles suspended in their centers. The warm air smelled like sharp pine, mulled wine, and cinnamon, along with a hint of woodsmoke even though there wasn't any fire beneath the dome. Above, you could see the unabashed glitter of Thistle Grove's diamond stars embedded in the night, the feathering drift of snowflakes that spiraled all around the dome. Some of the topmost plants were even enchanted to glow like chandeliers, shedding a natural luster on the witches gathered below.

And the moon was close to full, bright and enormous as a lantern, so radiant we could have celebrated by its light alone.

"Okay, well, maybe you *are* Bo," Jessa had said breathlessly when I'd led her into the dome with my arm looped through hers, Morty on my other side, Jessa's eyes wide and enthralled as she took everything in. "Because this is, *absolutely*, some other fairy shit."

"*Witch* shit, Kenz," I'd corrected gleefully, giving her a squeeze. "Though I will say I feel like you're bringing much more of that spicy succubus energy than I am tonight."

She'd shimmied her shoulders, bare above the black fur trim of her extremely clingy and low-cut black-and-silver cocktail gown, with an enviable lacy train included. "When one gets invited to their first witch party, one does not hold back, you know?"

Inspired by Morty's reasoning, I'd petitioned Emmy for an exemption to the oblivion glamour for Jessa, explaining that I wanted my best friend—my platonic life partner, someone who I knew would always matter deeply to me—to know who I truly was. *All* of who I was. I'd even suggested that this was something she might consider on a larger scale, from her Victor's perspective; making the glamour a personal decision rather than a sweeping autocratic mandate, by allowing witches the freedom to choose whom they felt safe sharing their secret with.

She'd told me that she would take it under advisement, but I could see immediately that the idea appealed to her. Unlike my grandmother, or any of the other Blackmoores who'd led before her, Emmy was an egalitarian sort of Victor. The kind of person who strove for justice and fairness in every aspect of her role.

I was really beginning to cultivate a new respect for her, along with a genuine liking.

In turn, Jessa had taken the news of my secret identity with her usual aplomb and passionate zeal for anything remotely interesting—and this development made me *much* more interesting than I'd ever previously been in our shared history.

"Are you for fucking real right now?" she'd demanded, grinning wildly as I lobbed witchlights around for her as proof, transformed her ceiling fan into glimmering sheaves of peacock feathers and back again. "I get why you couldn't tell me before—that good magic always comes with bullshit rules for the civilians—but *come on*, it's me! All those years of *Supernatural* and *Magicians*, and not even a dropped hint? Fuck, you owe me an entire decade of casting entirely at my whim."

She'd loved Morty in person, too, just like I'd expected, and would likely never stop patting herself on the back for her pivotal role in bringing us together. All three of us now wore complementary gowns, like a matched set; I was in red and gold, a fiery satin that the old Nina would never have chosen before, but that blazed beautifully against my blond updo and eyeliner-rimmed dark eyes. Morty wore grayscale, a velvet blazer over a silver corset and gray gown, his eyes sapphire against smoky makeup much more elaborate than mine.

I couldn't stop sneaking enamored glances at him, and from the warm admiration and spikes of desire that pulsed reliably through our bond, I knew the feeling was extremely mutual.

Even with whatever else might happen tonight, I couldn't imagine myself happier than this, flanked by the two people who mattered most in my little world.

And for several hours, they were *all* that mattered; sharing mulled wine and iced petit fours with them, dancing with Morty and Jessa in turn, whirling in the candlelight with the brighter-than-bright moon and stars winking above us like a goddess's coin. So much to be dazzled by, even in this, the year's longest and darkest night—the night before the balance finally tipped back toward the light.

Then Emmy swept up onto a podium beneath an evergreen arch studded with holly leaves and berries, and I knew the moment of truth had come for us.

The crowd stilled at once, before she'd even said anything; she glowed blue with Thistle Grove's distinctive light, from her eyes to her hands, where she held them clasped by her waist. She'd been wearing a dress the last time I'd seen her dancing with her partner, Natalia Avramov, but now she wore the Harlow family robes, the Victor's Wreath gleaming on her hair.

"Blessed Yule to all," she began, with a little smile. "And thank you to the Thorns for their gracious welcome, and the beautiful display they've designed for us tonight . . . with some assistance from the Avramovs."

So I'd been right about that, I thought, my gaze skimming over to where Rowan and Isidora stood near the podium, holding hands.

He wore a beautifully tailored but fairly staid navy blue suit, his long locs drawn back, while she wore elbow-length lace gloves and billows of gauzy black tulle like ectoplasm. Her entire freckled, milky back was bared down to the twin dimples at its base, her dark red hair braided into an almost sculptural updo. They looked like the most perfect mismatch in the history of time—highlighted by the subtle, elegant way Rowan bowed his head to Emmy, while Isidora dipped much lower than necessary, her black dress pooling around her, into what was clearly the sassiest of curtsies. How the two of them functioned as a couple was a mystery for the ages.

Then again, I thought, sneaking another glance at Morty, who was I to talk?

"Before we fully embrace the light," Emmy continued, her blue-tinged gaze sweeping over the gathered crowd, the wreath throbbing with sapphire light, "there are some things I'd like to share with all of you, knowledge that has come to light. First, a recent revelation, particularly well suited to Yule—we finally know more about Lady's Lake, what makes it magical. There's a statue of a goddess lying at the bottom—a deity named Belisama, to the best of our understanding. We still have no notion how and why she came to be there. But if you'd like to learn more about her, I'd direct you to Tomes & Omens, where both James and Delilah Harlow will be happy to share what we *do* know."

A moment of stunned silence followed, almost immediately splintered by an excited susurrus of whispers, as clusters of people began turning toward one another and breaking into quiet but urgent conversation. In the crowd, I could see my mother's and grandmother's icy blond heads snap toward each other like twin hawkish cameos.

Then they both turned, frosty gazes trawling the crowd—in search of me and Gareth, presumably. Because who else could have gone to Emmy, besides the two of us?

My stomach dropped instinctively, and Morty twined his fingers through mine in response. "You have nothing to be afraid of," he murmured to me, grazing a kiss over my cheek. "They can't hurt you, Nina, because you won't let them. And *I* won't, either. You know I won't."

"Of course I know," I whispered, squeezing back. "And I'm not afraid. Not of them, anyway. Not anymore."

Emmy lifted her hands to still the chatter, and all heads swiveled back to her.

"Unfortunately," she said, a cool, dignified determination settling over her face, that strobing blue light intensifying until it seemed to emanate from her entire person, "it has also come to my attention that Elder Blackmoore purposely withheld this vital information from me for weeks, with clearly malicious intent. Her actions contributed to the ongoing magical fluctuations most of you have experienced, the weakening of our communal power. And thus, I invoke the Rule of Victor's Justice, as is my prerogative as described by the Grimoire."

This time, a stuttering gasp raced through the crowd as everyone caught their breath, hands flying to mouths, astonished glances exchanged, along with a growing angry murmur. We all knew the rule existed, but it hadn't been invoked in generations; there had always been a tribunal instead, for every level of infraction.

Emmy was sending an unmistakable message here, and it was that a breach of trust had been perpetrated of such a shattering magnitude that she wouldn't even stand for a trial.

This time the punishment would be delivered by her edict, with no room for appeal.

"Elder Blackmoore," she intoned, her voice gaining a new, menacing knell that I knew must stem from her dual magical authority, "by the Rule of Victor's Justice, I hereby strip you of your status. Anyone willing to plot against the Victor and Voice of Thistle Grove—and willing to act to the community's detriment— is unfit to lead one of the four families. You will not be banished, but you *will* be severed, cut off from your magic for this act of treachery committed against both town and lake."

I could see my mother stagger in place, fury and shock blasting across her face.

"Mercy, Victor!" she cried out as she sagged, leaning against my grandmother for support. I didn't know how the blockage of magic worked, but presumably it was already in effect, stripping my mother of all the power she'd ever known. The worst sort of loss any of us could imagine. "We—*I*—plead for mercy! According to the rule, I am willing to atone, to suffer *any* other punishment—"

"No," Emmy tolled, simple and stony. "In accordance with my will as Victor, it is already done, the decision made. The role of Elder will transfer forthwith to Scion Gareth Aurelius Blackmoore, for a trial period of a year, at which time I reserve the right to reconsider. Elder Blackmoore, may you bear the burden and privilege of leadership with more grace than those who've come before you."

I glanced around frantically until I spotted Gareth in the crowd—slack-jawed and blushing, a strange mix of utter shock and pride commingled on his face. At any other time, I would have considered this a terrible call, an absurd mistake on Emmy's part, but not now; not given how hard Gareth had been working to build a better version of himself. She was giving him a proper chance to grow, to make good on all that potential he'd been wasting for so many years. Maybe he *was* capable of forging a new and better path for our family.

A road to being Blackmoores who contributed instead of inflicting damage, who molded themselves to the needs of this town rather than the other way around.

And then, as I knew she would, Emmy turned to me. Icy panic swirled inside me like a blizzard, a needling rush from my skull down to my toes as I steeled myself for her pronouncement.

"Nineve Cliodhna Blackmoore," she intoned, and then, more gently, "Nina. For your role in these events—for both the great good and the ill you've done—I sentence you to a year of limited magic. You will not cast any working at all, unless someone around you finds themselves in grave peril. And alongside Delilah Harlow and at her instruction, you will help restore the lost wardings at Tomes & Omens."

I inclined my head to her in acknowledgment, my heart pounding like a mallet as an intense wash of relief surged through me— because this wasn't terrible at all, nowhere near as severe a punishment as it could have been. This was only what I deserved. And even if I didn't have access to my own magic for an entire year—a prospect that, despite everything, filled me with an agonizing sense of preemptive loss—I would still have Morty to teach. I'd even be able to feel his own burgeoning grasp on magic through our bond.

"This is okay, right, babe?" Morty said, his thumb skimming the inside of my wrist, pressing down gently so he could feel my pulse flicker against the pad of his thumb. "You can handle this?"

"Yes," I whispered back. "She could have . . . it could have been much, much worse."

Not only that, Emmy had chosen to divulge nothing about what had really happened, granting me privacy. This way I could control the narrative, tell my story only if I wanted to, to whomever I deemed fit to hear it. It was both gracious and kind of her, the ultimate courtesy—and more than anything, it made me believe she didn't bear any real grudge against me.

And if I was going to be working with Delilah, that likely meant even she didn't completely hate me for what I'd done to her—and that meant almost more than anything.

"I would also call on you to serve as counsel to the Victor and Voice," Emmy went on, that fierce blue glow around her subsiding a little. "An advisor in a formal role, to me as well as the new Elder Blackmoore. I've found your perspective enlightening, and I suspect we would both benefit from each other's . . . lived experience, moving forward."

"Shit, I think you just got a promotion," Jessa murmured, with a little nudge. "That, and she wants a former demigoddess on her team."

"That will be all," Emmy concluded, the swarming blue light around her winking out entirely. "Have a blessed Yule—and may this solstice mark a new era for us all!"

As she stepped down from the podium, I smiled to myself, because, ironically, my grandmother and mother had been righter than they knew. This *would* be a new age for the Blackmoores, and for the whole of Thistle Grove, but not the kind the two of them had been envisioning.

The kind, instead, that would let us all step into power without trampling anybody else.

The kind that was going to let me be both Nina and Nineve, secure in my own skin, cherished by those who really mattered. Advisor to Emmy and my brother; lover and teacher to Morty; forever best friend to Jessa, no secrets lurking between us to undermine. Neither demigoddess nor mere witch, but everything I'd ever willed and wanted for myself, and would in days to come—because what we wanted for ourselves was ever subject to change.

What I wanted for myself now was all the light I could imagine, starting with the end of this longest night.

And I knew that somewhere, deep beneath the water of some very far-flung lake, a sleeping goddess stirred a little in her slumber. Her perfect lips curving with the suggestion of a smile.

Acknowledgments

))) ● (((

One of the many beautiful things about writing a series—especially a witchy one—is that each book not only allows you to explore a new facet of a magical town and its community, but also gives you the chance to lean into a totally different emotional experience. While *Payback's a Witch* was my safe and sparkly happy-place book, and *From Bad to Cursed* my opportunity to explore the darker side of Thistle Grove, Nina's almost-villain origin story was closer to therapy. It let me dive deeper into a more ponderous (and very adult) emotional journey than I'd ever done before, and gave me a lovely, healing outlet for personal trauma I was working through myself. That being the case, I'm even more grateful to have had the chance to write this particular book.

As ever, I'm indebted to my editor, Cindy Hwang, for her loving care and brilliant shaping of this story. To the entire team at Berkley—Stephanie, Elisha, Bridget, Angela, Katie, Julie, and everyone else so reliably making the magic happen behind the scenes—thank you so much for everything you do for me and Thistle Grove.

ACKNOWLEDGMENTS

Taylor, Jasmine, Holly, and everyone else in the Root Literary coven, thank you for your attention, wisdom, and hand-holding. Where/what would I be without you?! Quite weepy and messy, probably.

More than with either of the previous books, I leaned on my fabulous critique group crew (Jilly, Chelsea, and Adriana) to reassure me that the heavier subject matter, more intense magic, and predominantly Blackmoore narrative featured in *Back in a Spell* was hitting right. And massive thanks to my mother, my beloved OG beta reader, who loved Nineve Cliodhna Blackmoore so much that it gave me permission to love Nina like I wanted to.

As always, thank you to my family for the safety net you've always provided, and for the herculean efforts and sacrifice that allowed me to reach this relatively charmed writing life. It still feels like an impossible dream on many days; please know I never take it for granted.

Finally, to the Thistle Grove readers who've stuck by me book after book—you are the true heart of these stories. Thank you for your time, your money, your love for these characters, and every single Instagram, Twitter, and TikTok post celebrating these books (in visually creative ways I could never hope to mimic myself, because my photos/videos are . . . what they are!). You never fail to make my day, and I hope I get to keep surprising you with ancient spells and sleeping goddesses for many books to come.

Back in a Spell

LANA HARPER

Questions for Discussion

1. When we first meet Nina Blackmoore, she feels powerless and downtrodden, stuck in an "emotional fugue state" after having been all but ditched at the altar by her fiancée a year ago. Did her feelings resonate with you and if so, how?

2. Right before her first date with Morty, Nina has a very unusual experience at Lady's Lake. Did you have any thoughts about what might be happening beneath the water's surface, and how did your expectations fit with what we later discover about the lake?

3. Nina and her brothers have a deeply damaging and complicated relationship with their mother and grandmother. Can you identify with or recognize any of these destructive patterns, or are you more familiar with loving and supportive families like Morty's?

4. Did learning more about the Blackmoores and their toxic background shed a different light on Nina's brothers, Gareth and Gawain, for you? Did you find that your perspective on the Blackmoores shifted over the course of the story, or did it stay the same?

5. Nina loves Castle Camelot, and feels that it's much more of a home to her than Tintagel, the Blackmoores' ancestral demesne. What did you think of Castle Camelot after seeing it through Nina's eyes?

6. As a Thistle Grove "normie," Morty has a lot of (largely negative) opinions about the ethics of the oblivion glamour cast over Thistle Grove. To what extent did you agree with him, and could you see Nina's counterpoints as to why the glamour is necessary for the witch community's enduring safety?

7. Nina and Jessa have a very tight-knit relationship; Jessa even moved to Thistle Grove to be closer to her best friend. Do you think Nina's qualms about the fact that Jessa is unaware of her friend's witchy identity are well-founded? Do you think she's letting Jessa down by not trying harder to be more honest with her?

8. Nina's power grows exponentially over the course of the story. What struck you the most about seeing her grapple with her enhanced strength, while guiding Morty on his own journey of magical discovery?

9. What did you think of Nina's behavior at Tomes & Omens? Do you understand why she chose to take such drastic action, or do you condemn her for it?

10. Why do you think Belisama chose to bind Morty and Nina? Do you think it was ultimately helpful to Nina's development—and possibly to Morty's, as well?

11. On the whole, do you think you'd enjoy being the recipient of divine favor the way Nina experienced it? Why or why not?

12. What did you think of the punishments—and promotions—Emmy Harlow doled out at the Thorns' Yule celebration? Would you have chosen similarly or differently?

Keep reading for a preview of the next book in
The Witches of Thistle Grove series by *New York Times*
bestselling author Lana Harper.

In Charm's Way

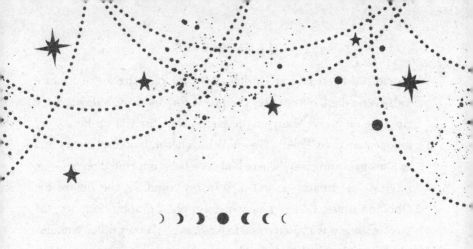

The Smallest Victories

THE VIRIDIAN TEARDROPS *should* have been in bloom by now. That much, at least, I had no trouble remembering.

But I'd been trawling the Hallows Hill woods for almost four hours, walking the forest in as methodical a grid as one could manage on terrain that tended to shift around you like a daydream if you let your attention wander, and I hadn't spotted even a glimmer of the distinctive, iridescent color that gave the flowers their name. A languid twilight had begun to gather above the rustling treetops; an early-summer wash of dusky violets and blues that dipped the already hushed bower in an almost melancholy light, as subdued as a sigh. If anything, I was more likely to spot one of the elusive flowers now than I had been earlier. Viridians unfurled at dusk, revealing glinting amber centers like fireflies—the stamens that contained the magically active pollen I was hunting for.

Six months ago, I wouldn't even have needed to traipse along a grid. I'd been hiking Hallows Hill for pleasure since I was a kid, even when I wasn't on the prowl for floral ingredients for a tincture or brew. Many of the plants that thrived up here were unique, native to Thistle Grove. Which herbs, blooms, lichens, and mosses grew precisely where had once been imprinted on me—an intricate schematic crystallized in my mind. In the Before the Oblivion times, I'd had a near-perfect photographic memory; the kind science wasn't convinced existed, even if every other wunderkind detective on TV claimed to have one.

But I'd *really* had one. The ability to recall whole pages of text I'd read only once; to summon up faded illustrations I'd pored over by candlelight; to confidently rattle off lists of ingredients for obscure potions I'd never even prepared. The Delilah Harlow of the BTO era hadn't had the first notion of just how much she took her mind for granted.

In my bleakest moments, I hated her for that smug complacency almost as much as I hated Nina Blackmoore for what she'd done to me.

Shaking off the creeping angst—in the months since I'd lost and regained most of my memory, I'd developed an excruciating tendency to brood over my own misfortune, a waste of productive time if there ever was one—I turned my attention back to the forest floor. Viridian teardrops often grew in little clusters of three, usually around the exposed root balls of deciduous trees. By this late in May, there should already have been a good crop of them ready for harvest.

But Lady's Lake had been a little tempestuous, lately. Nina Blackmoore's discovery of Belisama's statue at its distant bottom seemed to have stirred up the sleeping avatar, jolted the piece of the goddess that lived in our lake into some semi-elevated state of awareness. Among other things, we now enjoyed spectacular lightning storms crackling just above the lake on an almost weekly basis. Balls of Saint Elmo's fire had been seen drifting down Hallows Hill and through the town below, rolling through walls like ghostly, electrified tumbleweeds and scaring the entire shit out of Thistle Grove normies. (The oblivion glamour cast over the town prevented memory formation of spells cast by Thistle Grove's witches, but it was nowhere near broad enough to cover all the other unusual "meteorological phenomena" the town reliably served up.) Disturbances like that might have seeped into the forest as well, upset its natural growth rhythms or shifted them.

Just as I was about to cut my losses and call it a day, a flash of amber winked in my peripheral vision. I wheeled toward it, a flush of pure joy searing up my throat, like, *See? You've still got it, my bitch!*

It wasn't a typical cluster trio; only a solitary blossom, and on the smallish side as viridians came, growing in a nook just by a sycamore's base. But its teardrop petals were plump and glossy with health, a gorgeously vivid bluish green; nestled within, the stamens quivered with a rich dusting of that precious yellow pollen. If I was careful with it, this single flower would be enough to cast a full iteration of Marauder's Misery—one of the anti-theft wards I'd been restoring at Tomes & Omens ever since Fucking Nina Blackmoore undid three centuries' worth of them, in her brief and catastrophic rampage as a demigoddess.

Flames and stars, living in this town could be *exhausting*.

I sank down by the tree's base, pebbles and blades of grass pressing imprints into my bare knees. Then I closed my eyes and reached for the flower, cupping my hands around it without touching the petals.

Like most magically imbued flora, viridians couldn't just be plucked by mundane means. They needed to be harvested with the use of a particular preservation spell, to keep their potency intact. Magical botany was like that—infinitely fascinating and challenging, and also finicky as shit. Hence, why I loved it. It demanded both finesse and expertise, a deep understanding of theories and disciplines that the other Thistle Grove families largely ignored in favor of relying on their natural talents. Even the Thorns didn't bother with it much, given their affinity for magically coaxing plants into doing whatever they wanted them to do.

But arcane knowledge, and its practical applications . . . that was where Harlows excelled.

Especially *this* Harlow.

I took a slow breath, twitching my fingers into the delicate position called for by the spell, lips parting to speak the incantation. The words floated into my mind's eye in swooping antique copperplate; I could even picture the yellowed page on which the rhyming couplets had been inked.

Then the entirety of the charm sluiced out of my head, like water sliding through a sieve.

All of it, vanished in an instant. The words themselves, the lovely handwriting, the aged grain of the paper. Where the memory had resided, there was now nothing. A cold and empty darkness like a miniature black hole whorling in my head.

The panic that gushed through me was instantaneous, an icy, prickling flood that engulfed me from the crown of my head to the tips of my toes, a flurry of pinheads sinking into my skin. And even worse was the terrible sense of dislocation that accompanied it, as if the entire world had spun wildly on its axis around me before falling back into place awry. I'd *known* that spell, only moments ago. Now, I didn't. It was simply gone, lost, as if it had been plucked directly out of my head by some merciless, meticulous set of tweezers.

It felt nauseatingly like existing in two realities at once. One in which I was the old Delilah, a living library, a vast and unimpeachable repository of arcane information. And another in which I was a tabula rasa, almost no one at all. Just a facsimile of a person rather than somebody real.

The dissonance of it was horrifying, a primal terror I'd never experienced before. The way, I imagined, some people might fear death, that ultimate disintegration of identity if you truly believed nothing else came after.

I sank back onto my haunches, wrapping my arms around my chest. Goose bumps had mustered along the expanse of my skin, and I broke into a clammy sweat despite the buzzy warmth of the air, the humid heat that permeated the forest from the lake. "It's okay, Lilah," I whispered to myself under my breath, rocking back and forth, feeling abysmally pathetic and silly and weak. "You're okay. Try to relax, and let it pass over you. Like a reed in the river, remember? Don't fight against the current, because the current always wins."

Sometimes, the simple mantra Ivy had taught me worked, bleeding off some of the panic.

Other times, it did absolute fuck all.

The worst part was that no one understood why this was *still* happening to me. As a Harlow recordkeeper, I should have been shielded from a conventional oblivion glamour in the first place. Given our role as the memory keepers of our community, Thistle Grove's formal occult historians, we were all bespelled to be immune to such attacks. But Nina's form of the spell had been superpowered, whipped to unfathomable heights by the kernel of divinity that had been lodged inside her, the deity's favor she'd been granted by Belisama.

Why that entitled Blackmoore bitch had been deemed deserving of a goddess's favor in the first place was still beyond me.

In any case, even after the mega glamour dissolved—helped along by my cousin Emmy's and my uncle James's efforts—I wasn't rid of it entirely. Almost six months later, I still sometimes lost memories like this, little aftershocks of oblivion fracturing through me even after all this time. Other times, I reached for knowledge that I should have had—that I *knew* I'd once possessed—only to discover an utter, sucking absence in its place. As if some vestigial remnant of the spell lurked inside me like a malevolent parasite, a magical malaria that only occasionally reared up.

The lost memories did return sometimes, if I relaxed enough in the moment, or if I was able to revisit their original source— reread the page that held the charm, pore over the missing diagram. But sometimes they simply didn't, as if my brain had been rewired and was now inured to retaining that piece of information. And it was unpredictable. Just when I'd begun to tentatively hope that I might be on the upswing, I'd tumble into yet another mental vortex, shifting quicksand where I'd once reliably found the diamond edges of my mind.

But the relaxation methods Ivy had taught me were always worth at least a try. I repeated the sappy "reed in a river" mantra to myself several more times—trying my damnedest not to feel like someone who'd ever wear Spiritual Gangster apparel in earnest—all the while inhaling deliberately through my nose and exhaling out of my mouth. The familiar smell of Lady's Lake calmed me, too; the distinctive scent of the magic that rolled off the water and through the woods, coursing down the mountainside to wash over the town. It was the strongest up here, an intoxi-cating scent like incense. Earthy and musky and sweet, redolent of frankincense and myrrh laced with amber.

As a Harlow, my sense of the lake's magic was both more inti-mate and more acute than that of members of the other families—and the flow of it up here, so close to its wellspring, reassured me. Left me safe in the knowledge that I was still Delilah of Thistle Grove, on her knees on Hallows Hill; a Harlow witch exactly where she belonged.

Abruptly, the harvesting charm slid back into my mind. A lit-tle frayed around the edges, some of the words blurring in and out of sight, as if my memory were a dulled lens that had lost some of its focus. But it *was* back, restored, intact enough that I would be able to use it to collect the viridian.

"Oh, *thank you*," I whispered on a tremulous sigh, my limbs turning jellied with relief, unsure whom I was even thanking. Ivy's mantra, the goddess Belisama, the magic itself? When it came down to it, it didn't really matter.

Sometimes, you had to take the smallest of victories and run with them.

Sometimes, they were all you had to cling to.

Mystery Objects

IT WAS NEARLY nine by the time I got home, the harvested viridian pulsing contentedly in my backpack, safe inside the transparent little globe of magic I'd conjured for its keeping. I lived on Feverfew, only a few streets over from Yarrow Street and Tomes & Omens, the family occult and indie bookstore that was now largely my charge. Not even a five-minute walk away, but far enough and residential enough to cushion me from the relentless hubbub of rowdy tourists who overran Thistle Grove almost year-round.

Witch-crazy visitors were Tomes & Omens' bread and butter, but that didn't mean I had to *like* the noisy bumblefucks, or the overly familiar way they pawed my books and artifacts. You'd think tourists itching for a slice of occult history would approach it with more respect, and yet . . . That was people for you.

I paused in front of the renovated colonial that held my second-floor duplex unit, dipping into my cargo shorts pockets in search of my house keys. Protective candles always flickered in my windows, while my woman-about-town landlady's below were dark more often than not; the chick's social life was tantamount to an extreme sport. The summer night felt like a bell jar lowered around me, still and almost perfectly silent. A warm hush that pressed sweetly against the skin, disturbed only by the faint, whispery rustle of the elms that lined the street. The air smelled like honeysuckle, which grew abundant around the base of Hallows Hill and drifted around the town in fragrant currents every year, as soon as spring began its softening yield to summer.

Perfumed peace all around me, just the way I liked it. If I closed my eyes, I could almost pretend to be the only human left alive in the entire neighborhood, the sole survivor of some subtle apocalypse.

Sometimes, the idea of that much solitude was disturbingly appealing.

I located the correct pocket, still savoring my little triumph up on Hallows Hill as I fished out my key and jogged up the stairs to the porticoed landing, my hiking boots clomping against the concrete steps. I'd successfully snared a memory back from oblivion, something I'd managed only a few other times before. Maybe I *was* finally getting better; maybe the remnants of the oblivion were loosening their lingering hold, claws retracting from my mind.

Shifting the weight of my backpack to my left shoulder, I lifted the key to slide it into the lock.

And promptly forgot what I was doing, or what the serrated, ominous piece of metal in my hand was even supposed to be *for*.

The panic that slammed into me was like barreling face-first into a Sheetrock wall. My heart battered against my ribs with what felt like bruising force, my hand shaking so hard I couldn't even keep the—the *thing*, the Mystery Fucking Object—lined up with the lock.

Had my life depended on it, a cold blade pressed to the soft flesh under my jaw, I couldn't have divined what the object in my hand was meant to do.

The more I thought about it, the more sinister and wrong it felt, until some of that danger seemed to seep like welling blood into the texture of the night around me. Tainting it, turning it into the deceptively peaceful prelude of a slasher film. Why would something ever be *shaped* like this? That strange little circular head at the top, and then the menacingly toothy blade. Was it . . . a very small weapon, maybe? An artifact intended to facilitate some malign spellwork? What was I even doing, holding something so clearly forged to nefarious ends without even protective gloves between it and my skin?

I dropped my backpack with a thump, careless of the englobed viridian inside, and turned to press my back against the door, sliding down the varnished wood until my butt met the floorboards. My entire body was drenched in icy sweat, and I could hear myself panting, harsh breaths that sounded like they were being dragged by a fishhook out of my throat. I wanted to drop the Mystery Fucking Object more than I'd possibly ever wanted anything, but some deep-rooted stubbornness inside me resisted the impulse, the desire to take the easy way out.

A stupid, maybe-evil hunk of metal was *not* stronger than me.

But I needed help; that much, I did know, even if it felt like chewing on poison ivy, the sting of nettles down my throat. With my free hand, I fumbled in my pockets for my phone. Ivy was the first contact in my favorites, above Emmy and Uncle James, and she answered on the first ring, almost as if she'd been expecting my call.

Maybe she had; Thorns could be odd that way, as if they had a specialized sonar for long-distance emotional distress.

"Hey, Lilah," she said, her warm voice like a balm, an aural tincture with a honey base. Ivy had a beautiful singing voice; years ago, back when we'd still been together rather than best friends, she'd often sung me lullabies while I lay pillowed on top of her collarbone, the sweet vibration of her vocal cords thrumming through my cheek. Some of that natural melody carried over into her speech. "What's going on, boo? Shouldn't you be in bed with your tea and cheerios?"

Yes, I damned well should have been. Most nights, I'd have long since been snuggled under my weighted blanket with a book, a mug of chamomile-and-lavender tea, and snack cup of cheerios and peanut M&M's. Once upon a time, the ritual had included a nightcap, a lowball of negroni instead of tea; but I'd found out the hard way that alcohol didn't play well with the aftermath of the oblivion glamour.

Yet another thing, a small pleasure it had stolen from me.

"I went up to Hallows to harvest viridian teardrops," I said without preamble, my teeth chattering a little. My tank top was soaked through, stuck to me, and the balmy breeze felt almost chilly against the clinging film of sweat sheeting my skin. "I just got back, and I'm trying to open my door but then I—I *forgot* again, Ivy. Now I'm, I'm holding this *thing*, and I don't know what it is but it seems fairly awful and I . . . I'm afraid of it?"

A tiny mewling sob escaped past my teeth before I could call it back. I clenched my jaw, furious with myself, struggling to latch on to some semblance of control.

"Okay, honey, I'm with you so far," Ivy said, sounding sublimely unruffled; even just the timbre of her voice was soothing.

"You got home, and it sounds like you were trying to unlock your door. What does it look like, Lilah, the thing you're afraid of? Can you describe it to me?"

Gritting my teeth, I rattled off as objective a description of the Mystery Fucking Object as I could muster, without mentioning any of my suspicions about weaponry or baneful magics. I didn't want to bias her.

"Ah," Ivy sighed once I'd finished. Her pitch didn't change, but I could still somehow feel the wealth of aching sympathy rolling off her and through the line. "I got you. It's a key, honey. You're holding your house key—you know what that is. It fits into the lock, you turn it, and it undoes the mechanism keeping your door closed. Is that sounding more familiar now?"

A key. A fucking *key* had scared me out of my entire wits.

Because I remembered what it was, almost as soon as she'd begun explaining it to me. Often it worked that way, when the oblivion clouded my memory of mundane objects, infusing them with a pervasive sense of alien malevolence. It didn't happen often, but each time it did felt like the first—in the midst of an episode, I couldn't even recall that this displacement and confusion had crept over me before. I needed a grounding reminder, a brief, simple, externally derived explanation of what the object was.

But it had to come from someone else. I couldn't mantra myself out of a spiral like this, not when it was an everyday object that I'd suddenly forgotten. I hated this utter helplessness—this mortifying dependence on Ivy's help, the imposition and burden it turned me into, a flailing, needy creature instead of her steadfast friend— more than any other part of my miserable recovery. I hated it so much the loathing felt close to rage, a bubbling cauldron of vitriol

I couldn't tamp down, that threatened to boil over any minute and scorch everything around me into bitter dregs.

And beneath the fury was another, darker fear, a leviathan's shadow surging deep beneath the ocean's surface. What if, one day, the thing I forgot was my phone? How was I supposed to summon Ivy then, my best friend and my lifeline, the tether that kept me sane and reeled me back in to myself?

Flames and stars, what would happen to me then?

I started to cry, raw, croaking sobs that I could do nothing to suppress. "I'm sorry," I wept, swiping a hand over my horrid snotty face, succeeding only in smearing myself more. "Ivy, I'm so sorry to . . . to *be* like this. To do this to you."

"Lilah, honey, cut that shit out," she ordered, in the gentle and completely uncompromising tone she probably also used with the more overbearing tourists she handled at the Honeycake Orchards bakery. "Let me remind you that I love you, and that I volunteered for this. We agreed I'd be your person when you needed it. Tell me, did we not agree?"

"We did agree," I said damply, nodding as if she could see me. "We did. But you—you don't deserve this bullshit all the time. Having to, to fucking *handle* me like this, be on call at any time of day or night. Like I can't take care of myself. Like I'm this utter, useless waste of space."

"Welp, that's it," she replied briskly, and I could hear the soft rustling of thrown-back sheets—she, apparently, *had* been in bed. A shared love of early bedtimes had always been one of our mutual things. "I'm coming over."

I lurched back against the door, horrified. "No! Ivy, no, you have to be up at four tomorrow. You don't have to do that, you really—"

"Again, and I say this with love," she said, and I could hear the warm fondness in her voice, "but *do* shut up, bitch. Of course I'm coming over, this is no longer remotely a discussion. There's no way I'm letting you be alone right now, not when this is the prevailing mood. And have you had dinner, or did you forget to eat while you were up on Hallows?"

"It's . . . possible that I forgot," I admitted, chastened. "I had some trail mix, maybe? I was really focused on—"

"Harvesting the viridian, of course you were. Pearl Dragon should still be open; I'm going to stop by and pick something up. I had a light dinner, anyway, I could use a dim sum snack. Want bubble tea, too?"

She'd probably had a healthy, substantial, home-cooked dinner of the kind she prepared for herself almost every night, but of course this was what she'd say. I closed my eyes and tipped my head back against the door, awash in equal parts guilt and gratitude, and suddenly aware of the seismic rumble in my stomach that I'd apparently been ignoring for hours, possibly half a day. The friendship that had grown out of my former relationship with Ivy was one of the greater miracles of my life, one that I had no idea how I'd managed to pull off given how clumsy I often was with people.

Why she still chose to love me so hard was one of life's enduring mysteries.

"Thank you," I whispered into the phone. "Really, Ivy. I . . . I don't know what I'd do without you."

"Not much, because you'd have starved to death. Don't worry, though, fam—the dim sum's gonna be on you, to balance out the scales."

Photo by Gary Alpert, Deafboyphotography

Lana Harper is the *New York Times* bestselling author of *Payback's a Witch* and *From Bad to Cursed* in the Witches of Thistle Grove series. Writing as Lana Popović, she has also written four YA novels about modern-day witches and historical murderesses. Born in Serbia, Lana grew up in Hungary, Romania, and Bulgaria before moving to the US, where she studied psychology and literature at Yale University, law at Boston University, and publishing at Emerson College. She lives in Chicago, where she spends most of her time plotting witchy stories and equally witchy tattoos.

CONNECT ONLINE

LanaPopovicBooks.com
🐦 LanaPopovicLit
📷 Lanalyte

Ready to find
your next great read?

Let us help.

Visit prh.com/nextread

Penguin
Random
House